THE NURSE'S SPECIAL DELIVERY

BY
LOUISA GEORGE

HER NEW YEAR BABY SURPRISE

BY
SUE MacKAY

MILLS & BOON

The Ultimate Christmas Gift

*Best friends, a surrogate baby,
and a chance for love…*

Best friends Emma Hayes and Abbie Cook
will do *anything* for each other. So when
nurse Abbie asks Emma if she'll be her
surrogate and carry the baby she longs for,
of course she doesn't refuse.

But as Christmas comes it's not just the
new baby that turns their lives upside down.
Because for both women there's a chance for
love…if they're only brave enough to take it!

Read Abbie and Callum's story in

The Nurse's Special Delivery

And discover Emma and Nixon's story in

Her New Year Baby Surprise

Both available now!

THE NURSE'S
SPECIAL DELIVERY

BY
LOUISA GEORGE

HarperCollins
PUBLISHERS
Since 1817

Published in Great Britain 2017
By Mills & Boon, an imprint of HarperCollins*Publishers*
1 London Bridge Street, London, SE1 9GF

© 2017 Louisa George

ISBN: 978-0-263-92683-5

Printed and bound in Spain
by CPI, Barcelona

Dear Reader,

When the Medical Romance editors suggested Sue MacKay and I write another duet—our first was The Infamous Maitland Brothers, with *The Gift of a Child* and *How to Resist a Heartbreaker*—I was thrilled. Sue and I had a lot of fun the first time around, and I knew we'd have the same on our second duet.

Writing *The Nurse's Special Delivery* gave me the chance to share my love of Queenstown on New Zealand's South Island—one of my very favourite places in the world. It's a stunningly beautiful place: a town on the edge of a deep blue lake surrounded by snow-capped mountains. The area is a tourist haven and renowned for its sense of fun and adventure. I hope both Sue and I have captured a bit of that in these stories, too.

In this duet we've taken a few risks and covered a topic that is not often talked about: surrogacy. Abbie can't carry her own child, so her best friend Emma offers to do it for her in a completely unselfish act that embodies what their friendship has meant over twenty years.

These two brave, compassionate and feisty women need strong heroes, and we definitely found them in Callum and Nixon! Callum has demons of his own, and is only visiting New Zealand for a short time. He does not need or want to fall in love with a place and a woman, and he definitely cannot imagine himself being a father to someone else's baby. Meanwhile Abbie is preparing for her first child and has no time or space in her life for a man. So the road to love is a rocky one—with both parties resisting all the way!

I hope you enjoy Callum and Abbie's story!

Best wishes,

Louisa xx

Having tried a variety of careers in retail, marketing and nursing, **Louisa George** is thrilled that her dream job of writing for Mills & Boon means she gets to go to work in her pyjamas. Louisa lives in Auckland, New Zealand, with her husband, two sons and two male cats. When not writing or reading Louisa loves to spend time with her family, enjoys travelling, and adores eating great food.

Books by Louisa George

Mills & Boon Medical Romance

The Hollywood Hills Clinic

Tempted by Hollywood's Top Doc

Midwives On-Call at Christmas

Her Doctor's Christmas Proposal

One Month to Become a Mum
Waking Up with His Runaway Bride
The War Hero's Locked-Away Heart
The Last Doctor She Should Ever Date
How to Resist a Heartbreaker
200 Harley Street: The Shameless Maverick
A Baby on Her Christmas List
Tempted by Her Italian Surgeon

Visit the Author Profile page
at millsandboon.co.uk for more titles.

PROLOGUE

THE SOUND OF tinkling bells and Christmas carols floated into Abbie Cook's head. Followed by laughter. Hungry newborns grizzling. The chink of teacups. The smell of coffee that still made her nauseous.

Go away, world.

The babies' cries felt as if they had a direct line to her heart, tugging and stabbing and shaping it into a raw lump of pain. She kept her eyes tightly closed as she focused on keeping the contents of her stomach precisely where they were.

'Merry Christmas, Abbie. Wake up, the doctor's going to do his rounds in a minute. You might be able to go home. You'll want to be home, dear, on Christmas Day, won't you?'

Even though her eyes were clamped shut, Abbie felt the slide of the tear down her cheek and she turned away from the nurse's voice. The last thing she wanted was to go home to that empty house with an empty belly and a completely cried-out heart. Staying asleep, hibernating under the regulation hospital duvet, was just perfect, especially today.

Her third Christmas without Michael. The first had been a blur of condolence messages. The second a pretence of fun with people who *didn't think she should be alone*, when all she'd wanted was to be alone. And now this. Another year without decorations, another year gone by, without keeping her promise to her husband.

But it didn't do to feel sorry for herself on a ward in the hospital she worked in. There'd been enough pity glances from her colleagues these past few weeks. Actually, years. And enough self-pity too. What would Michael think of her? He wouldn't have wanted her to feel like this, that was for sure. He'd have wanted her to get up and make the most of her life regardless of what befell her. He'd want her to keep on fighting for happiness. He'd have wanted her to decorate the house, to celebrate Christmas and enjoy life.

She heaved herself up the bed and looked at the cup of steaming tea, hoping the well-meaning staff nurse would do a bunk and leave her on her own. 'Thanks. Yeah. Okay.'

'Hey, love.' A hand slid over hers. 'You'll be okay. You will—'

'Abbie! Abbie! Santa Claus been!'

'Uh-huh. Visitors.' The nurse's hand shrugged off as thudding footsteps sliced through the ward's white noise and a giggling, wriggling four-year-old scrambled onto the bed thrusting a box with sharp edges into Abbie's hands. 'Abbie! Look.'

'Hey, Scratch. Let me see.' It was hard to be sad around Rosie, who grasped her life with tight little fists and squeezed out every drop of every second. Abbie took the box and peered. 'What have you got here?'

'A tablet. For games and writing.' As the little girl spoke her dark curls bobbed from side to side and the tiny, jaded bit left of Abbie's heart squeezed.

'Oh. Lovely.' Abbie glanced up at Rosie's mum, Emma, and pigged her eyes. 'A tablet. Okay. Excellent?'

'Apparently the best present. In the world. *Someone* didn't realise I was holding off until she was older.' Emma gave a resigned shrug as she perched on the bed—against all hospital policies—but Abbie loved her for it. And she assumed *someone* referred to one of Emma's brothers who overcompensated for Rosie's lack of a father. At least this year he hadn't bought her another football. 'How are you doing, hun?'

Abbie dug very deep. It was Christmas Day. She wasn't going to spoil it for a four-year-old. 'Fine, thanks.'

'You look better.'

'Yeah. I'm okay.' She lowered her voice a little to prevent little listening ears from hearing. 'I've been thinking. A lot.'

'Me too!' There was a light in Emma's eyes that melded with the ever-present sadness that was there whenever she was around Abbie. She'd seen that sadness before, too, when Emma had been having her own troubles. 'You first—'

'You first!'

'Jinx!' Abbie laughed for the first time in what felt like forever. That was the thing about best friends—after almost twenty years of living in each other's pockets they finished sentences and had a strange and comforting telepathy. 'Okay. If you don't mind, I'm just going to say something and I want you to be honest. Okay?'

'Okay.' As she nodded Emma absent-mindedly stroked her daughter's curls. A simple action that was feral and instinctive and that Abbie craved to do to a child of her own with every atom in her body.

'Okay.' She sat a little straighter. 'The thing is, I can't do this any more. God, I want to; I want a baby more than anything in the world, you know that. But Dr Morrison was frank—I can't carry one to term. Ever. I've tried and tried and it's not going to happen. I can't put myself through that again so I have to face up to it. I can't have Michael's baby. I will never have it.' Her throat felt raw and her stomach tightened. It was reality and she had to deal with it. 'So. There it is. I'm not going to try *one more time* again. No more hormones or injections. No more baby books. Or bootees.' And now she was just being over-sentimental.

Emma's lip wobbled a little. 'Oh, honey, I'm so sorry. I really am.'

'I haven't been ready to stop for so long. I just wasn't ready to let go. I'm not sure if I really am, but I do have to accept that my husband is dead. That I won't be having his baby, because…because I just can't.' Abbie's chest felt as if it had a thick weight pressing on it. 'I tried. God knows, I tried.'

Twisting the edge of the duvet in her fingers, she rallied. 'So, I'm moving on. I'm going to leave NICU because I just can't face working with those little ones every day. I don't know what I'm going to do, but I'm determined that this time next year I'm going to be in a new job. At least, maybe my career can be my baby instead? That's something to look forward to, right? I've actually made the decision to let go. It hurts like hell, but…' Actually, it felt like a betrayal for everything she'd promised Michael, for everything they'd worked towards. She was betraying him and it felt like a knife in her heart. But… 'Anyway, no more hormones, so that's a relief. Well, happy Christmas to me. I may even put a tree up next year too. Who knows? Oh, and I got you both a present but they're at home. Right. What do you think?'

'Oh, honey, I know what it's taken for you to say that. I think you need a break and some rest and some time.' Emma wrapped her in a hug. 'But it is lovely to see you being positive.'

Abbie blew out a long sigh. 'Okay, so you don't think I'm giving up too easily? Good. Thanks. So, what do you have to tell me?'

'Rosie, love… Let me show you how to do this. Look, you can draw pictures…' Emma sat her daughter on a chair and gave her the little tablet device. After promising she wouldn't let technology become a babysitter, maybe she was learning it could be a good distraction tool for a few minutes. 'Okay, Abbie. I've been doing a lot of soul-searching. I…don't actually know how to say this…' Emma laughed nervously. 'I want to do something for you. Nursing a husband through cancer is bad enough, but losing baby after baby was killing you. And I love that you want a new job and everything instead of a baby and that you're trying to be brave, but I also know that that's something you've always dreamt about since we were little. You'd be a fabulous mum. You of all people deserve to have a baby—yours and Michael's. So…' Emma slipped her hand over Abbie's. 'I want to have it for you.'

'You…what?' Joy swam across Abbie's chest, swiftly followed by panic and anxiety and…well, guilt and shame that she couldn't do this herself. But, immense gratitude. And hope. Yes, hope fluttering in her chest—it was strange to feel something like this after so long. 'You want to have a baby for me? What? How?'

'I want to be the surrogate, the oven. I'll cook your baby.' Emma's eyes narrowed and she looked a little panicked now too. 'Is that a really bad idea? It's okay. I just thought—'

Her baby. Michael's baby. Carried to term. Their baby. A precious tiny gift. 'But there's so much… I don't know… It's a surprise. It's a miracle.'

'A good one?'

'Oh, yes! Oh, yes! Thank you. I can't even… I just don't know what to say. Wow. How? I don't know…'

'Ways and means. Let me do this for you, please. I've seen the way you look at Rosie and it breaks my heart that you have so much love to give. You've been with me every step of the way through the good and the bad and...' Emma smiled softly over at her daughter and Abbie knew she was referring to Rosie's dad '...and the very ugly. You've been my rock and now I want to be yours. Please say yes.'

Abbie's heart felt as if it would explode. But there were so many questions running through her head too. How would she feel with her baby inside someone else? What would they tell other people? Rosie? Would she understand? Would their families?

What if you change your mind?

Surrogates did. And battles started. Friendships broke. She shoved that away. That would never happen. Their friendship was tight, and, oh, what a gift. A baby. 'Yes! Yes. If that's what you want. Yes. I'd love it. Oh, my God! Imagine! Thank you. Thank you so much. I love you to bits.'

'Yeah, you'll do too. Oh, and happy Christmas.' More tears glistened in Emma's eyes. Commitment shone through, and love, as she hugged her again for the zillionth time in twenty-odd years. 'Excellent. Right then, let's get cooking.'

CHAPTER ONE

Ten and a half months later...

'ER... I THINK we're having an alien.'

'Or a windmill. Look at those arms and legs moving.'

Trying to make out the shapes on the black and white screen was getting easier the further the pregnancy progressed. Today, they could see the baby in its entirety, filling the screen, all the features as clear as day. A stubby nose. *Like Michael's?* The bow lips. *Mine?* The rapid-fire heartbeat filled the room. *Wow.*

With a mix of sadness and epic excitement Abbie blinked back tears and squeezed her friend's hand. 'Oops, it's pass-the-tissues time. I'm being such a wuss, but I just can't believe it's real.'

'You've said that at every scan and every appointment. And a million times every day since the positive test. Not believing it's real hasn't stopped you shopping up a storm, though.' Laughing, Emma patted her swollen belly. 'Should we find out the gender?'

The sonographer looked up from the scanner screen. 'You want to know?'

'No. No.' It didn't feel right for some reason. Abbie stared at the screen and convinced herself the images weren't that clear really. She wasn't ready to hear she was having a mini-Michael. When she thought about him she wished he were here with her, getting all gooey about their child. He should have been here, holding her hand. Hell, she should have been the pregnant one, not Emma. But life hadn't granted her all the wishes she'd had and everything was happening out of sync. Suddenly, she felt a little deflated. 'Let's leave it as a surprise. Is that okay, Em?'

'Hey…it's your baby, after all.' Emma grinned and Abbie just knew her friend was watching to see the sonographer's reaction. The story of their baby was pretty unusual; surrogacy wasn't something they came across every day in little old Queenstown. 'Anyway, I think I know what sex it is and I bet I'm right. I'm one of those people who knows they're pregnant before the test shows up positive, and I'm convinced I know the gender because I'm carrying in a particular way. But my lips are sealed.'

'The main thing,' Abbie ventured, because this was a question continually on her lips, in her thoughts—and after everything that had happened, who could blame her for having just the odd nugget of panic? 'Is everything okay?'

'Absolutely fine.'

'Are you sure?'

'Here's a picture for you both so you can see just how perfect baby is.' The sonographer smiled. 'I'll sort you out a DVD too. Yes, Abbie, baby is doing just fine for thirty-four weeks. And Mum…er…sorry, *Emma* is doing great too.'

Awkward. But it wasn't the first time and it probably wouldn't be the last.

Emma wiped the jelly off her belly and sat up. 'I feel great. And don't worry, we get that a lot. Okay, missy, you'd better get back to work, right? Busy day?'

Emma was always so chirpy at these appointments—

and every day in between—laughing and joking, but she'd been here before when she was pregnant with Rosie. How was she really feeling, though? Did she feel like the mum this time too? Would she be bereft at handing the baby over? Would she want to keep the baby herself?

'Abbie?'

'Oh. Sorry.' Abbie glanced at the wall clock and pushed back the little, silly anxieties she had—of course Emma was going to hand this baby over. 'Oh, yes. My lunch break has finished. Gotta dash. See you later. Enjoy the rest of your day off.'

'I have a few hours before I pick Rosie up from school. Do you want me to get any shopping in for you?'

Abbie gave her friend a hug. 'No. I'm good, thanks— do you want me to sort dinner out? No—let's have a quick coffee before we pick her up. Meet in the staff canteen? We can talk shopping and dinner then. Listen to us, we're like an old couple.'

'No man's got a chance.' Emma laughed again, but there was more than a kernel of truth in her words. 'No complications. Just how I like it.'

Just how they both liked it, really. Between them they'd had a rough ride where relationships were concerned. One husband dead, the other might as well have been, for all the good he was. After all the heartbreak they'd had, who needed another man?

As Abbie walked down the corridor towards the emergency department and the rest of her shift, she thought about how things had changed. Eight years with one man who'd been her life completely, then three years in the wilderness. But she was fine about it. No man would come close to Michael. She would bring this baby up on her own, in his memory... Or as much on her own as her next-door-neighbour-best-friend-for-life would allow.

As she turned the corner into the department she heard voices.

'Imagine if someone you loved couldn't have a baby, and you knew you could. Would you do it? For a friend? A sister? Would you have a baby for someone else? It's a long nine months, though, isn't it? What if something went wrong? What if they decided they didn't want it, what then?'

Another voice in a stage whisper that echoed around the quieter than usual emergency department replied, 'Honestly, I don't know how a mother could give her baby away. All those months inside her, kicking, hiccups, little feet under your ribs...you have a bond, y'know? You're not telling me that you don't develop a bond. It's living inside you.' There was a pause where Abbie imagined the gossipers all shaking their heads. Then... 'Oh. Er... Hello, Abbie. We...er...hello.'

'Hi.' She was standing where she'd frozen to the spot the second she'd heard the subject of their conversation, probably looking like a complete idiot with her mouth open and bright red cheeks. Her hand was still clutching the scan picture. Her heart was raging. Raging with all the things she wanted to tell them, but it was none of their business.

How she'd wanted to feel the kicks and the hiccups, but no pregnancy had ever progressed past fifteen weeks. How many times she'd had IVF. How many times she'd failed. Until she hadn't had the energy to do it any more and keep on failing.

It's my baby. Not Emma's.

Made with my eggs and Michael's frozen sperm. It's our baby. Just a different incubator.

It wasn't as if she hadn't been over and over and over

these thoughts every day since the minute a grinning, glowing Emma had shown her the pregnancy stick with the positive blue line. She'd loved her friend in that moment more than she'd loved anyone else ever—possibly even more than Michael—for doing something so precious. And she would love this baby as fiercely, no matter what. Finally, she'd have a family—a family of two. Other single parents managed, Emma did, so she would too. Just the two of them in a tight little unit.

And she'd always known she'd be the subject of gossip. How could she not be? Surrogacy wasn't common and people needed educating, otherwise the stigma would be with her baby for life. She gave them all a smile. 'If I could do it for someone else, I honestly would. I just can't even do it for me, which is why Emma's helping me out. She says to think of her as being the oven, but the bun is made from my ingredients. Does that make sense?'

There was a moment where they all gaped back at her, as open-mouthed as she'd been, and she hoped her message was getting through.

'Of course, Abbie, it makes perfect sense. Now, back to work everyone.' Stephanie, Head Nurse of Queenstown ED, and very well respected for her no-nonsense approach, turned to the group, thankfully distracting Abbie from the conversation topic and the need to defend herself. No one could possibly understand what she and Emma were going through—and that was fine.

With a few words from their boss, the subject of Abbie's baby's parentage and unconventional conception was closed. For now.

Thank you.

'Wait, Abbie. There's a Code Two call, and I want you to go with the helo. Tramper took a bad fall on Ben Lomond.'

'A medivac? On the helicopter?' Excitement bubbled in

her stomach and she pushed all her baggage to the back of her mind. Four months in and she still couldn't get over the adrenalin rush of working at the coalface that was emergency medicine. Every day, every second, was different from the last, with no idea of what she might have to deal with next.

'We've got enough staff to cover, so yes. This is your chance to watch and learn what it's like out in the field.'

'Sure thing.' Abbie controlled the fluttering in her chest. 'Thanks, Steph.'

'No problem.' Her boss smiled and said in a voice that everyone would hear, 'For the record, how you choose to have your child is no one's business but yours and I think it's wonderful. Put me down for babysitting duties. Now, out you go.'

It was the beginning of spring, so theoretically Queenstown should have been warming up from the previous long cold months, but there was still a good dusting of snow on the tops of the mountains and a cruel wind whipped across the helipad, liberating Abbie's unruly mane from the clips and elastic that were supposed to hold it all in place. Really, longer length was theoretically easier to look after but would she get a mum's bob when the baby came? Her heart thrilled a little at the thought, and she laughed at the image in her head of her being all mumsy with a short, neat, practical bob, at the thought of being a mumsy mummy after so long trying.

She was trying to fix the wayward hair neatly back under control when a chopper's chugging split the air. No time for vanity.

What am I supposed to do?

She ran through the protocols in her head and hoped she'd remember them under stress. But the Intensive Care Paramedics and crew knew what they were doing; she'd learnt that much over the last few months. She'd met them all and been impressed with every one so far.

Soon enough the chopper door slid open and a man dressed in bright red paramedic dungarees jumped down. Shane, the town's senior paramedic and old family friend, wrapped her in a hug, said something she couldn't hear over the chopper blades and bundled her towards the helicopter.

Through the open door she could see more crew. Oh. A new one. He had a shock of dark hair. Celtic colouring, like her late grandad. Irish heritage, maybe? Perfect skin. Blue eyes. Nice mouth. A smattering of stubble, which made him look rugged and a little dangerous.

Back to his eyes—because she wanted to take a second look—they really were quite the brightest of blues, like the Queenstown sky on a crisp winter morning.

Where the hell had that thought come from?

Mr Nice Eyes raised his eyebrows as he met her gaze. Out of nowhere she felt a strange fluttery feeling in her stomach.

A medivac! Exciting! She was moving up in the world!

Shane coughed, nudging her forward, and she drew her eyes away from the new guy. Now...what the hell was she supposed to do?

With the touchdown being as choppy as a protein shake in a blender, Intensive Care Paramedic Callum Baird's stomach had been left somewhere ten metres above Queenstown hospital. He breathed in the rush of cold air blasting through the open door.

November. New Zealand spring, apparently, and it was still freezing; as cold as a Scottish winter and windier than the top of Ben Nevis.

A diminutive girl had appeared in the doorway. Her face

was almost covered by earmuffs and a bright red woolly hat with huge pompom, plus a matching scarf pulled up over her mouth. All Cal could see was her eyes. A dark penetrating brown that showed her to be at once apprehensive and excited. A common rookie air ambulance reaction. She pulled down her scarf and grinned. 'Hi, I'm Abbie. Staff nurse in ED. I was told to hitch a ride, see what you do out in the wild.'

'Er...hello.' Cal shifted over in the tiny space, glancing over at his companion, Shane, who was leading this shift.

Shane nodded back and smiled at the girl; clearly he knew her and liked her.

'Where should I sit?' Her eyes danced around the cabin, her hands moving as she spoke, a vibrancy he hadn't seen before in anyone.

Shane lumbered up into the chopper, wheezing as he sat down. Poor bugger was just at the back end of the flu and letting everyone know about it. 'Shift over, Callum, make some room for our guest.'

It was none of Cal's business, but there was barely enough room in here as it was. Plus they'd have to fit the patient on the gurney and work on him if necessary. 'Going to be cosy.'

'It won't be for long. We can see Ben Lomond from here.' Abbie shuffled in next to him and buckled her belt. 'So, be gentle with me, eh?'

He looked at those dancing eyes and couldn't help smiling at her. 'First time?'

'First medivac. Not first time in a chopper. Don't you know, it's the only way to travel in Queenstown?' She bit her lip and explained, 'There's a lot of heli-sport here; heli-skiing, heli-hiking, that kind of thing.'

With a lurch they ascended. Helicopters didn't usually lurch. 'It's blowy, that's for sure.'

'Coming off the Remarkables. Along with snow, I reckon. There's a southern blast coming up from Antarctica.' She nodded and looked away, gripping her hands together. From this angle he could see the fine shape of her jawline and some tiny wrinkles by her eyes. Not as young as he'd first thought, then. Hair sticking out at all angles from under her hat. Long eyelashes. Geez, it was real cosy in here if he was paying attention to her eyelashes.

Kind of cute, too.

He gave himself a mental telling-off. He had no business thinking any woman was cute. Not when he had responsibilities elsewhere.

Still, a bit of window-shopping never harmed anyone...

'Great view, isn't it? I wouldn't live anywhere else on earth.' Having raised her voice a notch above the chopper blades' racket, Abbie pointed to the town below them. The deep blue lake stretched out as far as he could see, fringed on one side by the bustling centre of Queenstown. A string of gondolas swung directly beneath them, slowly scaling one of the mountains that framed the town. A zigzag luge was hundreds of feet below, where kids and adults alike risked life and limb—and had a lot of fun in the process—racing on go-karts down curved tracks to the valley. The girl grinned. 'You're not from here, right? Have you been on the luge yet?'

'Nah. But I've scooped a kid up from it and taken him to ED. Nasty grazes and a fractured elbow.'

'Makes you wary, then, does it? The adrenalin capital of the world?' Her eyes danced again.

If only she knew. Adrenalin was his best friend, and his worst enemy. Before he could answer, the earth started to come up to meet them and the pilot was saying something about a body at two o'clock. Cal scanned the snow, the steep ridge, the jutting rocks and thought he saw some-

thing that looked out of place. A flash of blue. Then, yes…
'He's over there. I can see him.'

'Yes. Yes. Watch out, it's going to be slippery,' the pilot
shouted back, his words barely audible under the chug,
chug, chug of the helicopter rotor blades. He'd made a
spectacular landing on the only flat bit of mountainside—
it took some skill to do that. 'Got your crampons?'

'Och, yes. I'll be fine, no worries.' If there was one
thing Callum Baird knew it was snow. Every kind. The
wet, seeping-through-your-clothes kind. The fluffy make-
a-decent-snowball kind. And this, the melted and frozen
again ice that meant getting a foot grip was challenging.
Especially in the sixty-knot winds and poor visibility at
the top of Ben Lomond. That last kind of snow was why he
was here in the first place. To learn how to make amends,
to try to fix things that probably couldn't be fixed, but to
make things better, at least.

He hoped.

Funny, how he'd travelled halfway around the world and
found himself on the top of a mountain bearing the same
damned name as the place he'd left. Almost as beautiful,
too. If the clouds disappeared, and with a bit of spring
sunshine it'd be stunning…but he wasn't here to admire
the view.

Bracing against the wind, he jumped from the helicopter then turned and grabbed his paramedic backpack. The
crampons slipped on as easily as the memories. He shook
the latter off. He was used to doing that. Some days they
did as they were told and slunk away, and he managed to
get through twenty-four hours before he was drawn back to
that fateful night of cold and wet and ice. Other days they
hung around him, a sopping, freezing bone-deep helplessness he couldn't shake. 'From what I could see, our guy's
up there, to the right—it's fairly rocky, so we'll have to do

a bit of scrambling. He told Dispatch he'd heard a snap, so we'd best take the scoop with us, too. Hope you enjoy a bit of ice-skating?'

'Preferably on the flat.' Abbie assessed the terrain, shook her head, then passed the scoop down. 'I'm not sure I'd manage a triple Salchow on this hill.'

'I'm not sure I'd manage a triple Salchow, full stop.' So, she had a sense of humour. That worked. Especially in conditions like this.

Due to the deteriorating weather, it had been touch and go whether to bring the chopper up here at all, but a man's life hung, literally, on the edge, so they'd made a call. A good one, as it turned out. The ride had been bumpy, but the wind seemed to be dying down, for now. Which meant hypothermia would be less of an issue for all of them. Two months living in New Zealand and the only thing he could predict about the weather was that it was unpredictable.

'You got crampons?'

'Doesn't every woman carry a pair in her handbag?' He watched as she delved into her backpack and pulled out a pair of ice shoes, which she fastened like a pro. 'Ready.'

Although giving him a reassuring smile, she looked frozen through. A tiny waif, with huge eyes and that mess of dark hair that was tumbling from clips in every direction. The huge hi-vis jacket swamped her, and she looked out of her depth on every level.

But determination shone in her eyes.

'Right. Let's get to it.' It was hard going—one step forward, steadying your grip. Another step. The snow had frozen to sheer ice in some places. In others, tufts of grass poked through. The wind pressed them back, the ice halted their steps, so they made it to their patient as quickly as humanly possible.

He was a crumpled heap in bright blue and black walking gear. Alone. Like many walkers here. Starting out on a pleasant day trip, but at least he seemed suitably dressed for the occasion, unlike some Cal came across. Still, even full walking gear didn't always prevent disaster from striking. You could be perfectly prepared for a night stranded on the mountain, but not for unexpected and complicated fractures, blizzards, nowhere to hide from the biting wind. Frostbite.

A brother lifeless in your arms and there is nothing, nothing you can do but pray. As they neared, Cal did a primary survey. Breathing. Bleeding from his forehead. Bluish lips. Thank God for cell-phone reception, or who knew when he'd have been found. Phoning for help had saved his life.

That was, if they could get him down quickly enough.

The wind might have died a little, but it was still fresh as all hell up here and their guy was shaking. Cold and shock, or worse. Cal remembered to keep his words slow. Enough people had told him they didn't understand his Scottish accent already. 'Hello, there. I'm Cal, your knight in shining hi-vis.'

Abbie rolled her eyes. 'And I'm Abbie. That guy down there is Shane, and we're going to help get you off the mountain. Now, can you tell us what happened?'

So, she was all about the process. Okay.

'I'm… Marty… I think I've…' Dazed and shivering, the patient tried to sit up.

'Whoa. Hold still, mate. Tell me what happened.' Secondary survey was underway. There was blood on the ground. Which meant consideration had to be made for internal bleeding too. *Blood on the floor and five more. Consider thoracic, intra-abdominal, retroperineal, pelvic, long bones.*

'Slipped. Fell down from the ridge. Hit my head, I think,

on a rock. Chest... Leg snapped...' He reached a hand to his right fibula and grimaced. *Long bones.*

Plus, a head injury—couldn't rule out neck damage too. 'So, first things first, we need to put a neck brace on to protect that neck. Steady as you go. Hold still. Stay still, mate.' Cal slipped the neck brace into place, watching as Marty clenched his fists to counter the pain. Then bent his undamaged knee. At least he could move all his limbs. Good sign.

Cal had a closer look at the forehead wound. 'Looks pretty deep, needs a few stitches. Luckily, they're very good at sewing down at Queenstown General.' He taped a dressing over the wound, noting other minor cuts and grazes that would need attention, when they had more time, and in the warmth of a hospital ward.

Cal felt Marty's radial pulse. Nothing. Carotid showed a rapid, thready heartbeat. 'Guessing the systolic pressure is lower than ninety. No radial pulse. I'll do a quick check. Needs some fluids.' Needed surgery, actually. Fluids and stabilisation were the best they could do, especially up here on the steep arc of a mountainside with thick black clouds coming in from the west. Cal's heart rate sped up a little.

Great. A suspected life-threatening injury and the mother of all storms.

Luckily, fighting the odds was what he was good at.

Shane finally made it up the mountain. Breathless and wheezing, he probably shouldn't have been up here at all. He should have said his chest wasn't up to it. But Cal kept that thought to himself.

The two-way radio crackled. It was Brian, the pilot. 'Weather coming in fast. We need to get off this mountain and quick. Over.'

'Things turn to custard pretty quick round here.' One minute it was sunny, the next it was a white-out. But they had to make Marty safe before they left. 'Okay. Let's have a look at your leg. I'm going to have to cut your salopettes. Okay? Damned shame, because it's good kit.'

Keeping the patient talking and conscious gave them a better chance, so Cal went with his usual patter. He nodded at Shane, who was assessing the obviously broken leg. The bone had cut through the skin. Needed a splint at least to stabilise it. Needed surgery.

Needed to get off the mountain, and fast.

Again, Marty pushed to sit up. 'I can't breathe... I can't...'

Cal shot a look at Abbie, who'd turned her attention to Marty's chest. Could be one of a dozen things. He prayed there wasn't any surgical emphysema. Dodgy lungs in thin air at the top of a mountain were a nasty prospect. 'I'm going to put a line in your left arm, mate. Give you some fluids to keep you hydrated and something to make you more comfortable.'

'Left lung clear, but can't hear much in the right base. You want to check?'

'Yep. Let me have a go. To check.' Not wanting to disbelieve her or undermine her, he listened as carefully as he could to the beat-up chest. Suspected right pneumothorax. Great. The odds were starting to turn against them. It was freezing up here; his hands were starting to ache with the cold.

'Oxygen in situ. Pain relief administered.'

'Leg splint inflated and in situ.' The distant clouds had become very real, thick and dark and heavy. Flakes started to spot their coats, Marty's hair.

'Pass me a survival blanket, will you? Right. Thanks. Now, we've got to get you onto this scoop.'

The radio crackled. 'Cal, come in. You have two minutes. Over.'

'Just getting Marty on the scoop. Over.'

Cal positioned the scoop alongside their patient and somehow they managed to shift him over, keeping his neck as still as possible.

'Let's go. You all okay?' Shane took the lead, carrying the scoop at the feet end. Cal was at the head and Abbie walked at the side, carrying equipment and making sure Marty was stable and as comfortable as possible. It was like a game of slip 'n' slide getting them all down the hill.

'You fancy some tobogganing, Marty?' It was only half a joke. Apart from a few rocks it was a vertical skating rink.

They started to inch gingerly down. The sun had slid behind a cloud and the wind whipped round them, biting through their clothes. They made it a few metres then suddenly the scoop lurched sideways and forwards. Next thing Cal knew, Shane was yelling and tumbling head first over rocks and ice.

Down. Down. Down.

CHAPTER TWO

'SHANE! SHANE!'

The boss had come to a halt a hundred metres or so down the hill, splayed against the rear of the helicopter. He wasn't moving.

Cal reassessed, looking from Shane to Marty and then back down the slope again, allowing himself the briefest moment for his heart to thump hard and fast against his chest wall. Damn. *Damn.* Then he closed off all emotion.

Panic didn't help. Helplessness didn't help. Just action. He'd learnt his lesson the hard way. Had been learning for two long years.

Two patients now. One scoop and a fledgling helper.

Their patient took priority. Getting him down the hill now was going to be a challenge.

Somehow Callum had managed to keep a firm grip on Marty's scoop. 'You okay, mate?'

'Holding on,' he groaned. 'Just about.'

The scoop listed at a sharp forty-five-degree angle, from where Cal had maintained his hold and height, to where Abbie had been twisted by the sudden lurch sideways and pushed to the floor. She was just about managing to hold the scoop aloft with her arms outstretched underneath Marty, bearing his weight in a desperate attempt to keep their patient still and secure. There was an ooze of blood on her head. 'Abbie? You okay?'

She grimaced, her body contorting in an effort to hold up the scoop and the man, who must have weighed three times what she did. 'I'm fine. It's okay.'

'You're bleeding.'

'It's nothing. I caught my head on a rock as I fell. It's just a scratch.' She shook her head, trying hard to pretend she was okay, but he could see right through it. 'You should see the other guy.'

'Sadly, I can see him.' The boss looked knocked out and flat. Marty was groaning in agony in the tipped-up scoop. And Abbie had a cut head.

It looked worse than just a scratch, but he had to believe her because he just couldn't do this alone. She seemed orientated and fine. Feisty, actually. He'd have a closer look once they were on safe terrain and out of danger. 'Right then. I'm going to lower him down so we can right the scoop, then we can wait for Brian to come help.'

'He'd be better staying down there, don't you think? To see if Shane's okay?'

'I'll talk to him.' Cal shouted towards the chopper but couldn't make himself heard. He flicked on the two-way. 'Hey. Did you see Shane? He took a bad fall, he's at the rear. Roger.'

'I'm on my way. How are you going to manage with the scoop? Slide it down?'

'Not sure yet. Over.' There were too many rocks sticking out of the ground to make sliding a feasible option.

'She's a little thing. Roger.'

'We'll be fine.' It was Abbie, glowering. She had the affronted air of someone who would not be underestimated. He knew that trait well. Too well. Someone who insisted on overstretching…and then paying the consequences. She'd lowered her side of the scoop now and was brushing the snow and ice from her clothes. As she bent to the left she winced. 'Just give me a couple of seconds.'

They barely had one. The weather was closing in. This was all falling apart, but he needed to stay in control. 'Are you hurt? Is it something more than your head? Did the scoop hit you?'

'Just winded me.' She shook her head again but he could see the way she flinched as she turned. 'Let's do this.'

'I can call back-up. You won't be able to manage.'

'Says who? I could be a champion weightlifter for all you know. I could have won the Queenstown Primary arm wrestling competition in 1997.' She flexed her arms, but all he could see was the huge coat covering her from neck to knee. With the head wound and her wayward hair and the enormous coat she looked like a bag lady rather than the professional she was proving to be. 'What do you think, Marty? Am I stronger than I look?'

'I hope so,' Marty groaned. 'Yes.'

She gave Cal an I-told-you-so grin that made her eyes light up and his stomach feel strange, then she shuffled to the end of the scoop and bent in readiness to pick it up. 'So, let's do this. What choice do we have?'

'We could wait for back up. Or Brian.' But even with the space blanket, Marty was shaking with cold; they had to get this done and quick.

'He's with Shane and it looks like he needs help too.' Too true. Brian was trying to lift Shane up, but the senior paramedic kept buckling forward. She glanced at the swirls of snow falling around them. 'There isn't a choice. We have to do this or we'll all freeze to death.' Without any further chance at a conversation she bent at the end of the scoop and shouted, 'Ready? On my call. One. Two. Three.'

They were badly matched size-wise, but if he kept his

arms straight and stooped down low they were just about able to maintain a satisfactory balance. But it was slow going. He could see every muscle in her hands tighten and strain as she bore the weight of the hiker.

She doesn't have gloves on.

Somewhere along the way she'd taken them off—to work the IV and draw up drugs, probably. And hadn't had the chance to put them back on. Her fingers were white—with strain? With cold?

That was all he needed. Frostbite.

Frostbite. The enemy of the winter hiker. Could do untold damage from the inside out.

The dread swamped him along with the memories. He wasn't going to let that happen. They were getting off this mountain without any further incident. Stooping low, he gripped harder and tried to take more of the weight. It was impossible without upending the whole thing. Regardless of how strong she thought she was, she was starting to tire—steps becoming slower as she navigated the rocks. She needed to rest without losing face, he got that. 'Stop. Stop, Abbie. I need a minute.'

'Oh. Okay.' Very gently she lowered her end of the scoop then straightened up, twisting slowly left and right to ease out her muscles. Her hands were still in crooked fists and even from this distance he could see red marks on her palms. More blood?

'Brian! Brian, come here and take over.' They were about fifty metres from the chopper. Shane was sitting slumped against the landing gear holding his shoulder. 'You go down and take over from Brian and he can come and help me with this.'

'I can do this.'

He kept his voice level despite his growing frustration. 'And I'm telling you not to. Your hands are cut and cold and there's no need for you to lift anything if we can get Brian to do it. I need you down there to sort out Shane. He's not looking happy. Brian's just a pilot—he can't assess anything. I need your nursing skills and his muscle.'

'Okay. I'm gone.'

He was impressed with the agility and speed with which she made it to Shane, crossing paths with Brian and stopping for the briefest of handovers.

He watched as she tripped lightly over the rocks, that jacket swamping her tiny frame. She had guts, that was for sure. In another life he might have…

No, he wouldn't.

No point in wishing. He didn't have space for a relationship; and definitely not with someone a million miles away from his home. That would never work. No point starting something.

He pressed forwards, forcing all his attention to the here and now, not the murky past or his short-circuited future.

Finally, they were all settled into the chopper. Two patients. One more than they'd bargained for.

Brian gunned the engine. 'It's going to be a bit bumpy, but we'll be back in no time.'

She looked a little green as they rose into the air and shunted sharply east as a rogue gust caught them. For one second she looked terrified, then she regained her composure and started to chat to Shane, keeping him orientated to time and place. Her voice was like music cutting through the grim roar of the engine and the beeping of the portable ECG machine that monitored Marty's heart trace.

She was laughing, but it was gentle and lyrical. 'So, Shane, your crampon front-ended and you did a spectacular cartwheel down the mountain. If you want to train for the gymnastic world championships you could do with finding a more level place to do it.'

'Er…what's…happening? Did we have a patient?'

There was a flicker of a frown, then she recovered. 'Yes. He's just here, next to you. Marty's had some ketamine so he's doing okay. No. No, stay where you are, love. We need you to keep as still as you can.' All the while she talked, her eyes roved over first one patient then the other, assessing, monitoring, smiling.

Dancing. Moving. Smiling.

There was just something about her that was mesmerising.

Cal shook himself and focused on Marty's observations. Mesmerising or not, he had promises to fulfil. Three months, he'd been given. Three months to train with the most highly skilled search and rescue team in the world and then he'd be back in Scotland to resume his duties and try to make amends for the mistake that had cost his brother his future.

By the time they reached the ED it was almost the end of Abbie's shift. Her head was thumping a little but the bleeding had stopped. And, okay, she'd lied. The scoop had been so heavy, her hands were cut and sore, but none of that mattered until Marty and Shane were sorted out. Having already taken Shane through to her waiting colleagues, she now helped wheel Marty's gurney into Resus and handed over to the ED staff. Into safe hands.

Theoretically, from this side of the process, she was done, but she hung around, feeling a little sidelined and a lot out of sorts. Actually, she was in pain and a little shocked at how things had progressed in those wintry conditions and how close they'd come to disaster. Cal was standing next to her. He looked up from his notes, those bright eyes catching her by surprise. He was a big man. Tall. Broad. Calm. He glanced at her forehead. 'You need to get that cut sorted out. I'll ask someone to take a look.'

'I'll sort it. Thanks. They're all too busy with Marty and Shane and a load of other things.' She swiped the back of her hand across her forehead. 'It's all dried up. I'll do it later.'

'Or, I'll do it for you, now.' He pointed to an empty cubicle. 'Grab a seat.'

'But I want to stay and work on Marty.'

'Tough luck. Not your job right now.' A straight talker, then. As he spoke Cal wheeled round and opened a few drawers, finding some gauze and saline.

'Actually, it *is* my job. I can't just abandon my shift.'

'I'm not asking you to, but you're my responsibility right now—you hurt yourself on my watch.'

'It was hardly your fault; we did what we had to do. This is just a bit of fallout. I'll live.'

'But I'm duty bound to fix you up. Plus, I can't let you tend to any patients looking like that—you'll scare them off.' His eyes glinted with laughter and she couldn't help joining in. Next thing she knew he was moving her to a seat and pressing the gauze onto her forehead. He'd been firm but fair up the mountain, having been thrust in charge of three—no, four, including the pilot—lives. Clearly, he was the kind of guy who took responsibility seriously. He hadn't been flustered or snappy, he'd just calmly told them all what they needed to do. A leader by example. And here he was doing it again.

He was also incredibly close. She couldn't remember being this close to a man who wasn't her patient for a long time. A long, long time. He was still being all calm and in control—if not a little bossy. And that made her nervous inside.

And…and he had the most amazing scent. A fresh air kind of smell. Something she wanted to inhale.

Stop it. She could feel her cheeks starting to burn. 'Look, give me the saline, I'll just wipe it—'

'No.' His voice was level and steady and she got the feeling he wasn't going to cave in to her refusal. 'Sit down and let me clean this up. This is going to sting.'

'Are you, by chance, an older brother?'

'Yeah. How did you guess?' There was a grim smile at that comment, his eyes dulling a little.

'Oh, you know, the take-no-crap bossiness. I bet your sibs love you.'

'As it happens, he does. One brother. Younger, by two and a half years. He hates me and loves me in equal measure.' There was a pause where Callum seemed to retreat into his own thoughts, his eyes clouded with pain that seemed to come from nowhere, but permeated his body. 'No, actually he just hates me.'

'Boys will be boys, I guess.'

'Something like that.' Cal took her hand and started to open the fist she'd made to try to keep the blood circulating, because to straighten out the broken skin hurt. A lot. Instead of thinking about the pain she focused on what he was saying, and what he was leaving out. It wasn't *something like that* at all; she could tell. His manner had changed. He'd shut down a little at the mention of his brother. Or maybe she was just imagining it. She couldn't fathom why she'd even noticed, and why his reticence intrigued her. He touched her fingertips lightly and they began to tingle. 'Let me see your hands properly.'

'Oh. Ouch. Remember when I said, *be gentle with me*? Yeah…that.'

Compared to the rounds and rounds of IVF she'd been through, the head wound was a walk in the park. Her hands, though—they were still frozen and cut and she just knew if he saw them he'd flip out. Because he was that kind of guy. The protective sort. The thought of which made her stomach constrict. She'd had one of them. A wonderful, amazing protective man who'd held her heart so tightly she couldn't imagine giving it to anyone else. She didn't need to, or want to. So she had no right to be thinking about Cal's eyes or manner, let alone getting carried away with smelling his scent. 'My fingers are starting to thaw out…you know that weird buzzy feeling?'

'Aha. Only too well.' He peeled her fingers open and sucked in a breath at the sight of her raw, bleeding skin. 'You shouldn't have carried such a heavy weight, or you should have put your gloves on to protect yourself.'

'Should have, would have, could have. There wasn't time, remember? None of it is important, anyway. Marty's safe and Shane's being looked at. That's all that matters. Right?'

But he'd zoned out, looking at her wedding ring. He was all matter-of-fact when he spoke. 'Yes, well, all fixed up now. How are your feet?'

She stamped her boots and wiggled her toes. Luckily she'd put extra-thick socks on today. 'Feet are just fine. Thank you. I'm good to go.'

'And I'm in charge of this shift now that Shane's indisposed, so finally, just one last thing: you need to get a hot drink inside of you and something to eat before you do anything else. We need to debrief before the next call if possible. Definitely time for a break. Paramedic's orders.'

'I'm fine.'

'You usually have blue fingers?'

Looking first at him then back at her hands, she realised there was no point in arguing. He was, in fact, right. She was still freezing and hadn't had a drink in hours. She'd be no use to anyone like this. But she wasn't letting him know that. And, if she was absolutely honest, she wanted a couple more minutes with him—it had been a strange day and debriefing was a great idea. With a theatrical sigh she rolled her eyes. 'Definitely an older sib.'

Could have done a lot better. Cal looked at the inexpertly applied gauze on her forehead and inwardly cringed. It looked as if it had been stuck on by a kindergarten kid.

It was because he was cold; that was what he was telling himself, anyway. And not because there was anything going on here—like attraction. Given he was heading out of town soon, attraction was a spectacularly bad idea.

Because of her wound, her bobble hat was pushed back, so more tufts of dark, coffee-coloured hair stuck out around her face. She looked as if she'd been…well, as if she'd been on the top of a mountain in a hurricane. It was lucky she'd been there as an extra pair of hands—albeit damaged in the process. She'd coped well, but his heart had only just about started to beat normally again. The SARS training had given him confidence he'd have been able to deal with anything up there, but he hadn't wanted to test it.

He paid for the flat white and handed it to her, wondering what this urge to chat with her was all about. He didn't usually buy Shane a cuppa and *debrief.* Yeah, right…great chat-up line; that'd have them all laughing back at base. The closest they ever got to debriefing for real was a quick chat on the ride to the next emergency, scoffing a lukewarm pie and bad coffee from the petrol station.

They steered through the busy cafeteria and found an empty table. Once they'd settled in, he broke up his bar of chocolate and offered some to her. 'Eat; you'll be better with something inside you to bring up the blood sugar.'

She blinked. 'You really *do* do a lot of bossing around.'

'Sorry. Bad habit of mine. You're not the first person to tell me that. It's a kind of misguided attempt to look after you.' Instead of analysing his faults—he was aware he had a few, because Finn made it his personal mission to highlight every single one of his brother's shortcomings—he went for a change of subject. 'So, you had a baptism of fire up there. You handled it all very well, though. Not bad for a newbie.'

Underneath the huge jacket, she bristled. 'I've been a nurse for a long time. I'm just new at ED, that's all. Well, I've been here a few months. But it's a big learning curve, right?'

'When you're out in the field, yes. You don't know what's going to be thrown at you.'

She took a sip and seemed to settle a little. 'I haven't seen you here before, though.'

'Different shifts probably, and I've been out at Wanaka a lot and with the SARS team. I've only been in New Zealand a couple of months all up.' Which reminded him that spending what little time he had left talking to women he could never see again was pretty pointless. Although very nice. Actually, more than nice.

'And you're from… Scotland? Is that right?'

'Aye.' The familiar tug of responsibility tightened in his gut. He needed to get back there. Wasting another month here felt as if he were killing time. Time he could be using to sort Finn out. But, he'd promised to get as much training as he could and he didn't want to go back unqualified, or to seem ungrateful to everyone who'd pushed him to come here in the first place. 'Another month then I'm gone.'

She nodded before blowing on the steaming drink. 'Of course you are.'

An odd reply. 'What does that mean?'

'The majority of people working in Queenstown are just

passing through, so I'm not surprised you'll be going, too. Where next? Aussie? Asia? The big OE we call it. Overseas Experience. A gap year?'

'At twenty-nine, I'm a bit too old for a gap year. Honestly. No travelling, I'm going straight back home.'

She looked surprised. 'So you did all your travelling before coming here?'

'No. I'm not travelling. I came to do specialist search and rescue training. For my job. I have…' And here was the thing—he was suddenly torn. The minute he'd been needed he'd pledged to spend the rest of his life looking after his brother. This trip had been the first glimpse of how life could have been, but nothing was going to stop him going back. Finn needed him. 'I have responsibilities back home.'

Was he dreaming or did she look at his hand? For a wedding ring? Laughable. He had enough to do without taking on someone else. 'Well, they'll be glad to have you back, I'm sure.'

He smiled. She didn't know the half of it. 'I doubt it. But I'm going anyway. What about you? Obviously a Kiwi…?'

She smiled right back. Looked straight into his eyes, and he got a warm sensation swimming through him. 'I've lived in Queenstown my whole life. Been out of the country a few times for holidays, but always came straight back here. It's where my family is.'

'You're not one of those New Zealanders who has the travel bug, then?'

'No. I need to stay here.' At his raised eyebrows she continued, 'Responsibilities too.'

'Oh—?' But of course. He'd noticed the wedding ring on her finger before. That was okay. He could do platonic. Yeah, platonic was good. Maybe then he wouldn't be so mesmerised by her.

Odd, but she quickly drained her coffee and looked at something behind him, her eyes darting and dancing, kind of nervous, kind of sad. 'Oh-oh, caught in the act. My boss is heading over. I've got to go.'

'Hey, Cal.' It was Steph from ED. 'Abbie, sorry to disturb you. I heard you did well today. Awesome job.'

'Thanks. It was…' She caught Cal's eye and smiled. A shared day, shared joke, shared rescue. There was always a bit of a connection after that. 'Interesting.'

'You left this on the desk, I thought you might want to keep it safe.' Steph handed her an ultrasound picture. He was no expert, but it looked like an antenatal one. Yep—even from here he could make out the shape of a baby.

She's having a baby.

'Thank you. Yes. Oh, goodness. My scan.' Abbie's eyes were filled with pride that gave Cal a strange jolt in his gut.

Steph ambled on chatting as white noise filled his head. 'Thought of any names yet? Did you ask about the gender?'

'No. We're going to wait. It's exciting, though. I can't believe that by Christmas there's going to be a baby here.

She's having a baby.

A bairn.

His overprotective gene fired into action. Finn would have laughed as usual and told him to back right off, but Cal couldn't help it. This was serious. He waited until Steph had gone, then, 'You didn't tell me you were pregnant. Up there. In the snow. You fell over. I let you carry a heavy weight. Why did you let me think you were okay?'

'I am okay. I'm fine, actually. Honestly.' She didn't even look a little contrite. What a dangerous game she'd been playing. And he shouldn't care, not at all, but for some reason he was firing on all protection cylinders today.

Maybe he was missing Finn. Missing the opportunity to care and be useful. *To fuss and smother,* as Finn would say.

'You carried that scoop, which would have put a strain on your whole body, and you hurt your side. You were wincing and it's obvious you still have some pain.'

She shook her head. 'It's nothing, just a pulled muscle. Really, I'm fine.'

Yeah, he'd heard that before. When his brother wanted him to believe everything was okay. It hadn't been. It had been far from okay. He wasn't buying it. He stood up. 'I want you to get looked over. I'm not listening to any excuses...you need to be checked out. An ultrasound or something.'

'Who are you? My mother?' But she was smiling. Smiling and moving and dancing. *Really?* He knew she was committed to someone else. Married, for God's sake. He needed his head looking at.

'I'm just concerned, Abbie. You could have hurt—'

'My baby?' she cut in, laughing. 'Don't worry, Callum. My baby is...' she nodded towards a pregnant woman walking towards them '...over there.'

What?

He did the maths, joined the dots, put all the jigsaw pieces into place.

Ah.

How could he have got it so wrong? His gay radar wasn't working today. 'Oh. I see. Your partner's having your baby...your *wife*?'

She rubbed her fingers over her wedding ring and laughed. 'You really have got it *so* wrong, I can't begin to tell you. But I've got to go. I've a very important coffee date. Thanks for warming me up.' Then she paused, blushed, her eyes meeting his in a very heterosexual kind of way. He could see something there that was just for him—a softening, a little bit of playfulness, a very timid flirt. Or was there? Was he going mad? There was definitely a connection here he just did not understand. She shook her head, dragging her gaze from his. 'I mean… Well…thanks.'

CHAPTER THREE

COULD I HAVE been any more tongue-tied? Eurgh.

It had been three days since she'd had that strange afternoon with Callum, and every time Abbie thought about it she cringed and blushed. Even when she was on her own.

She should have been upfront with him but she'd been cold and tired and excited about the baby and...flustered.

The man made her flustered.

Which was why she'd decided to go for a run—to purge those feelings, all of them, from her system. God knew she had enough on her mind without trying to work out why a man was making her lost for words.

It was the shoulder season, but in Queenstown that still meant a lot of visitors filling the buzzing town centre. A coach pulled up lakeside, spilling passengers for the *TSS Earnslaw* steamship cruise. The tourists, all rugged up in matching waterproofs and chattering excitedly, weren't looking where they were going, so Abbie had to zigzag round them.

'On your left,' she called out, hoping they'd move for a slightly uncoordinated runner. She could hardly blame them for being excited, though; the sun was out in the cloudless sky and it finally felt like spring. Although, that could easily change.

Not accidentally photo-bombing or running into the

crowds was difficult and Abbie craved some quiet thinking time, so she headed along past the gardens and out onto the lakeside bike trail.

For a few kilometres or so she shared the track with cyclists and other runners, but eventually she was on her own, breathing hard and trying not to trip over wayward tree roots and little rocks sticking up at irregular intervals as she navigated through bush.

Eventually, she found her rhythm, blissfully unaware of anything else but her feet hitting the ground, the rustle of the trees, birdsong. Then, the bit she liked best of all— the trail opening up from bush to a wide track, and the view of the lake, which, as always, took her breath away.

Up ahead there was a figure sitting on a bench. Great place to smell the roses, if you had the time. Sitting didn't do a lot for Abbie. Ever since Michael died she'd been running, exercising, anything to get rid of the excess energy that seemed to spiral through her. Anxiety didn't hang around when her lungs were pumping nineteen to the dozen. Endorphins worked too. Happy hormones— she needed them. Especially now.

As she closed in she heard talking. Bench Man was on the phone.

'What d'ya mean, you've been out on *The Cairnwell*? For God's sake, Finn, will you listen to me—? I don't care if it's the easiest one. You will not go there again, d'you hear me?'

Cal?

Just when she'd thought her heart couldn't beat any faster it sped up even more. She slowed right down. Even though she was feeling guilty about playing him along, now clearly wasn't the right time to fix things. He had no clue he was being watched and she felt a worm of discomfort twist in her tummy. If she entered the clearing he'd see her; right now she was camouflaged by the trees. But it felt as if she was eavesdropping on a very private conversation.

'Aye, well, I'm sorry about that. Did you take your meds?'

He was facing away from her, his back rigid. Shoulder muscles she hadn't seen the other day due to his hi-vis were well defined…taut. He was wearing sports gear too—a loose-fitting singlet and shorts. Running?

'Why the hell not? Well, you'd better start. Things are going to change when I get back. And how.'

He flicked his phone into his pocket and stood, staring out across the water, every sinew tense.

Now she didn't know what to do. Run? Walk? Say something? Nothing? Turn around and go home? Was he going to come towards her, or race off in front?

But he bent for a moment, lifting his foot onto the bench and checking his laces. If he turned his head even the tiniest fraction he'd see her. She'd be caught watching him. So not a good idea.

He looked the other way, along the path.

Now was her chance. She ducked out from behind the trees and sped along the trail.

'Race you!' she called as she overtook him.

What the hell…? Where had that come from? Her mouth had a mind of its own—and it was a little out of control. Damned endorphins must have kicked in early today.

'What?' He jumped at her voice, did a double take. 'Do I know—?'

'Come on.' Then, for some reason she didn't understand, she turned around and jogged backwards, slowly, until he caught her up. She threw him a gauntlet. 'Going to the bridge? I can give you a head start if you need it?'

'Abbie?' His gaze skimmed her body—for the first time ever she felt unbearably underdressed in full-length running tights and a razor-back top. And suddenly very hot. But then, she had been running. His amazing eyes met hers and he grinned. Not the faintest hint of breathless-ness anywhere in him. 'Well, wow. Unexpected. Hello.'

'I can hang back, let you go ahead if you need to.'

The irritation she'd seen in him while on the phone disappeared and he laughed. 'Not necessary. Challenge accepted.'

'To the bridge?'

'Seriously?'

There was a moment when she almost felt sorry for him. 'You underestimate me at your peril.'

Then there was no more talking.

They were evenly matched…at least, at first. She met him stride for stride and only when the path narrowed did she fall behind a little. All the better to get another view of those amazing muscles. He was either a climber, or he worked out. No one had that kind of upper-body strength just by lifting gurneys.

But when he sensed her close behind him he pulled sharply to the right to let her join him again. The bridge was in sight. She let him think she was going to let the friendly camaraderie continue, then, with fifty metres to go, she sprinted out. Hard. Fast.

He got there at the same time. Laughing, reaching for the stone wall to tag. 'Well, you're fast, that's for sure.'

She decided not to tell him her reasons for running these days. Some things should be kept private. Besides, she could barely manage words. She hauled gulp after gulp of air as she bent over, hands on knees. 'Ran for…Otago. Back…in…the day. School…cross-country champion.'

'What? Like, last year?'

'Over ten years ago.' She pulled up, hands on hips. 'I know, I know, everyone always says I look young…but I'm

as old as Methuselah really. Twenty-nine. Believe me…
I've lived a little.'

'Ach, the wild child of Queenstown?'

Hardly. She'd been married at twenty-three. Felt ancient
at twenty-five when she'd unexpectedly hit most of the age-
ing milestones far too soon—a married woman and then a
widow. Sadly, the family bit had passed her by. 'Not quite.
Let's just say, it's been an interesting ride.'

Without discussing where they were headed they started
to walk back towards Queenstown centre. Yes, she could
easily have run, but she didn't want to tire the poor thing
out. 'And you? A wild child of…?'

'Duncraggen.' He tipped his head back and laughed.
'The only thing that's wild up there is the weather. Oh,
and the sheep.'

'Where's that? Dun…crabbing?'

'The very tip of Loch Lomond, a tiny wee village near
Inverarnan. Not a lot about it, really.'

'So Queenstown must be the big scary metropolis,
then?'

'I did live in Edinburgh for a while. And I have travelled
a fair bit…in my youth.' He made a creaking sound. 'But
now, young whippersnapper, I'm over the hill.'

'Oh, don't be too hard on yourself.' Where was this
coming from? It felt natural to joke with him. 'You don't
look a day over seventy.'

'Cheeky.' He threw her a sideways look and she could
see laughter in his eyes. It was so nice to see that. A man
who didn't take himself too seriously.

But then she remembered the untruth she'd let him believe. Not quite a lie, because he hadn't outright asked her,
but not the truth either.

'Look, I've got a confession to make. I let you think that
I'm…that I'm married to Emma.' If her cheeks could have

got any redder they would have. As it was, she was puce from running and the cold wind on her face but having to put things straight was more than a little embarrassing. 'Thing is… It's, well…'

She'd got over talking about Michael's death without crying. The grief didn't overwhelm her as it used to. She could go a few days without that lurching feeling in her stomach when she thought about him. But explaining it to Cal felt difficult, for some reason. Never mind the whole *someone else is cooking our baby* bit.

'It's what?' Cal stopped, his eyebrows knotting together as he looked at her. They'd come up to a quaint old café overlooking the lake and he pointed to it. 'Tell you what, let's have a coffee. Something stronger? You look like you need it and I have to confess, I'm all intrigued.'

Sit down and analyse everything? No, thanks. 'You know, I'm actually happy moving and talking.'

He was still smiling. 'Yes, I got that the first time I met you.'

'Really?' He'd noticed her? There was a little thrill in her stomach. A strange long-forgotten feeling, as if her body was remembering how it was supposed to work. She'd been on autopilot for so long—just breathing and surviving—this was new and different and not a little scary.

They began to amble along the path and, even though it felt strange, she had to admit it was actually quite nice to be in the company of a man for a change. Emma was her best friend and they talked about anything and everything, but this was…different. Interesting. She drew the line at *exciting*, because she wasn't going to allow herself to feel that, despite her tummy going all out with its little butterflies. 'Anyway, Emma said I was mean to let you think we were in a relationship, when nothing could be further from the truth. Em is my friend, that's all.'

He cleared his throat. 'I see. You're not married to her. You're not gay?'

'Not even a little bit. She really laughed at that bit, said I wasn't her type.'

Did she imagine it or did his breathing hitch a little? Did his pupils dilate ever so slightly? Probably not. 'Ah, so it's her baby…but you're great friends, so you refer to it as yours too? Am I any closer?'

'Not exactly. Maybe we should have had that coffee after all.' She sighed and took a few more breaths of perfectly cold refreshing air. Everyone at the hospital knew what had happened to her husband. All her family and friends had been so very supportive, so she didn't ever have to explain it to anyone new. Because there was never anyone new in her life. Until now.

But wait! Cal wasn't in her life. He was just another traveller passing through. Regardless, she did owe him an explanation. It wasn't as if he couldn't ask anyone at work—Shane even, when he was discharged—and they'd tell him anyway. It just felt better if she said it. 'Okay…so, I'm wearing a ring because I was married to a wonderful man, but he got cancer and died before we could have any kids. So Emma's having one for us.'

She'd said it so fast she thought he might not have caught up with it all, but clearly he had, as it made him actually stop in his tracks. 'Whoa.'

'I know.' The thought of the baby made her smile. The thought of Michael made her sad. It was how it was: a see-sawing of emotion. Her life. It was so much easier talking about this as they moved along the track rather than face to face in the café, with all that intimate intensity and not being able to avoid the eye contact that brought with it.

But Cal was all amazing eyes and concern. 'You really have been through a lot. I don't even know where to begin here. There are so many questions—and I understand if you don't want to answer them. I don't even know if I should ask them.'

'It's okay.'

'I don't even know what to ask…your husband… So… how long ago…did he…?'

'Michael. His name was Michael. He died coming up to four years ago.'

He glanced down at the ring. 'I see.'

He didn't have to say another word. She'd spent so long wishing Michael were here, and she still did wish that. So much. She picked up the pace again. 'Yes, I still wear the ring. I'm still married in my heart, you see.'

'Aha. And the baby? This is where it gets confusing for a soft-headed man like myself.' He scratched his chin and frowned and she knew he was just playing her, but it was confusing, even for her, and she knew exactly what was going on.

'I can't, you know, have one. Have any. So Emma said she'd do it for me. Surrogacy. She's going to give me the baby when it comes.' *I hope.*

His eyes narrowed. 'You have concerns she might want to keep it?'

Had she actually said that out loud? 'No, not at all. It's just, I've been thinking long and hard about this recently, and I'm so very, very grateful to her. She's giving me my dream. We always wanted kids, you know? But when I look deep into my heart, I don't think I could do it. I don't think I could carry a baby and then give it to someone else.'

His voice was softer when he spoke. 'It's amazing what you'll do for someone you love.'

He was quiet for a few moments then—not a difficult

kind of quiet, more a sad one. And yet, it wasn't a sad conversation or a sad prospect, not really. She was getting the one thing that she wanted. So, she presumed, he must have been sad about something else. 'I'm sorry, I didn't mean to bring it up…to make you feel awkward or anything.'

As if brushing off a memory, he shook his head. The smile was back, although a little less spectacular than before. 'Not awkward. Not at all. When's it due?'

'Twenty-third of December.' A Christmas baby. She hugged that delicious thought to herself.

But, like a mind-reader, he nodded. 'Just in time for Christmas.'

'I used to love Christmas. This is just going to make everything better again.'

'I hope so. Sounds perfect. If that's what you want.'

Clearly it wasn't what he wanted.

Why had she even told him all this? Why had she told him any of it? It wasn't like her to just blurt out her past history and her worries to a…stranger. He was a stranger. With a nice face. And amazing eyes. But he was still a stranger. A stranger who obviously had troubles of his own, had known difficult times.

'Anyway. That's me. Complicated doesn't begin to describe it. But… I don't know, I just felt like I owed you an explanation.'

'Abbie, you don't owe me anything. What you do is your business. I'm sure it'll all work out and you'll be very happy.'

'I hope so.'

'After what you've been through, you deserve some good times.' Without any warning, he sloped his arm around her shoulder and pulled her into a sideways hug. Just a squeeze, really, a friendly you'll-be-fine kind of thing, not anything meaningful. But her heart thumped at his touch. Her skin prickled. She inhaled his smell and thought, *Nice*. More than nice. There was that little butterfly stretching its wings in her stomach again. She pulled away.

They were still a little way from town, so she couldn't do what she naturally felt like doing, which was running. Running away from this feeling. From his hug. From this very nice man who was making her heart trip just a little too much. So she turned her attention onto him. All the better to put her own emotions and history back in their box. 'What about you? Family?'

'Just the brother. For the foreseeable future and beyond.'

When he'd spoken the other day about having to go back to Scotland for his responsibilities she'd presumed he'd meant family. A wife. Kids, maybe. And then she checked herself, because assumptions were what had made her feel uncomfortable when the staff had been talking about her. Just a brother seemed a strange reason to take himself halfway round the globe—clearly they had strong ties. 'Is that who you were talking to earlier?'

He rolled his eyes. 'You heard, eh? He's being a jerk. But then he thinks I'm being a jerk. So it's situation normal for the Baird brothers.'

'The bossy sibling strikes again?'

'Yeah. But the less said about that, the better. Let's not dwell on my baby brother. Don't want to ruin a perfectly nice day.' And there wasn't anywhere to go with that; he had that set-jaw look that she'd seen too many times on Michael to know he wasn't going to elucidate.

'Okay. So, no wife? Or husband?'

'No. Neither. And, I'm not having anyone's baby.' The light was back in his eyes now and he laughed, flattening his T-shirt over very flat-looking abs. 'This is just beer and good New Zealand *kai*.'

'Let's run it off, then!' And they were back to being silly and laughing and doing little spurts of sprints and star jumps, then a final race to the big red and white First World War memorial archway.

She got there first. Obviously. 'You're going to have to do better than that next time.'

Next time?

'Ach, well, I don't want to tell you this, but I did slow up just to let you think you'd won.'

'Too funny.' She flicked her hand across his shoulder. He was a good guy. But a liar. 'You did not. I could see you really pushing all out.'

'Aye, well maybe. Or maybe not, you'll never actually know, will you? Besides, I have strength in other areas.' The way his mouth tipped up made her fixate on his lips. They were lovely. He had the best kind of smile.

She was still looking at his mouth as she spoke. 'Hmm… strengths? Sounds interesting?'

Flirting? Was she flirting?

'When's your next day off? I'll show you.'

'What? When? Me? No. I couldn't.'

His hands were on his hips now as he teased her. 'Scared? Don't want to be beaten, is that it?'

Was this a date? No, it wasn't a date. They both knew a date would be stupid. She didn't want a man…and definitely not a man who was leaving and who had something sad in his past that was dragging him back to places he didn't want to go. But he was going anyway.

She'd already had one man leave her. One perfect, irreplaceable husband. This was just…something to do with her day off. And a bet of sorts now, as well. She couldn't turn down a bet. 'Never. Tuesday. Day off.'

'Right. Meet you here at ten.' He tapped the stone archway. 'Prepare yourself for some fun.'

Fun? What the hell was that? She shouldn't be messing around with him. She had a whole heap of things to do to get ready for the baby. Her next day off should be spent shopping, cleaning, antenatal class tour of the maternity unit… 'I'll have to be done by two o'clock, though.'

'Right. See ya, then.' With a wink he turned and ran off around the edge of the lake, scattering the sleeping ducks and seagulls as he went, filling the sky with squawks and cries and feathers. His long limbs moved with surprising grace, his body clearly attuned to exercise.

There was so much adrenalin going through her she should have run too, but she hung back and watched him disappear into the milling crowds. A quick wave. That smile. And the butterflies began to dance in her stomach again.

But it was far easier to watch him run than to examine what was going on inside herself.

CHAPTER FOUR

'MAKE HER BREATHE. Make her breathe.'

The floppy toddler was thrust into his arms and Cal was on full alert. They were fighting the clock—hell, in this job they were always fighting the clock—but getting some adrenalin into this wee mite was the only thing that was going to fix her breathing.

With a history of allergies, she'd responded to the rogue peanut in her bestie's smuggled-in kindergarten snack like a pro. Many kids got flushed skin when they started to react to an allergen, but some went pale. Not pale enough to alert a carer necessarily, so warning signs weren't always noticed at first.

Ava was now ghostly pale and her face grossly swollen, so much so her eyes were barely visible. The allergic reaction was already in full flow. Tight wheezes came from her chest, otherwise she was eerily quiet as she stared up at him. The rest of the kindy kids had been ushered outside to play in the sunshine, their happy chatter the only noise breaking through that of the toddler's restricted breaths.

Geez, if ever he needed a distraction from the enigmatic Abbie, this was it. He'd not been able to get her out of his head for the last few days and every time he'd delivered a patient to the ED he'd found himself looking out for her.

Their paths hadn't crossed since the run. Which was of no consequence right now.

'Hey, sweetie. Not feeling too good today?' It was always the little ones that got him the most. They were the ones that kept him awake at night, no matter how much he tried to put them out of his head. It was their faces he saw when he closed his eyes. The sweet damp baby perfume that lingered, along with the smell of fear from their parents. At least then it wasn't Finn's face and the heavy weight of panic tight in Cal's chest.

Having run in from the first responder car, he'd brought no gurney, so he lay Ava on a blanket on the well-worn carpet and started to draw up the age-suitable adrenalin. 'I'm going to give you a little injection, baby girl. That's going to help everything. Okay? Okay, Ava. Can someone gently hold her to stop wriggling? Great. Here we go.'

'Wait.' Just as he was about to administer the injection the teacher gave out a wail. She was equally pale and shaking as she held the tot's legs. 'Mum's not here. I can't... I can't give consent. Can I?'

'Lady, I'm giving consent.' This really wasn't the time for semantics. He had a duty of care and right now he was the only one able to save this kid's life. He raised his hand again and jabbed the needle into the little girl's thigh, watching as she screwed her face tightly. But not a whimper. Probably didn't have the energy to, she was so busy fighting her body's reaction, and failing. Just the roll of a lip, and what he could see of her eyes filled. He stroked back thick blonde curls, trying to keep emotion from rolling thick and fast into his chest, all the time assessing. Assessment beat emotion, every single time. Later, in the privacy of his own home, he'd go over his actions and his reactions. He'd allow the brief jolt of fear, then he'd remind himself he'd saved another life. The numbers were stacking up in his favour but it was the near misses he re-examined over and over. His penance for one stupid mistake.

He tugged a mask over her face and gave her oxygen from the portable canister. 'Yes, I'm sorry, it hurts, it hurts, sweetie. I know. You'll feel better soon.'

He hoped. He watched, and waited. The kid's pulse raced. Her eyes closed...

'Whoa, baby. Come on.' He attached the stickies from the portable monitor to her chest. Fast heartbeat...but a rapid heartbeat was better than none. The swelling was still severe but it often took a while for that to go down.

'Breathe, kiddo. Breathe well. Come on, wee thing.'

'Where is she? Where is she? What the hell happened?' A well-dressed woman burst into the room, ran over and launched herself at Ava.

Cal managed to hold her off just enough to make sure the toddler was coming round. A little sigh then a big gulp of air. A whimper. Then a full-blown cry. Thank God. He breathed out long and hard. 'She's doing okay now, aren't you, little lassie?'

'What did you give her?'

'You are?' The last thing he needed was to be giving out confidential information to the wrong person. He thought he knew who she was, but waited for confirmation.

'Her mother, of course. She's allergic to peanuts, eggs, tree nuts and anything dairy. And they know this. It's in her notes and I have to remind them all the time. They should be more careful.'

'I gave her adrenalin. She's had an allergic reaction.'

'Her EpiPen?' The woman looked down at the ampoule. 'Not her EpiPen? It has her name on it. What the hell...? This is ridiculous. I'm going to write a letter—she could have died because of their incompetence.'

Now he understood why the teacher had been just a

little reluctant to hand over care. Cal stroked Ava's hair again and watched her blink more alert. He turned to her mum, not caring what fuss she was making. 'Now's not the time. She's getting better, but we'll have to take her in for observation. There's a chance she could have a rebound reaction.'

'But the Epi—'

'Let's leave the mystery of the disappearing epinephrine 'til later, right? I totally understand why you're upset, but she's okay now and that's the main thing. We can go over everything else when things are calmer. Now, let's get her to the ambulance. You want to carry her? I can come alongside with the oxygen.'

The mother opened her mouth, appeared to think better of what she was going to say, then nodded. 'Yes. Thank you.'

The ED was busy for a Monday afternoon, but he handed Ava and her very concerned mother over to Stephanie, wishing, not for the first time, that in this job he got to see how his cases panned out. It would be good to see this kid as her normal wee self, playing and giggling, or to see if she was as serious as her mum. But the chances of him seeing any of his cases in anything other than an emergency situation were dwindling with every day he spent here. Just under four weeks and he'd be gone, never setting foot in this place again.

So it was probably a good job he didn't allow himself to become emotionally involved after all.

He was on his way out when he saw her. Actually, he heard her first—that lyrical voice over the beeps and coughs and cries that were the soundtrack of the ED—and he turned to her as if tugged by a magnet.

She was laughing and talking to an old man who she was walking alongside, notes and X-rays in her hand. As if she sensed Cal watching her, she slowly turned and smiled. In amongst the stark, rigid edges of the no-fuss easy-to-clean ED furniture, the sharp antiseptic smells and raw life, that smile added a little softness. She was real and her empathy shone through, even in the most urgent of situations. Strange how his gut tightened instinctively. He wasn't generally one to pay any attention to the state of his heart either, but it definitely sped a little faster right now.

She said something to the man, who looked over at him too, then she walked towards Cal, her dark hair pulled back in a ponytail, eyes bright. *Dancing.* 'Hey there, I wondered if we'd ever get to meet at work.'

'It's all in the timing.' A quirk of the universe. A different shift, a busier day and he'd probably never have met her.

'Did you bring little Ava in? I heard she'd had another scare.'

'Yes. You know her?'

'I know her mother. We went to school together.'

'Lucky.' He was too much of a professional to say what he really thought.

'She owns and runs the Mountain View Hotel, which didn't get the reputation for being the absolute best for nothing. She can be quite demanding, so I've heard from her suppliers. I hope she didn't give you a hard time?'

'She's just anxious about her daughter. It's totally understandable. People react differently under stress.'

'Yeah…and the rest. I hear what you're not saying too.' Abbie smiled and shuddered. 'I hope I'm not that kind of mother.'

Not seeing her pregnant made him forget she was having a baby. Surrogacy. They sure did things differently here. Still, he hadn't had a child of his own but had experienced that surging protective instinct, that unconditional love that made people do extraordinary things when necessary. 'You'll love your kid no matter what and will fight for it too; a mother's instincts. One gurgle and you'll be a pushover.'

'Oh, believe me, I'm bad enough just looking at the scans. But you've only seen me on a good day. You wouldn't like me when I'm angry.'

'I'll remember that.'

'Abbie? Can you—? Oh.' The pregnant lady from the café the other day came over, her eyes giving him the once-over. 'Hello.'

'Emma. This is Cal. This is Em. She's my—'

'Best friend. Yes. Hi.' Cal nodded, instantly on his best behaviour. For some reason it mattered what Emma thought of him. He stuck out his hand and shook Emma's.

A strange look passed between the two women. Actually, it was more a flicker of anxiety that fluttered across Emma's face. She quickly hid it and smiled broadly. 'Hi. Abbie told me about the medivac the other day. Sounds a bit wild. Good job you were there.'

'Och, it was a challenge, that's for sure. But we managed, didn't we, Abbie?'

'Absolutely. The A Team, right?' Abbie's smile tugged at his gut. There was something unspoken between them. He'd felt it on the run, too—a fledgling friendship. She was fun and pretty and kind. More than anything she had guts and he admired that.

But there were plenty of women on the planet like that, some of whom lived a damned sight closer to Duncraggen. So why this particular woman in this particular corner of the world seemed to be playing with his head he couldn't be sure.

His phone started to ring. A good excuse to leave now because staying would be foolhardy. Like the date idea.

It had been agreed on the spur of the moment, but it was hardly something he could renege on now. 'That'll be another job, no doubt. Right, I'll be gone, then.'

'See you tomorrow?'

'Oh, yes. At the archway. Good.'

He left them to it, unable to put his finger on what it was that he was feeling. Conflicted was the best way to describe it. She was a lovely woman with a whole ton of baggage, none of which he could do anything about. Or wanted to. There was no point in taking on someone else's business, no matter how nice and fun and kind she was.

Hell, he hardly knew her, so taking her out for the morning had been a pretty dumb suggestion. But he was a man of his word, whatever else.

'At the archway?' It was Emma's voice floating over to him as he walked away. 'What's that about?'

He didn't hang around long enough to hear the answer.

Abbie felt like a kid playing hooky rather than a grown-up woman. But she had the distinct sense she was playing hooky more from her promises to Michael than anything else. This was the first time she'd been out with a man since the last date night with her husband. This wasn't a date, it was just a bit of fun, but should she even be here?

Her last words to Michael had been, *'I'll never love anyone like you. I'll never love anyone again.'*

'Of course you will,' he'd said. *'I want you to. I want to leave knowing you'll find someone else to make you happy.'*

She hadn't thought back then that she'd ever be happy again.

Which was all a bit morose given she was in a car with Cal going…somewhere. She looked over at him as he drove, a glimmer of a smile on his face. He was looking up at the mountains around them and in his eyes she could see a kind of wonder and excitement that was infectious. She was probably too nonchalant about it after twenty-odd years living here, but looking from a visitor's perspective… yes, the snow-capped mountains and deep slicing valleys did take your breath away. 'So, where are we going?'

She only hoped it wasn't a bungee jump, given that was the number one tourist attraction round here.

'Can't say.' The smile bloomed. 'It's a magical mystery tour.'

In truth, the whole thing was a mystery to her—the weird flutters when she looked at him, the lightness in her chest that seemed to squeeze back the sadness she'd worn for so long. The fact she was having a physical reaction to a man after all this time. That was pretty intense stuff. Was it real, though? Or was she just being silly? She swallowed back the apprehension and the nerves and tried to keep her voice steady. 'Then I should really be driving, seeing as I'm the local.'

'And then it wouldn't be my treat, would it?'

'Have you done much sightseeing while you've been here?'

'I've seen a lot, but I think you could live here for a whole lifetime and still not see everything. Right?'

'Definitely. I've hardly explored any of it. Bad of me to admit, I guess, but when you live somewhere so amazing you do tend to take it for granted. I've always wanted to do some of the great walks, but never have time. I certainly won't when the baby comes. I'll just have to add them to my bucket list—which is getting longer and longer, I might add.' Michael hadn't written one. They'd been so damned sure he was going to beat the cancer they hadn't wanted to cloud that vision with might-haves and wish lists.

Stop thinking about Michael.

Michael was dead. Cal was very much alive. But it was so hard, after all this time, to stop thinking about her husband. A betrayal of sorts. She looked at Cal's profile, a strong defined jawline, long eyelashes to die for, and her heart squeezed a little. 'So, you said to Marty the other day that you'd like to climb Ben Lomond. Do you do a lot of climbing? Tramping?'

'Hiking, you mean? That's what we call it, but it's the same thing. I used to, yes. But—' He stopped talking abruptly.

'But, what?'

Whatever he was going to say he changed his mind; she could tell by the little shake of his head. He consciously controlled what he was going to say, curling into himself a little. 'Now I just spend my time rescuing people from the mountains instead of scaling them for fun.'

'That's a shame.' She wanted to ask him why, but didn't know him well enough to go probing into his life. Something had happened, she was sure of it. But then, didn't everyone have something in their background? No one got to thirty without some baggage, or betrayal, or loss. If they did, then they were the lucky ones. 'You should really get out there and do what you love. Life's too short to do stuff you don't want to do.'

'You're right there, Abbie. That's for sure. But sometimes you just have to suck up the bad stuff and get on with it.' He pulled the car into a sharp left turn and drove through the huge gates and the entrance to the Lakes Shooting Range.

'Shooting?' How many times had she driven past this and never once stopped? This tourist was showing her around her stomping ground, go figure.

He climbed out of the car and waited for her to do the same, then started to walk with her up a gravel path.

'Abbie, please don't tell me you were the Queenstown Primary top shooter as well as best arm wrestler and fastest woman in the southern hemisphere.'

'Why?'

'You're a veritable superwoman and I'm feeling just a little intimidated by all your achievements.' But he didn't look it as he walked her to the large modern barn advertising shooting and hunting, and held the door open to her. 'Hey, Trent. How you doing?'

Which was Kiwi for *good morning* and sounded strange and quaint with a Scottish brogue.

He was tall and strong and had a confidence she'd always yearned for. She watched as he paid and shook his head at something the owner said, then Cal came over with two shotguns. Shotguns! But he kept hold of them both, refusing to hand one over. 'Before you touch this I need to do a safety briefing.'

'Good, because I've never held a gun in my life. But you clearly know what you're doing.'

'Ah…well, yes. I'm cheating, to be honest. I used to work at a shooting range, part time, you know, after school and in the holidays. I come down here to blast off sometimes.'

'Oh, so you're a world-cup hotshot, then?'

'Not exactly. But not far off.' His eyebrows rose and danced above his eyes, making her laugh. 'Just missed out on the Commonwealth Games in 2006.'

'Oh, my God. Really? You must be good.' Then the penny dropped. 'You really are the most competitive person ever, Callum Baird. You only brought me here because you knew you'd win.'

'Er… I seem to remember it was you who started the whole race thing on the lake path.'

'Me?' But she had. And it had been fun, just like this. Like him.

Once outdoors they walked to a cordoned-off area where there was a machine housing what looked like coloured clay plates and some banked areas called stands apparently, where they did the shooting. After he gave her a thorough safety briefing and she'd been so put off by the dangers of a loaded weapon she almost didn't want to actually hold the gun, he pointed her towards a cluster of trees.

He was standing very close behind her as he helped her adopt the right stance. So close, she was aware of his scent, much more than in the car. It was fresh and wholesome—soap, citrus shampoo. Male. And she was so busy breathing it in that she was barely concentrating on his words. Plus, being so close was making her hands shake a little. Actually, a lot. His voice whispered over her neck.

'Put your ear defenders on. Stand a little forward, leaning on your left leg. That's it.' She really, really wanted him not to touch her thigh like that. Or rather, she realised, with a shock, that she did want him to touch her thigh like that. And more. His words were fuzzy, but that was more about the way she was feeling than his accent. 'Okay, the clay is going to come from the left. Trace it with your gun. Then, try to get a little ahead of it and just as it's about to dip, squeeze your finger. And shoot.'

Whoosh! The clay was out high in the sky and crashing down to earth before she'd been able to breathe. She followed it, right down to the grass. 'I'm rubbish.'

'No, you're not. You just have to stand still. Concentrate.'

How the hell was she supposed to concentrate with him standing so close? 'Show me.'

'No. You do it.'

'Show me.' She nudged him and moved out of the way, offering the loaded gun.

He shrugged. 'Okay.'

Taking the gun from her, he placed the edge of it high on his collarbone, his cheek resting on top and... Bang! A shower of pink clay floated to the ground. Bang! And again. Bang! And again.

'Wow! You're really good.'

'I know.' His forehead crinkled a little. 'Actually, I should have asked. How are your hands? Are they still sore from the gurney? I should have brought you to do something different.'

'I don't think it's my hands that are holding me back, to be honest.' She held her hands out and showed him the rough healing skin on her palms. There were traces where the handles had gouged holes, but on the whole they were heaps better. 'Yes, they still hurt a bit, but not enough to hinder me. I can do that all by myself.'

'Then you've no excuse, woman.'

He handed the shotgun back to her. It was warm where his cheek had been and she tried really hard not to think of him in any way as a sexual, sentient being. All she knew was that she felt strange when she was around Cal. Strange and new and scared and excited and yet comfortable, all at the same time.

'You just have to steady yourself. Be mindful—that's all the rage at the moment, ye ken? Be in the moment. Breathe in. Focus.' A whizz and another clay shot into the air. They watched it together and she tried to trace it as he'd told her. It started to dip. He shouted, 'Shoot.'

Bang!

She let her arm relax as the clay hurtled to earth, intact. 'Whoa.'

He was all attentive, his eyes dark with concern as he

took the gun from her and propped it against the stand. 'You okay? Loud? Did you hurt your ears?'

'No. Not at all. But when I hold the gun up my heart's racing and my hands are shaking.' But she knew it had nothing to do with shooting and everything to do with him. He was making her nervous, making her shake. Which was silly. He was just a man. A very good-looking and lovely man. An almost medal-winning shooter. A very accomplished… Her gaze moved from his eyes to his mouth. A very accomplished kisser? Where the hell had that come from? *For God's sake. Stop it.* She did not want to kiss this man. Any man. But definitely not this one. *Focus. Be mindful.* 'It's harder than it looks. I don't think I can stay still for that long.'

'As I thought.' He stroked his chin and pretended to peer closely at her. 'I diagnose…ants in yer pants.'

Despite herself she laughed. She hated that she couldn't hit the damned target, but, well, he made failure very funny. 'It's hard. I can't slow. I never slow. I'm much better at running.'

She filled her spare time doing things so she didn't have to think too hard about her life. About the empty space in her bed. In her chest. About a future where she was the only parent the baby would have… Oh, yes, she had Emma and Rosie but, when it came down to it, she was going to be on her own. Every night. Every day.

Every night.

And that hadn't really concerned her until now. She didn't want to be alone.

Although, she wasn't thinking Cal would be the one to stop her being lonely. He had a one-way ticket out of here. So she wasn't investing in him. And, anyway, she'd have the baby to fill her every waking moment and no doubt most of her sleeping ones too.

He placed his hands on her shoulders and looked into her eyes. 'Settle. Take some breaths. That's it. Slow right down.'

'Okay.' She shook out her arms, made them loose and relaxed, did the same with her legs. Stretched her neck from side to side. 'I'm good. Okay. Let's do this.'

He gave her the gun and once again corrected her stance. Stood by her as she watched. Focused. Boom! Shot.

The clay fell to the ground. Intact.

Give me a break. Concentrating and breathing slowly were not happening with him so close. 'Cal, could you just step back a little?'

'Sure. Whatever helps.' There was a light in his pupils, a tease that tugged in her gut.

She was going to show him, if it killed her. She could do this. He was not having an effect on her. She would not let him. *Breathe. Don't think about him. Focus.* She closed her eyes and focused on her heartbeat. Opened them again. Caught the clay in her sight. Traced it. Anticipated the dip and— 'Shoot! Yes! Yes!'

The air was a fizz of pink powder.

'Yes! You did good.' He wasn't quite jumping up and down as she was, but she could tell he was impressed. There was a grin on his face the size of Lake Wakatipu. 'Do it again. Show me it wasn't a fluke.'

'How dare you? It was skill, not a fluke.'

It was a fluke.

The next clay crashed to the ground. And the next. 'Aargh. This is so frustrating. I did it once, I'm going to do it again.'

'You will. It takes practice. You've just got to keep going and going. You've so much grit you'll get the hang of it.' He stood back, but then bit his bottom lip and grimaced. 'Oh, and by the way, I have a confession to make. I…er…lied.'

'About?' Her heart jumped to warp speed. She couldn't imagine what he was going to say.

'About the Commonwealth Games. I was nowhere near good enough. Not even a little bit. Not even Duncraggen best. Well…maybe Duncraggen best.'

'Aargh, you.' She shook her head but laughed as she swatted his shoulder. Because…yes, she wanted to touch him. 'Why did you lie?'

Because she had when she'd met him?

'Just to see your face when you discovered I might be better than you at something. Priceless.' He went to tug her ear defenders back on, but paused. And then the strangest thing… The atmosphere went from funny to serious in a nanosecond. His thumb trailed along her jawline then across her cheek to her lips. His gaze became heated and focused on her and he smiled. Sexy and more. She knew what he wanted and she wanted it too. A kiss. She wanted to feel his lips pressed on hers.

Holy moly. She wanted to kiss him.

The air stilled. Her heart thundered in her chest and she felt the need to run, hard and fast…away. But she was rooted to the spot. She couldn't move if her life depended on it. She just wanted to see those eyes looking at her so intensely. To feel his mouth on hers.

But then his eyes darkened further, as if a cloud passed through his thoughts, and he took a step back, cleared his throat. 'Right then, lassie, you have about twenty more cartridges. Let's make them count.'

CHAPTER FIVE

HE'D ALMOST KISSED HER. Within an inch. Closer. He'd almost broken his promises; that nothing and no one would get in the way of looking after Finn.

And yes, he'd had some flings with women who were of the same mindset as him; who'd just wanted a good time, no questions asked. But with Abbie, things were different. She was the kind of woman who'd want more than just sex. Who was the whole package deal with a kid on the way—the *love of her life's* kid—and when Cal was with her he wanted a piece of that too. Something he hadn't ever contemplated. Something that was tugging hard. But he just couldn't. It wasn't in his future any time soon.

He had a debt to pay. And if it took a lifetime then it wouldn't be long enough.

A waitress brought over two glasses of pinot noir and placed them on the table, then fussed around finding blankets for their legs. Sitting outside to admire the view of rolling hills covered in vines had been a great idea, but didn't account for the cool wind whipping round them.

When the waitress had finally gone, he tipped his glass against Abbie's. 'You did well. I'll be phoning the New Zealand selectors and recommending you for the shooting team.'

'As if. I think you might need to hit the target more than

fifty per cent of the time to qualify, right?' She laughed. She was wearing a thick, baggy, candy-striped woolly jumper that hid most of the gorgeous body he'd seen on the run the other day, and skinny jeans tucked into knee-length brown boots. She looked the most relaxed he'd seen her, her hair in loose curls and her dark eyes sparkling. Always moving. Always dancing. So alive that he couldn't help wanting her, wanting a piece of that vibrancy too.

'It's early days. I'll have you shooting like a pro in no time.' And why he'd said that he didn't know. One minute he was making the decision to loosen the ties with her and the next he was making more plans with her. He was starting to lose the plot.

'Not sure I'm going to give up the day job just yet, though—' She tipped her glass against his. 'But, thanks. It's been fun.'

'That was my aim. Pardon the pun.'

She pulled a funny face. 'Oh, God, you're as bad at jokes as you are at running.'

'I told you, I let you win.' Tactics. Truth was, he'd already run fifteen kilometres that day and had been on his way back to town when he met her. Running to the bridge again hadn't exactly been on his agenda. But he'd never been one for backing down from a challenge. Especially not from someone like Abbie.

She was tapping her fingers on the table. Brewing something. 'Okay, so the score is one all. I won the run. You win the clay shooting. What should we do next? Something that neither of us are good at, or something we both are?'

He spluttered into his wine glass. 'I think you'll find I'm good at most things. Some things I'm exceptional at...' There was an edge in his voice that took the conversation from sweet to spice in an instant. Strange thing was, he couldn't control it even if he wanted to. He looked directly at her now, at her eyes and the perfect bow of her mouth. She swallowed. And again. But she didn't stop looking right back at him, too.

She licked her bottom lip and heat shot through him.

He'd almost kissed her and he still wanted to.

She leaned forward a little. 'I was talking about physical stuff.'

'So was I.' Because, why not test the waters? He'd assumed she was all about the kid and the package, but maybe not. Maybe she, like him, wasn't looking for anything deep. One last fun fling before motherhood hit.

His suggestion hung in the air and her cheeks coloured a deep, deep red, then a full all-out body blush. Cute. So, he made her feel a little of what he was feeling, then. Good to know he wasn't going mad and that there was definitely a mutual attraction here. It was just a very stupid idea. Seemed you couldn't break a habit of a lifetime. He was, after all, in his brother's words, the king of stupid.

He opened his mouth to say something about getting physical together, but the moment was broken as the waitress came out with their food.

Dragging some sweet mountain air deep into his lungs, he calmed himself. Thank goodness he hadn't actually proved his brother right. For one crazy minute he'd almost blown it. Abbie wouldn't want a fling. That had been his feral red blood talking, not his sensible educated brain.

After demolishing a huge helping of venison pie and salad she put her knife and fork down and leaned back in her chair. 'So, I've thought of the perfect thing. How about we climb Ben Lomond next week, then? I reckon I can just about fit you in on my next day off. Before things get really baby-crazy.'

'Absolutely not.' The words were out before he could

temper them. Truthfully, the thought of being up there on that ridge in the snow made his heart sing. But up there, *with her*, being responsible *for her*, turned the song from melody to high-pitched scream in his head. Not a chance. He softened his voice, relaxed his hold on the wine-glass stem. 'Hiking? In this crazy, unpredictable weather. No, thanks. You saw what happened to Marty, why we were up there in the first place. If we went up on our own there'd be no helicopter, no radio out.'

'But we'd be more prepared and there's two of us. I've been up it a thousand times, I've run up it in the summer in just trainers and a T-shirt. It's not that bad. Marty was just unlucky. Hell, you can get killed crossing the road. You can die—' She blinked. Swallowed. Blinked again. 'Well, you can just randomly die and there's no rhyme or reason for it.'

He knew she was talking about Michael, and he got that, but it wasn't going to change his mind. 'All the more reason to be sensible, then, especially with a baby coming.'

He'd thought that might put her off, but she became more animated, her hands open and moving, palms upwards. 'I want my child to be outgoing and adventurous, not to be afraid to take risks.'

'Taking risks is all very well until you have to live through the consequences. Not so exciting and life-affirming then, believe me.' He was not going to talk about this any more; they were steering into dangerous ground. Too close for comfort for him.

But she ran her forefinger round the rim of her wine glass, her mouth forming a pout, and he wasn't sure if she was angry or teasing or frustrated. 'What's really the matter, Cal? Are you fobbing me off? No? What is it, then? Scared?'

Of losing someone else? 'Actually. Yes, I am.'

* * *

That was so not what she'd expected him to say.

There was a moment of confusion as she reconciled the excitement in his eyes at the mention of tramping and then the shut down at the suggestion he did it with her. The grip of fingers on the wine glass and tightening of his jaw. 'But I thought you loved it.'

'I do…did.'

He wasn't exactly forthcoming, so she pushed a bit more. 'Scotland must be one of the best places for hiking. Did you climb Ben Nevis?'

He nodded. 'Sure. Me and just about everyone else in the UK. It's like a motorway in summer. Dangerous in winter, and unpredictable, just like here, the rest of the time.'

'I've never been, but it's a lot like here, though, isn't it? I've heard people say the South Island reminds them of the Highlands.'

'Yes. Similar in lots of ways. Lots of hills…' He took a deep breath and let it out slowly. 'There's this thing, a challenge for hikers; any mountain in Scotland over three thousand feet is called a Munro. There are nearly three hundred of them. The challenge is to summit them all. It's called Munro *bagging*. You can combine two or three in one day, others are multi-day walks just to get to the top of one. Others you chip away at one day at a time. Some are on the tiny islands in the Hebrides, some are hard scrambles, others are more gentle. Like I say, you're supposed to get to the top of them all and tick them off the list. All two hundred and eighty-two, to be exact.'

'Wow. I thought New Zealand had a lot of hills. And have you completed them all?'

He nodded, pride evident in the straightened shoulders and tilted jaw. 'I have. Twice, and then…well, I haven't finished the third completion.'

'I can see from the way you're talking that it's something you love.'

'Aye. But I do it alone these days, if I go at all.'

'Why?'

He tugged at the zip on his padded black jacket. Up and down. Up and down. 'Because that's how I like it.'

'Isn't that dangerous? More dangerous than if two of us go? There's safety in numbers, right?'

His foot was tapping against the table leg. 'I'm fully prepared and equipped. I don't take unnecessary chances. I know the risks. It's better if I go on my own.'

'Better for who?'

Cal stilled completely and held her gaze. 'For me. Look, I'm not having this conversation with you, Abbie. We are not going walking, tramping, hiking or anything up that mountain or any other mountain, okay?'

'Whoa. Bossy sibling alert.' No one had ever spoken to her quite like that. But he was deadly serious and there was no budging the man on this, clearly. 'Okay. So, no Ben Lomond.'

'No Ben Lomond. Not until the summer anyway, when there's less chance of horizontal winds and snow. Then, you can do what you want.'

'But you'll be gone by then.'

'Aye. I'll be long gone by then.'

There was a sudden wistful pang in her chest. 'Why do you go on your own?'

'I climb the mountains because I have to. Because I can't not. I love it. But I go on my own, at my own pace. Those are my rules.' He drained his wine and stared out across the vineyard.

She probably shouldn't have pushed it further, but she did anyway. Because—well, hell, there was a story there, on the tip of his tongue, and she was going to find out what it was. Maybe it would explain why he wanted to be the Lone-bloody-Ranger up on those hills, and why the shut-down thing occurred every time she asked a question. 'What happened?'

His eyes were fixed on the table, right hand curled into a fist. 'You don't want to know.'

'You mean, you don't want to tell me.'

'No. I don't.' Cal sighed low and deep and shook his head, and she knew she'd overstepped the mark.

'It's okay.' She reached over the table, took a gamble and wrapped her hand over his. Because she'd pushed him to an edge and she didn't want to watch him dive over it just because she wanted to get to know him better. 'I'm sorry.'

He tugged his hand away and sat up straight. 'Ach, it was in the papers, you can have a read if you want to be bothered. Short version is: we were on a ridge and my brother fell. A long way. He's…not the same as he was.' He drained his glass and she got the distinct feeling that the subject was closed. His eyes had dimmed and he wore a cloak of pain so intense she thought he was going to shout or rage or storm off. But after a couple of moments he gave her a smile that was half reassurance and half sadness. 'Let's get you back to town. Two o'clock, wasn't it?'

'Cal? Wait—' She wanted to apologise for pushing him into such a dark place, but he stood up and was striding over to the counter to pay. How terrifying to have a brother suffer so badly and still to wear the strain of that. All she wanted to do was stroke Cal's back and try to make things better for him.

Which made her stop in her tracks and take a moment to think.

Everything inside her was screaming not to get involved with this man. He played a dangerous game. He took a gamble with his own life while dedicating his time to saving others. He was fun and deep and sexy and stirred the sleeping dragon inside her. There were more butterflies in her stomach now, flexing wings and stoking a heat inside her. And she knew, if she wasn't careful, that heat might just burn her.

So, sense said it was better not to get involved with Callum Baird at all. But the more she got to know him, the more she wanted to know.

Emma was waiting outside the antenatal room, tapping her watch as Abbie half walked, half ran along the corridor, ignoring the *Do Not Run* and *Slippery When Wet* signs tacked to the walls. She wasn't exactly frowning, but it was a close-run thing with her pinched mouth and theatrical sigh. 'Two-oh-three. It's not like you to be late.'

Abbie grimaced. The last thing she wanted was for Emma to think she wasn't committed to this. She pushed all thoughts of Callum Baird and his roving thumb and mysterious past to the back of her mind. This was her future. Right here. In that blossoming belly. What the hell she'd been thinking, spending the morning playing, she didn't know. She'd been a fool to let him distract her from real life. 'I know. I know. Sorry. Sorry. Things ran late. I hope we're not the last.'

'There's a few in there already, but Sally's not here yet and she's the one taking the tour.' Emma held the door open and they squeezed into the crowded room. Women of all shapes and sizes stood around chatting. There were a few men, too, but certainly no match to the number of pregnant women.

'At least it's not all couples,' Emma said out of the corner of her mouth as she surveyed the others. 'Some grandmas here too, by the looks of it, and friends, girlfriends. At least we won't look odd being two women together.'

'The invitation said birthing partners. I don't care what anyone thinks. Mind you, if they start showing any birthing videos I may have to leave.' She was joking, of course. She'd delivered enough babies to know exactly what happened.

But Emma took the bait as Abbie knew she would. 'Hey, this is your baby. You're going to be there watching me suffer whether you want to be there or not.' She was laughing, but Emma didn't take her eyes from Abbie's. She had that no-nonsense look on her face that Abbie knew from years of being her friend. If she wasn't mistaken they were just about to venture into Emma interrogation territory. 'So, what's he like?'

Strike one for Abbie. 'Who?'

Emma rolled her eyes. 'Come on. *Outlander* guy.'

Abbie turned her back to the other class members and walked her to the window, all the better to chat a little without being overheard. Queenstown was a small enough place for gossip to spread between the locals as it was. How was he? Where to start? 'He's okay. I guess.'

Another eye-roll. 'Oh, please. Neither of us have had a date in years and all you give me is *okay*. Really? Really? This is so different from your first date with Michael.'

'Because it wasn't a date.'

'Yeah. Just like I'm not looking like a huge beached whale. How did *whatever it was meant to be* go?'

It had been a date.

There was no way of dressing it up in anything other than that. It had been a date and she'd enjoyed herself with a man. Really enjoyed herself, to the point of wanting to kiss him.

'Well…' It was fun stalling, just to see Emma's third eye-roll in as many minutes. 'On the downside he didn't turn up in a kilt. But on the upside he took me shooting. Like, a real gun. Clay things. I even hit some.'

That got a rise of the eyebrows. 'Interesting.'

'That's what I thought. A strange place to take a girl on a non-date, or even a date-date.'

Emma grinned. 'A rugged man like that looks more like the action type. Mountain biking, skiing…'

'Yes, well, having seen the way he moves in crampons I'd say that too.' Abbie fought the shiver that ran through her, wishing it were caused by the memory of the ice and not of him. 'He said he used to do more tramping but stopped. And then he went quiet, like he was dealing with memories.' And she knew all about that. She'd been there after all. Still was there in some ways.

But she'd decided to put Michael in a box and determined not to talk about him to Cal. Her chest tightened at the thought of that. It was hard to leave her former life behind. Hard to think of someone else filling Michael's shoes.

Not that anyone could. But maybe it was time to start moving forward. Baby steps.

Emma wasn't letting up at all. 'Sounds like Mr Scotland has a few secrets, then.'

The injured brother. The ridge. 'Hmm. I don't want to pry.'

'Really? Of course you do.'

Abbie giggled. 'Yes, of course I do. But I know I shouldn't.'

This elicited a smile from Emma that was warm and encouraging. Which wasn't exactly helpful. 'You have a strange look in your eye, Abbie Cook. And I'm not sure what that means.'

'It means I had a nice morning with a nice man, that is

all. I probably won't see him again. In fact…' She made a decision right there and then. 'No. I won't see him again.'

'But that look does not say nice, or that you don't want to see him again. It says interested.'

'I'm not interested.' *Liar.* 'He's heading back to Scotland to care for his injured brother.'

'Oh, be still my beating heart. The man's a saint, too.'

Abbie thought about the way his thumb had skimmed her lip and the look of desire in his eyes. He'd wanted to kiss her. Not very saintly at all. 'No. No, he's just nice.'

'If you say so.' Her best friend shook her head, then looked suddenly pensive. And protective. The way Abbie had seen her in the past when saving herself and her daughter from a painful relationship with Rosie's dad. She tucked some of Abbie's wayward hair behind her ears and smiled, softly. A look that said she knew what Abbie was feeling. That more hurt was not needed, for either of them. The message telepathically delivered through kind eyes and a gentle touch. *Don't get in too deep.* And then in words. 'Just be careful, eh?'

'I don't need to be. It's nothing. Just a bit of fun.'

But Abbie wanted so much to tell her about the near-miss kiss and how looking at Cal gave her a fit of butterfly stretches so hard it made her tummy tickle. And how she liked the way he smelled. She wanted to be back being sixteen again, the two of them piling into her bedroom, jumping on the bed and spilling secrets. *Did he put his arm around you? Open-mouth or closed-mouth kisses? How did he taste? How far did you go?*

She wanted the innocence and hopefulness of youth to wash through her, instead of knowing what she knew: that falling in love was lovely, but all it led to, in the end, was falling apart.

And she couldn't have that. Neither of them could.

The class leader bustled into the room and grinned as they took their seats for the introduction. 'Excellent, ladies and gents. I'll just go over the plan for the afternoon…'

It was all such bad timing. Emma had never thought she'd look at another man again and think…nice. She'd never thought she'd go on another date. Or start to heal her broken heart. Or that she wouldn't be able to tell her best friend for life the way she was feeling because she didn't want to break the spell. She wanted to hug this feeling to herself.

But also, she didn't want anything to come between her and Emma and the baby. They were a tight-knit little family, with Rosie. That was what they'd promised each other, after Alvin had gone, and after Michael.

So she said nothing and grabbed a chocolate biscuit from the table next to her and Emma smiled, and they were fine.

But Abbie wasn't.

Then the woman running the class clapped her hands and they were up and off on the tour, talking about birthing pools and gas and air. What to pack in the maternity overnight bag. When to call, who to call, what to expect.

A quick look in the labour suite, then an equally quick exit as a woman was wheeled in in a wheelchair, screaming, 'I need to push. Now!' And the red-faced man with her asking for a vomit bowl. For himself.

For a moment the group stood in silence, eyes wide and slightly panicked. Swiftly followed by little hiccups of giggles.

In another suite, a brand-new baby had recently entered the world and let out a hearty little cry that completely broke the panicked spell. And they all grinned. Emma glanced over at Abbie and her eyes widened. 'Feeling a little bit more real now?'

'Oh, yes.' There was nothing more that Abbie wanted than to be here, heavily pregnant with Michael's baby. But being here with Emma was a very close second best.

'Well, feel this too. Kicking. Your baby's a little soccer player.' Emma grabbed Abbie's hand and pressed it against her belly, as she'd done when she was pregnant with Rosie. There was such a softness in her eyes that Abbie thought she might cry.

'Oh. Oh, my goodness. So he is.' There was a raw thickness in Abbie's throat, but her heart felt light and fluttery. This was real. This was what she'd wanted for so long, what she'd endured days of pain and injections and interventions and heartbreak for. This baby.

This was what they had to look forward to.

And she wasn't going to let a sexy, blue-eyed Scotsman—saintly or otherwise—get in the way of that.

CHAPTER SIX

'THIS IS ERIC. He's eighty-four and was involved in a motor vehicle-versus-truck accident over in Wanaka. Took a knock to the right side of the head on impact. Neck tender at C-three and four. Right chest and shoulder sore from seat belt. Suspected fractured right tib and fib. Right ankle was crushed so it took a little time to dig him out. He's shaky and shocked but holding a decent BP all things considered. He's had pain relief and is feeling a wee bit better if he keeps still. Moving's the tough bit, eh, Eric?'

Abbie would know that accent anywhere. Her heart flipped as she turned to see Cal in his red overalls and hi-vis. That voice had been distinctly absent for the past week and she'd decided, resolutely, that if she heard it again her heart would absolutely not flip.

Traitor.

She'd also decided not to look up the Scottish ridge accident on the Internet, even though she'd typed his name more than a dozen times and let her fingers hover over the return key. It wasn't her business and she wasn't about to start nosing around behind his back. If he wanted to tell her, then that was fine. If not, well, that would have to be fine too.

The old man on the trolley looked familiar, although with the neck brace and facial bruising it was hard to tell.

A quick glance at his surname and she knew they were neighbours. 'I'll give you a hand through to Resus.' She nodded at Steph, taking the end of the gurney and wheeling him through, Cal following. Their patient was frail and shaking as she put her hand over the paper-thin skin of his knuckles. 'Eric, it's me, Abbie. From the apartments at the end of the road.'

'Eh?' Pale blue eyes darted to her and she thought he might just have relaxed a little bit. Good. Healing happened a lot more quickly if the patient wasn't fighting the whole time.

'I fed your cats when you were in last time. Remember?'

Eric patted her hand. 'Good…girl.'

'You've had a bit of a bump.' Glancing at his vital signs on the paramedics' mobile monitor, she could see he wasn't out of danger, and she was glad to have something to focus on that wasn't a Scotsman with a nice smile. Still, she wished it hadn't been someone she knew who'd had a head-to-head with a logging truck; Eric was lucky to have come out of that talking. 'This is Stephanie and there'll be a doctor through any second and they'll get you sorted out. I just wanted to say hi and that you're in safe hands.'

'Thanks.' His hand was cold and weak and she gave it a squeeze, found a blanket for him and started to attach him to hospital monitors.

Once she'd explained he was headed for immediate surgery and a long stay she whispered to him, 'Don't you go worrying about the cats. I'll pop round and feed them until you're home. Don't worry, I'll sort them out. Key in the same place?'

'Thank you. You're gold, you know that, Abbie?'

Cal's eyes met hers across their patient and he smiled and nodded.

She shook her head and laughed. She wasn't gold, she

was just doing what anyone else would do in the same situation. But she felt like gold bathed in Cal's smile.

Nixon, the ED consultant, bustled in then Cal left and she focused entirely on her patient's care and not on the memory of that smile and the tingle skimming across her skin.

'I'll get straight onto the orthopaedic surgeons.' After doing a quick assessment Nixon picked up the phone. 'In the meantime, we'll get more fluids into him and keep him comfortable with more pain relief. If you're a neighbour, do you know his next of kin, Abbie?'

'No, but he's been in before, so it'll be in his notes. A son, I think. In Dunedin.'

'Excellent.' Nixon finished his call and gave her a quick smile. 'Hey, I just wondered...how's Emma doing?'

Unexpected. 'She's fine. Getting a bit tired these days. Why? Is there a problem?'

Nixon shook his head and his face flushed a little. 'No. No problem. I was just... Nothing. It's okay.' And with that he picked up the internal phone and started dialling. Conversation closed.

She watched him for a minute and tried to work out what that had been about. Then she heard the dulcet tones of the ward clerk and the auxiliaries discussing the love lives of one of their colleagues and decided he was probably concerned about her being the subject of gossip. Or, more likely, concerned about her pulling her weight at work. Or...then the Arrest Code alarm went off and she put everything else bar saving lives to the back of her mind.

Later, as she was pulling on her coat at the end of her shift, she felt the little hairs on the back of her neck prickle and awareness ripple over her. Cal was close somewhere; she could sense it. Sure enough, he was outside the staff café talking to the helicopter pilot.

She was going to try to sneak past and not allow her fluttering heart to take charge, but her words tumbled out before she could stop them. 'Hey, Cal.'

He ambled over, all smiles that sent ripples of need over her skin. 'How's young Eric?'

'He's a lot more comfortable now he's back from Theatre.'

He fell into step with her as they walked out into the bright sunshine. Queenstown was putting on a very summery attempt with a gentle warmth and pretty flowers in huge barrels along the pavement. Cal slipped on sunglasses that at once elevated him to rock-star status. 'Do you often take on the feeding of other people's animals when they're in hospital? You don't have to do that.'

'I know, but it's a small place, you know. We help each other out when we can.'

'I know all about that. You can't sneeze in Duncraggen without someone handing you a tissue. Where are we headed, by the way?'

She hadn't a clue, in all reality. 'I'm going to the primary school to pick up Rosie. I don't know where you're going.'

'Home, I guess. I'll walk with you to the school—my car's parked nearby.'

'So you can regale me with the tale of Eric's rescue along the way?' And it felt stupidly and refreshingly normal to walk side by side across the car park. It was these little things she missed: having someone to talk to about what to have for dinner, the sweet peck on the nose for absolutely no reason, a hand to hold in the middle of the night, walking across a car park. Hell…she really hadn't realised at what point grief had turned to loneliness, but now she felt acutely that Cal had slashed through all of that. He was filling her up with good feelings, but also turning the loneliness into a longing. A longing to be touched, held, kissed, and she wasn't sure how to deal with that.

After he'd talked about cutting Eric from the car he asked, 'You got to your appointment in time on Tuesday?'

'The visit to the maternity ward? Yes, thanks.'

'How was it? You learnt how to have a baby?'

She laughed, thinking about that poor man and the vomit bowl and his wife or girlfriend who was in the throes of labour. 'We've been there before. Emma's got a five-year-old—hence the school—so we know the drill. We have the birth plan and everything all agreed on.'

The walk to the school took them past a little park that smelt of fresh spring blossom. Magnolias hung full and ripe and pink from spindly branches. Cal didn't seem to notice any of it, maybe because it was just plain old pretty and not stunning snow-capped peaks. He seemed much more focused on her impending parenthood. 'That must be interesting. I mean, what if she wanted something— drugs, or whatever—and you didn't agree with that? How does all that work? Who's in charge? This surrogacy thing raises a lot of questions, doesn't it?'

'Like, whether she'll even give the baby up? What if there's something wrong with it? Will I still want it? Yes, I know. It's very complicated and wrought with questions and ethics. But bottom line, she's helping me out and we know each other well enough to know how we feel about most things.'

Emma was the only person who really knew what Abbie was going through, but it felt good to be able to share these thoughts—thoughts she'd kept away from Emma for fear of upsetting her—with someone removed from the situation. It felt a little disloyal, but he was a good sounding board, just letting her get her jumbled thoughts out without judging her.

Whatever he thought about the surrogacy set-up he didn't say, and she couldn't read it from his body language, but he seemed to take it in his stride. 'Something I've always wondered… Does she…do you pay her?'

'No, it's an altruistic surrogacy. I'm not allowed, legally, to pay anything but her expenses.'

'And then, afterwards…how do you see that panning out?'

'She'll always be involved, obviously. She's my friend and she's already brought up one baby—I'm going to need all the help I can get with that. Good thing we live next door to each other.'

'What if you didn't, though? What if you decided to move… I don't know, to the other side of the world, for example. Or Australia. Or even Auckland?'

They'd come to a halt as a taxi pulled away from a taxi rank. Abbie pressed the pedestrian crossing button and they waited for the red light. She was fighting the urge to slip her hand into his and feel his heat on her skin. 'I would never move. I couldn't. How could I? I'm the mother, but she's so involved. It wouldn't be fair to any of us to be separated. Why are you asking?'

'Ach, I was just interested in how it all works.'

'Queenstown is my home. I have my…memories here. I could never leave.'

His eyes softened as he looked down at her ring. 'Michael?'

She rubbed her finger. Would she ever take this off? Could she? 'Not just him. Everything I've ever known is here.'

Cal shrugged, scrubbing a hand through his hair. 'I couldn't wait to leave Duncraggen. I wanted to see the world. Rule the world, if I'm honest. I was a cocky wee bairn, I have to admit.'

'But you went back.'

He stiffened. 'Of course. He needs me.'

How? Why? Maybe if she just looked on the Internet she'd know…but no. She was going to resist that temptation. It was his story to tell, if and when he wanted to. 'Now you rule your small piece of Duncraggen.'

There was a wink and a rueful grin. 'Well, Finn believes he rules it, to be honest…but I just let him think that.'

Abbie unlatched the school gate and dipped in to pick up Rosie. There she was, all pink-cheeked and a mass of dark curls causing the usual squeeze of Abbie's heart. What this kid had been through, and been protected from, sometimes haunted her. Out of all the men in the world, Emma had somehow fallen for one of the bad ones. Ever since, she'd determined that the only person she was going to love unconditionally was her daughter. Oh, and Abbie…and their bun in the oven. Abbie wondered if she could possibly love her own child any more than she loved Rosie, and decided that that kind of love was simply unimaginable.

'You can have five minutes to play before we go home; either the play park here, or the one near the house. One, Rosie. You can choose.'

The little girl's eyes narrowed as if she had to make a life-or-death decision. She looked over towards the park and the shiny slide, so much higher and better than the one closer to home. The choice was hardly difficult. 'This one.'

'Good choice. But no tears when we go past the other one.'

'Okay, Abbie.' Her eyes darted towards Cal. Luckily, with a couple of uncles close by, Rosie had had a lot of positive men in her life. 'Who's that?'

'A friend of mine. This is Cal.' Friend. It felt strange saying that, but that was what they were. Nothing more.

He was leaning against the gate, hands stuffed deep in his pockets. He tugged one out and waved at Rosie. 'Hi!'

But the little one had lost interest and was careening towards the slide.

What had they been talking about? Oh, yes. Finn. 'So, how is your brother?'

Sighing, he shook his head. 'Don't even ask.'

'Not climbing mountains without your permission again?'

He grimaced, shoulders stiff. 'Planning a skiing trip. With one leg. I ask you.'

Rosie slowly climbed each step, putting both feet on each rung as she went. Finally at the top she gave a little wave. Her smile splitting her face.

'Hold on with both hands, sweetie.' Abbie waved back and nodded encouragingly for her to sit down. Sweet, sweet girl. Then turned back to Cal. 'You can't protect him for ever.'

'Why not?'

'How old is he?'

'Twenty-seven.'

She coughed, dragging her eyes away from little Rosie and back onto him. Childminding and chatting was serious multitasking. 'Really? From the way you were talking I thought he must be under eighteen.'

He shrugged. 'You think I'm overprotective.'

'I think you love him very much and don't want him to get hurt again. But it's his life, Cal. Let him take some risks.'

'But what if…?' He shook his head. 'I know, I know. Well everything's easy in theory.'

How to say this without sounding hurtful? 'I don't know

what your relationship with your brother is really like, okay? But I do know that when you hit adulthood things aren't as basic as limiting a five-year-old to this park or that park. Your brother sounds like he was a pretty competent athlete before his accident, so I'd say he's trying his damnedest to get back to some semblance of that. To get his life back. You want that, right?'

'Of course. Yes, of course I do. But what if he—?'

He couldn't say it. He couldn't imagine it, and she was glad he hadn't had to face that kind of thing as she had. But, for Abbie, it was getting easier to say these things. It had been something that she couldn't shy away from when reality hit. No amount of euphemisms would change the facts. 'What if he dies? Then he'll die doing something he loves.' She put her hand on his arm and looked up at him, hoping he'd take this with as much kindness as she meant. 'Let him live again, Cal.'

'It's not that easy.'

'I know it isn't. Believe me, I do understand. You want to wrap them up in cotton wool and save them from pain and hurt. Let me tell you something—' She dragged in a deep breath. This wasn't something she shared often, but she hoped it would help. 'I spent so long trying to make Michael better, chasing cures and looking up miracle treatments on the Internet, that I forgot about spending good times with him. I just wanted him well so we could restart our life. I couldn't think about the alternatives. But all I ended up doing was alienating him, pushing him to do things he didn't want to do, trying different remedies, making him feel worse in the end, making him fight when he didn't want to fight any more, when he was tired of all that *brave* talk. All he wanted was to spend his last months doing fun things and being surrounded by love, but I was on a crack hunt for a cure and couldn't rest until I found one. It wasn't him who didn't have a bucket list, it was me who wouldn't let him.'

'You were only trying to help, you were fighting for him—that's a good thing, isn't it? You loved him and fought for him.' Cal nodded then as the penny dropped. 'I see. Yes. I get what you're saying. It's his choice.'

'Life's too short to force people into corners. I think, if I could, I'd just try to support people chasing their dreams... even if I didn't think those dreams would work. Even if they sound like a really rash idea.' She hoped it didn't sound like a lecture. 'And I need to apologise for last week. I tried to make you talk about things you didn't feel comfortable talking about.'

His hand covered hers and his thumb stroked over her skin. Such a simple gesture, but it stoked something deep inside her. Something more than lust. Although there was a good deal of that there too. His voice was soft when he spoke. 'And I should apologise for ruining a great morning with my *greeting*.'

'Greeting?'

'Whimpering. Whining. You know, carrying on.'

'It was nothing.'

'I'm not good at this.'

'You are.' She could have looked up into those eyes for hours. So demonstrative, so clear and bright. There was a funny feeling she got when she looked at him that she'd never had before. Or at least, she'd forgotten it. The keen ache down low. The straining of her breasts for his touch. The crazy ideas that popped into her head, the hope, the feeling that maybe things could be better.

She'd forgotten, or hadn't wanted to remember. God, she'd forgotten how that all felt and just looking at him it seemed almost in reach. Her eyes drifted to his mouth and she wondered...could she? Could she reach up there and put her lips on his? How would that feel? How would she feel deep inside? How would he taste? Would he kiss her back? Did he want to?

There was a little cry. Her name. Abbie turned and saw Rosie with her hands on her hips. 'What is it, sweetheart?'

'See-saw, please.' She pointed to the large plastic see-saw, each end shaped like a bright blue horse's head, the mane twisted into a handle for little hands. 'Okay, then. Two minutes on the horses.'

After a couple of moments of her bouncing up and down off her heels, Abbie's eyes naturally sought Cal out again. She was drawn to him, like a magnet. *Like a stupid infatuation,* she told herself.

It would all blow over when he headed back home. He was still watching and smiling. Waving. He must have thought she was dreadfully dull and domesticated, but this was her life and she was looking forward to more of it, not less. But instead of looking bored he looked actually quite animated.

Eventually she managed to convince Rosie it was time to go home for dinner, but as they came through the gate he said, 'I've had a thought about our next dare. If you're still willing?'

She tried not to look too pleased at the prospect, but her heart kicked up a little. Dare not date. She liked that idea. It sounded a lot less committed to a path she couldn't take a single step on. 'Maybe?'

He leaned in, his finger curling round a strand of her hair, and whispered, 'How are you in the saddle?'

Her gut clenched and fizzed and she giggled.

Like a teenager. Grow the heck up!

'In truth…rusty.'

'Excellent. Me too.' He grinned. Winked. 'Day off?'

'Thursday.'

He was still very close, his nose in her hair, mouth very close to her ear. Warm breath skittered over the back of her neck, making her shiver. 'I'm on an early. Meet you at our usual place at three-thirty?'

Our usual place. Her heart rate doubled. And she was probably reading far too much into it all. She grimaced, unsure as to what to do. Her heart screamed yes, but her head was being far too sensible. 'But—?'

Far from being playful, he was kind and genuinely concerned. He drew back and looked at her. 'What's the matter? Scared?'

She nodded, resisting the urge to curl into his heat and his touch. Scared didn't begin to describe how she was starting to feel when she was with him. 'A little, to be honest.'

He tipped her chin up and for a moment she thought— *hoped*—he was going to kiss her. But that would have been foolhardy with little eyes on her and a tiny chubby hand tugging her to *go home now, Abbie.*

He smiled. 'Don't worry. You know enough about me by now to be confident I'll make sure you're safe.'

But that was the problem. Given the way her body was reacting to the tiniest of touches and the slightest flirt, she wasn't sure her heart would ever be safe around him.

CHAPTER SEVEN

THURSDAY COULDN'T COME around quickly enough. The work Cal had been so invested in, and the training he'd come here to do, barely held his attention these days, only enlivened when his thoughts drifted to dancing eyes and loose dark curls. Things he did on his day off, rather than things he spent the majority of his time doing. For a woman who he'd only seen a couple of times, she was seriously starting to get under his skin.

The thought of not being here gave rise to a weird feeling in his chest. And he knew he shouldn't take it out on his brother, but he felt trapped by one world when part of him wanted to be in another just for a little bit longer.

Having arrived at the archway early, he was taking the opportunity for a catch-up. And beginning to regret it. 'What I don't understand, Finn, is why the hell you're bothering to ask my advice? You're hell-bent on killing yourself, so just go off and do it.'

That was what Abbie had suggested he do, right?

Let them follow their dreams, she'd said.

And okay, he knew he wasn't handling this well.

Finn was stretched out on the sofa in their lounge at home. It was the middle of the night there, so curtains were drawn. Ever since the accident, he'd had difficulty sleeping and often rang to while away the dark hours. Behind him, Cal could see the detritus of his life: dirty cups, beer bottles, pizza boxes. A stack of laundry. Books. The wheelchair. Fidget, the cat, sat aloof on its seat cushion; the only sentient being that used it these days, after Finn refused to sit in it ever again the day he came back from the rehab ward. Against medical advice, obviously.

That was how he was, how he'd always been; an independent, single-minded, beat-the-odds kind of guy. Somehow his whole life had been preparing him for the accident. His eyes rolled. 'Ach, you could at least listen instead of rage at me. I want you to come skiing with me. A week in Austria.'

'And watch you kill yourself? No, thanks.' But actually, he'd sworn to do whatever it took to get his brother a life, so he'd have to do this too. And enjoy it, for Finn's sake. Maybe Abbie really did have a point about supporting his dreams—instead of smothering him with overprotection. 'When is it?'

'February.'

'February? I won't have accrued any leave by then. You know this trip is taking most of it.'

'You'll be able to scrape a few days, though? Look, if you don't want to I can find someone else to come.'

February in Europe meant cold and sleet and snow. Here in New Zealand it meant the height of summer. Cal looked out across the lake, imagined what it'd be like here. Imagined what she'd be like in the summer. Those curls hanging loose over naked shoulders. Swimming, sun-kissed. Holding her baby. Being a family.

The brakes went on that thought as his chest squeezed tighter. He'd no more envisioned a family—a baby, and someone else's baby at that—than he'd imagined himself flying to the moon. But recently the scenario had started playing in his head…a maybe, a what if. Which was all kinds of weird and unsettling.

He looked at his brother and remembered cradling him in his ice-cold arms, and the promises he'd silently made back then. And how he'd begged him to hold on and told him he'd do everything—absolutely anything—to help him live. And if that meant giving up any kind of future for himself, then so be it.

These two halves of his life weren't going to gel any time soon. And, above all of that, whatever he wanted didn't matter. He owed his brother, he'd promised him and he was sticking to that. For ever. 'Nah, I'm with you, mate. Every step. Remember? Every. Single. Step. Sorry I've been so down on you, Finn. I'd like to blame jet lag or something, but I'm—well—'

He wasn't going to mention Abbie because that would only complicate things.

'Just a moody bastard?' Finn smiled. Something of a rarity these days, especially in their conversations. The break had been supposed to help—absence making the heart grow fonder, and all that. He wasn't sure it had.

'Yep. Okay, you got me. I'll make it work. Skiing, eh? I'm looking forward to it already.' He'd make sure they stuck to the nursery slopes, even though he knew Finn would make a beeline for the moguls. Suddenly his senses fired into action and he knew she was here. Before he turned around to see her and gave his game away to his know-it-all brother he stood up. 'How's everything else working for you? Maggie bringing food in? Pete still doing the morning and evening shifts?'

'Aye. It's smooth. I told you it'd work. The timetable you made is a dream and I get some peace and quiet when they've all stopped fussing.' He didn't need to add, *unlike when you're here*, but it hung there between them.

'Good, well, I'll be back soon enough, irritating you and cramping your style. But I'm going now. I've got things to do. I'll call you in a couple of days. Email me the details of the trip and I'll forward it to the boss.'

'Hot date, is it?' Did the guy have an X-ray into his head? 'What's she like? Knowing you, she'll be blonde and well…developed.'

He cringed. How much of this could Abbie hear? He lowered his voice. 'Going horse riding.'

'Lucky you.'

He was. He knew that. Having two working legs was damned lucky. It could just as easily have been him who'd fallen from that mountain. 'There are plenty of places that could help you go riding. Everything's possible these days. We can get you on a horse if you want, when I get back.'

'I meant the date part. Scars might be hot these days, but I'm not sure false legs are up there in the Top Ten Sexy Body Parts lists.'

'Finn…' There was a time when Finn had literally had women queuing up for him. When being the scrum half for the Swans had been a big deal. When he'd earned the country's yearly annual wage in a month. 'It'll happen.'

'Yeah. I can't move for hot women wanting a piece of me.' Finn rubbed a hand over the two-day stubble on his chin and pulled a thick wool blanket over his shoulders. 'Go. Have fun, you big idiot.'

'And you, ya *bampot*.' And things were back on an even keel again. God, he missed him. But he wasn't about to let him know that.

'Bad timing?' Abbie was leaning against the grey stone wall that edged this end of the lake, a little distance away, obviously giving him space to chat to his brother. She'd tied her hair into a long plait that fell over one shoulder, a half-circle of another tiny plait framing her face. She was wearing those skinny jeans from the other day and a navy-blue padded sleeveless jacket over a pale pink sweatshirt. She looked horse-riding ready, but he wanted to skip that bit altogether and take her straight to his bed, peel those clothes from her and run his mouth over every inch of her soft-looking skin.

God, keeping his wicked thoughts—never mind deeds—to himself was going to be damned hard.

He walked over to her, resisting the tug to wrap her in his arms and, instead, giving her a chaste wee kiss on her cheek. She smelt of apples and something flowery and the tug intensified. He stepped away and pointed over towards his car. 'Just climb in. Actually, I took your advice about supporting him and things weren't too bad.'

She laughed. 'I'm looking forward to hearing you say things are good.'

'You might have to wait a while. Right, let's get going, Calamity Jane. Did you remember your cowgirl hat?'

Her eyes glittered. 'It's been a long time. I think I'm going to need something a lot harder than that.'

'I'll see what I can do.' He wasn't sure what to make of her statement, whether she was playing with him or was woefully innocent of the reaction she'd achieved low down in his gut. Her perfume filled the car, a sweet softness that had him hot under the collar. Somehow he was going to have to keep that burning heat under wraps, while the thought of skiing in Europe left him colder than the snow he'd be sliding down.

'Horses are always so much bigger than you think they are.' Abbie leaned her head against the warm equine throat and stroked the chestnut nose of Kelly, her ride for the afternoon. There was something very soothing about a horse's deep breathing. And God knew, she needed all the help she could get with Cal around. The hard hat made her look a bit silly, but she didn't mind; Cal had one on too and he looked gorgeous. 'It's been a while since I rode, so please tell me she's a good-hearted soul.'

Bryn, the woman who ran the stables, gave her a reassuring smile. 'She's a sweetie and very used to nervous riders. I'll be coming along, so we'll keep an eye on you.'

'And what kind of route do we take?' Cal was up on his bay horse, Boss, looking as if he'd been born to do this. And, no doubt he was a champion horse rider or something.

Bryn flicked the reins towards Abbie and nodded at her to climb up onto the step, grab the reins and then hoist herself into the saddle. 'Just a meander through the farmland and then down along the riverbed. Nothing too strenuous, unless you want to gallop—there's space down there to let loose and Boss loves a good run.'

'Let's take it slow and see how we go. I haven't ridden in a very long time.' Abbie jabbed her heel softly against Kelly's side and clicked her tongue against her teeth. 'Come on, girl. Walk on.'

They filtered into single file; Bryn up front, Cal second and Abbie taking up the rear as they made their way from the farmhouse, downhill, to the forest. It was cool and fresh down there, an eerie glow bouncing off the tree bark covered in moss, as if someone had washed the view with a green filter. There was little noise save for birdsong and the clomp, clomp, clomp of hooves.

This had been a great idea; a chance to unwind and force her muscles to relax in a different kind of exercise compared to what she was used to. Abbie breathed deeply, all the better to steady her head, taking note of the altogether nice view of Cal's back. The man had fine posture. Great shoulders. Her eyes moved lower. A gorgeous—

He turned and gave her a wave, pulling to a halt and

waiting until she'd caught up with him where the path widened enough for two. 'You okay there?'

Why did he have to be so considerate? It just made her like him more. 'Yup. Just plodding, as I like it.'

'I thought you'd be galloping ahead, blazing a trail.'

'Kelly and I have only just met. I don't want to push her too hard. Later, maybe, at the river.' She ran her hand down the soft coat and patted, receiving a little whinny in reply. 'This is lovely. You really do know how to spend a day off.'

'Just trying to make the most of things. I hope we didn't mess with your schedule? Whoa, wait, watch your head.'

She bent at the sight of a low-hanging branch coming towards her just a little too quickly. 'Wow. Thanks. I do prefer having two eyes. Although I do feel very guilty being here when I should be painting the nursery and… well, doing adult stuff. Nesting. But I don't have the hormones to kick me into action, so I'm just putting up with Emma's periodic nagging.'

'All in good time. You're allowed a little bit of fun before the parenting thing kicks in.'

Was she, though? If she wasn't carrying this baby the least she could do was be ready for it when it arrived. 'I have so much to do.'

'You've got a few weeks before Christmas. Plenty of time. Besides, how many times have you heard new parents say they could never be prepared for what hit them?' He grinned at her wide-eyed response. 'How are you feeling about it all?'

'Excited. Nervous. Scared. It doesn't seem real to me, even though I know it is.'

'Yes, it would be weird seeing her carrying your child.'

That was exactly how she felt. Weird. Excited, nervous, amazing, and…weird. 'I can't quite believe it. It's almost like seeing her pregnant with Rosie again rather than with my baby.' Then, the truth of it fell out of her. 'I hope I love it. I mean… I will, of course. But what if it doesn't bond with me? What if he or she wants Emma and not me? What if we don't get along?'

He let out a low sigh. 'Of course you'll love each other. Of course he'll love you.'

'You think it's a boy?' She had no idea, alternating between the genders depending on the shape of Emma's belly, what her cravings were and what Abbie secretly wished for: a daughter. And then, sometimes, when she saw a little boy kicking a ball, or charging breathless around the play park, she wanted one of those too.

Of course, Cal didn't know any of this; no one did. She had no one to share her crazy higgledy-piggledy thoughts with. But given they made little sense, maybe that was a good thing.

Cal looked nonplussed. 'How would I know? I just couldn't imagine having a baby girl. I'm not sure I understand the female of the species too well. Mind you, given my brother, I'm not sure I know a lot about the males either.'

'I've been reading a lot of "what to expect" books and have followed the pregnancy from being two little lines on a stick, every moment, every scan, every ginger biscuit for morning sickness. Emma knows what she's doing. She'll help me.'

If we're still friends at the end.

Truth was, Emma hadn't given Abbie one single hint that she wasn't happy doing this. But you just never knew, did you? In the end? Guilt rolled through Abbie again. Here she was riding a damned horse and Emma was waddling around work, looking after Queenstown's injured, carrying a baby, thinking about how she was going to entertain her five-year-old later.

How could she ever repay her?

The route opened up to rolling hills covered in tussock grass, past an old dilapidated shed and duck pond, then downhill. Abbie remembered to lean back a little to stop her from falling. It was a long way down to hard earth.

Cal's eyebrows rose in question. 'So, you've got no family around, then?'

'None here.'

'They're where?'

Abbie thought about her parents, who'd given her the choice to move overseas with them back before she'd even met Michael but she'd waved them off on a mid-life adventure never thinking for a moment how alone she'd end up being. 'They semi-retired to a little village in the South of France. They have a small bed and breakfast there and three apartments here. The one I live in, next door where Emma and Rosie live, and the one on the end of the block. They rent the end one out as a holiday let, and use it when they come home. Which is getting less and less frequent. They've really got into the ex-pat lifestyle in Europe and the weather helps Mum's asthma.'

'You must miss them.'

'Of course. Especially...when Michael... Sorry, I shouldn't keep talking about him.'

Cal shook his head, giving no emotion away, certainly no frustration. 'You don't, not really. He was a big part of your life. I understand.'

She wasn't sure if he really did or was just being kind. Because he wasn't exactly going to tell her certain subjects were out of bounds, was he? 'So, anyway, yes... What with a new baby and getting ready for Christmas, I have lists coming out of my ears.'

Callum shifted in the saddle and peered closely at her head. 'No. Nothing there that I can see.'

'Okay, smart guy. My phone's stuffed full of lists, I'm nowhere nearer putting up a tree or anything and yet here I am with you. Again. Playing hooky.'

'It's my animal magnetism. Women just can't resist it.'

If she could have swatted him she would have; as it was, all she could do was tut. Loudly. 'Don't flatter yourself, Mr Baird. I'm only back here because I don't want to show you up. Otherwise I'd be off in the wind, galloping across the grass.'

'Sure you would, honey.' He grinned, holding the saddle and rocking forward and back on his horse like a cowboy from a film. So sure of himself, so confident. So damned—

He interrupted those thoughts. 'Why did you tell me—that first time, I think it was—that you didn't like Christmas?'

'Oh, you remember that? Well… Christmas always used to be a big thing for me and Michael. He loved making things magical for me. Then…' She swallowed at the memory of how they'd known that the last Christmas was going to be exactly that. So she'd gone all out to make it special and it had been. Nothing could beat that, the little cocoon of intense emotion. 'Then it was just me. And it kept on being just me. Of course, I had lots of invitations to go out and Emma made me talk to people and socialise at some point. Last Christmas I spent in hospital after a miscarriage. A failed IVF.' She wasn't sure if she should have said anything because Cal seemed to close down a little at that. 'Sorry, too much information?'

He shook his head. 'No. Not at all. You've had it tough, Abbie. I'm sorry.'

'Not your fault.' She didn't tell him about the other four miscarriages before, during and after Michael's illness. The IVF, the waiting game. The hopeful Christmas songs that made her feel as if her heart was breaking. 'Anyway, let's not spoil this day. All that's in the past.'

'Aye well, the past has a way of hanging around a bit, doesn't it?'

She determined to throw off this air of sadness and so she made herself smile and breathe in the fresh air. 'No. Not today.'

Up ahead Bryn had stopped and was waiting, but Cal waved her on. 'We're good, thanks! We're fine.'

She waved back, then started to trot on towards the almost dried-up riverbed covered in gravel and stones, and a small beach area. When they caught up she rubbed her hands together. 'Okay, you two. You're doing very well. Cal, you say you've ridden before?'

'Aye.'

'And, Abbie? You used to ride?'

'A bit, yes. I can trot and canter a little.' She didn't want to think about how long ago it was. She was hardly a pro, but she'd aced pony club when she was seven.

Bryn pointed forward. 'Well, the river stretches on for miles and it's like this all the way to a small wooden bridge. When you get there wait for me, okay? I'll keep back and make sure you're okay. Whenever you're ready.'

Cal raised his eyebrows. 'Ready?'

No. But she wasn't about to let him see that. A good gallop would shake off the doom and gloom that she'd introduced into the conversation. What they needed was another race. 'Any time, mate.'

'Yes, because I can see from your white knuckles that you're very relaxed and ready to gallop.'

She opened and closed her fingers, then grabbed the reins again. 'Like I said, I'm just getting back in the saddle.' And if that didn't sound like a come on, she didn't know what did. 'I mean...'

'I know exactly what you mean.' There was a tease in his eyes and he laughed. 'How do you feel about going just a little bit faster?'

'Fine, I think.'

He reached out and stroked her arm, his eyes intense. 'Okay, just relax and stop thinking about all the things you should be doing and everything that's happened before. Just enjoy this. This moment. Live in this moment—or whatever thing you're meant to do.'

'Okay. I'd never pegged you for New Age, but okay.'

'Great. Relax. Breathe in. That's right. Excellent. In again. Out. And…race you!' He kicked hard and sped off, disappearing in an arc of water that curled high around him.

'Hey!' Typical! Always trying to out-run or out-shoot or just plain beat her. Laughter bubbled up from her gut and she squeezed her ankles against Kelly's flank. 'Come on, Kel. Let's go. Let's show him.'

It was like flying. Well, a bit soggier than flying, but with the wind in her hair and spray on her face she felt the most alive she'd felt for years. This was absolutely the best way to spend a day off. Freedom from thinking about anything but the moment. And Cal.

Yes, Cal.

He was standing in the stirrups now, one hand raised in the air, a loud cry of something joyous splitting the air.

So she stood up too, raised her hand and was just about to scream when Kelly stopped. Just stopped. And lowered her neck.

The next moment Abbie was falling forward and somehow sideways and tumbling and there was no way she could stop it. The great hulk of horse seemed to shift, or Abbie did or something, and the ground was rising up to her, too fast. Too fast.

Reaching her hand out, she tried to ease the impact but her bones bumped and crunched onto gravel and stones and water. All breath was pushed from her lungs and she felt the impact reverberate through her like shock waves. She wanted to cry out, but there was no air. Just pain. A sharp pain in her left wrist.

And right then—in that moment that she had been so concerned about living in—she realised what an utter idiot she'd been. What a risk she'd taken.

Because how could you look after a newborn baby with a broken arm?

'Abbie! Abbie! Are you okay? Hell.' She heard the thump of hooves and the splash as Cal dismounted. But she didn't want to look up and see him because that would admit to all the rules she'd broken. How stupid was she? Why would she do something so reckless?

He was by her side, kneeling in the shallow water as if it didn't matter, and then looking at her as if she really did. His hands ran over her face, down her shoulders. 'What happened? Where do you hurt?'

'It's nothing. I fell, that's all. She just stopped. I don't know why.'

He turned to the horses and caught the reins that were dipping into the water, tied them around a large rock. Then he turned back. 'Let me look.'

She didn't want him to look, didn't want to look herself. Because it would only scream how irresponsible she'd been. She could feel the prick of tears. Humiliation. Guilt. Shame. But most of all because it actually bloody hurt.

But instead of looking at her wrist he kept on looking into her eyes. 'You're not okay at all.'

'I am.'

'Stop being brave and come here.'

The next thing she knew she was pressed against his

chest, his arms tight around her. He was hot from riding, his breathing hitched. His hand clasped the back of her neck, stroking her hair as he whispered soothing noises and words that seemed to reach into her heart and tug so tightly she wanted to cry even more. 'You'll be fine, wee lassie. You're okay. You're safe. It's okay. It's okay, we'll fix you up.'

But she wasn't okay at all. Because the longer she stayed wrapped here in him, the more she couldn't bear the thought of tearing herself away. Everything hurt; every bone and sinew in her left hand, every riposte she shot at herself was like a knife jabbing at her. She was stupid and foolish and reckless and what kind of an almost-mother did that? What kind of a responsible person would take such a risk?

But she was also a woman. A widow.

A *woman*.

A woman whose only thought right now was that she was in the arms of a good man. A sexy man, hell, not just sex on legs, but gorgeous and kind, and who stirred something deep inside her.

She'd been through enough heartache to last her for the rest of her years, and was going to devote all her energy to her child when it came, so she deserved just one moment in the arms of a strong man.

So she let her body be lulled by Cal's heat, let her mind be hypnotised by his voice and she lay her head against his chest and breathed him in. Breathed in a man who wasn't her husband, who wasn't the father of her child, who wasn't someone who could offer anything other than comfort right here and now. But she didn't care; she wanted that. Just a moment where she could be a woman who was being comforted, protected, cherished. By a man like Callum Baird.

Suddenly she realised her heart was raging fast and it

wasn't from the fall. Her body was hot and buzzing, but not from the exertion of exercise. The stroke of his hand on her back made her press harder against him. Her mouth was wet and yet dry. Her breathing fast and unsteady. Like her thoughts. She liked this. She liked him. She wanted him.

'Hey.' He edged away from her, holding her shoulders, tugging gently. 'Are you all right?'

'No. No, I don't think I am.' She closed her eyes, suddenly unsure. Did he want her the same way? And then what? Kissing him was a one-way ticket to heartbreak.

But she wasn't sure she could stop it either. She opened her eyes and touched his cheek, ignoring the sharp twist of pain that shot up her arm. This was one moment she was going to take for herself and to hell with broken bones and broken hearts.

He was so close, his gaze on hers, the heat there mirroring the way she felt. He wanted her. She didn't need to ask. 'Where do you hurt, Abbie?'

'Here.' She touched her heart, feeling raw and exposed and turned on all at the same time. 'Because I'm going to kiss you and I don't know what will happen next.'

He sighed and laughed and ran his thumb over her lip in that way of his that made her knees buckle. 'Well, let's find out, shall we?'

CHAPTER EIGHT

IT WAS NO USE. He couldn't resist any more. There were too many emotions swirling in his chest and all of them were because of her. For a moment he'd thought she'd done some serious damage, then it was just relief she was alive and okay, and then hot on the heels of that the sharp tang of need.

Cal lowered his mouth an inch from hers. Seeing the desire in her eyes, but a struggle there too, almost broke him. 'Abbie, are you sure?'

Because, despite all the bravado, he had no idea what the hell was going to happen either, or even what could happen.

The struggle was still there as she nodded and edged towards him, but it had been overridden with longing. He cupped the back of her neck and tilted her mouth towards his, his reservations exploding into a thousand pieces the second his lips touched hers.

There was a tentative moment that was almost innocent exploration, then she opened her mouth to him and he couldn't stop the very *un*-innocent groan coming from his throat. His mouth slid against hers as sensation after sensation pumped through him. She tasted of the mountain air and fresh river water, so good. So damned good.

Her hand snaked around his neck and she shifted in the

water until they were both on their knees, pressed together, his palms cupping her face. Her scent was all around, and he couldn't get enough of it. Of her. There was something about her that tugged and tugged and tugged at his heart, at his groin.

At his heart.

He deepened the kiss, seeking out her tongue as a heat started to build inside him. This was what those little games had been about; the races, the give and take, the push and pull, dancing around what was so inevitable— that despite every single sensible reason not to, everything would lead to this. *This.*

His gut contracted at the feel of little beats of pressure as her soft body pressed against him, a perfect fit in his arms. There were so many things he wanted to do to her, and with her, right now he could barely think straight. He slid his hand down her neck, down the side of her jacket and under her jumper, a riot of stars bursting in his head as he touched the soft skin there.

But then she was pulling away, breathing fast, and there were tears in her eyes that she was trying to blink away.

He wasn't sure his heart would be able to take much more. There was something about her that made him putty in her hands; he would give her the world, just for another kiss. To kiss those tears away. 'Are you okay?'

'My arm.' She was cradling it in her good hand. 'I think I've done some serious damage.'

'What? Let me look.' He'd been kissing her while she was hurting and needing medical attention? Stupid bloody fool. Then he wanted to curse loudly as he took her hand and saw her wedding ring glinting in the sun. All desire leached away. At least, in his head, anyway. In his gut he still wanted her. In his heart he still wanted her. But wanting her was a hiding to nothing. She had more baggage than anyone else he'd met—apart from him. 'You always seem to get hurt when I'm around.'

'It'll be okay. It's nothing, I'm sure.' She gave him a smile, but it seemed a little wobbly and unsure and he couldn't help wondering if she'd looked at her wedding ring and thought the same thing he had. Or whether she was just in pain. 'I hope it isn't broken. The last thing I need is a plaster cast and a new baby.'

'Could make things interesting, for sure.' That hadn't even occurred to him. He was going to say the cast would probably be off by then and that he'd help all he could, when he remembered he couldn't. There was a thundering in his chest. What a big mistake this whole thing had been.

'Ahem.' It was Bryn. God knew how long she'd been standing there; he hadn't heard her approach and she was on foot, leading her horse. 'Sorry to interrupt, but are you okay?'

Wincing, Abbie jumped up, water dripping from the knees of her jeans. She held up her hand, which was swollen and starting to colour in deep purples and reds. 'Kelly wasn't in the mood for a runabout. She clearly just wants to eat.' Abbie nodded towards the horse, who was tugging at the tussock grass with her large teeth, oblivious to what she'd just done. 'But I think I might need an X-ray on my hand.'

Bryn's eyes widened. 'Oh, my God. I'm so sorry. Are you okay? Only, I wasn't sure and I didn't want to…er… interrupt.'

Because we were too busy making out when we shouldn't have been.

Cal's chest constricted. He'd kissed her without thought for anything other than that moment.

Kissed her.

He wrapped an arm around Abbie's shoulders, making

a mental vow to look after her, but not to start any more kissing or…anything else. There were too many reasons not to. 'We just need to get her out of these wet clothes, and then down to the hospital.'

'No problem, let's get you back to the farm and we can take it from there.' Bryn took hold of Kelly's reins and handed them to Cal. 'Abbie, can you manage to get back on? Do you want to?'

She was shivering now. Shock. Cold. Passion? That had taken a very definite downturn. 'I don't know. But I guess it'd be quicker if I did.'

'Absolutely, we've come a long way and it's an uphill hike home. There's a boulder over there. If we walk Kelly over you can climb up onto her again—if you're sure? She's a real plodder usually. That's why I give her to the less experienced riders. I can't imagine what she was thinking.'

Abbie gave a wry smile, her shoulders sagging a little. 'She was just interested in the grass, and I was propelled forward. I shouldn't have been standing up in the saddle for a start.'

And that was his fault. He shouldn't have been messing about; he should have been much more concerned about her welfare instead of charging ahead. One slip. One slip was all it took. It wasn't as if he didn't know that. He should have been paying more attention. Should have protected her.

That was another reason why he couldn't do any more kissing; he was dangerous to be around.

Bryn called over, 'Can you help, Cal?'

'Sure thing.' The only thing he wanted to do more than help was rewind the whole morning. The taste of Abbie was still on his lips and hers were red and swollen. Regardless of what he'd vowed, there would be no forgetting that kiss. Ever. It was the best thing that had happened to him in his whole sorry life. He gave Abbie a hand to mount the horse, making extra sure she was safe and secure and out of his reach. 'Come on, Abbie. Up you go.'

'I have clothes you can borrow.' Bryn took her phone out. 'Do you want me to call ahead and get Tane to phone someone?'

Cal bristled as he fashioned a sort of sling from his T-shirt, then wrapped his jacket around Abbie's front, pulling her good arm through the sleeve and zipping her in, hoping to help her get warm. He was going to sort this out. 'No. Really, I'm a paramedic, Abbie's an ED nurse. We just need to dry off and get back to town. We know what we're doing.'

But after the kissing and the wanting to do it all over again, even though he shouldn't, it was clear, without a shadow of a doubt, that they didn't have a clue.

'Stop fussing, please. I'm fine.' Of course it had been Emma that was the first one to see them as they walked into the ED, red-faced and bruised and still a little damp and dishevelled. Of course it had been her who had filled out the forms and shaken her head and given her that teasing naughty-girl look behind Cal's back, along with her *hottie* and *phwoar* looks and the thumbs up, as if they were really sixteen again.

So, of course, it was Emma who was now trying to get Abbie to take more painkillers and elevate her arm on cushions in Emma's apartment. Rosie was fast asleep in bed and Cal had gone home. Been sent home, actually, because there wasn't anything more he could do and Abbie needed some space to get her head together. Which was difficult given the analgesics she'd already had.

The memory of the kiss had lingered between them as she'd looked for words to say to him on the drive from the stables and hadn't been able to find any. What could you say after one smouldering kiss that had ended so abruptly?

It had lingered as they'd walked from the car to the ED making polite conversation and as they'd sat waiting in X-Ray and not even made real meaningful eye contact.

But something had changed between them and she thought it was right about that moment he'd looked down at her hurting wrist and seen her wedding ring.

'It's a nasty break, and even with a plaster cast on you still have to keep it higher than your heart to help the swelling go down.' Emma stopped plumping more cushions and frowned. 'I know, I'm teaching my grandmother how to suck eggs. But you need looking after and I wasn't sure whether you wanted Cal to stay on. Plus, once he was satisfied you were going to be well looked after and that he could come back tomorrow, he didn't seem all that keen on staying. What's going on there? Horse riding not quite the perfect date after all?'

'It was a dare, not a date. And it was great. Really. Lots of fun…until the fall. I'm worried about what I'll do, when the baby comes, with a cast on.'

'You'll manage. *We'll* manage. But I get the feeling it's not just your arm that's bothering you.'

'I'm fine. Really.' Thing was, Abbie just didn't know how she felt about the kiss and she didn't want to tell Emma about it for so many reasons. It was so hard to even begin working out what she was feeling. Yes, it had been divine. Yes, it had made her want him more. Yes, he was perfectly perfect in every way and made her heart thrill completely. But…well, he wasn't going to be around and she'd had her fill of getting attached to men who didn't stay.

Worst thing of all: she didn't want to get attached to

Callum, but she actually thought she probably was, just a little bit. Even a little bit was too much.

'Well…' Emma rubbed her large belly and rocked from one foot to the other as if trying to get comfortable. 'Missy's certainly been active today. I think she wants to join the fun out here.'

The painkillers didn't dull Abbie's panic. 'But you're only thirty-six weeks. I'm not ready. She's not ready. We're nowhere near ready.'

'Hey, calm down. She's just been doing somersaults, that's all. She's got lots of time to cook yet.' Emma grinned and sat down next to her on the sofa. 'So, without wanting to pry too much, I really do want to know what's going on.'

'With Cal?'

'With Cal. I don't want you getting hurt. I mean, getting your heart broken…given that you're already in physical pain.' Marriage for Emma meant pain. Men, for Emma, meant pain. Physical as well as emotional. She'd been hurt badly by a man who'd used her to get what he wanted. Commitment and love weren't ever really in the picture.

Cal wasn't like that. 'It was just an afternoon out, that's all.'

'Hey…' Emma grabbed a cushion and held it against her chest. 'You remember when we were kids and we used to imagine what our lives were going to be like and we said we didn't need princes to make us princesses?'

They'd been six or seven and had had the whole of their lives to look forward to. It had been very straightforward back then; girls ruled. Girls could surmount anything. Anything at all. Including a dead husband and an abusive one. If only they'd known what the hell was going to hit them. 'I most certainly do remember.'

'Right. So, then we discovered that princes could actually be quite good fun. And then, well, then we learnt that nothing is ever perfect. Thing is, we've been through a heap of stuff together and I really do want you to be happy...' There was a soft mist in Emma's eyes. She was a strong, independent woman, but she had a squishy heart. 'I can see he makes you happy. You have a look, you know? You seem excited by him and that's amazing. I love to see you like that; it's been so long. Too long...'

She squeezed the cushion tighter against her chest and Abbie wondered if there might be a little bit of envy there, or at least a fear of being left alone, pregnant and not horse riding with gorgeous Scottish men. Or any men. But no, surely not. Cal wasn't going to be a permanent fixture; Emma knew that.

There was still a little ache in Abbie's heart at the thought of the kiss. 'He's a nice guy and we had some fun, but that's all.' If she said it out loud she might actually start to believe it herself. Then, the words just tumbled out. 'We kissed.'

Emma clapped her hands together. 'I knew it. Or at least I guessed.'

'Can I not have any secrets from you?'

'No. Don't you ever dare. Do you like him?'

'I do.' The pain was starting to break through now and Abbie lifted her wrist and looked at her fingers. They really were a kaleidoscope of colour. 'But he's not worth spending time on, right? I mean, there's no point getting attached to someone.'

'Because of the brother.'

'Callum takes his responsibilities very seriously, obviously. So, to him, I'm probably just a dalliance, a Kiwi fling.'

'He could be your Scottish fling. A Highland fling! God, I'm funny!'

'Seriously? You're suggesting this just before I become a mother. With a broken wrist.'

Emma shrugged, then smiled. 'Good point. Probably not one of the best ideas I've had.'

Oh, but it was. For a few moments Abbie had been wrapped in his heat and it had been heavenly. She smiled to herself, hugging that thought close. At least she had the memory of one amazing kiss with Cal to see her through to old age. 'So, I'm going to call a halt to it all. I don't want another relationship. I don't want to think about anything else other than my baby, my family. Me and the little one.'

'Are you sure?'

'With him around the place I can't give the pregnancy or anything else my full attention.'

Emma patted Abbie's good hand. 'You don't have to. I've got this.'

'That is not the point. You're doing enough. Being a mother is everything I've wanted and dreamed of for years, you know that. I don't want to be distracted.' *Or feel guilty about you.* She sighed. It had all seemed so uncomplicated before she'd climbed into that helicopter. 'I like having an easy life.'

'Life isn't easy when you have kids, trust me. But it's your call. If I were you, I'd have a bit of fun. You might not get another chance for a while. This way you get to play a little, no strings.'

'Would you, though?'

'I might.'

'You wouldn't. I thought you were completely off men. With who?'

The smile Emma gave her was wistful. 'No one really... Sometimes I get lonely. Sometimes I think it would be nice to have a little play.'

'No! I thought you were sworn off men for ever?' But

that didn't stop men asking after her, though. Abbie still wondered about the subtext of the Nixon conversation, but shoved it away—it wasn't her business and she knew that, after the nightmare of her marriage, Emma was still bruised emotionally. Trust would be hard earned with that woman.

But her friend laughed. 'Hey, a girl can still window shop, right? There are some good-looking men around and I appreciate looking. Or maybe it's just my hormones playing up. Still, if I had the chance, maybe I'd be tempted by a hot man like Callum.'

'But then what? What if I fall for him?'

Emma looked at the arm in a cast propped on the cushions and smiled softly again. 'Honey, I think you already did.'

CHAPTER NINE

THERE WAS SOMEONE knocking at the door.

Was there? Had she dreamt it?

There it was again.

Abbie dragged herself from the drug-induced sleep and sat up, her neck sore and her arm buzzing with pain. She looked around, wondering for a moment where she was. Then remembered she'd left Emma's last night for the comfort of her own bed rather than sleeping on the sofa.

Picking up her phone, she checked the time. Nine twenty-four! She'd slept fitfully but had fallen into a deep sleep after more painkillers in the early hours.

Another knock.

She climbed out of bed, pulling on her kimono-style dressing gown—tugging the sleeve hard over the cast—and walked through to the hall, trying to peer through the bubbled glass, but she could only make out a shape.

'Hello?' She opened the door and her stomach fluttered. The usual response she had to Cal. There he was, his lovely mouth smiling broadly. Those teasing eyes with their laughing, glittering with concern. His gaze ran the full length of her body, taking in her bare legs and navy silk pyjama shorts peeking out from her robe. When his eyes locked with hers there was so much heat there she was at risk of catching fire. There was no way she was going to be able to forget the kiss and the way it had made her feel, no matter how much she tried. 'Hey. How are you?'

He gave her a cheeky grin. 'Morning. Sorry, did I wake you?'

'No.' Abbie ran a hand over her hair and imagined how she must look with her plaits all out of control and fuzzy—and then decided that he'd have to take her or leave her. This was who she was. 'I've just been lazing around, y'know... D'you want to come in?'

Did she want him to? Hell, yes. But she wasn't sure it was such a good idea.

His eyes flitted down to her arm. 'In a minute. I just wanted to check you're okay. How's the wrist?'

It was throbbing as she hadn't taken her meds yet. She stretched it out a little, testing, twisting the cast back and forth. 'Sore. But okay. I won't be shooting clay things for a while.'

'Luckily, that's not what I had planned. I've got something...' He looked a little abashed and for a moment she thought he was going to say something about yesterday, about the kiss. But he pointed over the balcony towards the car park. She stepped out into the surprisingly warm fresh air and looked down.

Whoa.

There was a Christmas tree roped onto the roof of his silver hatchback. The stump hung down to the car boot and was roped there too. 'Is that...is that for me?'

'The tree, not the car.' He laughed. 'You said you had a long list of things to do and, while I didn't know what else was on it, I did know this was. I thought you probably wouldn't be able to manage with your hand, so I got you one.'

It was huge; probably far too huge for her small apartment. A big bushy conifer, like something out of a magazine. It was such a thoughtful gesture it made her heart squeeze. 'It's lovely. Thank you.'

'And I have some decorations too. I didn't get many because I assumed you'd have some already, somewhere. If you want me to get them for you I can.' Cal paused. 'Did I do something wrong?'

There were tears pricking her eyes and she blinked them back. Because he was carving a way into her heart and she couldn't stop it. 'No. Not at all. It's really lovely.'

He looked relieved. 'I feel bad about the arm, to be honest. It's my fault you fell from the horse. I shouldn't have been acting the way I did.'

She thought about his brother and the way he was always so protective of him and realised that was his way. He saw himself as responsible for people, for making sure they didn't get hurt. 'Don't be silly. You didn't make me stand up in the saddle.'

'But I knew you would if I did.'

'I'm not that gullible.' But he was right, she'd been so competitive and determined to play that she hadn't given any thought to her own safety. Well, things were going to change. No more games. She would invite him in, thank him and then explain that the kiss had been the beginning and end of anything between them. Stepping back, she opened the door wide. 'You'd better come in.'

'Wait right there. I'll just grab the tree.'

And so he did. Then he went back down to get a box of baubles and tinsel and it was, *almost*, the nicest thing anyone had ever done for her. Because nothing could ever beat carrying a baby for you...but this was pretty special.

So she didn't have time to have a shower or anything except a face wash and teeth clean while he was at the car, and he didn't seem to mind that she was in her pyjamas—in fact, he'd looked at her clothes and grinned. Smiled, actually, a slow sexy smile that seemed to reach down into her gut and stroke it.

She pulled herself together. 'Right, well, I have a box in the top cupboard, just here, we'll just need to drag it out.'

'Okay. Lead on.'

'Just up there. At the back. Behind those boxes...yes, it says "XMAS" on it.' In the tiny hallway she watched the shift of his T-shirt across his taut stomach as he stretched, and the pull of his arm muscles as he dragged down the box with strands of red tinsel trailing down the side.

Since when had she found arm muscles attractive? Biceps brachii. Extensor carpi radialus longus. Abductor pollicis brevis. That was all they were. Not arms that had wrapped around her and pressed her against his chest. Or hands that had cupped her face and stroked her skin.

Just muscles. Nothing to get worked up about.

She hadn't even had time to tidy things up. But she looked at the place through his eyes—heck, he was a man, he wouldn't care that her huge red cushions weren't exactly straight, or that there were parenting magazines still open on the large window seat that looked up to the mountains. Surely he'd gloss over the piles of baby things she'd left out, just so she could see them.

She loved the place; decorating it in the bright blues and greens had been part of her healing process. She'd wanted to cover the drab beige that reminded her of illness and disease with something vibrant and alive. It had given her and Emma something else to focus on for a while.

When Cal had brought the box through to the lounge and she'd managed to control her wayward feelings she flicked on the music system. 'I never, ever dress the tree without Christmas music, so hang on. Let me find a play list.'

He pulled a face. 'Oh, God, it's too early. Way too early. I should have offered to do some painting or DIY or something. Anything but death by "I Saw Mommy Kissing Santa Claus".'

'How dare you? This is the first time in years I've been excited about Christmas.' She flicked some tinsel towards him and it caught him under the chin. He chuckled. She laughed, and it felt so nice to be looking forward; her heart was fluttering a little at the anticipation of new beginnings. 'Don't you spoil it for me, Callum Baird.'

'I wouldn't dare.' His eyes widened as if he knew the kind of things she'd like to do to him. 'I know I can't out-run you, so I'm doomed.'

There was an ease with which they started to put things on the branches. As if they both instinctively knew where things should go; even the childish hand-painted baubles that Rosie had given her. But too soon they were reaching to the bottom of the box and the only ones left were the named ones Michael had bought in Sydney. Callum picked up the one with her husband's name on it and handed it to her. 'I think you should put this one on.'

'Thanks. Yes.' She put it where it always went: near the top of the tree, next to hers. It had been a fun anniversary weekend when they'd stumbled on a little market in Paddington. She'd been looking at a jewellery stall and he'd surprised her with these Christmas baubles. One each. Just one each. She'd been on pregnancy number two and they hadn't dared tell anyone as yet. They hadn't bought Bump a bauble, or done any baby shopping at all because they'd learnt the first time that putting all those things into tissue paper and into a box at the back of a cupboard was heartbreaking. By the time that Christmas came around they'd already started grieving for the second baby they'd lost.

In hindsight, they'd had a bad run of Christmases all round.

But for the first time in a long time she didn't well up

at the thought of Michael missing another one. Sure, sadness still came in waves, but she knew now that no amount of wishing was going to bring him back. She had to move on. She'd never forget him, but she was going to make the most of every day.

Cal was watching her as she hung the bauble up.

'Are you okay?' he asked, his voice quiet and concerned, but loud enough that she could still hear him over someone dreaming of a white Christmas. The lights twinkled on the tree and she wondered if Michael was looking down from somewhere and whether he was happy she'd found Cal, even for a few weeks, or whether he'd be disappointed, or sad. And then the tears did threaten.

Make the most of every day.

'Yes. Surprisingly. I am. I'm fine. Thank you for doing this. It's lovely.' Fine, but she didn't want to dwell on things. She also wasn't sure whether she wanted to walk into his arms to hold him, one last time, and what kind of reaction she'd get if she did. So she held back, even though every atom in her body was tugging towards him. 'What kind of Christmas will you be having back home?'

He shrugged. 'Knowing Finn there'll be a lot of booze; we usually go to our neighbours' house for turkey and the trimmings. We've known them all our lives.'

'What about your parents? Won't they be around?'

'Mam died a couple of years ago, just before the accident, thank God, because she'd have been so upset by that. She had a bad stroke and never recovered. Dad left us years before that. We don't see him. Don't even know where he is.'

'That's a shame.' So they had no family close to support them. No doubt that was why he took the job of looking after his brother so seriously. There wasn't anyone else to do it.

'It is how it is. Can't change things.' He reached deep into the bottom of the box and pulled out a rather bedraggled angel with bent wings, which he handed to her, because clearly he knew exactly where that was going. The very top. She took hold of it in her sore hand, forgetting that it was so bruised, and winced. 'Angel Gabrielle, yes, I know...' She cringed. 'I couldn't think of a better name when I was six. She has been passed down in the family since for ever. I will never ever have anything else on top of my tree.'

He held her good arm as she stood on a dining chair and placed Gabrielle on the top. 'Funny how everyone has their own traditions. We have a few silly ones too. Or did have—me and Finn can't be bothered these days.'

'Like what?'

'Ach, you know...putting coins in the pudding, dousing it in whisky and setting fire to it, you know...'

'You should keep those traditions going.' Easy for her to say when she'd avoided Christmas altogether for the last few years. 'Although, do be careful with the setting-fire thing. And do you really not cook at all?'

'No. Mam was the heart and soul of the village, so everyone's only too happy to make sure we don't starve and there's no end of invitations. You can't ever be lonely in Duncraggen, believe me.'

Abbie stepped down from the chair and there was a moment again where her body seemed magnetically attracted to his, and she was sure he was feeling the same because his eyes misted the second they touched. All he was doing was steadying her, but she needed a little more than a strong hand to shift her equilibrium back.

It was no good. It didn't matter how much she told herself to forget him, she just couldn't. She wanted to kiss him. And more. She wanted to...*calm down*. He was leaving—dammit; he was talking about the place he was going back to.

'It sounds lovely. I imagine Christmas in Scotland will be very snowy and magical, like something out of a film.'

'I suppose it is.' He was quiet for a moment. 'It's because of the people in the village that I'm here at all. They clubbed together and paid my fare and we made a roster of who was going to look after Finn while I wasn't there.'

She sensed they were heading into emotional territory and wouldn't have been surprised if he'd clammed up again, because that was his way. But she so wanted to know what had happened, to understand him, to help... possibly. She didn't even know why. Why did Callum have such an arrow straight to her heart?

Even though her fingers had hovered again and again over the keyboard, she hadn't looked him up. It was almost killing her, but she'd stayed true to her word. She wandered over to the window seat and sat down, trying to sound nonchalant and not too intrusive, while hoping he'd open up just a little. 'So the accident was two years ago? That's still very fresh, then.'

He came over and waited while she shovelled the parenting magazines onto the floor, then he sat next to her, leaning against the corner between the window and the wall. 'Aye. It's why I've made sure we have a SARS team now in the village and why I'm here to learn as much as I can and take it back to them.'

'So what did happen?'

'A blizzard, a white-out. We lost our bearings and he fell. It took them a while to find us. The roads were all cut off and visibility was so bad they couldn't get the helicopters in. It was too risky for anyone to come find us at first. A total disaster.'

'So how long were you up there? What the hell were you doing all that time? Finn was injured? How badly?'

He shook his head, his eyes drifting to the mountain peak, still covered in snow. 'It doesn't matter.'

She shuffled forward. 'Actually, it does matter. It matters to me. It matters to Finn. And clearly it matters to you. Tell me?'

'Why? It only brings it all up. I don't talk about it. Full stop.'

He was retreating again, shutting down, and she didn't want him to. It wasn't good for him. Or her. 'So help me out a little. There are so many gaps in this story and I'm filling them with my own bleak thoughts.' She watched as he shook his head and turned away. 'It's okay. Honestly, I don't need to know. I understand you might not want to dredge all those things up again. But, even if you don't want to talk to me, you need to talk to him. Definitely you need to talk to Finn. One thing I learned with Michael was that we needed to communicate about how we were feeling. Otherwise you end up guessing. Guessing's no good. You need to know if someone needs your help getting through stuff, not be shut out.'

She thought he might recoil at the mention of Michael in amongst all of this, as if they were having a competition about who'd suffered the most, but he didn't.

'We're all different, Abbie. We don't all have to put our feelings out there to be stamped on. It's not my way.'

She pressed her good palm onto his hand. 'I know. But right now you can't even say the words. That can't be healthy, right?'

'But if I start I might not stop. If I don't even go there, I get to control what happens in here.' He tapped his head, then looked embarrassed at his outburst. He shrugged. 'It's difficult.'

'I didn't say it was going to be easy. But you'll be surprised how much it helps to give voice to those feelings—they do tend to float away for a bit.'

'I want them gone for good.'

'So make a start. You were on the Munro, right? It was snowing, you got lost.'

His eyes rolled as if he was being pressed into something he really didn't want to do, but knew he couldn't get out of it. Worse, actually, his tone was emotionless, as if he'd subsumed all feeling. She guessed it was the only way he dealt with this. 'Ben Arthur. The mountain. It's usually not too difficult in the summer. But we thought we'd have a challenge and go up in January. It's a scramble at the top, challenging, but anyone can do it with a bit of care.'

He stared out of the window, his features hollowed out somehow as he retreated into his memories. 'Going down's always the tricky bit. You know? I mean, the uphill always hurts the most, but, when you're tired after all the exertion, it's the going down that can be the most dangerous. We were pretty high, though. We'd got up in record time; it had been an easy stroll. We were chatting about what we were going to do that evening to celebrate when it suddenly started to snow. Not little wisps, I mean huge flakes, thick and fast, that were sticking to the ground. So we upped our pace. Nothing to worry about. But after a few minutes we couldn't see anything around us; we were *in* the snow cloud. It was freezing and it was like we were walking blind. We couldn't see our outstretched hands, never mind the path, and we must have wandered off somehow. It's easy to get disoriented in those conditions.'

'Yes. It's scary too.' She gave words to the feelings she thought he might have, hoping that to name them would help him acknowledge them. They were easier to let go that way.

'We argued over which way to go. He wouldn't listen to me. I wouldn't listen to him. Things got pretty ugly.'

He sucked in a deep breath and she didn't know how to respond to any of this so she just let him go on. 'I insisted we should go one way. He disagreed, told me I always thought I was right... I pulled at him to listen, there was a bit of rough. Brother stuff. Nothing and everything; panic rolled into sibling rivalry and then some. Then the next thing, he disappeared. Just disappeared in front of my eyes.'

'God, that's horrific. I can't imagine.'

'There was a steep drop, a sheer cliff, and he just fell over it. I mean, how could that happen?' He shook his head. 'I didn't mean to...'

'To what?' Her heart was thundering now.

He didn't answer her. 'I could just about make him out at the bottom, motionless, I didn't know what the hell to do. All my training just faded from my head and I just shouted. Like an idiot. I'm shouting into the air for someone to come and help us. To save us.'

At least with Michael they'd had help, so much help. They'd been frightened, but there had been no end of assistance and advice and love. Being alone on a mountain and unable to do anything must have been desperate.

His voice was still completely flat. 'You know the rest. The snow, the delay. I managed to climb down to him using some rope we'd taken with us to do some rock-climbing practice before we started the hike. And he was just... cold. So cold.'

'I can't imagine how you must have felt, what you thought.'

'He was so badly broken I thought he was going to die. I made my peace with him. I promised him that if he held on then I'd do everything to help him get better. He kept his side of the bargain and I kept mine.'

'I'd say you did more than that.'

'Hell, yes. He should never have gone over in the first place.'

There was something in his tone that she didn't understand. 'You're saying that was your fault?'

Cal looked broken, bleak. 'I'm saying that if we hadn't tussled and I hadn't been so cocksure which way we were heading, he'd still have two damn legs. Yes.'

'You can't possibly put blame on anyone. It was an accident.'

'That could have been avoided. I, more than anyone, know that.'

He needed to understand—believe—that there was either no blame, or equal blame. 'He walked up that hill just the same as you did. Don't tell me he doesn't feel responsible too.'

'I shouldn't have suggested we took that route.'

'It was dark, snowing. You couldn't see. Who knows what might have happened if you'd just stayed where you were. You could have died of hypothermia.'

He shook his head. 'He might have two working legs.'

'And he might be dead. So might you.'

They sat in silence for a while as they both went over the events of that night. It had scarred him very deeply, and clearly he wore that responsibility like a brand.

'So you gave up your job to look after him? Moved back home?'

'Aye. I was going places in Edinburgh, you know, in the ambulance service. Promotion, awards... But I'm okay with going back to Duncraggen. Really. It's a lot smaller, but I love being a paramedic and I can give so much back to the community that saved us...that saved Finn's life.'

But he took that responsibility very seriously now, that was clear; he'd given up his career to care for his brother.

There were a few more moments of quiet and she waited for him to say more. He didn't. He just stared out of the window at the mountains, and her heart contracted a little. Because she knew how he was feeling—that he was trying to make sense of something and he couldn't.

Because life happened and sometimes it was amazing and sometimes it broke your heart into tiny little pieces and you just couldn't put them back together again. She imagined him up there making all those promises to his brother, to himself, staring death right in the face. Wishing he'd made better decisions. Wishing it had been him who had fallen. And her heart started to break a little more.

She reached out to his arm, stroking and stroking, and after a while his shoulders relaxed and he breathed deeply. After a few moments he covered her hand with his and looked at her, smiling and shrugging off the emotion and the memories.

He sat forward and reached out to her hair, ran a stray lock of it through his fingers. 'So that's the tale of the infamous Baird Boys.'

'Thank you for letting me in.' She found him a smile. 'Feel better?'

'I don't know.' As he let the lock of hair drop he glanced down at her legs that she'd pulled up onto the seat cushion. His fingers trailed over her ankle, drawing tiny circles in the little dimple on the inside of her foot. She knew she should have pulled away, but it was so delicious to have his hands on her again. To feel the sadness evaporate and to see his gaze change from haunted to heated. To know that she did that to him.

She knew, oh, she knew a zillion things, but she didn't

say a word about any of them, or about the decisions she'd made about calling a halt to all this.

When he leaned in and tilted her chin up she let him.

And when he slid his mouth over hers she let him— no, she encouraged him. She wrapped her arms around his neck and pulled him close so she could feel the beat of his heart against hers, so she could breathe him in and feel his heat. So she could tell him with her body and her sighs that she wanted him, that he wasn't to blame, he'd saved his brother's life. Because, hell…she wanted him to kiss her, to make love to her, to hold her into the night.

One thing she'd learned was that there were few moments in life that were truly beautiful, and this was one of them. This was one that she didn't want to let go, one she didn't want to forget. So she kissed him back, hard and deep until she didn't just want him inside her, she needed him there.

When he pulled away he was breathless, his eyes glittering with more than just desire. 'Abbie, tell me to stop if you don't want this.'

'I don't want you to stop, Cal. I know it's crazy. We shouldn't do anything more, because I know this can't go anywhere, but I can't stop.'

'You and me both.' His fingers ran down the opening of her dressing gown. 'Tell me the truth, lassie. I woke you up, didn't I?'

'Yes. Yes, you did.'

'So, you want to go back to bed, aye?'

She'd never been outright asked before, not like that. Heat pooled low in her gut. 'Yes.'

'Good. Because I want to take you to bed and kiss every inch of you.' He gave her a wry smile by way of explanation and the mood got lighter. 'You did say I should voice my feelings.'

'You're talking about sex, not feelings.' Sex. Yes. Sex was good. Simple. Animal. Natural. Sex.

And now it was her turn not to want to acknowledge the emotions swirling around her chest.

His forehead was against hers. 'You want me to lay my heart out for you, do you?'

'Yes. No. I don't know. It's so hard, Cal. One minute I think I know what I want, then I get confused.' She didn't want to lay her heart out to him the way he just had to her; to admit there was a raw heat under her ribcage and it was all mixed up with images of him desperately trying to save his brother. Of his kisses that were so consuming. Of the thought of him getting on a plane and never coming back.

'Okay, Abbie. Let me tell you what *I* want.' He pressed a kiss to the dip at the base of her throat, making her shudder with desire. 'I want you like I've never wanted anyone before.'

Another kiss to her collarbone, a trail of little presses to her shoulder. 'I want to peel these clothes off you. I want to take you to bed and watch you come. I want to hear you sigh. I want to kiss you from head to toe. I want to be inside you, hell…more than that. So much more.' He closed his eyes and swallowed. When he opened them again they were burning with heat. Over the top of her robe he palmed her breast, his breathing ragged. '*Just* sex is something different altogether.'

And so what did all this mean? Was he hers to take and have and then give up?

The thought of him leaving made her gut curl and her head hurt. The thought of keeping him here, just for now, was so overwhelming, so delicious she couldn't contemplate any other outcome. She pressed her palm against his chest, felt the strong, fast beat of his heart, ran her fingers up to his neck, his jaw, tried to make light of something that was very, very momentous indeed. 'I will, if you will.'

'No more games, Abbie. Not this time. This time we both get to win.' He took hold of her broken wrist and kissed along her knuckles so gently it made her heart contract.

'Yes. Yes.' She'd never felt more certain about anything in her life. She wanted him and she wasn't going to let anything get in the way of that. Because tomorrow, later, for the rest of her life she would be Abbie the mum, Abbie the widow, Abbie the nurse, Abbie the friend...

'In that case, what are we waiting for?' Cal's beautiful blue eyes danced over her fingers as he sucked one gently into his mouth. The sensation of his hot wet tongue on her skin sent her body into overdrive. Her eyes connected with his and the connection between them seemed to tug tighter and tighter.

She was going to bed with him.

He smiled a wicked smile, that stoked more heat in her belly, and looked back down at her hand.

And she saw the exact moment doubt clouded his head.

He went completely still, focusing on her wedding ring. 'Actually, no. We've both made promises to other people. We'll stop right now.'

CHAPTER TEN

WHAT THE HELL had they been thinking?

There was her wedding ring glinting in the Christmas tree light and, no matter what, he couldn't make love to another man's wife. She had so many things going on in her life, getting involved with a man who was duty bound to go halfway across the world would only muddle all that. He couldn't take on the responsibility for her happiness or heartbreak too.

Cal tugged away from her, letting her hand go, gently—because she was still hurting.

And, dammit, he was hurting her even more by pushing her away, but it was for her own good. 'I can't, Abbie. *We* can't.'

She looked down at her ring and pressed her lips tight together, eyes now shimmering with the sheen of tears. She shook her head. And again.

And his heart just about melted. 'I understand, Abbie, it's okay. You loved him. And I'm not...' *Him.* He had no words. He wasn't about to cuckold a memory for the sake of a roll in bed. And yes, he knew his feelings were more than that; that somehow he'd become all tangled up with this woman. But there was a line he wasn't prepared to step over no matter how much his body begged him to.

She was wearing Michael's ring. She was still in love with his memory. 'We can't.'

She touched his arm, breathing out long and slow. 'Yes. We can. I can. It's time, Cal. I've been putting it off for too long and I should have done it a long time ago.'

'Not on my account. I don't want you to do anything like that for my sake.'

'This isn't about you, it's about me. About letting go of the past and moving forward—we both know we have to do some of that, right?' She tugged off her wedding ring—more difficult, given her swollen wrist—felt the weight of the gold in her hand. And he saw in it all the promises she'd made to her husband.

Short of begging his brother not to die, this was the most intimate thing he'd ever done. And he wasn't sure if he could handle it. Yet even so, far from this being a killer of his desire, it only made the ties to her feel stronger. Because of all the men in the whole damned world she could have done this with, she'd chosen him. There was a hitch in his chest, something shifting, making space. It felt blown wide open and yet also crushed tight.

'Can you unfasten my necklace for me?' She gave him a wobbly smile and he could see she was holding back more tears.

He frowned. 'No. Not for me, don't do this for me.' It was too much to ask of him, too much responsibility.

'It's for me. Help me, please, Cal. I want to kiss you again. I want to go to bed with you.' Now she laughed, a little. Decision made. She looked as if she believed the words she was saying. 'Don't make me beg.'

'I wouldn't dare.' He was all thumbs as he turned her away from him and gripped the fragile chain, eventually releasing the thin gold clasp, then after he'd handed it to her she slid the ring onto the chain and he fastened it back around her neck.

She turned, fingering the ring for a moment then letting it drop to hang loose at her throat. Her eyes glistened as she looked up at him. 'To be absolutely honest with you, I don't really know if I am ready. I don't know if this is going to be the best decision I've ever made or the worst one, and I certainly don't know what the hell is going to happen to us in ten minutes, never mind tomorrow or next week. But I've spent years avoiding hurt by not getting close to anyone. Now I'm scared about how much I'll hurt if I don't. All I can think about is that I want you. So badly.'

That was some huge admission, but she was right. He hadn't wanted to get close to her either, but trying to pretend it wasn't happening wasn't getting them anywhere. He reached for her and pulled her close, wrapping his arms around her, because he couldn't stop this. Couldn't fight the stirring in his belly and the overwhelming need for her that came from nowhere. He couldn't fight it, didn't want to, not today. Not in this moment.

'Come here.'

She slid her arms around his waist and laid her head against his chest and they stood, locked together, not fighting, not playing, not racing. Just feeling the beat of their two hearts as they mingled into one steady rhythm, and still listening to the Christmas music that was now harking on about it being cold outside.

Actually, the sun was shining on a late spring day, but it was no match for the heat in here. Because, regardless of all his principles, he was still very hot for a gorgeous woman in a silk robe. Hot for *this* woman, who was a combination of all things sexy and funny, kind and sincere and yet a fighter. A survivor. The whole package. Perfect.

Whoa.

Perfect was a lot to get his head around.

'You okay?' she asked him. 'I haven't frightened you off?'

'I'm good.' But his heart started to hammer and he had to admit to being spooked. If she was perfect, that meant he might just fall for her. Completely.

Maybe he already had. Too hard. Too quick. But even though all logic told him to leave right now and get his head straight, his feet were stuck to the floor, his arms locked around her.

He felt her smile against his chest. 'Me too. I'm very, very good.'

'And, I've finally found a way to keep you still,' he whispered into her ear, rubbing his cheek against her head, breathing her in.

'We'll see about that.' She wriggled away from him, tipping her head back and laughing. 'Race you to the bedroom.'

'But—' This wasn't how he did things—leaping from intensity to humour, from comfort to need. He usually did the slow build, or hot and raw, not zigzagging from one to the other and everything in between. Or maybe it was how he did things now. Maybe this was his new normal; experiencing the whole range of emotions in as many minutes. Maybe this was what *she* did to him and would continue to do to him until he left. 'What about…?'

'It's this way…' There was a sparkle in her eyes as she ran back to him and pressed her mouth to his. 'Surely, Callum Baird, you're not going to let me get there first?'

'Never.' Cal's arms snaked round her waist and he picked her up, scooping her legs into his arms as if she didn't weigh any more than a feather. Abbie hadn't got a clue what all this meant, why taking her ring off had felt like the right thing to do. All she knew was that there had been no way she could let Cal walk out of that door. There was a wave of guilt but she tried to convince herself that Michael would be happy for her. He would.

The atmosphere was changing lightning fast from intense to fun and she was struggling to catch up. It felt as if they were trying to make up for all the hours, weeks, years they hadn't known each other, trying to fit a lifetime into these moments. It was breathtaking, scary, exhilarating and tilting her a little off balance. When it came to Callum Baird she felt so many things. Too many.

He smiled and she felt that ping in her heart. 'If I carry you through we'll get there together,' he growled.

'Seriously, I can manage to walk.' She made a play of struggling, but in all truth it was divine to be in his arms. She leaned her head against his chest and breathed in his spicy scent, felt the bristles on his jaw scrape her forehead, felt the muscles on his arms contract and stretch, and everything tightened in anticipation of another kiss, of how he'd feel inside her.

He shook his head. 'Knowing you, you'll be racing to get undressed and in bed before I get the chance to take those clothes off your body. But believe me, lady—*I* am taking those clothes off.'

She pretended to weigh up her options, when the only reply was *how quickly*? 'Only if that means I get to undress you too.'

'I think we can manage that.' He laid her on the unmade bed and climbed in next to her, looking at her as if she'd saved his life, as if she'd hauled him off that mountain herself. 'But first, thank you. For being right there and listening.'

'Anyone would have listened, Cal.'

'No one would have known how right it was to say it out

loud, no one would have pushed so gently, yet so perfectly. But you did, Abbie. You did.' He leaned over, cupped her face in his hands and angled his mouth over hers in a bone-melting intimate kiss born of all the emotions they'd just shared. It was a caress, a promise of no more hurt, a wiping away of pain. It was the seal of something—a connection so raw and genuine and pure that she thought her heart was going to burst open. She needed him and, miracle of miracles, he needed her right back.

But when he groaned into her mouth the kiss turned feverish, kindling hot need inside her, spreading fast through her body. It deepened into seeking out his tongue, clashing teeth, a biting-lips kind of kiss.

Dragging her mouth from his for the shortest second she could bear, she tugged at his T-shirt, pulling it over his head and throwing it aside. Ran her hands over finely sculpted muscles, sighing in pleasure at this beautiful man, ignoring the wrist twinges and the heartache and the knowledge that this could only be temporary, fleeting — because nothing was going to stop her exploring every inch of him.

As she kissed across his chest, from one nipple to the other, making him laugh, his fingers tore at her robe, then her pyjama top and he was groaning again as he looked at her, half naked and all turned on. 'God, Abbie, you drive me mad.'

'I hope that's a good thing.' She straddled him, pressing fast kisses to his throat as his hands palmed her breasts, shuddering as he sat up and caught her nipples in his mouth. Beneath her bottom she could feel how much he wanted her and she writhed against his erection, desperate to be relieved of her shorts and him his jeans. She arched her back as he sucked her nipple, intensifying her need to fever pitch.

'Aye, it's a very good thing.' He flipped her onto her back and ground against her, breathless, his hand now stroking the tender part of her hip. She reached down and unzipped his jeans and he wriggled out of them, then discarded them on the floor. He, in turn, stripped her of her shorts and within seconds they were both naked.

Somehow he was standing next to the bed and she was lying on the duvet, momentarily transfixed by his body. He was…*oh*, he was impressive. Her mouth dried just looking at the rock-hard abs and the trail of fine hair down, down, down… He was divine. She knelt up and reached for his hips, tugging him towards her, taking his erection in her good hand, her mouth inches from the tip. But at her touch he sucked in air, covering her hand with his own, cursing and laughing.

'Abbie, if this was a race, I'd definitely be losing right now. So give me a fighting chance, won't you?'

Then he pushed her back onto the bed and his mouth was on her thigh and his hands under her bottom, his stubble grazing her skin, and it felt amazing. A sweet pleasure and pain, which she never wanted to stop.

For a fleeting moment she wondered how it would be, with him. Whether she'd please him. Whether she'd be enough for Cal. Because she hadn't done this for such a long time…

But Callum's fingers pressed against her core and all thought shut off. Then his mouth found her centre and the wet heat on her thighs and his rhythmic kisses hypnotised her, drugged her, completely took over her brain and her body.

She felt her release rising and bucked against his mouth, hanging on, hanging on… 'Cal, Cal! I need you inside me.'

'Soon. Soon. Not yet.'

But just as she thought she couldn't hold on any more, he pulled away. And smiled.

For one cold second she wondered what he was doing, then she understood.

Condom.

She could have told him it wasn't necessary. She wanted to shout out, she wanted him inside her. *Now.* Nothing else mattered, the world could wait. Only he mattered. Them. This.

But then he was over her, pushing gently...so gently, too gently, so she raised her hips to meet him and he filled her, stripping her breath on a moan. She felt her core contract as he began to move inside her, his kisses greedy. Hungry. She tried to hang onto a single thread of control, but with Cal all control was lost.

It was scary and yet wonderful. Something she'd never thought she'd experience again; to meet someone, to do this.

His gaze connected with hers, his fingers entwined with hers, his body moved in time with hers as if they were two halves of one whole. Harder. Faster. Her release started to build, more intensely now, as she met him thrust for thrust. Then he rocked hard against her, moaning into her hair, her name on his lips over and over and she tightened around him. He was crying out and she with him, both racing to the edge. Both winning.

She couldn't let him go. As the high began to recede she pulled him back to look at her, covering his face in kisses that came straight from her heart. And he stroked her hair, surely a derailed mess by now, and he smiled his heart-melting smile. 'Well, I think I'd call that a draw, wee lass.'

'Yes. That was definitely a win-win.' But as she looked deep into those bluest eyes, at that beautiful face, as she breathed him in and wrapped him close, her heart squeezed so viciously at the thought of him leaving.

And she knew…

She was irrevocably lost.

It took Callum some time to find his equilibrium—actually, he doubted he'd ever find it properly again while he was under Abbie's spell. He rolled onto his back, dragging in ragged breaths, and she wrapped herself into his arms, her legs lazily draped over his.

Meanwhile, he felt the furthest from lazy. His heart was thudding along at a rapid pace and his brain was whirling with a whole load of questions. How could it be possible to feel so connected with someone when logic told you it was a stupid idea? How could she have taken possession of his heart so quickly?

He wanted to move, to be alone with his thoughts and work out what the best thing to do would be for both of them, but didn't want to disturb her. She looked so comfortable, so thoroughly satisfied; as if nothing was troubling her at all.

Maybe when he left here today, she'd slip from his mind. Maybe he'd forget her the moment he got on the plane.

Yeah, that was just wishful thinking. Reality was, he'd never forget her. She was bruised on his heart now.

She sighed and for a moment he thought she was falling asleep, but then she spoke. 'I wish you weren't going back to Scotland. I know it's immensely selfish of me, but I really do wish you were here for a bit longer.'

Her honesty hit him hard in the solar plexus. She put words to the feelings he had and tried to hide from himself. 'Yes. But I've got to go home. There is no debate there.'

'For your Scottish Christmas.'

'For my job, my brother. My life. I just happen to be

going back in time for Christmas.' Today had been the closest he'd be getting to the best of Christmas cheer, he reckoned. He couldn't remember a time when putting up a Christmas tree had made him feel so much.

'Do you have a going-home date?'

'My ticket's booked and paid for. I leave on the eighteenth.'

'So soon?' She wound her legs around his calves and tugged herself closer, and he kissed the top of her head, breathing her in and trying to commit her scent to memory.

She had so much to look forward to, she'd easily forget he'd ever been here. Even her house pulsed with the anticipation of the baby and a future; bags brimming with tiny clothes, nappies, toys in the corner of the lounge. She was moving forward while he was going back. 'Ach, you'll have the baby soon and I'll just be the guy who bridged the waiting time until you got your family. You won't miss me.'

'Oh, I will.' With a sad smile she squeezed against him and he caught the scent of her again. It felt as if it were part of him now. 'What do you do for him? For Finn?'

Cal sat up at the mention of his brother's name and the reality of what they faced. 'He's had a difficult recovery. Complicated. There was the frostbite, lower leg amputation, broken pelvis. Dislocated shoulder. Displaced collarbone. Minor head injury. He couldn't drive for a long time so I took him back and forth to appointments. He had a lot of adjusting to do. A hell of a lot. He's a physiotherapist, so he had some understanding of what's required, but he's so damned impulsive and impatient. And he loved playing rugby—any sport, really. So his whole life has changed. He was down for a long time.'

'By down, do you mean depressed?'

He kept looking straight ahead because to see her soft eyes would make him give in to the emotion he kept firmly locked inside. 'Aye. I had to keep watch…you know. A few times. I was worried he might…well, finish the job off altogether.'

He'd almost lost his brother over and over. Unable to do anything but watch as drink had almost pushed him over the edge. As darkness had shrouded him too many times. Abbie hitched herself up next to him and stroked her fingers down his cheek, pressed a kiss there.

'That would have been so hard on you. Did he get help?'

'In the end, yes. He did. Don't get me wrong, he's a natural optimist, but he was badly broken in body and spirit. It took some working out in his head to try to get better. But he still struggles with sleep and some pain, and yet with planning a ski trip and more climbing I get the impression he thinks he's bloody Superman.'

She laughed and prodded his shoulder. 'Don't all men?'

And now it was time to put all that darkness aside, and relish these fleeting moments. He dug deep and found her a smile, flexing his biceps. 'I don't *think* I'm Superman, I know I am.'

'God, yes.' She straddled him again, and his body reacted exactly as it always did when she was around. And for the next few minutes he showed her just exactly what he meant.

Afterwards, he brought coffee through to the bedroom and he could see by the dancing in her eyes that she was brewing an idea and her body was restless. He gave her a cup and perched on the bed next to her. 'Ants in yer pants again?'

She grinned. 'I feel like I need to get out in the fresh air. Come for a walk with me?'

'Are you sure that's a good idea with your injured hand?'

'I use my feet to walk. I'll be fine.' She put out her

hand and rotated her wrist, clearly trying to mask the grimace. 'It's fine.'

'It still hurts.'

'Of course it does. I can't use it properly, but if I just sit here ruminating I'll focus on the pain. If I get outdoors I can focus on other things.' She ran her good fingers over his chest. 'Or… I can think of other things to focus on too.'

There was nothing more he wanted than to stay here in bed, but every kiss, every stroke chipped away at his resolve and his heart. 'Give a man a chance to recover.'

'Oh? What's happened to Superman all of a sudden?'

'He needs some down time. Literally.' Something purely physical, rather than emotional, might help his heart and head settle down a little. Now he understood why she kept on moving; it meant she didn't have to dwell on what was really going on. 'Okay, a walk sounds good. The lake path again?'

She shook her head. 'There are plenty of lovely walks around here. We can stop off and get a packed lunch and then decide.'

It was only just past midday, but it felt like a lifetime ago that he'd turned up here with the tree. He looked down at his clothes strewn over the floor. 'Okay, swing by my place and let me find some decent walking clothes.'

She looked at him over the steam from her mug. 'Yes, oh, and I mustn't forget to feed Eric's cats.'

'And pick up Rosie? The play park?'

'Not today. Emma's picking her up after her shift, but I do have to be back in reasonable time because I promised them we'd put the cot together tonight.'

For some reason this simple statement made Cal's chest hurt. He imagined the two women screwing bits of wood together to make a whole lot more than a bed—it was a life. A life so full she definitely wouldn't miss him. He almost offered to help, then realised he'd be butting in on something very intimate, something that didn't involve him.

So what kind of idiot would willingly walk this path when the reality was staring him in the face? There could be no future here; he could not stay. His responsibilities were to his brother, the village, another life.

Finn would laugh and tell him to enjoy the ride. But when the ride became so addictive that you didn't want to get off, what did you do?

Finn. The thought of his brother and the accident gave Callum pause. He was trying to hang onto his emotions, but he felt as if he were watching himself go over the cliff. Like his brother, he was falling too hard and too fast and there was only one guarantee—he would hurt like hell when he landed.

CHAPTER ELEVEN

'IF I DIDN'T know any better I'd think you were taking me up Ben Lomond.'

'I thought we could do just go up in the gondola, maybe have a coffee and see how we feel.' Yes, she was going to take him up Ben Lomond, because why the heck not? She liked the walk and he would too, if he ever gave her a chance. Although, she noticed his voice had an edge to it and she wasn't entirely sure if she should push him.

Abbie told him to pull the car into the gondola car park and tried to pretend everything was fine. It wasn't. Something had happened during their lovemaking that had made her feel so totally connected to him and utterly bereft at him leaving.

In her roundabout way, she'd asked him to stay and he'd again pointed out all the reasons he couldn't. So now she wanted to exercise off the weird feelings running through her. She needed to protect herself and her heart from falling in love with him. That couldn't happen.

So, not spending any more time with him would have been the best approach, but there was one thing she wanted to do, for him…and she didn't want to think about anything past that. 'It's a lovely day, and there are wonderful views. And the gondola ride's always fun. Hey, we could luge our way down.'

'Or we could just luge all day and not go up the mountain.' He grinned, although she could see the guarding in his eyes. He'd gone from being honest and open to closed off. 'Be honest, Abbie, you're pushing me again. I told you I didn't want to do this with you. You know what I think about it.'

She tucked her arm into his and smiled innocently. 'Oh, come on, it's a lovely day and we won't go all the way to the top. Trust me.'

He let out a heavy sigh. 'It's not you I have a problem with.'

The gondola swung precariously in the wind as it inched up the mountain. It was a spectacular day of sunshine but there was still quite a breeze. In the big metal and glass cabin with them was a heavily pregnant woman and her husband. Abbie smiled. 'When are you due?'

'January.' The woman ran her hand over her belly, but even though she looked thrilled at her condition she didn't look particularly enamoured with the ride. Every time the wind blew she grabbed hold of her husband's fist. 'This is our babymoon. We've come down from Nelson for a few days. I wanted some down time before the chaos hits.'

'First one?'

She beamed. 'Yes. I'm so excited. It's our miracle baby, you see. We tried so hard for so long and now here I am. I never thought I'd hit forty-one and then get pregnant. To be honest, I'm a bit nervous about it all.'

'Yes, I can imagine you would be. I'm sure it'll be wonderful.' Now was the time Abbie should have mentioned her own impending parenthood, but it would be too hard to explain. And she felt guilty that she was up here having a trip out when Emma was working.

But she was due to go on leave at the end of the week,

so Abbie would make a double fuss of her then. Instead, she pointed out the sights to the holidaymakers.

As if reading her mind, Cal squeezed her hand and she squeezed back, glad that, even though they hadn't discussed what was next for them, he still wanted to stay physically close at least.

'Does it always swing like this?' The woman stared out of the window, her hand moving from her belly to her mouth. 'It makes me feel a bit sick.'

It hardly appeared to be moving at all now to Abbie. 'We're nearly at the top. The fresh air will help you. Take a few deep breaths when you get off. I'm sure you'll feel better.'

But the woman still looked green a little later after Abbie and Cal had had their coffee overlooking the town. And her ankles were suspiciously swollen under her maxi dress. She was sitting in the café with her head in her hands. Her husband was telling her she'd be fine and that she just needed to rest.

Abbie's nursing instinct made her stop and check. *Just in case,* she told Cal. 'Hi there, are you still not feeling great?'

'I'm just a bit dizzy and out of breath, that's all.' The woman grimaced, red-faced, but Abbie didn't think that was just from embarrassment.

'She's just been sick. I told her to try and eat something, but she doesn't want to.' The partner grimaced. 'The minute she feels well enough, we're heading back down and I'm going to make her go straight to bed.'

'Good idea. Maybe a quick trip to the doctor's en route.' Abbie smiled, knowing her face was a mask of friendliness, meanwhile assessing for any obvious signs and symptoms. 'Your husband is probably right—some rest would be good.'

Cal was also clearly a little concerned if his frown was anything to go by. 'Headache?'

The woman nodded. 'I've had it for a few days and I can't seem to get rid of it. I thought the fresh air would do me some good.'

Pre-eclampsia. All well and good to deal with in a hospital setting, but not so great at the top of a huge hill with only a swinging box to get them back down again. 'And the swelling in your feet, is that normal for you?'

The woman looked down at her shoes. 'No. It's not. But then, I've never been pregnant before so I don't know what normal is. I just thought that's what happened. You get fat all over, right?'

'Hey, well sometimes. My name is Abbie and I'm a nurse. Cal here is a paramedic. Is it okay if we sit with you for a while? Just to keep an eye on you until you feel better?' Cutting short the walk was nothing compared to making sure she was okay.

Cal nodded and joined them at the table, his voice gentle but probing. He'd gone straight into professional mode and Abbie was glad there was something to buffer the weird atmosphere between them. Only, she wished it weren't this: a potential emergency. 'What's your name?'

'Ashley. And thank you, you don't need to go to all this trouble. This is Mark, my partner.'

Cal patted her arm. 'It's no trouble. I was just wondering, when did you last see a midwife or obstetrician?'

'Oh, a few weeks ago. I should have gone last week, but I was too busy at work. Then we came here and I've been trying to relax, but I do feel a little strung out.'

Alarm bells started ringing. She could have dangerously high blood pressure, be at risk of seizures and even a stroke. Death. The baby was at risk too. Abbie wasn't going to panic her, but she'd have felt better dealing with her in the ED. At least she'd have the equipment there; here she had nothing except her observation skills. 'I think it's probably a good idea to just get yourself checked out when you get down to town. No harm in checking, right?'

'Sur...' But the woman's words didn't come out properly and she started to slump to the side, into Cal's lap. He caught her and helped her back in the chair. 'Ashley? Ashley? Hey, we should stop meeting like this.'

Back to his black humour and Abbie loved him for it because it got a smile from both of the expectant parents. Although, Ashley's was pretty weak.

Mark grabbed Ashley's hand. 'Hey, girl. Hey. What's happening?' Then he looked over to Abbie, his voice rising. 'What's happening?'

'I'm not one hundred per cent sure, but she may have pre-eclampsia, or just be dehydrated.' Or a dozen things that they couldn't deal with up here. *Please don't start fitting. Please, just don't.* 'We need to get her down to the ED as quickly as possible.' Trying not to look panicked, Abbie glanced over to Cal.

'I'm going to call my mates and get them to bring some reinforcements.' Cal fished his phone out of his pocket. 'There's a helicopter landing pad just outside. It shouldn't take them long to get here.'

But in the meantime there was little they could do apart from make her comfortable. Abbie moved her chair to be closer, stroked Ashley's hand and smiled. 'Got any names chosen yet?'

'Jessica Rose,' Mark answered when his girlfriend didn't seem to be able to make the words she was clearly trying to find come out of her mouth.

'Pretty. You know it's a girl, then?'

'Yes. Can't wait to meet her.'

'Not…yet…too…early.' Ashley was groggy and suddenly inhaled sharply, her head jerking back.

'She's having a seizure.' Abbie's heart started to beat rapidly. *No. No. No. No.* This couldn't happen.

Abbie sent Mark to ask for some space to be cordoned off and for blankets, and to make a makeshift bed on the floor. She rolled Ashley onto her side to protect her airway and held her head gently in a safe position. Time for mum and bub was starting to run out.

Meanwhile Cal had run outside at the sound of the chopper blades and was now reappearing with two of his colleagues.

'I have never been so glad to see you,' she whispered. Would she ever get sick of seeing that beautiful face? Of breathing him in? Right now she wanted to be in his arms in bed and not here facing this. She made it her priority not to get involved with men or patients, and yet here she was doing exactly that. She could barely breathe for worry about Ashley and that precious baby. And could barely look at Cal without the tug of desire and need.

Within minutes, Ashley was in the helo with Mark and it was lifting from the ground, but keeping as low as it could carrying a patient with dangerously high blood pressure. The magnesium sulphate had been administered to manage the fitting and she'd been given something to sedate her.

So, as they waved them off, Abbie should have been feeling more positive. She wasn't. She felt an overwhelming sense of dread.

Cal's arm was loosely wrapped around her shoulder. 'Hey, are you okay, Abbie?'

No. She wanted to lean against his chest and tell him about her fears. That the baby might not survive, and neither might Ashley. That she felt bad about being here, fit and well and not pregnant. For the first time ever, she was glad she wasn't pregnant and that made her feel very strange indeed.

She wanted to admit she was lonely and that he was the best thing that had happened to her in a very long time and that she didn't want him to leave. But couldn't ask him to stay either.

What man wanted to take on a woman and a baby and an almost co-dependent friendship set-up? Especially if that man had other reasons to go back to Scotland. Good, honourable reasons that she had no argument with.

'More, now than ever, I need to get rid of the adrenalin. I need to walk. Or run.' Or sex. Yes, sex would definitely bring her blood pressure right down. But she dragged on her backpack as best she could with one hand in a cast. 'Come on, let's get going before it gets too late.'

She started to hike, hard and fast, trying to put distance between them, concentrating on putting one foot in front of the other for as long and as fast as she could. Trying to wipe away the images of him in her bed and the hurt in her heart.

Soon her heart began pounding with the exercise and her head began to clear as the endorphins kicked in and she thought less and less about all the things pressing into her brain and more about just breathing.

After a good hour of pushing up and up and up through tussock grass and along thin gravel paths edged by tiny alpine plants, she heard his voice behind her. 'Abbie! Abbie, stop. For God's sake. Stop.'

She dropped her bag to the floor and grabbed a drink bottle from the side pocket, waiting for him to catch up. 'What's wrong? Can't keep up?'

'I just wanted to stop and admire the view. You know...

smell the roses…instead of marching up to the top of the hill and marching down again.'

'Oh. Yes, of course.' That had been the reason to bring him in the first place—to show him how lovely it could be instead of worrying about danger and disaster and search and rescue. And his brother. 'Stunning, yes? And no issues, you see? Neither of us have fallen over or off and it hasn't snowed. We're not lost—the path is pretty easy to follow. We're fine. We're absolutely fine.'

They weren't fine, she knew that. But neither of them was prepared to talk about it. His eyebrows rose. 'I suppose.'

'How do you feel?'

He took a long deep breath and looked over the panoramic view of mountains and valleys and the bluest of blue lakes. His hair was tousled in the breeze and there wasn't a drip of sweat on him. It was as if he'd just gone for a stroll instead of scaling a peak. 'Great. Pretty damned good.'

'It's always good to face your demons.'

'Ach, how can I not when you're around?' He winked and then looked across the exposed terrain. Wind sliced through them and the grass bowed and swayed in one direction and then another. 'I admit, I was playing it cautious, but I'm learning. Live and let live. Give support and don't overpower. Right?'

'Right. And learn to trust in other people's ideas and dreams.'

'It's harder than you think.' He tilted her chin so he could look at her. 'But thanks for that, Abbie.'

'Oh, you're absolutely welcome. But who am I to give advice? I don't have any kids….yet.' She couldn't help but press her good palm to his cheek. It was cold from the fresh southerly breeze, but his eyes were warm and she stood for a moment basking in their heat.

'Not long though.'

He smiled and her heart melted all over again. He was a good man. A damned fine man, with demons. But then, didn't everyone have something? It just meant he had faced and fought and lived. Scars, even mental ones, were proof of survival.

'You did well back there, with Ashley.'

'We both did. I mean, it wasn't as if there was a lot we could do to actually help, but I hope we made them less panicked at least. I could tell you were thinking the same thing as me—get her the hell down the mountain.'

'Aye. We did good.'

'Yes.' She ran her fingers down his cheek. 'Here's to us.'

'To us.' Then his lips were on hers and all the emotion of the last few hours was infused in his kiss. He hauled her against him, not gently but with a need her body matched. There was no denying this. She was his and she wanted him to be hers. Everything they did together seemed to deepen the connection between them; she was falling harder and faster.

He tightened his grip around her and she held onto him, not wanting to let him go.

After a few minutes she became aware less of his amazing mouth and the hum of the wind in her ears and more aware of another kind of hum.

Abruptly, she pulled out of his arms. 'Did you hear something?'

'What?'

'I think it's my cell phone. Wait, let me look. It might be Mark, about Ashley. Or one of the paramedics or someone… I hope she's okay. And the baby.' Abbie shoved her hand into the bottom of her bag and pulled out her phone.

Texts, so many texts. And missed calls. She scanned down the messages, her heart in her throat. 'She's in labour. She's been in labour for...'

'Well, they'll probably do a Caesarean just to get the baby out and then put her in an induced coma until they can get the blood pressure—'

'Not Ashley. *Emma.* Emma's in labour.' There were messages spanning back to when they'd started the walk. 'Well over an hour. Oh, damn. Damn and blast. *My* baby's coming and I'm up a stupid mountain trying to prove a point.'

And having the best kiss of her life.

Flinging the pack onto her back, she turned around and looked down the path. An hour's walking. A gondola, then a drive. She was going to miss the birth of her baby. How could she have done this?

How would she help Emma with a broken wrist? How would she hold her child?

Cal was looking at her as if he'd been punched in the gut. 'It's a bit early?'

'Yes. Yes. It's early, Cal,' she snapped, but couldn't help it. She needed to go. She shouldn't have even been here. 'Too early. She's not due for another few weeks. Oh, God, I hope they're okay. She must be going mad, wondering where I am.'

She fired back a text.

On my way. Don't you dare give birth without me!

Emma replied.

I've got my legs crossed, but I don't know how long I can do that for.

We'll be there as soon as we can.

We?

Me and Cal.

Emma fired back almost immediately:

Interesting...

Not interesting. Confusing.

'Come on. We've got to hurry.'

'Stop. Wait a second.' He was frustratingly slow all of a sudden. 'What did we talk about before? Going down is always tricky. One bad footstep and you're going to go head over heels. Take it easy.'

'Take it easy? Really? This baby is the only good thing in my life. It's the only good thing that came out of Michael dying. I promised Emma I'd be with her every step of the way, and here I am with you instead of with her.'

And yet, she wouldn't have given any of today up. Meeting Cal had been the best thing that had happened to her in a very long time. Today had been hugely emotional and intimate and the more she got to know him, the more he was chipping away at her heart. Coming up here had been her idea, not his. She'd wanted to trick him into facing his demons but here she was, facing hers instead.

'Look, I didn't mean that the way it sounded. I really didn't. Today has been so, so lovely. I'm just scared I'm going to miss one of the most important moments of my life. I have to be there. I have to go for my baby. Now.'

CHAPTER TWELVE

'OF COURSE YOU DO. And I'm going to get you there safely, okay?' Cal took her by the arm and made her stand still. 'If you start getting het up you might hurt yourself.'

Or worse. He knew how that went; getting emotional only made things less controllable.

'I can't imagine anything would make me hurt as badly as I do now, to be honest.' She shook her arm out of his grasp, but he made sure she was steady and not at risk of falling.

It was starting to rain now, to add to the mess. He had to take some control here. He couldn't stay. He couldn't be the father, or her lover, he couldn't walk into that labour room and help, or witness the birth of her child. But he could make sure she got there safely at least. 'I'm going to go first, okay, to set the pace I think we can safely go at. You will not run down this hill in the rain. Do you hear me?'

Her nostrils flared but she nodded. 'Yes.'

'You'll be no good to your baby or to Emma with two broken limbs or a damaged back.'

'Okay. Okay. Yes, I know. Just make sure your pace is fast.'

The path became slippery underfoot and her mood became equally dangerous.

And he knew she was blaming him.

And she was right to.

If she hadn't met him none of this would have happened. If she'd met some other man she could have a real future with, she wouldn't be grasping for little bits of joy or trying to prove to him that he could do things he was afraid of.

But she had met him, a man who already had enough responsibility and couldn't take any more on, who couldn't change his life to fit hers, no matter how much he wanted to.

He stopped to check she was okay, but she rushed past him and he let her. Because how could he stop her rushing towards the one thing she deserved more than anything—a future?

He watched the sway of her ponytail and the clip of her feet and his heart clenched like a fist.

He wanted to take her on. He wanted to stay. He wanted to be a father to her child.

He wanted to love her. He wanted her to be his responsibility.

Maybe he already did love her.

He tried to fathom it out. And every which way he turned he couldn't ignore the fact that he was falling for her. Loving her.

Because who the hell brought someone a Christmas tree if they didn't love them even just a little bit?

Trouble was, he didn't think it was just a little bit. He thought it might be a whole lot.

Could be. If he stayed.

He groaned inwardly and upped his pace. It was a hell of a mess all round. And letting her in had been the most stupid thing he'd ever done. Almost.

The gondola ride and journey back to town were made in silence, save for the incessant tap of Abbie's good fingers on the dashboard as he pulled the car into a parking space at the hospital. She'd wanted to drive but he hadn't let her.

'I can absolutely drive. I know the roads better than you,' she'd railed at him.

But he'd climbed into the driver's seat and refused to move. 'You have an arm in a cast—how the hell can you grip the steering wheel?'

'How will I hold my baby? Or help Emma? I don't know, but I'm damned sure I will. So I can drive too.'

'Like hell.' And he'd gunned the engine and driven like a maniac, but it still wasn't fast enough for Abbie. Her body was coiled and tense, ready to jump and spring at any moment.

'Let's go through ED. That's the quickest route to the lifts.' She pushed him out of the car, assuming he was going to go with her. Once outside she took him by the hand and all but dragged him through the emergency department. Excitement rippled over her, as if someone had given her the best birthday present ever—and yet it was laced with trepidation. Fear. Panic.

As they rushed past ED Mission Control she paused briefly to speak to Nixon, one of the doctors. 'Hey, did you hear? Emma's having contractions.'

'Yes. She's up in Maternity. Her waters broke while she was here, working. Give her my regards, will you?' The doctor nodded hello at Cal and he nodded back, still unsure what the hell he was doing here. He should have just dropped her off. He was going to be no use up there; Emma wouldn't want him in the room.

But he couldn't let go of Abbie's hand. It was as if his body was clinging to the very last moments, to the last touch before it was prepared to let her go.

'Sure will, Nixon. Bye.' Abbie's face crumpled a little and she bit her bottom lip. 'I hope she's okay.'

'She'll be fine.' Cal squeezed her hand and she looked up at him, registering he was still there, still holding on, still marching along with her.

'Oh, Callum, my head's all over the place.'

'I'm not surprised. It's been a big day. A lot's happened.' So much.

The hospital had been transformed to a Christmas wonderland at some point over the last few days. Streamers zigzagged across the ceilings and someone had sprayed fake snow onto every window. There was a huge Christmas tree in Reception, and tinny Christmas music filled the air. It felt like another world. He thought about the real snow that was awaiting him in Duncraggen. So many thousands of miles away.

And of his brother who needed him. And how much Cal wanted to be there to look after him, and here to look after an amazing woman and her baby.

So much had happened. Too much for his poor, pathetic heart.

She gave him a sad smile as she pressed the lift call button. 'I can't believe it was this morning…that we…wow, Cal.' There were tears shimmering in her eyes. 'It's all muddling up. I didn't want it to be like this. I wanted… I don't know what I wanted. I'm going to be a mum and we just made love… I'm so confused. I have so many feelings. I don't think I'm making sense.'

Always so honest, putting his feelings into words for him. He tugged her against him, his heart contracting into a tight, fierce ball. Because, she was right. None of it made sense. How could it? It was all muddled. He needed to make things clear for her. For himself. He pulled away from her. 'Abbie, I'm going to just drop you up there on the ward, okay? You understand? I'm not going to stay.'

The lift pinged and the doors slid open. She jumped in

and jabbed the seventh-floor button. 'Come on.' She looked back at him, confusion in her eyes. 'Wait…you mean… you're not coming in to see her?'

'No. You don't need me there. This is private. This is your family and your time. You don't need me.'

'I bloody well do.' Then she seemed to join up the dots of his thinking and her eyes grew wide. She tugged him into the empty lift just as the doors started to close. 'Oh, no. No. Don't do this right now, Cal. I haven't got time to even think about this. I can't just say goodbye and this be the end. Not of us. Not like this.'

He shrugged, his heart fracturing as his arms strained to hold her again, but he managed to control himself. 'We both knew it was going to happen, Abbie. Some time.'

'Not now, though. Please come with me. I want you there. You…you feel like family.'

How could he break her heart so swiftly?

Because he loved her, and it was best for both of them if this ended now. He loved her. Dammit. He loved her and was going to lose her. 'But I'm not family, Abbie. I can't be. It's best if we don't get even more involved. I can't watch your friend give birth to your baby—that's not something I should be there for. I hardly know her. This is your time. Yours and Emma's.'

And Michael's.

Fourth floor. The door swished open. There was no one there.

She shook her head again, jabbed the seventh-floor button one more time and paced to the other side of the lift. 'No! I can't believe… I don't know what I believed. That somehow we'd make it through this. That somehow we'd make it work, Cal. You and me, we'd make it work.'

How could they? He pulled her to face him, felt the lurch in his gut and knew it had nothing to do with the lift jerking upwards. 'You'll have everything you want right here. And, what's more, you need to concentrate on Emma. Not me, or us, or whatever we just did.'

She blinked quickly. 'We made love, Callum.'

'Aye, we did.' It was the most amazing thing he'd ever done. *She* was the most beautiful thing he'd ever known. A huge weight pushed on his chest. There was absolutely no way he could stay and watch her hold her child and not be part of it. She didn't need him here and, hell, he couldn't bear to be here and not be able to hold her again, not be able to make love to her. Not be able to be part of this. For ever. He had to cut loose.

His fingers went automatically to that crazy lock of hair that always fell differently from the rest and he wound it round his fingers. So soft. So strong. Like her. 'Your family is the most important thing to you, Abbie. Mine is to me too, and I have to be in Scotland. If we spend any more time together it'll just make things harder in the end. You need to focus on your baby and your new life. You'll forget me soon enough, when you're up to your arms in nappies and baby poop.'

'I don't think I'll ever forget you, Cal.'

Aye, she was imprinted on his heart, branded there, and there was no way he'd forget her. Ever.

The lift doors pinged open before he could say any more and they stepped into the very busy maternity corridor. Little children raced back and forth laughing, new mums waved goodbye to visitors. New dads clutching fresh bright flowers and balloons wandered around with tired, proud grins.

They found a nurse aide who pointed them to the labour suite and soon they were standing outside Emma's room.

Abbie went to open the door but he tugged her hand gently. It was time to go. To actually take that step away.

To give her the space she needed for her family. For her future, without him. 'Good luck, then, Abbie.'

I love you.

'No. No. No.' *Don't go,* her eyes pleaded. But then they flicked to the ward door and he knew he had to go right now, make it easy for her to leave him behind.

'Have the very best life, wee lassie.' If he faltered one step he might say or do something that had huge ramifications for them all. He had to go. He had to walk away. But first he ran his thumb over her lip—because he loved to do it. And knew she loved it too. He watched her eyes mist and saw the curl of her hand as it came towards him. He couldn't let her touch him, couldn't let her hold him.

He stepped away.

Her lip was trembling. 'Will you wait for me, Cal? Somewhere? Downstairs? In ED? The café? Please? Somewhere? I'll come down…soon. I don't know when… I don't know…when I know what's happening.' She looked bereft and his heart hurt; he'd done that to her. 'You will be there, won't you? When I come down?'

'Aye,' he whispered, hoping she wouldn't hear, or believe him.

Because they both knew he wouldn't be.

'Hey, there. Where's the hero of the hour?' Emma was sitting up in bed, and across her belly were tapes that fed to a monitoring machine. She looked like a Christmas present all wrapped up.

Abbie had barely had time to wipe her eyes, never mind find her happy voice. She'd watched him walk away and prayed he'd look back, turn back. *Come back.* But he'd done none of those things. Her gaze had followed him the length of the corridor, his confident swagger a little less sure than normal. His shoulders had sagged. And her heart had broken.

Because even though she'd known it was going to happen she hadn't expected it to be so soon. She hadn't expected to feel this much.

She hadn't expected to love him this hard.

And she did. Her eyes filled with tears, so she busied herself looking at Emma's charts and trying to speak through a throat that was full and raw. She loved him. And he was leaving her. Right when she needed him most.

But that was pure selfishness, really. She needed him, but she was asking far too much. 'Hey, gorgeous girl. Couldn't wait just a little bit longer?' Her heart felt as if it were twisting against her ribcage. 'Er... Callum, do you mean? He's gone.'

'Oh. As in...gone home? Or *gone* gone?'

'Gone downstairs. But very likely gone altogether.' Abbie cleared her throat and dug deep for her smiley voice. 'You seem very happy given you're in labour.'

'This is baby number two. I know what to expect. Plus, there's a lot to be said for gas and air.' Emma patted the bed. 'Come and sit down and talk to me. You look bloody awful and you're not the one in a hospital bed. What the hell happened, hun?'

I fell in love. He broke my heart.

'You're in labour, my lovely friend, let's focus on that. On you and the baby. How did it start? How do you feel? How long have we got? Isn't it a bit early?'

'I'll tell you all that soon enough. We're going to be here for a few hours yet, I think.' But there was no getting past this. Emma was a terrier when it came to interrogation. 'You have probably about four minutes before the next contraction hits. I need some distraction, so talk. Or I'll scream the place down. Talk, woman.'

Abbie took a deep breath. She would say this once, get it out, then not mention him again. 'It hurts. I'm hurting all over again. But somehow this is almost worse than Michael, because he didn't have a choice, but Callum does. I do.' But how could you choose between families and their needs? She pressed her hand to her mouth to stop herself from crying, but it didn't seem to do much good. Tears began to drip onto the green hospital blanket leaving bleak circles. 'He said family was more important and that we didn't need him here. I knew it was going to happen. I just didn't think it'd hurt so much. I just hoped we'd have a bit more time. A lot more time.'

'You love him.' Abbie had expected Emma to be irritated by this, but she wasn't. She linked her fingers into Abbie's. 'I'm so sorry. I shouldn't have encouraged you to have a Highland fling. I should have known you'd fall for him.'

'How? Why?'

'What's not to like about the man? He's your Mr Perfect.'

Yes. 'This isn't helping. Let's talk about the baby. The plan. Right, so Rosie's staying at school until her uncle picks her up—'

'Coward. Yes, the plan's going fine. My bag was in my car, as we discussed, so Nixon went and got it for me. Which was kind of him.' Emma ran her hand over her stomach and the monitor printout started to jump. Another contraction was building. One step closer to holding her baby.

'Yes, it was.' Abbie still hadn't mentioned that weird conversation with Nixon earlier this week and now she definitely wouldn't. Not the right time or place. 'Yes, let's distract each other. Are we sure we're happy with Michaela for a girl and Michael for a boy?'

'Your call. If you want to honour your husband, then that's great. Really great. If you want to move on, then that's good too. This is your baby.'

'*Our* baby. Yours and mine and Rosie's. A collective effort for one very longed-for child.' She looked at her beautiful friend wince in pain, and wondered how she could have agreed to put her through this, but knowing she'd have done the same if given a chance. Because families did come first and, above everything, Emma and Abbie were sisters in everything except blood.

She wanted to ask her how she felt about handing the baby over after all of this, but couldn't go there. It was something they'd have to deal with at the time. Nothing could prepare them for that moment. She stroked Emma's hair back from her face.

But Emma leaned forward, frowning. 'What's the matter? Why are you looking at me like that? Like *I* just broke your heart?'

'I'm not. It's not… I'm not.' Abbie made herself smile.

But Emma was starting to tense with the pain. 'Am I imagining it, then? When I said it was your baby, you jumped right in and said *ours*. It's not ours. It's yours, Abbie. What's the matter? Don't you think—? Oh, my God! You don't think I'm going to give it to you, do you?'

This.

On top of Cal leaving. It was too much. One moment Abbie had almost had everything and then…so close to losing everything. 'I just thought… I couldn't give my baby away. I don't know how you can.'

For a moment, Abbie thought Emma was going to growl at her, but her eyes softened and she covered Abbie's plaster-casted hand with hers. 'Oh, honey. I thought you were being a bit weird about it. Every time we talked about this moment you referred to the baby as ours, as if you were suggesting I wanted it and you were trying to keep me sweet. Don't worry, okay? Whatever happens, I will give you this baby. I love it, yes, of course I do. It's been inside me for so long I've definitely grown attached. But, not to the point of wanting to keep it all for me.'

'So, you're okay about handing it over? Are you sure?' Relief rolled through Abbie; she'd been secretly so worried that at the end of these nine months she'd still have no baby to call her own. 'I should have said something. I'm sorry. I should have trusted you more.'

'Yes, you should have. Or we should have talked more about it. I thought you believed me, but I can imagine how you've been worrying. I know what you're like, Abbie Cook.'

'I heard some women gossiping at work and it sent my head into a spin.' Seemed that happened a lot these days.

Emma's eyes closed for a moment and she seemed to be controlling her breathing; either riding the contraction or just pretending to feel better about things than she wanted to let on... Abbie would never really know. 'I am absolutely one hundred per cent certain I do not want to keep your baby. I have one of my own, thanks, a sweet five-year-old, and I'm done with nappies and toddler tantrums. Plus, to be honest, I'm a little over heartburn and sleepless nights too. And this, yes, this, lying on a bed in agony...is not exactly fun. I don't want to be pregnant again for a very long time. If ever... No. Never again!' Her grip tightened around Abbie's bruised fingers. 'Okay. Here we go. This. Bloody. Hurts.'

'I know. I know. I'm so sorry. I wish it was me. You know I can't thank you enough for this, but...can you hold the other hand, please? This one is damaged enough.'

'Sorry. Sorry. Not sorry. Pass me the gas and air.' Emma screwed her eyes closed as Abbie ran round to the end of the bed and grabbed the cylinder and mouthpiece. Once back at Emma's side she let her friend have some long puffs and then stroked her back. 'You're doing so well. So very well.'

Emma puffed out as she breathed through the pain. 'Things haven't got interesting yet. We'll see. Now, no more talk about who's going to bring up this baby, okay? He's yours. She's yours. All yours. With love.'

'Okay. Thank—'

'Hello!' A midwife came into the room. 'How are we doing?'

'Managing.' With a grunt, Emma hauled herself up the bed and Abbie rearranged pillows, feeling useless.

The midwife looked at the monitor printout and nodded. 'We can take this off now. Everything is fine there. I just need to check on a couple more things, see how well you're dilating. You want your friend here?'

'No. She's going to the shop. I'd like some magazines and mints, please.' Tired eyes looked over. She was hurting but pretending she was fine. Story of Emma's life. 'Go. You never know who you might meet down there.'

Cal had long gone, Abbie was sure. 'Okay. Don't do anything while I'm gone.'

'I wouldn't dream of it. See if you can find him. Talk to him. Phone him. Tell him how you feel.'

'Why?'

'Because this is one chance you won't have again.'

'But, what about… Scotland? He lives in Scotland.'

Emma was being draped with a towel and the midwife was about to get serious, but Emma flashed a smile that was filled with love and a positivity that actually hurt Abbie's heart. 'We'd get by. You saved me from myself, Abbie. You helped me when I had nowhere to go with that bastard of a man trying to hurt me. I owe you. So what's a few thousand miles between friends?'

'I wouldn't go.' She couldn't. She couldn't leave her friend, her family.

Besides, he hadn't asked. He understood. Which made it all so much harder.

One last weak word as the midwife snapped on gloves. 'Mints?'

'Oh. Yes. Sorry. I'll go now.' Abbie tiptoed out and pulled the door behind her, pausing for time. Because she didn't want to go downstairs and see that he wasn't there.

CHAPTER THIRTEEN

CAL HAD MANAGED to keep a lid on things in the hospital, but out on the lake path he let rip; running at top speed for as long as he could push his body, until every muscle screamed for relief. Then doubling up as he hauled as much oxygen as he could into his lungs.

He'd done the right thing. He had. But everything felt wrong. Everything was wrong. He should have stayed with her. He should have told her how he felt.

But then what? What good would that have done? It would have just mired them deeper into a situation they couldn't fix.

The lake was so calm today it was in direct contrast to his insides. He needed to run again. And fast. But, in perfect, typical timing, his phone rang.

Cal was not in the mood to talk to his brother, but every time he saw the name *Finn* flash up on his display his heart thundered. Emergency? Depression? Who was watching him? 'You okay?'

'Yes. Fine.' A long sigh. 'What are you doing?'

Cal fought for enough breath to manage more than two words. 'Running. By the lake. Trouble sleeping?'

'Aye. The usual.'

'Maybe you need to do more exercise during the day, Finn. Tire yourself out physically, you know.' Although right now it didn't seem to be working for Cal. He felt painfully, hopelessly alive.

There was a pause. 'What's wrong?'

'Nothing.' Cal walked to a lakeside bench. The same bench he'd been at when she'd run past him and challenged him to a race. *Damn.* Everything about Queenstown would be tinged with memories of her. *Good job you're leaving soon.*

'Look, pal, you're my brother. I know when there's something wrong. Your voice is flat. You're not your usual sunny self.' Finn laughed. Because Cal hadn't ever been described as sunny and certainly never by his brother. 'What's got your goat this time? Job? Me? A woman?'

There was a catch in Cal's throat and he wheezed. 'Nothing.'

'Ah. Woman.'

'None of your business.'

'Spill the beans, man. I have all night, literally.' As if to prove his point Finn stretched out on the sofa and Cal got a glimpse of the lounge. Tidy. Neat. Clean. Finn had shaved. Wow, things had taken a turn for the better, just from yesterday. There was something about him that was different too. He was…lighter somehow. His mood was better. Hope underpinned his voice.

Unlike Cal's. 'I don't feel much like talking.'

There was another pause. Finn ran a hand over his jaw and smiled. Another unusual thing. 'That's not like you. I remember that long night on the ridge and how you blathered on and on and on. I couldn't shut you up.'

'I was trying to keep you awake. To keep you…you know…with me.' They'd never talked about that night before. Never gone there. He wasn't minded to go there now either.

'And you did. And you have, many times since, Cal. I

know. I'm grateful. I mean it.' Finn actually looked a little embarrassed. 'Really. I owe you. So talk again now.'

'Ach, it's nothing.' It was everything. But if he started he might just never stop.

When had he said that before? Ah yes, to her. And she'd made him talk and he had and he'd felt better. She'd made him better, had helped to heal some wounds.

'What's her name?'

'Abbie.' There was a fist of pain under his ribcage just saying it. He rubbed to make it go away. It didn't.

Finn's eyebrows rose. 'And what's the problem with this Abbie?'

Where to start? He couldn't be in two places at once. Didn't know if he had enough space in his head or his heart for her and a baby when he was already brimful of responsibilities. Plus, the distance. So many problems. But his subconscious seemed to be one step ahead as he blurted out, 'She's having a baby.'

'What?' First time in a while he'd seen his brother's eyes shine. 'Way to go! You wee randy devil.'

Cal kept a small smile to himself, because no way would anyone believe him if he tried to explain the whole story. 'No. Not mine.'

'But you want it to be yours, right? You want her?'

'Aye.' More than anything. A huge admission, but yes. He wanted her and this baby.

'So what's stopping you?'

You. Me. Fear. Duty. He cleared his throat; no point in going there. 'How's everything going?'

Finn raised his hand and pointed to the clean room. 'Better, so much better. It's about time I got my act together and smartened things up—so don't go thinking I miss you. I've got news too. The old boss said I could go back one day a week in the new year. See how I go.'

'Back to work?' Cal didn't know how he felt about that. He thought for a moment. A ball of heat filled his chest. Proud, actually. A bit of trepidation. Feeling his brother slipping away a little. In a good way. Cutting some ties. 'Good. That's great. You'll have to sort your sleeping out, though.'

'I'm working on it.'

It was something they could work on together. 'Okay, well, we can make an appointment with the doctor and talk it through. When I'm home. I've been reading up on sleep routines—'

'Leave it, Cal. I'm managing.' His brother's jaw had set. Not a good sign.

'I'll see you on the nineteenth. We can talk more about it then.'

'Ah—yes. About that.'

'I've got a shuttle booked from the airport and Maggie can get some food in. Don't worry about anything.'

Finn's hands were palm up towards the screen. *Stop. Stop. Stop.* 'Enough, Cal. Stop it. Stop.' He scrubbed a hand over his hair, the sheepish look coming back. 'Thing is…' He took a big deep breath and blew out slowly. 'Thing is… I don't want you to come back.'

What the hell? 'Why not?'

'I know you feel responsible for what happened, but you're not. We made a stupid mistake and we don't both need to spend the rest of our lives paying for it.'

'But I said—'

Finn nodded. 'Yes, I know what you said. I heard every word through that freezing night. Your voice kept me alive Goddammit. *You* kept me alive.' He actually did sound grateful and humbled, not angry. Even a little choked up. 'And thank you, but all of this…living-with-me thing…it's too much. You can't put your life on hold for me in some sort of penance.'

There was no question or debate; he had to look after his brother. 'It's not a penance.'

'It's a pain in the arse, is what it is. I can't do anything without you telling me how to do it. I know it's just your way, but I need to live my own life.' Now he was back to his normal annoying self. *Brothers.* 'Oh, and I'm sorry, but I have a confession to make.'

'What?' Cal's interest was piqued along with his mood.

Finn did that funny grimace men did when they didn't want to say something but knew they had to. A sort of *sorry, mate but…tough love* kind of thing. 'It was me who spoke to your boss about an exchange to New Zealand in the first place, and he agreed you needed some space. It was me who paid for the airfare—we didn't get nearly as much as we wanted to by fundraising. I needed you out of my hair. I needed you to learn how to live without guilt. Everyone else just helped with the organisation and amped up the idea to make you go.'

The last few months had been a set-up? 'But I wanted to help you. I still do. It's my job—you're my brother. You're family.'

'Aye. And I still will be whether you live here or in New Zealand or Timbuktu. So—you're free to do what you want. Go wild, have fun. Or…you know. Go get her.'

'I can't stop worrying about you just because you want me to.' Depression sometimes came back. Cal wanted to be there in case it did.

But Finn shook his head. 'I'm fine. I'm getting stronger every day. Stop using me as an excuse not to live your life.'

'I'm not. What about the Search and Rescue? My job.'

'Excuses. Just excuses, trying to find reasons why not instead of, *why the hell not*? I should know, I've been doing the same for long enough. You're scared to commit to anyone or anything in case it goes wrong. But look at me—things do go wrong, but we survive. We survive, Cal, and we live. Time to face reality and make the most of it.'

'Well, now I want whatever it is that you've been taking.' But Finn was right. Cal had worn his duties as a shield, held his job and his brother up as reasons why he couldn't give his heart to Abbie. But she had it anyway, in the palm of that damaged hand of hers. He'd been afraid of letting her in, because the simple truth of it was that he hadn't thought he had enough space in his life to take on more. But at what cost? Losing her altogether? Losing the chance of happiness? A life? A family of his own? He was losing all that by not even considering any other way.

Could he let Finn go, though? Could he stand aside and watch him falter? He wanted so much for him to be well—maybe this was a first shaky step of actually allowing him to be.

They had daily conversations across the world as it was—nothing there needed to change. And he could still be a brother and a husband and…a father. Something hopeful bloomed in his gut. 'Er… Finn, you know that skiing trip?'

'Aye?'

He needed to get back to the hospital and tell her. He hoped she'd be willing to have him in her life. Was it too late? Had he already hurt her enough by leaving her right when she'd needed him most? Would she even want him, when she had her own little family already? He had to try at least. 'I don't think I can make it after all.'

His brother grinned. 'Well, thank God for that.'

'You're doing so well. So bloody well. I'm so proud of you. Keep breathing, that's it. Pant. Pant.' Abbie gripped

Emma's hand and let her squeeze as hard as she wanted
to. For the last two hours they'd been in a tight, half-lit
cocoon of contractions and hand-holding and tears as the
contractions had become closer and stronger.

But now things were really starting to happen. The
midwife peered over Emma's legs. 'Good girl. The baby's
crowning. I can see the head.'

'Oh, my God. Oh! This is it. This is real.' There was
a moment when Abbie didn't know whether to laugh or
cry, so she did both.

And Emma joined in. But hers were mixed with screams
and grunts. 'I'm…so glad…you didn't miss this.'

'It's thanks to Callum that I'm here at all. He drove—'
*He drove me here. He made sure I was safe. He made
me love him.*

He was missing out. His loss. She couldn't believe he'd
walked away like that. Or how much she'd hurt at the
thought of him not being around. She didn't want to think
of waking up tomorrow and not seeing him. Or being at
work hoping for the sound of his voice that would make
her day so much better.

She didn't want to think of Christmas Day. For so long
she'd been looking forward to Christmas and now it felt
tarnished without him. But she couldn't change the fact
he didn't want to be here, couldn't be here.

She pushed thoughts of him as far away from here and
now as she could. She wiped her friend's face with a cool
damp flannel, wishing there was more she could do to
help. 'You're amazing, Em. Not long to go.'

'Whoa…! I need to push. Right now!' And with that
Emma took a huge breath and groaned and squeezed and
pushed and pushed.

And Abbie watched and waited and worried.

'Good. Excellent. Yes…yes. Here! A girl. You've got a

darling girl. All fingers and toes accounted for. She's gorgeous.' The midwife handed a squirming, wriggling, waxy baby into Abbie's waiting hands, but she couldn't hold it properly and her gut contracted. She dug deep and found enough strength to hold her long enough for one falling-in-love rush. 'Here. Put her on Emma's tummy.'

'You want to cut the cord?' The midwife again.

Scissors were placed in Abbie's good hand. Which was shaking as much as her heart was thumping. 'Oh, yes. Yes, please.'

And then the room was filled with fledgling wails and Emma's little sniffles as she stroked the baby's down-covered back, and Abbie snipped. And they were all in tears. Because this really was the most beautiful thing. The best gift anyone could ever give.

'Let me help you.' The midwife lifted the baby up and went to put her on Emma's chest, but Emma shook her head.

'Give her to Abbie. Give her to her mum.'

Abbie couldn't fight tears any more. *Mum*. She was a mum. A mum. Wow. 'Are you sure? You don't want to hold her first?' There were tears streaming down Emma's face and Abbie didn't know if it was a good thing or not. 'Do you...how do you feel? Is everything okay?'

Wiping her face with the back of her hand, Emma smiled. 'I'm fine. Really. Just hormonal, and emotional. And I just love the look on your face. You look so, so happy. It's a big thing, being a mum. I know. I already am one. Now you are too.'

Then Abbie was sitting down and holding the most precious, the most adorable, the cutest baby, in the whole world. And yes, she was biased, but she didn't care. It was true. She looked deep into those big eyes and her heart was lost. For ever. This was it. Hopelessly in love. Funny, how that could happen twice in one day. This one, though, this one would stay for a while at least. She looked up at her best friend. 'Thank you. Thank you. I just want to make sure you're okay with this.'

Emma sniffed and sat up a little, trying to make herself comfortable after her ordeal. 'Of course I'm okay with it. She was never mine to begin with, Abbie. She's yours. All yours. Look, she's got your eyes.' Emma looked straight into Abbie's eyes and blinked quickly. 'Oh. She's so beautiful.'

'Of course she is. And very few tears, look, she's just quietly watching. Such dainty fingers and toes. So graceful. Right. I've decided, I'm going to call her Grace.'

'Not Michaela?'

A wave of sadness rippled through Abbie, and she let it go. 'That can be her middle name. I don't want to feel sad every time I call to her. She deserves her own name. And I need to move forward. In so many ways. This is a new start. My new family of two.' Abbie squeezed her friend's arm. 'I don't know how the hell I'm ever going to repay you.'

'For what? Being a friend? You've done it a thousand times over since we were muddy-kneed with toothless smiles, and nothing but trouble.' With a sigh, Emma lay back against her pillows. 'Just love her, okay?'

'I already do. I'm besotted. Completely. And I love you, and Rosie, with all my heart.'

And it was true. So very true. But there was one corner of her almost full heart that would never be the same, that would never heal. Because Callum wasn't here to share in all of this.

He found her in the nursery. With her back to him, she was standing over a crib whispering softly to a baby.

A boy? A girl? He couldn't tell from here. It was swaddled in a white sheet and just stirring from sleep, its tiny arms and legs jerking in the air.

She leant in and twisted her wrist to pick it up. Flinched. Twisted again at a different angle.

No way was she a quitter.

Not like him. One sniff of emotional trouble and he was off.

Not any more. 'You want some help?' He kept his voice low, but even then she jumped and turned round.

'Cal?' There was pride glowing in her eyes, but caution too. And love. She was scared. She'd been through so much. He'd hurt her, he knew, and she wasn't going to let him do it again. She pressed her lips together and shook her head. 'I'm okay. I can manage. We can manage, thanks.'

'Do you want to sit down and I'll lift her? Him? Into your arms?'

'Her. She's a girl. Grace. My daughter.'

My daughter. It was a swift blow to his heart. He'd chosen to walk away from this? A fool. Stupid really was his middle name.

'Hey, wee bairn. Abbie, she's so beautiful.' There was a fierce possessive streak in him; he knew that very well. Finn had called him on it and Abbie had too. But it was because he cared. Cared deeply and wanted to protect the people he loved from every potential harm. And right now that same streak was running through him as he looked into the black button eyes of this little scrap of life. He wanted to be a part of this. He wanted this child to be his daughter.

He choked that all back—it was too much to think that she'd refuse him, refuse this. But he wouldn't blame her if she did. 'And Emma? How is she?'

'Sad, I think, but she won't admit it. She did so well.

So very well, but she's tired now and resting. I take over from here, so I'm on a steep learning curve.'

'So let me help.' Without discussing it further, he took her hand and sat her down in one of the large, soft feeding chairs. She looked exhausted and this was just the beginning. Every part of him craved to look after her. He wanted to hold her—and the baby—and keep them safe.

But she was still guarded. 'Why are you here?'

'Two things.' He went with the easier one first. 'I've just been talking to Nixon. He's had word that Ashley's okay... Ashley, from the gondola, with pre-eclampsia... She's still very sick, but they're confident she'll pull through. And baby's in NICU, but doing fine.'

'Thank goodness. I was so worried.' She looked over at Grace, who was starting to make little chirruping noises, and her eyes misted. She pressed a fist to her chest. 'I couldn't imagine...'

'Don't. Don't even think about it. You want to hold her?'

There was a smile. 'Yes. All the time.'

'I don't blame you. Wait there.' His heart was racing as he bent to pick little Grace up, but it just about melted as she wrapped her tiny fingers round his thumb. *This.* This was what he craved. There was something raw and thick in his throat. 'Here you go. She's beautiful. Like you.'

'Callum. I can't...not here.' She took the babe into her waiting arms and looked down at her with such tenderness that he didn't think he could hold himself together for much longer. He loved her and loved that child—a miracle that he could feel this way so quickly.

'So...' He wondered if he was making the same kind of face as his brother had a few hours ago. There were so many important things he had to say, he just didn't know if they'd come out right. 'I want you to know that I love you, Abbie. That I'm staying here, in Queenstown, indefinitely.'

'You love me? You...love me? You walked away, Cal. You walked away when I needed you.' Her eyes widened. 'Why the change of heart?'

He pulled a chair over to sit next to her. 'There was never a change of heart. I always wanted to stay. I just couldn't be in two places at once. I couldn't be a brother and a...partner...boyfriend.' *Family.* 'I couldn't give everything to everyone. At least, I didn't think I could. But I want to be here. With you. And little Grace. I want us to be a family.'

'And Finn?'

'He's fine. He's a lot better and I actually need to let him get on with his life the way he wants.'

'You've come a long way.' Abbie gave him a very gentle smile and placed her palm on his cheek the way she'd done so many times before. And it gave him some hope. 'It's a lovely thought. It really is.'

But... He could tell from her tone that there was a *but* coming. Hope faded.

'But how do I know you won't walk again? How can I let you in when you might leave? You're a bit of a flight risk. Don't you have a ticket for home?'

She wasn't going to make this easy for him, and who could blame her? He grabbed his phone and showed her the airline app. The cancelled flight. Nothing booked, nothing planned, except staying here. On that point, he was absolutely certain. 'This is my home, Abbie. Here. With you and Grace, if you'll have me.'

His home. The words struck her chest in a hard blow. Abbie watched as he shoved his phone into his pocket and she started to believe that maybe this was the new fresh start she craved. Him. A man who had been through so much, who'd shown he was good and honourable by knowing his limits, by not making false promises. A man she loved hopelessly. 'We're a lot to take on, Cal. I know that. It's complicated and messy. It's a lot of responsibility.'

'Which I want. I want you, both of you. We'll make it work. *I'll* make it work.'

And his voice was so ardent and the passion in his face so honest and true she believed him. Almost. 'Grace deserves someone who'll stay around.'

'I intend to and I'll prove that to you every day. Just know that I love you, and that's never going to change.' He was leaning closer now, his mouth inches from hers, his eyes filled with love, and she could feel the tug into his arms. 'I want us to be a family, Abbie. And that means I want it all; the wedding, everything.'

'What? A wedding?' He really was serious. 'Is this…? A mother and a wife in one day! Are you asking me to marry you?'

'Aye. I suppose I am.' He ran his finger over her necklace and came to a halt when he connected with her wedding ring. Held his breath, his eyes capturing her gaze. 'Yes. Yes, I am asking you to be my wife. Marry me, Abbie?'

And she wanted so much to stay like this, feeling like this, being with him for the rest of her life. Placing her palm over his, she nodded, because words were just too hard to say through a throat so thick with emotion. And she was concentrating on not crying because that might wake the baby.

'Is that a yes?'

Not crying wasn't happening. She felt the first tear, then the rest roll down her cheeks. 'Yes. Of course. Yes! Oh, I love you, Callum.'

'I love you too. Both of you.'

And then he kissed her. A promise. For ever.

EPILOGUE

IT WAS VERY early on Christmas morning, but Callum had been up for hours. He was standing by the Christmas tree, rocking his darling daughter, trying to get her to go back to sleep. He'd been the last to bed and up in the small hours and again now. At some point, they'd manage a whole night's sleep, but probably not for a few years. 'Shh, you'll wake Mummy.'

Abbie was watching from the doorway. Every time she saw that big strong man holding her tiny little daughter—their daughter—her heart pinged with a rush of love. 'Too late. I'm already awake.'

'Ach, sorry, love. We managed a nappy change and a feed but I think she wants entertaining.'

'Presents?' She looked over at the huge pile that had accumulated over the last few weeks. Gifts from her parents, from Emma's family. From work. And, of course, gifts from Callum. So many, too many.

But this was the best one: to watch him being a father to her child. To know he was staying. That he was part of her family. She didn't know if she'd ever felt so happy. 'No, we'll do presents when we get back. Now that we're all up, should we go now?'

'Aye. We're all dressed up in our Christmas best, aren't we?' He kissed Grace on both cheeks and secured her in her pushchair, grabbed the toys and entertainment, then wrapped Abbie into his arms. The place she always wanted to be. 'I love you. Did I ever tell you that?'

'I know you do. And I love you too. But hurry, or we'll be too late.'

Their route took them out through the botanical gardens and along the lake path. There weren't many other runners out so early, but they did pass some exhausted-looking parents with excited kids on sparkly new bikes and scooters, and they gave each other that tired grin that said, *happy*.

When they reached the bench, they unpacked, dialled and waited for him to answer. It was still Christmas Eve there and he was going out, so they didn't want to miss him.

'Hey, how's my beautiful girl doing?' Clearly, being soppy but pretending not to be ran in the family. Finn had been besotted with Grace and being an uncle from the minute he'd set eyes on her—distance didn't mean a thing with technology these days. 'It's snowing, look. This is snow, Gracie. This is Scotland at Christmas. Cold. Damp. But there's lots of whisky, so not too bad at all.'

'I think she's a little young for whisky, Finn.' But the little girl followed his smile and gurgled. Abbie grinned, snuggling into Callum's arms, her favourite place in the world. 'It's just how I imagined it would be. Magical. Look at this, Cal, your village really is like a film set. Isn't it beautiful?'

'Hmm? Beautiful? Yes. You are.' He kissed the back of her neck, then the side of her head. And she turned and kissed him full on the mouth.

'Hey, guys! Children watching!' Finn was shouting and laughing thousands of miles away. 'Please be mindful of our innocence.'

'Yeah, says the guy who was dating well before his

188 THE NURSE'S SPECIAL DELIVERY

older brother. Happy Christmas, Finn. Have a great one. And, please, be good.'

'I'm always good. I'm golden, mate. Happy Christmas, everyone.'

'Now, where were we?' With one sweep of his hand, Cal closed down the app. With a sweep of his other hand he'd picked up Grace and buckled her into her pushchair again. Then with both arms he wrapped Abbie into a hug.

'I think you'll find we were right here. Doing this.' She kissed him hard, then pulled out of his arms. Ready to race. 'Last one back to the flat is a turkey.'

'Or cooks the turkey.'

'I'm definitely going to win, then.' But she didn't shoot off. Instead, she stopped, taking it all in. One minute to smell the roses. Two. Three. For ever. She gazed first at her man, then at her child...then out across the deep blue lake and the soaring mountain backdrop. Their first family Christmas.

No need to race any more. She'd already won.

* * * * *

Read on for the next great story in
THE ULTIMATE CHRISTMAS GIFT *duet*

HER NEW YEAR BABY SURPRISE
by Sue MacKay

And, if you enjoyed this story,
check out these other great reads
from Louisa George

TEMPTED BY HOLLYWOOD'S TOP DOC
HER DOCTOR'S CHRISTMAS PROPOSAL
TEMPTED BY HER ITALIAN SURGEON
A BABY ON HER CHRISTMAS LIST

All available now!

HER NEW YEAR
BABY SURPRISE

BY
SUE MacKAY

Published in Great Britain 2017
By Mills & Boon, an imprint of HarperCollins*Publishers*
1 London Bridge Street, London, SE1 9GF

ISBN: 978-0-263-92683-5

Our policy is to use papers that are natural, renewable and recyclable
products and made from wood grown in sustainable forests. The logging
and manufacturing processes conform to the legal environmental
regulations of the country of origin.

Printed and bound in Spain
by CPI, Barcelona

Dear Reader,

A woman having a baby for someone else has to be one of the most unselfish gifts she can ever give. I know people who have children from surrogate mothers and how this has changed their lives in a very positive way. This has always been a story I've wanted to write, and when better than in a duet with the wonderful Louisa George?

Emma Hayes is a solo mother with a big heart, and when her best friend cannot carry her pregnancies to full term it is only natural for her to offer to have Abbie's baby.

It is this generosity and kindness and her courage that has Dr Nixon Wright sitting up and taking notice of Emma as more than a nurse and casual friend. But while his heart is leading him into love, his history is hauling on the brakes and trying to keep him safe and single. Of course his heart's going to win, but Emma won't make it easy for him. If she's going to love him back she wants the whole deal—not just the pieces Nixon offers.

I hope you enjoy reading this story to find out how Nixon wins over Emma as much as I enjoyed writing it.

Cheers!

Sue MacKay

sue.mackay56@yahoo.com

To my duet partner and wonderful writing friend,
Louisa George.

Loved writing a duet with you again.

Hugs, Sue.

Sue MacKay lives with her husband in New Zealand's beautiful Marlborough Sounds, with the water on her doorstep and the birds and the trees at her back door. It is the perfect setting to indulge her passions of entertaining friends by cooking them sumptuous meals, drinking fabulous wine, going for hill walks or kayaking around the bay—and, of course, writing stories.

Books by Sue MacKay

Mills & Boon Medical Romance

Visit the Author Profile page
at millsandboon.co.uk for more titles.

CHAPTER ONE

'JUST LOVE HER, OKAY?' Emma Hayes told her best friend as exhaustion from giving birth ripped through her aching, painful body and threatened to tip her into sleep. Sleep, where she could hide for a while. Then she'd wake up and still have to face up to the fact she'd had Abbie's baby for her and now her own arms were empty.

Abbie didn't raise her eyes from the precious bundle she held against her breast as she replied, 'I already do. I'm besotted. Completely. And I love you with all my heart.'

Aww, sniff. More damned tears. 'I know you do.' There'd never been any doubt. Love had been why she'd done this crazy, amazing, scary thing in the first place. 'This wouldn't have happened if you didn't, and if I didn't reciprocate those feelings.'

Sitting carefully on the edge of the bed, Abbie leaned into Emma, mindful of the baby cradled between them. 'I can't describe my feelings. All the waiting and hoping and now here she is.' She brushed a kiss over Em's wet cheek. 'Thank you so much. Again.'

Emma lightly wound her arms around her friend and their precious bundle. 'Stop saying that, okay?' She didn't want gratitude; she didn't need to be thanked. That they'd come through the pregnancy without an argument said a lot for their friendship, but then, it'd been strong since the day they met at Queenstown Primary more than twenty years ago. But at the moment, the only thing she knew for certain was a few minutes to herself were imperative if she was to keep her equilibrium now that she'd given birth. 'Go be a mum while I get some shut-eye.'

She needed to fall into the haze filling her head to forget the pain of the birth and remember only the relief that everything had gone well, despite the baby arriving early. Happiness and sadness wound together in her heart at the wonder in Abbie's eyes as she gazed down on the tiny, beautiful little girl tucked into a pink hospital blanket. A child who'd never know her father; who had been created through artificial insemination.

One of the two most beautiful girls in the world. Emma's heart swelled with love and longing. 'Rosie.' Suddenly, more than anything in the world, Emma needed to hold her own daughter. Her other daughter, barely five and full of energy and mischief.

No! Don't go there. Grace is Abbie's. Always has been, always will be.

Snatching up the phone, she texted her mother.

It's over. Baby's gorgeous. Please bring Rosie to me.Xx

Abbie looked up, her eyes filled with awe and trepidation. 'This is for real, isn't it? This is where I get to step up to the mark and be a mum in all ways possible except carrying her myself.' Tears streamed down Abbie's cheeks. 'This is why you gave me such a precious gift. To be a mother.' Her voice trailed off in a whisper, the last words barely audible.

'Isn't it the best?' Emma whispered back around a lump in her throat and a dash of emptiness. But not one regret. Abbie deserved good things. If there'd been a moment when being the mummy tummy might've been difficult, Emma suspected it would've been minutes ago when the midwife had handed Abbie the baby, not her. But no. She'd been fine about it, hadn't had a sudden change of heart, so she now reiterated, 'Grace has been yours since conception.' Abbie's and Michael's, though he would never get to see his daughter, never hold her or know her. His only role in the pregnancy had been to leave sperm in the bank for this very day.

Emma bit down on a soft smile.

I did the right thing by them.

Abbie and Michael had stood by her through the hideous, violent days of her marriage as much as her family had. They'd helped pick up the scattered pieces of her dreams afterwards, had shown with their own strong love for each other that she could make a life with Rosie without looking back. That they could be a family without a man in her life. Not that she'd ever been in the market for a new husband. No, thank you very much. Been there, had the bruises and fractures to show for it.

Her friends had also made sure she and Rosie never went without fun and laughter. This had been her way of returning the love. Knowing the baby would be living next door in the adjoining apartment would make everything easier to come to terms with. Abbie was not rushing out of Queenstown to some place else in New Zealand to keep her daughter to herself. Though who knew where she might end up if the Scotsman pulled his head out of his backside and found he couldn't live without Abbie. Right now, she wanted to throttle him for hurting Abbie with his uncertainties.

They'd always been there for each other on the days when Rosie wouldn't stop crying and Emma needed a break, or other days where Abbie couldn't cope with losing Michael. Their friendship was solid, and it would take a hurricane of massive proportions to break it. Today, with a baby and a broken heart to deal with, Abbie needed her support more than ever.

'If only I had that with a man.'

'Had what?' Abbie asked without taking her eyes off Grace.

'The same trust and sharing and loving and laughs—and tears—you had with Michael.'

Abbie's head shot up, surprise widening her eyes. 'That's a shift in your thinking.'

'Told you I needed sleep. Must be baby brain.' She did not want a man in her life. The only man she'd loved unreservedly had developed a pair of fast and hard fists along with a cruel mouth. She wasn't going to repeat that experience in an attempt to find love. Only the unwise didn't learn from their mistakes, and Alvin had been a *mistake*. Definitely better off without a man in her life, and the reason she turned down any—the few—date invitations. Her body was safe, and, more importantly, Rosie was protected. There was already plenty of love in her life—Rosie, Abbie, and her fiercely protective brothers and father, and her ever patient mother. Who needed someone special when she was surrounded by those guys? Talk about greedy. Not everyone got so lucky.

'Any man in particular causing this left-field idea? An emergency specialist by any chance?' asked her cheeky friend.

'Nixon and I get on fine as friends. I turned him down for a date once.'

'You never told me.' Abbie eyeballed her, then grinned. 'Mr Cool isn't as uninvolved as he'd like you to think.'

Sigh. 'Yeah, right. I had enough going on with the pregnancy and Rosie. I didn't need complications with a man.'

Abbie smiled sadly. 'Guess I can't argue with that today considering Cal has just dumped me.'

Ping!

Saved by the phone.

Nearly there. Princess couldn't wait any longer. Mum. Xxx

Then the baby—

Grace, Emma, her name is Grace.

The baby gave a small cry and Emma's breasts tightened painfully. Breasts that did not have a role to play in feeding this gorgeous infant.

Abbie looked up, panic in her eyes. 'What now?'

'You feed her. Food, warmth, love.' Under the blanket, Emma's hands clenched against the urge to reach for the baby to place her on her breast. No surprise here. Her body didn't understand it was no longer the mother, despite the repeated messages from her brain. All it heard were the calls from her heart.

The midwife bustled into the room. 'Did I hear Baby cry? She'll be wanting to be fed.' Her eyes flicked to Emma, and she gave an almost imperceptible lopsided nod as if to ask, *How are you doing?*

Emma nodded back. Okay, she mouthed.

But take them away so my breasts can settle down.

'She's making noises like she's hungry,' Abbie muttered, still gazing at the baby, only now with trepidation.

'You'll be fine, Abbie.' The midwife had all the reassuring words and actions. The baby hadn't latched on when first placed against her mother's breast, but hopefully now she would. 'We'll go along to the nursery and I'll start you learning to breastfeed. Emma needs to rest.' She helped Abbie to her feet.

'Right.' Abbie held Grace as though afraid of dropping

her as she moved out of the room. With her injured arm, it was a distinct possibility, so it was no wonder she held her daughter carefully.

Emma's eyes tracked her until she disappeared around the corner, a lump the size of Lake Wakatipu in her throat and her chest painfully tight. Abbie and Grace. Her friend and her daughter. Her daughter? Or Abbie's? Definitely Abbie's. But…

No buts.

Where's Rosie?

A fierce ache throbbed in her breasts and there was nothing she could do to appease it. Bizarre didn't begin to describe the fact that Abbie was able to breastfeed her daughter. 'The wonder of modern-day drugs.' Emma carefully slid further down the bed. The irony being that she would need something to help with stopping her milk supply, or at least to dull the pain while nature ran its course. Uncomfortable days were ahead, then hopefully everything would settle down and she'd get back to life as she knew it—raising Rosie and working day shifts in the emergency department downstairs; saving for a deposit on a house and keeping her head below the radar when it came to men.

'Mummy, where's the baby? Can I hold it?' Rosie raced into the room, staring all about. 'I can't see the baby.' She leapt onto the bed and lifted the cover to peer underneath.

Emma gasped at the sudden movement. 'Easy. Mummy's sore.'

'Where is it?'

'It's a little girl and her name is Grace, darling. She's gone to the nursery with Abbie,' Emma explained and had to bite down on the chuckle brought on by her daughter's disappointment.

'But I want to hold her.'

At least she wasn't jealous. The midwife had warned that Rosie could initially be anti the baby, might see her as competition for her mother's affections. But these were unusual circumstances.

'Rosie, love, remember what I told you?' Emma's mother appeared in the doorway. 'The baby will be tired and only Abbie can hold her just now. You'll get a turn soon.'

Really? Would Rosie go along with having to wait? Emma raised an eyebrow at her mother. They were good at talking like this around a certain little madam.

A nod. A frown. An eloquent shrug. Then in real speak, 'I've been fobbing off demands to come see you since I picked her up. Daniel got tied up with a client and couldn't make it,' she explained. 'When I received your text we were already pulling into the car park, the word "no" having long gone out the window. She was far more interested in the baby than what happened at school.'

'That's saying something.' Emma laughed. Rosie believed school had been created just for her.

'Where's the nursy?' Rosie bounced up and down on the bed.

'Nursery,' Emma corrected automatically as she tensed against the sharp pain brought on by the bed turning into Rosie's trampoline. 'Can you sit still, love?'

'What's the nursy?' The bounces reduced in severity but didn't stop.

'Nursery. It's where the babies sleep while they're in the hospital.' In this case anyway. Emma reached for her girl. 'Got a hug for Mummy?'

Little arms wound tightly around her neck. 'A big, big, big one, Mummy.' And a sloppy kiss apparently.

Not to mention the elbow in her belly. Carefully dislodging Rosie's arm, she kissed her daughter's forehead. 'Thank you, darling.'

'Do you like my hug, Mummy? It's special for you.'

Tears sprang into Emma's eyes, and she tightened her hold on her daughter. Pressing her face into the abundant dark curls, she sniffed and croaked, 'It's the best hug ever.' It really, really was, and she might need plenty of them over the coming days.

'How are you, sweetheart?' Her mum kissed her gently on the other cheek and passed over a handful of tissues.

'I'm good. About everything. Though I feel like a freight truck's driven through me.'

There was doubt in those knowledgeable eyes that she'd known all her life. Not even shock tactics had diverted her mum from her real mission. 'When do you see the psychologist?'

Give me strength.

That was the last person she wanted to talk to, but there'd be no avoiding that particular conversation. It was part of the surrogacy deal she'd signed that she talk to everyone this side of the Crown Ranges about her feelings. If the shrink lady didn't come looking for her then her mother would be hauling her to the counsellor's rooms herself.

'In a couple of days, unless I need her sooner. Honestly, Mum, I'm fine. When Grace cried, I felt a tug on the heartstrings, but she has always been Abbie's baby and nothing's changed.'

Nothing I can't handle. I hope.

Hell, what if she couldn't manage, was crippled with longing for the baby that wasn't hers?

Her mum cut through the sudden pain in her head. 'If you're sure.'

'I am,' she answered more forcefully than she intended.

Pushing the demons back into their box? 'At the moment I'm more in need of sleep.'

Her mother smiled her special mum smile and gently pushed the hair away from Emma's forehead. 'I'm proud of you. I don't think I could've done what you have.'

More tears. 'Thanks, Mum. You got a hug for me too?' Why did she need so many?

Rosie squirmed in close, pushing her way under Emma's right arm. 'Me, too, Mummy. I love hugs, don't I?'

'This a hug fest?' The booming question came from across the room.

Emma's eyes flew open. Nixon stood at the entrance, looking uncertain of his welcome. 'Hey. You want to join in?'

'Me? I don't think so. There's a crowd already.'

'Chicken.' The challenge slipped out with no input from her brain. No problem, he'd refuse. He'd asked her out about six months ago. With every other available female, and some not so available, swooning at his feet, she knew she'd shocked him by saying no. She wanted nothing more to do with dating men, or so she'd told herself over and over since that day, trying not to wonder what it would've been like going out with Nixon. Once he learned she was pregnant, he'd got over his shock quick smart and they'd started getting on great guns as friends. Perfect. Really? Was it perfect?

A wriggle, a squirm, and Rosie shrieked, 'Nixon, have you seen the baby? Mummy won't take me to see it and I want to hold her.'

Emma's mother stepped back, rubbing her ear. 'Quieter, Rosie.'

Emma ran her hand over Rosie's curls. 'That's not what I said. Abbie's feeding Grace so you have to be patient.'

'That's like asking a cat to ignore the mouse running

across its paws.' Nixon winked. 'Especially with this one.' He knew Rosie from the times she used to be dropped off at the department after pre-school on the days Emma was running late signing off. Her daughter had fallen under his spell in the flash of a chocolate bar and a wide smile. Easily bribed, her girl.

Nixon moved up, leaned over and wrapped his arms around Emma. 'You're looking good for what you've been through.'

A warm sigh trickled across her lips. This hug felt special. The perfect elixir for lurking emotions left over from handing the baby to Abbie. Emma leaned forward ever so slightly to rest against Nixon's chest and breathed deeply, absorbing the man scent and strength. She lurched backwards. This was all wrong. They were pals, not lovers.

There had been one time she'd said too much to him. At the end of a particularly hectic shift she'd been tired and achy, heavily pregnant and despondent, and when he'd walked out of the department with her and suggested a wind-down drink over the road at the café, she'd burst into tears. It had to have been the tea that loosened her tongue, or otherwise why had she spilled her guts to Nixon about her feelings over giving up the baby? The feelings she wouldn't share with Abbie so as not to rattle her friend's confidence that she would hand over Abbie's baby.

He'd listened without interruption as she'd explained her fear of not being able to let go the baby, which would break her friend's heart along with her own. Not once did Nixon say it was her fault she was in that predicament. He'd shown another side to himself. He'd always been popular, but also somewhat wary, and known to be a focused, caring doctor. She doubted anyone at work had seen Nixon so thoughtful and considerate about something unrelated to work. Which made her wonder what else he was hiding behind his everyday face. And glad she'd turned him down for that date. She had enough of her own problems to be carrying on with, without taking on anyone else's.

Now he stepped back, those thoughtful eyes watching her too closely for comfort.

'Mum, you haven't met Nixon, have you? Nixon Wright, this is my mum Kathy Hayes. Nixon's our emergency specialist,' she added for clarity. No point raising her mother's hopes that she'd found a man. How her mother could want her to get married again was beyond Emma. Not after her last fiasco. But then, all her family held onto some guilt over that. They'd fallen under Alvin's spell too and had encouraged her marriage.

'You're not a local.' Her mother shook Nixon's hand, appraising the tall, strapping specimen before her as if she was about to interview him. Which, being her mother, was definitely on the cards. And her mum had nothing on her brothers or father. Emma wouldn't put it past them to tie any man she might be interested in up to the fence and throw icy water over him while proceeding with an interrogation about whether he knew his hands were not made to be used against their sister and daughter.

He gave a light smile. 'I shifted here from Dunedin a year ago, so, no, most people don't know what I like to eat for breakfast or what grades I got in school.'

There were few secrets in Queenstown amongst the locals, for sure. Hurrying to cut her mother off before she got started on in-depth questions, Emma said, 'Grace weighs three point seven kilos, has ten fingers and ten toes, and is cute as a button. Abbie's besotted.'

Nixon agreed. 'I saw her in the nursery on my way here. I think we could have a Force Six earthquake and she wouldn't notice.' His smile dipped. 'You're all right?'

The same loaded question her mother had asked. No doubt she'd hear it a few more times yet. 'Yep.'

He locked eyes with her, as if he was looking for more. But what could she say? Especially in front of her mother, who had had misgivings about the whole surrogacy thing from the day she'd told her family she was having Abbie's baby. 'I have no regrets. Okay?'

'I didn't think you would.' Nixon looked away, and got caught in the beam of her mother's stare. 'You've got one tough daughter, Kathy.'

'She had to learn to be.' It was so unlike her mother to say such a thing. Her family never talked about her past unless she brought up the horrible subject herself, which she rarely did. Why go back to hell when she'd finally found her way out?

Emma shivered. Her mum was certainly assessing Nixon thoroughly. Too thoroughly. Something she needed to stop doing. 'Nixon's my boss.' For some inexplicable reason that gave her a stabbing sensation in her chest.

Her mother nodded once, abruptly.

But Nixon surprised Emma with his suddenly widening eyes and flattening mouth. What had she done other than tell the truth? He *was* her boss. And one hell of a man, who had the broad shoulders to cry on and endless patience when she'd needed to let off steam. Those shoulders were filling her vision now, tightening her tummy in ways it shouldn't.

Then a deep yawn pulled her mouth wide. The day had caught up with her in spades. 'Sorry, everyone. I need to catnap for a bit.' She reached for Rosie. 'Another hug for Mummy?'

As Rosie obliged Emma glimpsed Nixon over her daughter's head. There was a strange longing filling those grey eyes as he watched them. Something she'd never seen before. Something that strummed on her heartstrings. Nixon was lonely for love? Was that it? Couldn't be. He could have any woman he set his eyes on.

But wait, wasn't there a rumour that he had a three-dates rule? He also shunned invitations from individual staff members to work social occasions, but that was probably sensible. Yet he'd asked her out. Strange.

She chose to be alone too, but that didn't mean she didn't want family and love. Nixon hadn't said a word about his family when she'd talked about hers the day she'd blubbed all over him. He'd only said he was too busy for commitment. What with running a small but busy emergency department here in the Queenstown Hospital, where extreme sports injuries were as common as the tourists that filled the town all year round. Being a mountain-biking addict alongside his busy job, he didn't have the time required for a full-on, permanent relationship.

Nixon might be surprised to know everyone knew he avoided relationships. It was fairly obvious when he only ever dated women who were visiting Queenstown, getting his testosterone fix without getting entangled. Emma hadn't been able to decide if she should've been flattered or insulted when he'd asked her out. Apparently she'd been the exception to his rule. He socialised without getting involved, so he'd have been a perfect date for her. She'd have had fun. It wasn't as if he were dull, weird, or afraid of his own shadow. Completely the opposite, in fact. Tall, built, fun, sincere.

Sexy.

Gasp.

Was it all right to think that of a friend?

Emma's heart slowed. Sadness rocked in and darkened her mood; she closed her eyes so she didn't have to see Nixon watching her with a hunger in his gaze that confused her. To her he was someone she worked with who'd become a good friend over the last few months. He was a man in need of a shake-up. Who amongst her old friends could she find to knock his knees out from under him? No one. What about—?

No one. Or—?

No one.

The thought of Nixon getting all cosy with someone she knew felt like a lead ball swinging at her head.

A phone sounded loud in the still room. 'I'd better get back. The heli's five minutes out,' Nixon said as he read his message. 'I grabbed a quiet moment to check on you.'

As her boss? Or as a friend. 'You want to give me a lift home later?' What was wrong with her? As if she wanted Nixon driving her home. But he'd ask less questions than her family.

Her mother got there before him. 'I can come back in whenever you're ready. You and Rosie should stay the night with us anyway.'

'Thanks, Mum, but I'd prefer going to the apartment, taking a long, hot shower and curling up in my own bed.' That was the truth, even if it meant having to stay awake until Rosie went to bed, which these days could be any-where between seven and nine. The kid didn't get bed-time rules at all.

'Your brothers will be disappointed. Not to mention your father.'

Exactly. An inquest about her feelings was not on her agenda. 'I'll see them tomorrow.'

Nixon turned his formidable gaze from her to her mother and nodded. 'I'm going to be tied up for a long time with what the paramedics are bringing in.'

'What happened?' Emma asked.

'A mountain biker here for the Lake Hawea challenge

went off the edge of the road somewhere on Cardrona while on a training ride and hit the rocks way below.' Nixon headed for the door, and paused, one hand on the frame. 'I'll drop by later to see if you want me to give you a ride somewhere.' A hint of challenge coloured his voice, which disappeared before he nodded to her mother, who was nudging Rosie towards the door. 'A pleasure meeting you.'

Then he was gone, leaving a void in the room Emma wanted filled. By whom? By what? She had no idea, she only knew her head and heart were all over the place at the moment, and that had nothing to do with Nixon and all to do with the baby she'd delivered not so long ago.

Yet she felt that challenge even if she didn't know what it was about. As if Nixon had handed her the baton and she needed to run with it. Now. When she'd just had a baby? When she did not need—or want—a man in her life? Forget her earlier longings. That had been baby-brain talk.

Baby. Her hands slid over her empty stomach. I had a baby today. And she's nowhere to be seen.

Abbie's baby. Not mine. Abbie's baby. Abbie's baby. My baby.

Emma cried herself into a restless, baby-filled sleep.

CHAPTER TWO

NIXON WRIGHT EASED himself onto the chair beside Emma's bed, and, with his elbows on his knees, dropped his chin into the palms of his hands. The cyclist was in Theatre. He was done for the day. His own cycle at home beckoned but he'd told Emma he'd drop by before he left; hadn't told her he needed to check on her for his own peace of mind.

Watching Emma as she slept tugged him deep inside. Her short, light breaths lifted an errant curl from one cheek, let it fall on the outward sigh. Dark shadows resembling bruises darkened the pale skin beneath her eyes, her coppery hair striking against those cheeks. She looked small and defenceless under the covers, bringing all his protective mechanisms to the fore, making him want to crawl onto the bed and hold her close, keep the world at bay until she was ready to face it again.

He'd never seen her so lost. Oh, sure, she'd deny that faster than a blink, but she was confused, dealing with emotions she knew and expected and didn't want. She'd been brave today; so very, very brave. Not a hint of regret apparent, but there had to be a lot of tugging towards that baby going on inside.

Emma was a loving soul. Since he'd learned she was pregnant, he'd seen how she'd loved that baby growing inside her. Yet not once, even on those bleak days when she'd felt wobbly about it all—and there had been some, though she'd only ever talked to him about her feelings once—had she said anything to suggest she wouldn't give up Grace to her rightful mother.

From what he'd seen, Emma and Abbie had a strong, unbreakable bond so that had never been going to happen. Apparently the two women had seen each other through some terrible times. Abbie's husband had passed away from cancer, and from idle gossip in the department he knew Emma had been married to a violent man—which made him seethe with impotent fury just thinking about it. He shoved the anger aside. It had no place here, and if Emma had managed to walk away from that husband then *he* had no right resurrecting her history, if only in his head. She needed positive vibes.

Nixon's heart expanded. If ever there was an amazing gift, Emma had given it to her friend. Her generosity knew no bounds, but in the coming days she'd need someone to lean on and he was putting his hand up. As the friend he'd already been for her.

Oh, really? some strange, illogical emotion deep inside asked.

His phone pinged with an incoming text. Nixon read the message his uncle Henry had sent to all the family.

Hope everyone has a lovely time at the birthday party in Wellington this weekend. I'll be thinking of you. Sorry you can't make it either, Nixon.

Henry could be joining his children and grandchildren if he eased up on his belief he was doing his family more good leaving them a large inheritance than using some of his money to be with them for special occasions. Instead, he ignored the pleas to spend the money now when everyone could enjoy the benefits.

Guilt snuck in. It was brought on because his uncle had taken him in when he was six and raised him with his cousins until he left school. Henry had never been generous with money and especially not with his heart, but Nixon had been fed, clothed in hand-me-downs and given shelter. He'd always be grateful, but he'd have been happy to go hungry if instead there'd been open and happy love such as he'd known in his six short years with his parents and brother before they died in a plane crash.

'Nixon, your mum and dad and Davey are not coming home ever again.'

The terrifying words had cut him off from his family, from love and happiness. From ever giving his heart unconditionally again.

But had Henry giving him a roof over his head been his way of showing love? Fundamental perhaps, but that was his uncle's approach.

Well, he could do the same. Nixon texted back.

Book flights and hotel. I'll fix you up tonight.

Henry would go for the most expensive flights and hotel room, but, hey, those were the breaks. If it made his uncle happy then what did it matter? It was only money and he wasn't short of a few dollars. These people were his only family. They had cared about him as one of their own, looked out for him when he hadn't been able to grasp what not ever coming home again meant. If only Henry had shown his love with hugs and games and laughter as his own parents had, then he mightn't have felt quite so lost and alone.

Nixon's gaze drifted to Emma.

He'd cried off going away with his cousins and their kids, using a bike endurance he'd entered as his reason. While it was true, he'd also been reluctant to be out of town when Emma had her baby. He'd wanted to be around when it happened in case that despair and fear she'd once sobbed out onto his shoulder returned, stronger and harder to move past. He might've made sure she was all right when her waters broke and retrieved her bag from her car for her yet he'd waited 'til well after the birth to visit her, suddenly afraid of where his feelings about Emma were taking him. They'd become such great friends that he'd even felt grateful she'd turned him down for a date because when he walked away at the end of it, which he surely would have done, he'd have missed out on so much. While she was pregnant, he'd felt restrained about further-ing their friendship. She'd had enough issues to deal with. But now where did they stand? He believed he didn't want involvement, couldn't risk his heart only to lose her when she decided she didn't need him, but...

But ask him why he'd felt he should be here and he couldn't find a satisfactory answer. Emma didn't need him at her side. They got along fine, and sometimes she opened up to him, though lately he'd pulled back, afraid of where this was headed.

Be honest. You like that she talks to you about things she can't tell her best friend.

Yeah, well, all very good, but all the more reason to pull away. That thinking could lead to deeper involvement, a place he wasn't planning on going. If he ever chanced fall-ing in love with a special woman—Emma?—he'd want to be able to leap in, boots and all, heart and all, be open, have fun, share the highs and lows. He wouldn't want to be this uptight, afraid version.

His phone received a text. Henry.

Thanks, lad. Appreciate it.

No problem.

Had Henry shut down on his open loving side when his wife died in childbirth? Gone further into the deep when Nixon's mother died? Did he hold the same fears?

Oh, man.

Occasionally Nixon had wondered about this but had always shaken it off as wrong. He wasn't Henry's child, he'd inherited different genes, and his mother, Henry's sister, had been a happy, always laughing person. From what he knew and remembered. None of this had crossed Nixon's mind before. He could very possibly be a chip off the old block. Might've learned from his uncle how to hold everything in. They both kept their feelings close to their chests. Didn't rush around hugging friends and family.

You hugged Emma earlier.

Yeah, well, Emma.

Now what? Carry on with no hope of it being anything more? Or try to let go of the restraints and open up, risk his heart and see where that led? Instantly his belly tightened and his heart slowed as though it were withdrawing from this crazy idea, protecting itself. It was far wiser to stick with the current way of doing things. But was that truly what he wanted?

'You going to sit there staring at the floor all evening?' Emma muttered from the bed.

'It's a damned nice floor.' Grey vinyl wasn't really his thing.

She chuckled.

That chuckle crept into places that had remained cold since the day the social worker had picked him up from school and delivered him to Uncle Henry. The warmth

Emma engendered made going for a diversion imperative. He wasn't ready to follow that warmth. 'Easier than
deciding who to employ for the summer rush.'

'Which started a week ago, in case you hadn't noticed.
The day the spring rush finished.' Emma shuffled up the
bed, wincing. 'We've already had numerous broken bod-
ies in ED from mountain day trippers going off track and
getting caught by unseasonal storms.'

'I'll never understand why visitors to the region don't
read the weather warnings.' Nixon stood to arrange the pillows more comfortably behind her back. Doctor mode to
the fore. Really? Yes, really. 'Tell that to the CEO. We're
up to our ears in patients and he's still saying wait. My
problem is the doctor I want to take on won't hang around
for ever. She's had another offer in Christchurch, a better
one I suspect, but with a sister already working here she'd
prefer our neck of the woods.'

'The joys of being the boss. Glad I'm only a nurse.'

'No such thing as just a nurse.' Especially Emma, a ded-
icated carer if ever he'd met one. 'How's the body feeling?'

'Like it fell off Ben Lomond, rolled down the mountain
and finished up in a ravine. Just like your earlier patient.'

'That good? Want to go mountain-bike riding tomorrow?' he teased.

'Sit on one of those hard, narrow bike seats after what
I've been through?' She shuddered and scrunched up her
lovely face. 'Haven't you got work to do? Paperwork if
nothing else.'

'I'm done for the day.' He gave an exaggerated sigh.
'The weather forecast predicts no wind and warm tempera-
tures. Perfect for hitting the trail out to Jack's Point Pass.'

Emma shook her head at him. 'Your calf muscles must
hate you sometimes.'

If he were open to more than casual friendships, he'd

suggest they pack a picnic and take Rosie up the track out of Arrowtown one day soon. *If.* A friendship on that scale with Emma and her daughter could eventually expose his need for more and as he was her boss that couldn't happen. He never dated women he worked with. It got complicated when the three-date rule was enacted. He still didn't understand why he'd asked her out that time. Except that she was gorgeous. 'You decided where you're going to spend tonight?'

'I guess I'll go out to the Valley. It's the soft option but sometimes it's nice to let Mum take over with Rosie. I kind of want my family around too.'

Not him. Friends only. Not so close they shared everything. 'You don't want to stay in town without Rosie, do you?'

Emma stared at him, blinking twice and swallowing hard. 'No.' Another swallow. 'I need to hug and touch her, or just watch over her. I need to be a mum tonight.' Sadness flicked through her eyes and was gone.

It was hard not to reach for her hands, wrap his fingers around them and give her his warmth and strength. He all but sat on his hands in case Emma misinterpreted the gesture. 'You are allowed to be shaken up by it all, you know? No one's going to give you a hard time for feeling down about not having this time with Grace.'

Her left foot jiggled continuously as she nodded slowly. 'I get that. But knowing that and experiencing it are different. I'm not saying I'd change a thing. Of course I wouldn't. That baby's always been Abbie's. I don't even want another child. I've got the most adorable daughter and no time or energy to spare for bringing up a second child.' She stared out of the window.

She was an awesome mum, the kind he'd want for his children. If he was ever to have a family. He'd love his own kids, sometimes imagined holding his daughter, playing ball in the yard with his son, pouring into them all the love he knew he held inside. After he found the right woman and loved her to the edge and back—but that wasn't happening. He was a screw-up, had loved his family too hard and deep so that the loss had cut the ground out from under him, left him unable to understand who he was any more. Left him afraid to love without reservation. Hence flings were the way to go. Fun, carefree and over before the trouble started.

Nixon's heart pushed the barriers back in place that Emma didn't know she'd shunted sideways. What was he thinking here? *Get back on track.* Concentrate on Emma and what she wanted. 'Rosie's a lucky girl with a great mum. What more does she need?' Nixon felt that protective surge for Emma stir, the one that came to the fore at inopportune moments. It sat up and expanded into…? What? The need to look out for her shouldn't cause this sense of leaning too far out over a cliff, of hovering on the point of no return.

Leave. Now. Go home and grab the bike, put in a couple of hours' hard pedalling. Break out a sweat, make the muscles ache, and silence the infuriating brain.

His legs weren't behaving; they were suddenly lifeless, keeping him stuck on the chair. As though they were saying Emma needed his strength at the moment and he couldn't take it away, no matter the cost to him. Whatever the hell that cost might be. Just some strange, gut-tightening, emotion-expanding thing going on in his head, his body. His heart. *His heart? Get away.*

'She's unlucky not to have a dad.' She blinked at him. 'Forget I said that.'

Slap. Rosie's father. Nixon slowly leaned back in the

uncomfortable chair. Did she still love the guy? 'How long were you married?'

'Nearly three years.' No emotion coloured her voice, or her gaze. None at all. Hiding her feelings?

Talk about derailing the conversation off post-birthing blues. Only problem was, he seemed to have hit as big a bump in the road. 'Sorry, I shouldn't have asked.'

'Why shouldn't you? It's no secret.' Was that anger firing up in her eyes? 'Broken marriages are as common as muck.'

'I suppose.'

'Alvin saved me the hassle of a divorce by getting himself killed in a pub brawl up north in Kaikohe.' Emma's mouth was tight.

'Jeez, Emma, you've had a rough time of it.'

'You have no idea.'

'Yet look what you've done for Abbie. You're tough, and kind, and full of love.' That love word was cropping up a lot today. Best find another subject to talk about. For both their sakes. 'Your mother coming back to get you or do you want me to drive you out to Gibbston Valley?'

She blinked, shuddered. Then finally dredged up a weak smile. 'Would you?' Relief began lightening those teal eyes, nudging aside the gloom that had overtaken her minutes ago. 'If Mum comes she'll bring Rosie and my girl has had more than enough excitement for all of us.'

An odd happiness filled him. Because she was accepting a ride with him? Pathetic. 'Are you allowed to go yet?'

'It's entirely up to me. The midwife has done her final checks for the day and says she'll see me tomorrow, so any time that suits you. I'll have a quick shower and change into something half decent.' She began easing off the bed, obviously feeling every movement.

Nixon stood up, rolled his shoulders. 'I'll go see how that cyclist's doing. He should be out of surgery by now. Back in ten?'

'Sure.' She was already digging into her daypack for clothes.

Nixon found his patient's orthopaedic surgeon writing up notes on the operation he'd just performed. 'How's our guy?'

'That shoulder is nasty, and he's in for a long haul getting back to—' Cameron flicked his fingers in the air '—normal. The skull fracture's of concern, though we're fairly certain there's no lasting brain injury. I'll operate again tomorrow to insert rods in his leg and arm. He won't be a happy chap when he comes round.'

'He's lucky to be alive. That was some fall.'

Cameron stretched in his chair and linked his hands behind his head. 'You cyclists certainly keep me busy. Shoulders are my expertise these days. You still as crazy on your bike as you were when you first arrived in town?'

Nixon grinned. 'What's crazy about racing down a mountain on two wheels? It's an adrenalin fix like no other.' He loved it, needed it at times. Used it to pretend all was right in his world.

'Could also be the end of you, is what else it is,' Cameron retorted. 'Your family ever worry about you?'

There was another question behind the obvious one. 'They're long used to me doing hair-raising sports.' His cousins had more than enough to focus on with their families and jobs without worrying about him.

'You ever think you should slow down?'

'Yeah, but then I get on the bike and that idea goes out the window.' If the worst happened then he wasn't hurting anyone else, because there was no one close enough to be affected if he didn't come home one day as his family hadn't. His cousins would miss him, as would Henry, but not in a life-stopping, future-changing way. He'd chosen to live like this. If he couldn't have love then he'd have adventure.

'You're mad.' Cameron was studying him far too closely. 'Find another fix, something less dangerous. Collect stamps or play bowls. Or…' and the guy drew a breath, warning Nixon he wasn't going to like this next pearl of wisdom '…a woman. As in a woman you go home to every night. They can be as addictive as anything else out there.'

'Bikes are cheaper to run,' he flipped back.

'You don't mean that.'

Did the guy ever give up? Nixon put some grit in his voice. 'You're right, I don't. What I meant is I'm not getting involved with anyone. End of.' He headed for the door. Time to collect Emma, whether she was ready or not. *And that's not getting involved?*

'Nixon,' Cameron called after him. 'Give me five and we'll go across the road for a beer. I promise to drop the subject of looking after your bones.'

'Sorry, already got some place I need to be.'

Disappointment warred with annoyance in Cameron's eyes. 'It's only a beer, not a lifetime commitment.'

Blast. He did not want to get offside with the man. 'I'm taking Emma out to her family in the Valley.' *Don't you say a bloody word.*

But he should've known better. This was Cameron. 'Watch out for her family. They don't like men hanging around their Emma.' Then he was busy filling in paperwork.

Dismissed. That was how Nixon felt. Cameron had got the last annoying word in. Except he was glad to learn there were people looking out for his friend. After the mistake her husband had turned out to be, it was only right her family would check out any bloke Emma became interested in. He could handle that. Besides, he was only her boss and a casual friend wanting to see her home.

Wasn't he?

If that was the case, why was he rushing up the stairs to the maternity ward with fingers crossed that Emma's mother hadn't come to pick her up? He'd be free to hit the road on his bike, put some wind through his hair if she had.

Yeah, but he wanted to be the one driving Emma out to Gibbston Valley tonight.

Glad Cameron wasn't around to hear that one. He'd be laughing for days.

Emma stepped into her parents' dining room and shook her head at her mother. The solid wood dining table was all but bending under the weight of food. 'I had a baby, I didn't run a marathon.'

'Everyone's here,' was her mother's explanation, meaning her brothers' girlfriends were hanging around too.

As long as she wasn't in for a grilling about her feelings for the baby, she was okay with their presence. They might keep the boys quiet. And she had wanted to wrap herself in family, right? What about Nixon? He'd chatted all the way out, saving her the need to fill in the gaps. Yet she'd known if she'd wanted to broach the events of her day he'd have given her one hundred per cent focus. She was glad she had accepted his offer of a lift, and what better way to thank him than dinner? Her mother would never, ever, not have enough food prepared to feed everyone twice over, so Emma turned to Nixon. 'Don't even try to get out of staying for dinner. Mum can be stubborn if she has to.'

'I do have to get back to town.' His gaze was cruising the banquet of cold cuts and salads of every variety imaginable.

'Might as well eat here as there.' Emma would swear he was drooling.

'But—' Nixon seemed to be having a battle with his stomach. He cut a look to her mother. 'Okay. Thank you for inviting me, Kathy.'

Technically she hadn't, but then she expected people to stay. Her favourite saying was 'Everyone gets hungry, I enjoy plugging the gaps.'

'You brought Emma out. It's the least I could do.' Her mum's smile was genuine. No hidden agenda, no lurking doubts, no worries about Nixon being with her daughter.

Oh, boy. This was getting tricky. She didn't need her mum getting all fired up about a man in her life. If, and that was a huge if, she stepped out into the dating world, she would not introduce the poor guy to her family until she was absolutely certain he could take the grilling that would come his way, but one glance at Nixon and she knew he'd handle it, might even expect it. Not that he'd be getting the opportunity. Dinner now and then he'd be racing back to town, away from her family and any risk of being slowly pulled in by the mantle known as the Hayes blanket—so called by one of the many strays her parents had taken in throughout her life. Not that Nixon was a stray. Just a little adrift. Alone.

Emma sighed. It was out of her hands. 'Sorry we're late, Mum, but I slept longer than I intended.'

Remember, Mum, he's my boss, not a potential lover. Definitely not a future husband.

One of those had already been one too many. She would never marry again, even if—heaven forbid—she did fall in love and move in with a guy. She was Emma Hayes for ever.

Her mother shrugged. 'No problem.'

Oh, boy, again. Emma spun away from her mother's knowing look and said, 'Nixon, you'd better meet everyone else.'

'Why does that sound like a threat?' he asked, sounding and looking as comfortable as any man could when about to walk into the bull's paddock. Could he be a skilled bull tamer? She was about to find out.

Out on the back deck she said, 'Hey, Dad, everyone, I'd like you to meet Nixon from work. He gave me a ride out here,' she added pointlessly, more in a pickle than Nixon appeared to be.

'Nixon,' Rosie shrieked from the swing. 'You came.'

'Hey, Rosie. Of course I did.'

The handshakes were testing, and the locked-eye looks were designed to undermine any man not strong enough to withstand a tsunami of questions and probes.

Nixon took it all on the chin, smiling and individually acknowledging her father and brothers, Shaun and Daniel, then the girlfriends. 'Glad to know we're all on the same side when it comes to Emma.'

That had each of them tipping their heads back and staring at him before smiles broke out on their faces, as if they shared some man secret or something. Even Shaun's girlfriend was getting in on the act. Emma had the distinct feeling she'd missed the point and should head back inside to help her mother. At least she'd feel at home in the large, country-style kitchen with her mum, her lack of cooking skills excepted.

'Hey, Em, how're you feeling?' Daniel asked, not quite taking his probing gaze off Nixon. 'I presume you're sore.'

'Tired, and still all right with what I've done,' she said

pointedly. Just in case there were any misconceptions going round that she might be howling on the inside for baby Grace. Right now it was the physical aspects of giving birth making her uncomfortable. A dull, throbbing ache in places best not sat on or pressed too hard a constant reminder that her day hadn't been about helping patients and all about giving Abbie a daughter. 'I'm going inside.'

Don't kill Nixon, or hold him over a flame while I'm gone.

'Nixon would probably enjoy a beer.' Her parents might own a vineyard but beer was the preferred pre-dinner beverage with the men.

'I like him,' her mum told her the moment she'd checked Nixon hadn't followed Emma back to the kitchen. 'He comes across as solid and kind and honest.'

That made him sound a tad boring, and Nixon was anything but. 'All of the above as well as a bit of a daredevil on his bike apparently. Also, he backs people when they're being wronged.' As he had her when one of the nurses had criticised her for carrying Abbie's baby. That day, she'd heard for the first and only time real anger in Nixon's voice, seen it in his tense body and taut shoulders. That was when their friendship had taken a step further along the sliding scale of acquaintances to soulmates. It also helped that he was deep, funny, and a little bit lonely. And, damn it, sexy. There, she'd admitted it again. And he still wasn't going to become anything more than who he already was. A friendly, caring boss. Saying it often enough would stop these errant thoughts popping up. Thinking of him as sexy was not a good move. But how to stop?

Little crinkles appeared at the corners of her mother's eyes. 'Just how friendly are you two?'

'Drop it, Mum. Please? I'm tired and sore and want to eat dinner before hitting the pillow.' Suddenly, curling up in her old bed, curtains shut tight, pillow tugged around her neck, and her eyes and ears closed so she became completely and utterly alone was all she wanted. To try and relax, to let go all pretence that today had been easy. To be able to study every moment again, to look at everything from all angles without anyone twittering in her ear saying how great she was for what she'd done. She wanted to hold the unabridged facts and emotions and absorb the truth of it all. Only then would she fully accept the birth was over, Grace was not hers, and she had her own life to be getting on with.

Her mother's arm was around her shoulder, tugging her close to that chest she'd always gone to in times of sadness growing up. 'Give yourself time, Em.'

'Can everyone see through me?' *Blink, blink.*

'We know you well.' Her mum's smile was lopsided. 'I'm thinking Nixon might too.'

Her shoulders sagged. Her mum was not one for letting go a bone once it was between her jaws. She conceded, 'He does seem more understanding than most men I've met.'

'Which makes him a treasure.'

Emma slipped free and slid her hands down her tee shirt over her heavy, full breasts and onto her flabby stomach. 'He doesn't belong in the local museum, nor does he have a place in my life. Nor I in his. We're too different. Seriously, Mum, I want you to drop this because nothing is going to come of it. I don't want it to. I'm not ready to get involved with a man again.' She only had to shut her eyes and she could see Alvin's rage as his fist slammed into her stomach. Until images like that one went away, she'd never be ready to give her heart again or to put her safety in another man's hands. Though if there was one thing she knew for certain it was that Nixon would not hurt her physically.

'I want you to be happy.' Her mum always got the last word. Or so she thought.

'Me too, Mum. Me too. And you know what? I am. I don't need a man to make me happy. I have to do that for myself otherwise I have nothing to offer.'

'Fair enough.'

Huh? The fact that was all her mum was saying rang alarm bells. The subject of Nixon was clearly not over, merely on the shelf for another day.

Over dinner, Nixon answered questions about himself without giving too much away—a fact the male members of her family seemed to grasp and accept. The guy was allowed his privacy as long as it didn't hurt Emma, was the silent message. It didn't matter that Emma reiterated bluntly that they had no right subjecting her friend to this. She was ignored. Her brothers and her father could be pains in the backside, and yet she understood they worried about her. These were the men who had run Alvin out of town with the promise of pain if he ever so much as thought about returning. *So, sorry, Nixon, but welcome to my family. Take them as you find them, or leave.*

Glancing across the table, she met his scrutiny and knew he'd received her message loud and clear even when she'd been staring at her clasped hands in her lap. He nodded, smiled that smile that lately had begun taking on a tummy-tugging element, and remained in his seat. He was staying.

The only problem was that tummy-tugging smile caused an ache in her solar plexus. Post-birth pains? Not likely to be anything else. Not longing for something special with Nixon? Emma pushed her plate aside still over half full. 'My appetite's done a bunk.'

Shaun stopped eating to stare at her. 'You're kidding, right?'

She shook her head. 'Favourite food and all, I can't take another mouthful.' Something was cutting off her throat, refusing to allow food post, and what little had gone down before was bricks in her stomach.

'Nixon, you're a doctor. Take her temperature,' said her smart-ass brother, Daniel.

Nixon was still watching her; summing her up, she suspected. There was that astute, didn't-miss-a-thing glint in his gaze. 'You're all right?' he asked quietly, making her brother sound louder than ever.

'I feel like I've been run over by a bus, but medically I'm fine. Think I'll go to bed. Sorry to be disappearing on you, Nixon, when you've only just met this lot, but I doubt I can keep my eyes open much longer.'

'We'll look after him.' Shaun grinned.

That was what she was afraid of. 'Don't feel bad if you want to bolt while you can,' she told Nixon as she clambered to her feet.

'I've had a glimpse of what's for dessert and I'm staying.' His smile was soft and enveloped her in hope and a longing for what she'd sworn off. A good sleep and she'd be back on track, no left-field ideas knocking her sideways.

Through the haze filling her skull she heard her father say, 'In other words, he's no coward, this friend of yours.'

Thanks, Dad.

At the moment, she needed reminding of that as much as her mum did. Especially while this longing for something—someone—squeezed her tight and forced the air from her lungs. 'Goodnight everyone,' she muttered as she headed down the hall, aiming for the bathroom, ignoring the tears pouring down her face.

Crying wasn't a rarity for her. There'd been too many times when she'd not been able to stop in the past.

But not knowing why she was crying was new. And unsettling. All in all, it had been a huge day. Now she wanted it gone, finished, wrapped up and delivered, like the baby, and tomorrow's sun coming up, bringing the beginning of the rest of her life.

CHAPTER THREE

'GRACE'S FACE IS red but she's pretty.' Rosie bounced up and down in her car seat as much as the safety belts allowed while they headed to school for a special trip to see the llamas.

'Isn't she?' Emma swallowed a yawn. There'd been little deep sleep last night, more a smattering of moments of not being aware and many long, agonising minutes of being fully alert and trying to ignore the emptiness in her heart. No, not in her heart because the baby would always be in her life one way or another. In her maternal soul, perhaps. She had carried the child and her body wasn't ready to let her forget it. But she would—in the nicest possible way. During the pregnancy, she'd talked to other women around the country who'd been a mummy tummy and everyone had said they'd been able to move past this feeling within a few weeks. It'd continue to give her nudges but those would come less often as time passed. It seemed that women who were able to interact with the baby had better outcomes more quickly.

Her phone played 'Jingle Bells', and Rosie clapped her hands. 'Santa's coming to town. He's bringing me presents.'

A glance at the screen. Nixon. Pulling over to the side of the road, she answered. 'Hi.' *Why are you calling me?*

You don't usually get in touch outside work. 'You got home all right after the inquisition?'

Maybe he was phoning to demand compensation.

A deep-bellied laugh rumbled into her ear, and sent waves of warmth—make that heat—to her toes and tummy. No, couldn't be. This was Nixon, Mr Super Avoidance. And she was Ms Super Avoidance. Concentrate. Nixon's talking.

'Checking how you are this morning.'

'Doing good.'

'I hope you're not rushing things. You're officially on leave now.'

'Thanks. Hopefully I'll be up to light duties and part-time hours not too far away. I'll get sick of my own company pretty damned soon I reckon.' Through sheer determination, her body would handle returning to the department more easily than her head and heart.

His boss voice switched off. 'Where are you now?'

Did it matter? Nixon didn't usually want to know what she did in her own time. It wasn't as though she was leading an exciting double life. No, she was a single mother of a loud and boisterous five-year-old, nothing more. Or less. But it was kind of nice he cared. 'I'm dropping Rosie at school to go on a short trip to see llamas.'

'On a Saturday?'

'It was meant to be last Wednesday but weather wrecked the plans. The kids were so disappointed the trip is happening today with some parents going along as help. I'm sure they're going to hear all about the new baby.'

'How do you feel about that?'

'Had to happen. It's not as though people didn't know I was pregnant with Abbie's baby. Though there is the sister factor to work out. Are these girls sisters or not? Abbie and I reckon they are.' They'd sort it but not today. Today she couldn't make Rosie's toast without burning it, twice.

'Rosie's a bit young to understand any of that,' Nixon surmised.

'Bang on.' He wasn't having any trouble with straight thinking, so she couldn't blame the hot weather for the mess in her head. 'Rosie met Grace and had a cuddle as soon as Daniel dropped us off this morning. There was no stopping the little minx from racing straight inside where Abbie was happy to oblige.' Emma released a tired giggle. 'You'll never believe who else was visiting, looking like he'd already received his Christmas present. Callum.' The speed at which Abbie's life had turned around was mindboggling. And wonderful. 'He's proposed, and Abbie's accepted.' Lucky girl. What a day she'd had yesterday. 'Everything's coming together for her at last.' Her sigh was not filled with envy. Okay, maybe a teeny bit.

'Fantastic news. They're meant for each other.'

'They are. Callum's besotted with Grace. Anyone would think she was his and he'd done all the hard yards.'

'We blokes are like that.' Then Nixon dropped a surprise. 'Are you going to be home around lunchtime? Thought I'd call by, check out my nurse and make sure she's getting back on her feet.'

'I was never off them.' Not true. There'd been hours lying and panting and pushing, but she knew what he meant. He'd said my *nurse*. Disappointment slowed her heart. Which was plain dumb. She was one of his staff. Just because he'd driven her home—probably because she worked with him—and stayed for a meal didn't mean she could expect something else. Then again, he was coming to visit her. Why this sudden yearning for more? For more with Nixon? Then it hit her. Avoidance. By trying not to think too much about Grace her head was filling up with

thoughts about Nixon. That was all there was to these
ideas and longings. Might be better to let Grace, and the
sense of loss that snuck up on her when she wasn't looking, get in so she could deal with it and move on, no Nixon
thoughts in sight.

'Hello?'

Where was she? Apart from parked outside the youth
hostel. Nixon, and something about lunchtime and a visit.
'I'm here.'

'Say no if it's inconvenient.' He paused, then seemed
to be drawing a big breath. What was coming? 'I've still
got a shoulder available if you need one.'

Tears pricked her eyelids. How about right now?
'Th-thanks.'

'And a box of tissues,' he said in a low voice as if he
really needed her to know he was still there for her now
that the pregnancy was over.

'I've got to see the midwife at ten but should be home
by midday. I'll fix us something to eat.' She would?

Relief underlined his next question. 'Your appetite's
back?'

'With a vengeance. Think I had emotion overload
last night.' And just like that, the tears spurted down her
cheeks. A vision of Grace filled her head, held by a glowing Abbie, Callum watching on in awe. Picture perfect.
Lots of love in the air when she and Rosie had dropped
into Abbie's apartment. Really beautiful. Sniff. Her boobs
hurt. Her heart was heavy. 'Got to go. See you later.'

'Emma, wait. Are you sure you're all right?' Nixon's
concern spilled from the phone.

'Just having a moment. A good one.' Liar. 'Promise.
Bye.' Bigger liar. She tapped 'off' before he could ask
any more telling questions. 'Right, missy, let's get you to
school.' She pulled out into the traffic, wiping the back of

her hand across her cheeks. Rosie didn't need to see her mother's meltdown when she got out of the car.

'Mrs Watson showed us how to draw a cat yesterday. Can I have a cat, Mummy?'

Last week it'd been a puppy. 'No, darling, we're not having any pets.' So Nixon was leaving work during the day to drop by her place. He wasn't walking away from their friendship now that she no longer feared not being able to hand the baby over. Cool. She didn't want him gone out of her life. She loved hearing him laugh, the way he talked with his hands, how his eyes widened when he got all thoughtful, those long legs. Ouch. Friends, remember? Yeah, but seeing Abbie so happy she was fast moving on and wanting more in her life.

'But I want a cat. Why can't I?'

Reality moment. Talking about a pet was what was important right now. Why couldn't they have a cat? It would be good for Rosie and less work than a dog. 'We'll talk about it another day. Here's school.' She swung into a park outside the main gate.

'Mummy, there's Colleen,' Rosie shrieked. Her finger was jabbing the window in the direction of the gathering of excited kids.

Colleen and Rosie had become inseparable since starting school, and Emma hoped her daughter had found her Abbie.

Undoing Rosie's seat belt, Emma lifted her out of the car seat and handed over her bag. 'There you go, young lady. Does Mummy get a kiss first?'

'Yes, but hurry. I have to see Colleen.'

Blasted tears threatened again. Crouching down, she wrapped her arms around Rosie. 'Love you, darling. Have a good morning.'

'Mummy, hurry up. I want to tell Colleen about the baby.'

Here we go. People would be watching, talking about her—good and bad. She'd cope. As long as those who mattered to her were onside it didn't matter. Nixon's support and friendship being the benchmark. Friendship. That blasted word again. She needed to look it up in the dictionary and check that it didn't include hot zaps of need and heart-melting longing for a man.

Watching Rosie race up the path to her friend, Emma slashed away the tears on her cheeks. 'Sod off, mood. I'm happy with my lot.'

Had she been like this last time she'd had a baby? Absolutely. But there'd also been the Alvin factor thrown into the mix. He might've been gone for three months by then but she'd lived with a deep dread he'd turn up and demand to see his daughter, or snatch her away. It hadn't happened, but it wasn't until the police had arrived on her doorstep two years ago to tell her that her husband had died as the result of a fight that she'd fully relaxed the crippling fear.

'Jingle Bells' blared again. 'Nixon, did you forget you just rang me?' she choked.

'That's better. You're not crying.'

How wrong could he be? 'You rang because I sniffed a couple of times?'

'Just checking. See you later.' Gone.

Leaving her smiling and pinching herself. What was going on here? Would this feeling of excitement crash and burn as her hormones settled back in their cave? Had post-birth hormones temporarily heightened her awareness of Nixon as a man; a hot man? She stared around the car park, up at the sky, over at the main school building. There were no answers waiting to drop on her. She'd have to play the waiting game, to see the hormonal rush through to its end and look at what was left afterwards.

* * *

Nixon sauntered up Emma's path and raised his hand to knock but the door opened before he had a chance. Loud music spilled out. 'You're a rocker?'

'I'll turn it down.' Emma lurched forward as if she was about to plant a kiss on his cheek, then as rapidly she pulled back, her face burning.

His face untouched.

'Emma?' He followed her through the apartment to the small but neat lounge where she killed the volume.

Her shoulders were tense, her neck stiff, and her hands now fists at her sides. 'Sorry about that.' She looked—fragile. Yes, definitely delicate. As if she didn't know if she was coming or going. Not surprising. The birth must've caught up in full force. 'I was trying to block out stuff.'

'Baby crying next door stuff?'

An abrupt nod. 'I'm probably adding to the problem as Grace won't be able to sleep. But I'm going up the walls and had to do something, and going for a run is not an option.' Emma's bottom lip quivered.

Nixon wanted to hug her, to send that crying packing, but sensed a hug might make things worse. He swung the paper bag he held in one hand. 'I got pastries from the French patisserie. That okay?'

Her lips softened, a small smile creeping in. 'I got some ciabatta from the bakery and ham from the superette. I thought we could sit on the deck.' She stared around the room as if it were foreign to her.

'Perfect.' Hopefully it would be further away from the baby's cries if they happened again. 'Emma, look at me.'

Her reluctance stabbed him in the chest. He shouldn't have come. She didn't want him here. But then she said, 'Take no notice of me. I'm all mixed up.' She drew a breath. 'I'm glad you came. I need sane and sensible at the moment.'

So he wasn't about to be kicked out. He wasn't sure he liked being labelled sane and sensible but if that was what she wanted then that was what she'd get. But as she headed into the kitchen his gaze scoped her body and that thick, wavy copper hair falling down her back, causing a pang of need to slide under his skin. Emma was beautiful. Alluring. What? Nixon tensed. What was that? Emma was captivating? Yes, she was, but he wasn't going anywhere with this. He recognised that she was attractive, but he wasn't admitting to wanting to follow through on that. Not likely. Oh, man, he was an expert in caution so what had gone wrong that his gut had tightened when he'd looked at his *friend*? Better get back on track with why he was here. 'About coming back to work. Don't rush it. We can cope.' She really was exhausted and would need time to recuperate.

'I know, but it's a bit confronting being this close to the baby so you'll probably see me sooner than later.' Emma sort of laughed. Strained and unhappy laughter.

It wasn't up to him. 'Why not move in with your parents for a few days? I know Kathy would love to spoil you.'

'And Rosie.' Emma sighed. 'It's like my family have always got my back and this time I want to be strong. I chose to have a baby for Abbie, and I need to see it through to the point I'm past these annoying hormones and accepting that I don't have another baby to raise.'

'I think I can understand that. But don't feel you're on your own. I'm here if you need a punching bag.'

Emma winced.

Wrong term given her history. 'You know what I meant. Come on. Let's eat.' He took her arm to lead her outside. 'You can fill me in on how you're really managing now that you've come back to earth. With a thud, I'd say, if those dark shadows under your eyes are any indicator.'

She swayed towards him. Where was this going? The scent of strawberries reached him. Her shampoo? Then she placed a hand on his arm and gave a gentle squeeze. 'What do you want to drink?'

'Water's good. Unless you've got a commercial coffee machine?' Strong black coffee was his weakness.

At last a full smile, aimed at him what was more, turning his toes and filling him with warmth. 'You see the size of my kitchen?'

He gave a perfunctory glance around. 'If you got rid of the toaster and kettle, put the tea, *instant* coffee and sugar containers away, we could make one fit. Just.'

'You're going to be visiting that often?' Those stunning eyes filled with happiness and laughter.

He shrugged up a smile for her. 'Who knows? Come on, let's go eat.' *Before I say something like, 'Hell, yes, I want to call in every day.'* He waved the pastries in front of her. 'You told me you're starving, remember?'

'I've munched on some biscuits since then. So not healthy.' She headed outdoors. 'Anything interesting happen at work this morning?'

'Surprisingly quiet really. Suspected stroke, sprained ankle and a couple of broken bones.'

'You'll never get away with that. This afternoon will be diabolical with every emergency imaginable.' Her smile was lopsided. 'Call me when that happens.'

'You're not serious?'

'Of course not. Even I get that I need to take things slowly, but it's so frustrating. Getting in the groceries is about as exciting as my day's going to get. Until Rosie gets home anyway. How come you're working today?'

'Braden got called out of town by his family.' Braden being his second in charge.

Plates and food were set on a tiny wrought-iron table

under the pergola attached to her front wall. There was a bottle of water in a bowl of ice and mismatching glasses beside it. Emma winced as she lowered herself onto one of the two metal chairs. 'Right, help yourself.'

'After you.' Suddenly he felt awkward, and, worse, he didn't understand why. It was a bit like the very first time they'd shared a tea break in the department.

You're kidding yourself, buster. This is more difficult.

Back then Emma had been just one of the staff he was getting to know by having one-on-one sessions over coffee and cake. Now she'd become a friend as well as a great colleague, and a woman he couldn't seem to ignore, try as he might. A woman hurting and confused whom he longed to hug and kiss better.

Like it's that simple. Let alone the consequences. Friendship ruined, working together awkward. Keep the kisses to yourself.

'Thanks,' she muttered and picked at a piece of ciabatta without any butter or ham to make it edible.

Putting a thick sandwich together, he placed it on her plate and took the mangled ciabatta away. 'Eat. Properly.'

'Yes, boss,' she muttered.

'Give yourself a break, Emma. It's less than twenty-four hours since you gave birth, and it wasn't, isn't, the most usual of situations.'

'I'm fine, just making the most of having a few days off work, that's all.' Pick, pick, pick. Her finger moved faster, as if it was trying to destroy something. Him for raising the subject of Grace? It needed raising. How else was she going to move forward?

Nixon slapped some ham between two chunks of ciabatta and bit into it, chewed slowly. There wasn't a hope in hell Emma was about to start talking freely about what was eating her up. It was beyond her at the moment. She wouldn't know where to start. 'Remember the day I arrived in the department? When those two toddlers were brought in after apparently swallowing bathroom cleaner? Crying and screaming?'

Emma nodded slowly, and the eyes that met his said, *Where are you going with this?*

'Turned out they'd drunk gin from the mother's drinks cabinet, not cleaner, and they were tiddly.'

Emma began chewing slowly.

'The mother wasn't even embarrassed, more annoyed that the kids had disturbed her afternoon.' Nixon recalled the thin, young woman with more attitude than parenting skills. 'You picked up one toddler and handed him to me and said cuddle him as he needed that more than anything. Then you wrapped the second child in your arms and started telling a story, almost crooning to her. Within a couple of minutes both of them were quiet, hanging onto every word you uttered.' She'd had him thinking what a wonderful mother she'd make, not realising she already had a child.

That look was still fixed on him. 'So?'

He wasn't sure what he'd started out to say, only that the memory had suddenly filled his head and he knew he had to share it. 'Days later I met Rosie when she was dropped off. She was relaxed, funny, cute; well rounded. That came down to her having an amazing mother who knew what a child needed and how to give it. I understood then that those toddlers had had a special moment.'

'They don't get enough of them.'

'You've seen them since?'

'This is Queenstown. We all know each other, or of each other, through business, schools, you name it. The ones who've grown up here, anyway.'

'I've seen you give other patients you've known in ED

hugs that have stopped the crying, or softened pain. Give yourself a big one, Emma. Or I can…' No, he couldn't. He might want to but he was not going to hug her. Hugs could be too involved, at least any he had with this woman would be, and involved wasn't in his vocabulary.

'I don't want to cry,' she snapped as tears burst from her eyes and streamed down her cheeks.

'Hey.' Now what? Nixon sat, transfixed.

Through the open window next door came the soft sound of a baby crying. Emma drew a long breath, her hands gripping her sandwich so that the ham slid out and onto the deck.

'You've only seen Grace once today?'

A nod. 'When we first got home from the Valley.' Her left leg was bobbing up and down, up and down.

'You're not ready to see them again?' Shut up, Nixon. Keep your sticky beak out of this. No, this was why he was here.

'Of course I want to,' Emma continued quietly. 'I want to drop in and out all the time like Abbie and I always do for each other. But this is different. What if she thinks I'm trying to hog Grace's attention, or that I can't let go, or…? I don't know.'

'When Rosie was born did you live next door to Abbie?'

'Yes, Abbie and Michael. Without them and Mum I'd still be trying to work out how to change nappies.'

'How often did Abbie come in here when you first brought Rosie home?'

'Seemed like every five minutes.'

'Did you mind?' Nixon asked.

'Of course not. I'd have been upset if she hadn't.'

'I rest my case.'

Hope spilled into Emma's worried gaze. 'You make it

seem simple.' Then her shoulders lifted, her spine straightening. 'Thanks. You're right. I'm being a dope.'

'You're dealing with a lot. Go easy on yourself.' He stood and reached for one of the pastries. 'Now, I'd better get cracking.' The guy never seemed to stop working.

Emma turned to him. 'Nixon? I'm really glad you dropped by.'

'So am I, Em.'

So am I.

Screech. Tyres on hot tarmac. *Screech, screech. Thunk. Bang.* Glass tinkling.

The music stopped.

The air was too damned quiet. As if it were poised, waiting in anticipation. Something terrible had happened.

CHAPTER FOUR

NIXON SPUN AROUND to peer down the lawn towards the street. 'Sounded like a vehicle hitting something solid.'

'Electricity's gone off so I'd say a power pole.' Emma snatched up her phone and charged down the steps and across the lawn.

Nixon was right behind her. 'Go carefully. There could be electric wires on the ground.'

The wires were still attached to the insulators, swaying in the light breeze, while the pole was at an odd angle, but nothing dangerous for them or bystanders. 'Call 111. Need power, fire and ambulance,' Nixon ordered.

'Already onto it,' came the calm voice of his very competent nurse.

Screams rent the air. Lifted the hairs on his arms. A young child's screams, filled more with panic than pain, Nixon thought. Hoped, anyway, and crossed his fingers to make doubly sure.

Very medical, buster.

Reaching the vehicle, he did a quick walk-round, making doubly certain a stray wire hadn't dropped to touch the metal with arcs of electricity.

'All good.'

Peering inside, the female driver appeared unconscious,

the steering wheel jamming her tight against the back of her seat while the airbag was all but smothering her.

'Everyone's on their way.' Emma was beside him. 'I'll see to the wee one.' She had the back door open and was feeling for the buckles of the belts that had kept the child safe. 'Shh, there. I'm going to get you out of the car, sweetheart. I know you've had a big fright, but you'll feel better out on the grass. Shh.'

The screams weren't abating, but Nixon had to ignore them while he dealt with the woman. If he didn't get that airbag deflated immediately she might suffocate.

'What can I do?' Abbie appeared behind him.

'Get me a sharp knife fast,' he called over his shoulder. It was an old model and wouldn't self-deflate.

Abbie was gone, not wasting time talking, her baby bouncing in her arms. She was not going to be able to help them much unless she could put Grace down.

'What's your name?' Emma was asking the child. 'Mine's Emma. You can call me Em, if that's easier.'

'Mummy, I want my mummy.'

'Need a knife here too,' Emma told him. 'This car seat's twisted and the buckle's not releasing.'

Nixon felt for a pulse at the exposed side of the woman's neck. 'The child got any obvious injuries?'

'Not that I can see. But he'll have been thrown hard against the belts. When the shock quietens he'll notice some pain. How's the driver?'

'Can't find a pulse. Yes, I can. Weak and irregular.' An event causing the accident? Or as a result of impact?

'I brought two knives.' Abbie was back already. 'Not sure which is best.'

Nixon took the pointiest and stabbed repeatedly at the airbag. Whoosh. Yes, good result. He held the woman's head so she didn't drop forward too hard. 'Emma, going to need you here.'

She was sawing at the seat belt. 'Two ticks. Need someone to try to calm our little man.'

Abbie stepped closer, her arms full of baby Grace. 'I'll talk to him while you help Nixon.'

'Can I do something to help?' a man asked.

Nixon glanced around, saw a gathering crowd and then the young guy standing near Abbie. 'Can you try to get that belt undone or cut apart?' He didn't wait for an answer, turning immediately back to the woman. 'Em, I don't want to move her until the ambulance is here and we can get a neck brace on but I need to see what the damage is.'

'I'll get in from the other side.' She was gone, and almost immediately inside the car, wincing as she hurried.

'Hold her head still for me.' Nixon tore open the woman's blouse and cursed silently. Left side of ribcage stoved in. Probable punctured lung.

'You need to check her pulse again,' Emma said. 'Her resp rate is non-existent.'

He placed two fingers on her carotid again. 'You're right. Got to get her out of here.'

'Mummy, I want you.'

Nixon flipped his head around, stared into the anguished eyes of the child—a boy if his fire-engine shirt was an indicator—saw the terror, and shock. *Felt* the fear. *Knew* those crippling emotions as if they'd happened to him yesterday. And the kid didn't understand he might be losing his mother. Didn't have a clue in Hades what that meant. How his life could be tossed up and down, round and round, with no chance of ever righting itself.

Not on my watch.

He knew the cruel blows coming to the boy if he didn't save this woman. Knew how love could switch to fear that swamped all emotion. 'Do what you can to hold her head steady and I'll get others to help lift her out.'

Sirens filled the air, the fire truck suddenly beside them and men swamping the area. Would've preferred the ambulance, but he wasn't going to be picky. 'Hey, guys, here, now.'

'They'll have a neck brace,' Emma informed him.

She wasn't forgetting the important stuff. Not like him. Of course fire crews carried basic emergency equipment for patients.

Within moments their patient was out of the car and lying on the ground, and Nixon was doing compressions. *One, two, three, four. Come on, lady. Don't you dare not come back for your son. Ten, eleven, twelve. Do you even have a clue what it's like to grow up without your mother there for you? Thirty.*

Nixon lifted his hands, nodded to the fireman ready to squeeze air into the woman's lungs with a ventilation bag.

Faster, man.

Of course the guy was doing his job correctly; it only felt as if it were taking for ever.

One, two, three. More sirens. Six, seven, eight. *Lady, you'd better start breathing or I'm going to get angry. Your son is crying for you now. Think how he'll feel if someone has to tell him you're not coming home. Ever.* Twenty-one, twenty-two.

'She stopped breathing shortly after we arrived.' Emma was talking to paramedics as she stepped away to allow them access. 'There's a little boy too. He's just been freed.' She reached out for the child being held by the man who'd helped cut him out of his seat. 'Hey, sweetheart, let me carry you away from the naughty car.'

At least Emma was thinking straight. The boy did not

need to see his mother in this state. Thirty. Nixon stopped compressions for two puffs of oxygen to be given.

'We have a pulse,' the fireman at the woman's head said.

Relief snapped through the air. Nixon glanced along the path to where Emma stood holding the child, talking quietly, trying to soothe him.

We did it, buddy. Your mum's alive.

Though still in big trouble. Now to get on with saving her from those injuries. Hopefully not a flail chest. The compressions wouldn't have helped there but he'd had no choice.

As Nixon checked her ribcage he began to think luck was on this mother's side. And her son's. 'Let's get her loaded and down to the hospital. I don't think those ribs are as bad as first expected but I don't want any delay.'

'We've got her,' one of the paramedics commented as he attached leads to the defib, reminding Nixon that out here he took second place. These guys knew what they were doing.

'I'll see you in ED, Jeff. There's also a young boy who needs transporting to hospital.'

'A second ambulance is nearly here,' the paramedic informed him.

'You okay?' Emma was at his side.

'Sure.' Now that the situation was under control the adrenalin rush was quietening down.

Emma shrugged as if she didn't believe him. 'Guess this takes care of your appointment with the CEO.'

'Definitely. I'd better get cracking. Talk later.' Nixon shoved his hand in his pocket for his keys. 'You were great with that child.'

'Poor kid. I couldn't find any serious wounds, only two abrasions, but the head stuff—that's going to be hard to fix in a hurry.'

Oh, yeah. And if the worst happened then there would be no fixing him. He would carry today in his head and heart for the rest of his life. It would form the basis of everything he did from now on. 'Do you know if anyone's contacted his father? Or relatives?'

'The police are onto it.'

Being focused on saving the mother, he hadn't noticed their arrival. 'Good.' As long as there was a father to step up for his son, and the woman wasn't in Emma's position.

'You sure you're okay?' Emma asked, her gaze fixed on him, studying him intently.

Had she noticed his anguish? The urgency driving him to resuscitate the mother? Had Emma seen his fear? His need to save a boy from the pain and bewilderment he'd suffered? Please no. He didn't need other people to know how he still hurt, how he was still afraid he'd lose someone else he loved. He did not want Emma's sympathy. That would squash any sense of awe he might feel with her. 'Why wouldn't I be?'

'I don't know. You looked desperate while doing compressions.' Yep, she'd seen through his façade to the screwup inside.

Where did that leave him? More screwed up, or letting go some of the fierce grip he kept on his emotions? In an effort to curb her interest in his background, he forced all emotion out of his voice as he told her, 'Of course I was. That woman's life was in the balance, and I had to save her.'

'Of course you did.' Disappointment tainted with hurt glared out of those soft green eyes. 'Thought there was something more going on, that's all.'

Once Emma knew his history she'd be in, under his skin, behind the barriers he held in place with sheer determination and not much else. When that happened, he'd be lost. For ever. 'Isn't that enough?'

Emma's gaze locked on him. 'Not for me. You're hiding something.' Her eyes widened. 'From me or from yourself.'

Nixon strode towards his vehicle, hoping she wouldn't follow. He'd love nothing more than to wind his arms around her, let her warmth push out the chill that had gripped him when the boy had screamed for his mummy. But he couldn't take the risk. What if he found himself wanting more and more from her? It would be like falling into something deep and dangerous from which there'd be no turning back; a place where he'd open up and expose his needs and fears and take everything she had to offer, and he wouldn't know how to give back half as much. He would always hold a part of him back in case he lost her.

So, Emma Hayes, I am not going to be any more than a friend, a close one maybe, but not a lover or more. You deserve so much better.

Emma watched Nixon charge down the footpath to his fancy four-wheel drive with its bike stand on the back. Those long, toned legs ate up the distance. He'd say he had to get back to the hospital in a hurry for that woman, and, while there was truth in that, there were other medics on duty. His unreasonable hurry was most likely to get away from her questions. She'd pushed him when he didn't want to talk. Something had been going on inside that clever head. Something deep and painful. Which was why she shouldn't be surprised he hadn't answered her query. Did he not understand how much she cared? How much she wanted to help him, as he had her? That was what friends were all about.

Wary, remember? Non-involved, remember?

He had no qualms when it came to asking about her past,

her family, Rosie's father. None at all. Sure, he sheathed the questions in concern for her, but he still damned well put them out there. Almost as if he wanted to get closer but was afraid of where that might take him. He needn't have worried. She might be noticing him as a man, a sexy, desirable hunk even, but she wasn't going anywhere with this.

Back at her apartment she cleared the outside table. Nixon wasn't into sharing about himself, which meant no real closeness. Good friends shared some private details about themselves. Lovers a lot more. There were no secrets between two people in love. There was her answer. This had nothing to do with love because she couldn't tell him how weak and feeble the past had made her. She certainly wasn't going to explain how his care and concern piqued her interest, made her think there was a life out there involving a man—love, sex, commitment.

The baby cried on the other side of her lounge wall.

Her boobs squeezed tight, diverting her from Nixon and the improbable to Grace and reality.

The sound of Abbie murmuring sweet nothings to her daughter drifted through from her open windows to Emma's straining ears. Nothing like a baby's cry to hit her heart, pull on the strings.

Emma crossed her arms carefully over her breasts. *Down, girls, down. Not your job to feed Grace.* Sharp tugs of pain said it all.

She could go visit, maybe hold Grace. She had to if she wanted to move forward, past this hurdle of longing. Deal with this and put Nixon on hold. She was using him, if only in her head, to avoid the emptiness from handing the baby over.

She might as well deal with the real problem here. It was baby Grace who made her ache with pain and longing and love, not Nixon. With a huff she headed across the lawn and up the steps to Abbie's deck. Never before had she been reluctant to drop in on her friend, while at the same time she couldn't wait, needing to reassure herself they were still on the same page, that nothing had changed between them.

'Hey, how're you doing?' she asked softly as she stepped inside the apartment identical to hers in size and layout and the exact opposite in décor. While Emma went for soft and feminine Abbie had chosen a strong modern style.

Abbie looked up with wonder in her eyes. 'Amazing. I still can't quite believe I'm breastfeeding my daughter.'

Emma's boobs were still doing that tightening, painful thing, but she just breathed deeply and waited until they got tired of the game. 'It's great for bonding. I still remember those feelings when I first fed Rosie, and many times afterwards. It's so special.'

'You want to hold Grace when I'm done?' Abbie was watching her too closely. As if she could see the need inside. No surprise there.

Suddenly the turmoil that had kept her busy doing unnecessary things that morning dropped away. 'I'd love to. And for the record, I'm fine about it all.' It was the truth, just not the whole truth.

'I know. Just don't push yourself too hard and fast to get up and running again. You're going to be pummelled with emotions for a while, but I'm here, okay? We can talk any time, about anything.'

'Someone else with nothing to keep their mind occupied but me and my problems.' What was it with people today? Was this their way of looking out for her? To tell her what to do, and how and when?

'Nixon giving you grief, was he? I couldn't believe it when he turned up earlier. Then again, maybe I could.'

The downside of living next to each other was they both

knew who their visitors were, what music they were listening to, and what was cooking on the stovetop. 'Just as well for that woman he was here.'

'You can say that again.' Abbie shuddered. 'That poor little boy was so scared. I hope he didn't see his mother lying on the ground.'

'Me too.' Emma watched Grace feeding. 'Sorry about the loud music. Hope I didn't wake the baby. I was trying to distract myself.'

'I guessed. Don't worry, it wasn't that loud. Maybe she's going to be a rocker because she wasn't fazed at all.'

'I'll move apartments before she's old enough to know how to download tunes.'

'Why did Nixon visit?' Persistent. 'It's not like he ever has before.'

See? Abbie didn't miss a thing. Two could play at that game. 'Callum left for work early this morning.'

Abbie blushed. 'He stayed the night—not that it was very restful with little miss making herself known every hour.'

'Bet she wasn't the only cause of lack of sleep,' Emma retorted around a grin. 'Did he get called in early?'

Abbie nodded. 'There was an accident on Lake Wanaka. Two boats were racing and crashed into each other.'

'Morons. No one ever thinks it'll happen to them.' In ED they'd seen and dealt with every scenario and nothing much surprised either of them. 'I didn't hear the helicopter.' Callum was a paramedic on the rescue helicopter.

'They came in while you were taking Rosie to meet up for her llama visit.' Abbie lifted Grace from her breast and laid her over her shoulder for a back rub. Just like an old hand. 'Nixon? Don't think you can avoid my question.'

Hadn't thought I could.

But she had given it her best shot, hoping Abbie had

baby brain too. Got that wrong, hadn't she? Bloodhound Abbie never dropped a question she was bursting to know the answer to, and Nixon's visit was right up there. 'He was checking up on me. Brought some pastries for lunch so I didn't mind being looked in on.'

'Oh, right. His phone wasn't working, then. I hope you were nice and friendly.'

'Why wouldn't I be?' Emma could feel her hackles rising. *Down girl. This is Abbie, who says whatever she likes to you.*

'Because you need a man in your life, and who better than Nixon? He's got everything a hot-blooded woman needs. At least I presume he does.'

'I do not need a man. I do just fine alone. Okay, not alone. There's Dad, Daniel and Shaun to annoy the heck out of me with all their checking and telling me how to run my life.'

Abbie grinned. 'They're not the sort of men I was thinking of. A man, as in sex and kisses and holding hands and—'

'Shut up, Abbie, and give me Grace.' Emma reached for the baby and hugged her carefully against her achy breasts. This time the ache didn't bother her. Instead she felt right holding Grace and knowing she would be giving the cute little dot back to her mum shortly. Her hackles had returned to their normal position, quiet and submissive. 'She's gorgeous.'

'Absolutely,' Abbie sighed through her perpetual smile. 'Do you think Nixon's hot? Because if you don't I'll never mention him again in connection with you.'

She should've known Abbie hadn't finished. 'This is me you're telling that ridiculous lie to.'

The smile widened. 'So? Hot? Or not?'

The air limped out of her lungs. 'Hot.'

'Yes.' Abbie punched the air. 'I knew it.'

'Don't go there. Every female in Queenstown over the age of ten would agree with us. I am normal in that respect. Nothing's going to happen between single mum me and Mr Uninvolved. Nixon's devoted to his career and lives most of his life in ED. When he's not there he's outdoors on his bike. He's not the type to drop by for a glass of wine.' Except he'd sat on her deck an hour ago. 'He doesn't like knowing why people are upset or not coping with something.' Yet he was always there when she needed help.

The more she said, the more Emma realised she'd nailed what was worrying her about him. She didn't really know Nixon. He appeared to do the avoidance thing yet made his shoulder available whenever she needed it. More importantly, today he'd known exactly why she was so moody. Too easily, what was more. Leading her to see through that reserve he kept in place more often than not. Had Nixon let her closer than anyone else? Still not close enough to talk about what put that anguish in his gaze while trying to save the woman. What had that been about? He'd been shaken up badly, off the Richter scale. All she'd wanted was to hold him until that pain and desperation disappeared.

Get real, Emma. You're looking for trouble. Tomorrow, or next week, or next month, when your hormones are back in place, you'll recall this and have a bloody good laugh for being so naïve.

Fingers crossed.

Abbie screwed up her nose. 'Wonder why he does keep himself aloof more than most people. Look at that three-date rule he's supposed to have. It's kind of strange when he can be social and always keeps tabs on his staff if there's something going on in their lives that's causing problems. No denying he holds a piece of himself back. An important piece, I reckon.'

Grace blew a bubble and Emma gently wiped the goo away. She was so cute. Time to change the subject. 'Thanks for understanding. I will move on, still hang around, and try not to watch you like a hawk over how you're doing with Grace.'

'You don't think I know that?' Abbie came and wrapped her arms around Emma and her daughter. 'Silly woman.'

'I've had some doubts over the past months,' Emma admitted.

'Knew that too.'

'Know-it-all.' Emma relaxed totally for the first time since Grace's arrival. There'd be days when she struggled with letting go but with Abbie being so understanding she'd make it through the murky patches. She would.

Nixon had made a valid point though. She shouldn't rush the process; she needed to deal with errant hormones and emotions as they arose, not tease them into existence and then get upset because she couldn't beat them into submission.

Abbie had more to say. Nothing new there. 'You're so generous of spirit to those of us you hold in your heart. You'd do anything for us. Carrying my baby was never going to be a stroll in the park but you did it, and did it graciously.' Abbie wiped the back of her hand over her eyes. 'If Alvin hadn't done all those hideous things to you and you hadn't had my shoulder to cry on, do you think you'd have given me Grace?'

'Of course I would've.' Emma paused, thought about it some more. 'I might not have known to make the offer, because I wouldn't have understood the pain of never having something I'd grown up always believing would be my right. But I would've said yes if you'd asked.'

'See? You gave me Michael's baby when I couldn't carry a baby to term. I love you to bits but the love you thought you'd have with Alvin, that raising kids and growing older together love, the thing you believed was your right, didn't happen. You understand loss.'

Where was Abbie going with this? She didn't have to wait long to find out.

'Nixon won't hurt you. I'd swear to that.'

'You're forgetting, I never pegged Alvin for the monster he turned out to be. Nor did you.'

'True.' Abbie's smile finally faded. She'd always felt bad about not working out what had been going on behind Emma's closed door during her marriage. Not that they'd lived next door to each other then. That had come after Emma had gone solo and started looking for her own place. It had been Abbie who'd suggested she move into the apartment next to hers and made her parents take Emma as a tenant. The move had turned her life around and got her back on track, this time as a solo mum.

'Hey, don't go there. I could've told you long before I did.' They'd also had this part of the conversation more than once. 'For the record, I think you're right. Nixon doesn't have a nasty bone in his body.'

'You've seen his bones?' A wicked gleam lit up Abbie's eyes.

'No.'

'I saw that. You want to.'

Emma screwed up her nose, and gave up trying to remain coy. 'Is it possible to have a fling—okay, sex—with a guy for as long as it takes to get the need out of your system and then walk away without being hurt?'

'For you and me, no.'

'Then this conversation's redundant. Nixon remains in the boss and casual friend category.' A sharp pain stabbed behind her ribs. Nothing to do with boobs that were full of milk not needed, and all to do with a longing she hadn't known existed until very recently, and which she couldn't—but had to find a way to—deny.

'Em.' Abbie nudged her. 'Don't be so hard on yourself. Or on any guy who comes along showing some interest in you. Your life isn't over.'

Said the woman who'd believed for a long time that her life was finished when Michael died. It was Emma's turn to slash tears away from her cheeks. Staring down at the gorgeous bundle tucked into her arm, she gave a wobbly smile. 'I have Rosie.' She didn't need anyone else. But there were days when she wouldn't mind a man in her life she could trust and rely on not to beat her up. And to love her for who she was. 'My life's pretty darned good these days.' She'd had lunch with a friend on her deck. That never happened.

She'd ignore the longing for strong arms and a warm male body tucked against hers lying in bed that sometimes woke her in the deep of the night and kept her awake for hours. It only happened occasionally. She could handle that. It was how she stayed safe.

CHAPTER FIVE

Rosie ran around the park, shrieking and laughing as only little girls did as she held onto the kite's string. 'Mummy, look what I can do.'

Emma tightened her hold on the wooden baton holding the rest of the string, staying in the centre of Rosie's circles. 'Awesome.' The kite dipped and came close to the ground before soaring on a chilly gust of wind. Summer had taken a leaf from winter's book and dumped a load of snow on the Remarkables over night.

'Do you think Santa can see me?' Rosie spun round and round, her head tipped back to watch the caterpillar-shaped kite until vertigo won out and she tumbled over, landing on her back, feet in the air.

'Hey, careful.'

'Must be all right. She's still laughing.'

Emma's head shot up too fast, and her neck cricked. 'Nixon?' Who else had a voice that lifted her skin and tightened her gut? So, the hormones were still out of whack.

'Heard you two were down here creating havoc. This one's just like her mother.'

'Naturally. All kids pick up some of their parents' ways, and as long as Rosie's got my better ones we're doing okay.'

'I guess.' Nixon strode across to giggling Rosie and

pulled her to her feet. 'You've got to look where you're going, missy.'

'Did you see me crash, Nixon? Watch me with the kite.' She was off, racing across the park, her little legs pumping fast. Once again her focus was on the kite as it began rising back into the air, and not on where she was going.

'I've got it,' Nixon tossed Emma's way and chased after Rosie.

'You need this,' Emma called. Just like her daughter, he wasn't watching anything but the kite, but he'd heard her and took the baton. Ignoring the flare of heat where his fingers brushed hers, she followed at a leisurely pace.

Why was he here helping Rosie launch the kite after a sudden nosedive into the bushes? 'How did you know where to find us?' she asked.

'Abbie.' Nixon stood hands on hips, his eyes tracking Rosie, wariness on his face.

'You weren't meant to say?'

He shrugged. 'It would've been better if I hadn't, apparently.'

'Abbie will want to live a little longer.' She wouldn't admit to being happy Nixon was here.

He smiled, and her stomach dived. 'I dropped by to see how you're getting on.'

'Nixon, are you coming to our picnic?' Rosie burst between them. 'We're going to have it after I finish flying my kite.'

He flicked Emma a silent query, and she nodded.

'We've got chocolate biscuits,' Rosie enticed.

'I can't say no to those, can I?' Nixon laughed. Very carefree today.

'Yippee.' Rosie was off running more circles.

Emma watched her as she said, 'About work, if it fits I might do some mornings later in the week. I can be the bandage nurse, fix cuts and bruises. Nothing heavy.' She looked up into his eyes. 'I'm going to start painting stripes on my walls soon. Purple and red ones.'

'Stripes?'

'Or a large snakes and ladders board.'

'You're bored at home?' Nixon hiccupped. 'That's why you're down here?'

'Sort of.' No. 'I needed to get away from Grace crying.'

The beginning laughter faded instantly. 'You're looking for diversion. Is this doing it for you?'

'Sometimes I feel a ball of tears building up and I'm afraid to let them out. Especially when Abbie could walk in any moment. She doesn't need to see me losing it. That would make her sad at a time when she should be happy.'

'You're feeling empty?'

Bang on. 'There's a big hole where normally the baby would be. It's not unexpected, but it's hard all the same. Then I see the love and joy in Abbie's eyes and the hole disappears for a while.'

'To come back when you're tired or Grace is crying.'

She nodded. 'I have to be patient.' It hadn't started getting any easier yet.

'You're being honest with yourself, and that's got to help.' Nixon stared across the park. 'You've got Rosie, too.'

'I'd be lost without her. I only hope I'm not putting any pressure on her as a substitute.'

I'm being honest with you, too. Understand? I'm telling you how I feel. Think you could do the same next time I ask about your feelings?

'Rosie looks as happy as ever.'

'Thanks,' she said neutrally, and waited for more comments on how she was doing, because they were coming. Plain as day in that intense gaze.

Nixon looked down at her, his steady, deep gaze making her feel warm and cared about. 'You're amazing, you know?' Then he blinked, as though he'd shocked himself.

Amazing, huh? She'd take it, even if it wasn't true. A girl could get used to compliments. Could even start believing them.

It still rankled that he hadn't opened up even an incy-wincy bit about his reaction at the crash, but she could've got that wrong too. Reading people wasn't always her forte. Sick, injured, frightened patients—yes. Joe Average on the street, in her apartment, at Rosie's school? Not often. She'd used to have that skill, but maybe she needed to start trusting herself again?

'Nixon, Mummy, the kite's in the tree.'

'I'll get this,' Nixon laughed.

'All yours.' She loved his laugh, deep and sexy, and, today, so relaxed.

Shouts and hilarity came from the other side of the trees where teenagers were kicking a football and some were throwing a plastic disc. On this side couples were strolling with toddlers and dogs. A typical Sunday afternoon. Enjoyable, fun, and a little bit dull, if she was being honest. But she was out of the house and doing *something*.

'Don't break it, Nixon,' ordered a certain little madam.

'Would I do that?' he answered around a smile aimed solely at her daughter.

I'd like one of those, solely for me.

Emma shrugged off the pathetic despondency. He was here, wasn't he? 'How did the endurance race go?' He'd mentioned he was doing today's Lake Hawea challenge during that aborted lunch.

'Cold, and exhilarating. Came in ninth.' Satisfaction flooded his face, those dark eyes turning charcoal. 'The weather knocked some of the contestants off their pace.'

'But not you.' He'd have been totally focused, snow, rain or sun.

He handed the kite back to Rosie. 'Try to stay on the other side of the park. If it gets caught high up in one of these suckers we won't get it back.'

'Okay, Nixon.' Rosie headed for the far side, at the water's edge. Lake Wakatipu might look beautiful and inviting but it was glacier fed and dangerous for unsuspecting souls. Other children playing on the foreshore would be temptation in full dress for Rosie.

Emma immediately followed. 'Rosie, wait up. You're not to go near the water until I'm there.'

'Okay, Mummy.' Except she didn't stop.

'Rosie, stop.' Emma picked up her speed. 'Now.'

Nixon strode out, those long legs gobbling up the distance to reach her daughter where he matched her pace and redirected her as he chatted, as though he were used to wayward little girls. Which was fictitious, as far as she knew. He didn't have a clue. So he was a natural. All charm. Don't forget wary. A cautious charm. Yeah, she could see the potential in that. It won him everything, and lost him nothing. Nothing except involvement. Go, Nixon.

Nixon watched Emma helping Rosie bundle up the kite. Perpetual vigilance with her daughter meant she didn't do relaxed in her down time from the department. He was used to seeing her constantly on the go, watching, caring. She'd carried the same instincts into motherhood. Rosie was one lucky little girl.

Talking of luck. The young boy from the accident had collected too. 'The woman we pulled from that car wreck will make it with few consequences,' he told Emma.

'That's great news. And her son?'

'Paddy. His dad met the ambulance.' Paddy hadn't been on his own, nor had he lost his mother.

He had relaxed on that score. There'd been a sleepless night afterwards, reliving his own day of fear and reality, but those horrid memories had been overlaid with pride for helping another boy avoid collecting similar memories.

Emma walking beside him made him happy. As if they were right together. Whoa. Where was this going? Foreign territory for certain.

'Remember, don't put your hand in front of its mouth,' Emma told Rosie, who was talking to a Labrador.

'It's cute.' Rosie leaned forward, her hands clasped behind her back, almost rubbing noses with the dog as the owner told it to stay.

'Don't even ask,' Emma muttered. 'Not until you make up your mind between kitten and puppy anyway.'

A shadow, a brief glimpse of movement and Nixon spun around. Saw a disc hurtling through the air at head height. 'Watch out,' he yelled as he swung his arm to snatch the spinning disc before it hit Emma. Bloody maniacs using one of these when the park was busy with families enjoying the summery afternoon.

'I'm sorry.'

Emma's words barely registering, he flicked the plastic dome to the teen who'd thrown it, sending a stern glare with it. Then he heard her strangled gasp. 'Em? Are you all right?'

'I'm sorry. I didn't mean it.' Her words were halting and filled with—fear.

Nixon stared as Emma huddled in on herself, her arms wrapped around her body, her hands white where her fingers dug into her sides. What was going on? 'You haven't done anything wrong.'

'Don't hit me.'

Whoosh. All the air was driven out of his lungs by those three words. Without thought he reached for her, to hug her, to show she was safe with him.

She jerked backwards, tripping. With fast steps she righted herself, but still didn't look at him.

Be calm, don't add to her misery. 'Emma. It's me, Nixon. I am not going to hurt you.' That bastard had a lot to answer for. 'Emma, please look at me.' He stood still, his hands loose at his side—not easy when rare anger raged through him.

Her head lifted slowly. Fear from those green eyes sliced into him. Fear that began dissipating as she studied him from under lowered eyelashes. 'Nixon?' Her tongue lapped her bottom lip. 'Nixon.' Her relief was rapid and enormous, lifted her head further. 'Hell.' Glancing around the park, she took in where she was and who was nearby before her gaze came back to him. The fear had gone. 'Sorry.' This time it didn't sound like a plea.

'Now can I hug you?'

'Would you?'

She shook like a puppy in a thunderstorm. Every protective cell in his body held her from danger. His chin rested on the top of her head as she wept against his chest. OMG. Emma. This was what her ex had done to her. Hopefully her father and brothers had beaten the guy to a pulp. They were very protective of her. The other night they'd been friendly and accepting, but, deep down, how had they really felt about him being there with Emma?

'I reacted without thinking. I saw your hand flying through the air and responded instinctively as I learned to do a long time ago. It's something I've tried to control but there are times when I act first, think second.'

'Did that save you in the past?'

Her head moved back and forth. 'Not often. He was

usually too quick for me. He'd be there hauling me out of a corner. There was never anywhere to hide. Best to get it over with than rile him some more.'

Nixon couldn't help the expletives that spewed across his lips. And got a nudge in the ribs from a sharp elbow.

'Young ears.'

Talk about being out of his depth. 'I was catching that flying toy before it hit you.'

'I never saw it.'

'That's why I put my hand up.'

Sniff, sniff. His shirt was rapidly becoming soaked. 'All I saw was a hand flinging through the air in my direction. I haven't reacted like that in a long time.'

'I hate that you ever had to.'

'Mummy, I want a hug too.'

Emma jerked in his arms. 'Rosie,' she sniffed. 'Of course, darling.'

Nixon reached down for the sweet little girl he was becoming too fond of and lifted her up between them. The three of them stood bound together by arms and concern and...

No. Not the L word.

That wasn't what this tight feeling in his chest meant. If it was he'd be pushing away. Loving anyone was dangerous. Loving these two in particular even more so. They could decimate him with their power to tug him in and wrap their magic around his heart. Give him the things he refused to expose himself to. He needed to stick to being fond of them both.

But he couldn't step away, couldn't lower his arms or deny himself this brief moment. Not of joy, considering what had precipitated it. But he felt good; that protective streak of his was wired and ready to hold the world at bay for this brave, strong woman. With a quick, barely touching kiss on the top of Emma's head he finally managed to pull away, leaving the child in her mother's tender hold.

'Why are you crying, Mummy?'

Emma rubbed her arm across her face and dredged up a parody of a smile. 'Not crying. I got dust in my eyes, sweetheart.' Placing Rosie on her feet, she looked across to the lake, around the trees, over at the gatherings of people. Everywhere but at him.

Hurt lanced him. Why this sudden avoidance? He'd seen her break down. They had this between them now. But he hadn't been where she'd been, didn't know what it was like to have the confidence beaten out of him. That could account for any number of reactions, and yet she was still here with him. He'd take that as a good sign. 'Do you want to go home now?'

'We haven't had the picnic.' Rosie bounced up and down between them. 'I'm hungry.'

'When aren't you?' A soft, sad smile appeared as Emma ran her hand over her daughter's head. 'We've got orange juice to go with those biscuits,' she told him, 'plus bananas and apples.' Tipping her head around, Emma finally eyeballed him. 'If chocolate biscuits and bananas are your thing then you're welcome to join us.' The smile dipped. 'I'll understand if you've changed your mind.'

'Hey, stop that. You're allowed a bad moment without expecting me to think the worst of you.' Now he understood her need to appease people over some of the least likely things. 'If you want to talk about it some more, then I'm here for you.'

'I've never been one for prattling on. It's hard, you know?'

'I imagine it is. But not with me, okay?' *Never with me.*

'You didn't like me mentioning your reaction to that little boy's predicament the other day, yet at the same time you think I should spill my guts about what's turned me into the blithering wreck I can sometimes be?' Astonishment glittered out at him.

Way to go for the throat, Emma.

'I'm a better listener than talker.'

Glib, man. Also true.

'Same here, especially with someone not prepared to share what's made them who they are, not willing to open up. I thought we were friends, Nixon.'

He wanted to be angry, but he couldn't when every word she said hit the truth on the head. Instead, his heart was skittering all over the show. They were on the brink of something here, something huge. Something he didn't understand. Something he'd already stepped back from once. Now he tried again, took a pace back physically and mentally, saying, 'I'm unable to talk about certain things. I don't know how to vocalise my emotions.' Like Henry? Where had that come from? Was there any truth in it?

The astonishment softened. 'Unfortunately, the result's the same. You expect more from me than you intend sharing about yourself.' They'd reached her little car and she flicked the locks before facing him. 'I can't work like that, Nixon. For me it takes a lot to trust someone and I've found that with you, but I need the same back.'

Another truth slammed him. 'I do trust you, Emma.'

'You want to explain why you were so desperate to save the boy's mother? Apart from that you're a doctor and you want to save everyone.'

Forcing his mouth open to answer her, to give her what she was asking for, he found that nothing came out. Not a word. Zip. *Nada.* Bloody hell.

Say something...anything.

No, not anything. Emma will turn her back on me. For ever.

'I see.' Her body slumped. 'Come on, Rosie. We'll take our picnic back down to the lake's edge.' She lifted the lid of the boot, retrieved a shopping bag and slammed the boot shut. Pinged the locks. Held her hand out to Rosie. 'Let's go.'

'Nixon, race me to the water.' Rosie didn't pick up on the tension crackling in the air.

Emma didn't acknowledge him, kept walking away. Her hand gripped her daughter's tight, the bag swinging hard in her other hand.

With every step she took, cracks opened deep inside him. He couldn't drag his eyes away from that tight, straight back, those short, sharp steps. He'd hurt Emma as hard as one of her ex's fists had. He took a step after her. Stopped. This needed thinking through, not some rash compromise he couldn't fulfil. Getting it wrong would only compound the hurt.

Pain flared in his chest, as if his heart had been sliced in two. But love had nothing to do with this breakdown in communication. He liked Emma a lot, admired her strength and bravery, enjoyed being with her, wanted to spend more time with her, but love didn't—couldn't—feature. He'd shut that emotion down for so long, so deep, it was beyond being resurrected.

Chocolate biscuits and bananas weren't going to be a sweet fix for what ailed him. He turned away, aiming for his vehicle. What was required for that was impossible.

He would go back to being her boss and hopefully, eventually, they'd put this behind them and return to their comfortable friendship. Some time in the not too distant future. Only problem with that scenario—his body craved intimacy with hers. Got hot and flustered at the sight of those lush curves, the swell of her breasts, that copper-shaded hair spilling down to her waist, the multitude of expres-

sions flitting across her face. Oh, yes, he wanted Emma
Hayes as he'd never wanted a woman before. Friends? Ba-
loney. Not any more.

Emma glanced over her shoulder as Nixon all but ran to his
four-wheel drive. He was so desperate to get away from her
he hadn't said goodbye to Rosie. That stunk. Her daughter
had done nothing wrong.

Did I? By being honest did I wrong Nixon?

For once, tears did not appear to track down her face.
Sure, she wanted to cry, loud and ferociously, to shout at
Nixon that he was wrong to keep everything so locked up.

But how could she when she was guilty of the same
thing? Her family had often heard about her marriage and
the horrors it held. Abbie more often. But they knew her,
they'd been there all of her life so naturally she turned to
them when she finally opened her gob.

She doubted Nixon had ever talked about what was eating at him. Not to a soul. There mightn't have been anyone
to tell, so he'd become a master at keeping quiet. No denying that horror and determination in his eyes the other day
when he'd looked at the little boy screaming for his mother.
But talk about it? About as likely as winning the lotto.

Then it hit her. Hard. Did Nixon know how it felt to lose
his mother at a young age?

Emma's stomach sucked in. That was it. Had to be.
Or, if not his mother, then his dad or someone very close.
Whoever it had been, the raw pain that had been there at
that crash site spoke of loss. A loss he'd been determined
to prevent Paddy learning. It had been in Nixon's actions,
his steady, determined compressions and dark voice count-
ing to thirty. Paddy had not been about to lose his mother
if Nixon had anything to do with it.

He'd beaten the odds, brought the woman back from

death's door. Apparently she'd coded in Resus too and again Nixon had been her saviour. Driven by those ghosts, Emma bet.

'You're holding too tight.' Rosie tugged at their joined hands.

'Sorry, sweetheart.' She looked around for an available picnic table and came up short. 'Let's sit on the grass and have some biccies.' An engine started up, probably Nixon leaving. So he wasn't coming back to join them. Not today. Probably never.

Rosie had other ideas and was waving frantically towards the car park. 'Doesn't Nixon like chocolate, Mummy?'

'I'll eat his.'

If only life were so easy. Emma wished hard for Rosie to know only this sun-kissed version for many more years. She hated that one day her sweet little girl would learn that not everything went her way, that sometimes things went belly up very badly.

'Can I call my puppy Nixon?'

Despite everything, Emma could not stop a shout of laughter.

No, you can't.

'You're not getting a puppy.'

But if you do I'll make sure it's a bitch so you have to think of a girly name.

'I will one day.'

Shades of her own determination as a young girl were shining through more often lately. Where had that determination gone when she'd needed it the most? Into the mine of pain riding on a hard fist. That was where. Now she was getting closer to a man determined to keep her on the edge of his life who at the same time kept dropping in as though he couldn't stay away. What was going on between them? She was seeing possibilities for a new, happier life, shared with someone she might one day care a lot about. But every time hope lifted, Nixon went and proved how wrong she was. He did not want to get involved.

'Right, let's eat.' Swallowing was going to be difficult when there was a lump of bewilderment and disappointment in her throat, but she'd give it her best shot. Chin up. Tomorrow she might drop into work and apologise to Nixon for raising an obviously painful subject. Then she'd put on her mother hat to go pick Rosie up from school, cook dinner and go to bed to get up in the morning and start all over. By the end of the week the routine would surely have settled her down on all fronts. Baby hormones needed to start backing off and give her breasts a break, and then her head space could calm down and return to being rational.

The same needed to happen with the yearnings for Nixon that cranked up whenever she was around him. They had to go away so she could get on with her comfortable, safe, single-mother life.

Except she'd acted totally out of character when she'd stood up to Nixon about his reactions to that boy's mother's situation. Where had the cowering, be-nice-or-get-hit woman gone? She'd actually told him what she thought, and then watched him walk away. Was she finally getting a backbone? Standing up for what she believed to be right and true? She sank further onto the ground, her bones resembling jelly.

She hadn't backed down when Nixon had got upset, because it was important for their future. Not that they had one.

Determination in spades. Yes. Good. Great, even.

So why did she feel so tearful and pleased and worried?

Blasted hormones. Hadn't taken a hike at all.

CHAPTER SIX

'IT FEELS GOOD fitting into my old-size scrubs again.' Emma laughed at her reflection in the changing-room mirror, ignoring the stretched fabric across her breasts and the tightness around her waist. Slightly forced laughter, but hey, whatever it took to start out the day on the right note.

Her colleague Steph laughed too. 'Like you were huge when you were carrying Grace. You made most of the other girls jealous with your lithe figure right up until you gave birth.'

'For that I'll work twice as hard this morning.' And keep as far from Nixon as possible.

'You will take it slowly, and you won't go rushing around like a mad thing.' Steph got all serious. 'You sure you're ready to come back? I'm not only talking the physical effort.'

'Best you don't give me babies for a few days. There's no guarantee I won't have a crying fit with these hormones swirling around my system. Every time I think they're on their way out they give me a right old beating up.'

'I'm putting you on triage. You can't get into too much mischief there. No heavy lifting or pushing wheelchairs either.'

'Yes, ma'am.' Emma saluted. It was good to be away from those blasted walls in her apartment she'd been all but climbing with frustration. She was probably pushing herself too hard. It was Wednesday, five days since the birth, but she had to get out of the house.

She scanned the department for a certain person, while her ears did an imitation of radar shields trying to hear his low, gravelly voice.

'Hi, Emma. Surely you're not back to fighting fit yet?' one of the younger nurses asked.

'No plans on doing anything crazy strenuous but otherwise feeling A-okay, thanks.' Not spilling the beans about the head stuff.

'Hard to believe you've had a baby,' another nurse said. 'Look at you, all slim and attractive again. Make that still.'

Okay, getting embarrassing now. 'Cheers. Thanks for the vote of confidence. Can we get on with something, like work?' Emma looked over at the white board where patients were written up when they were brought through. 'Not a lot going on yet.' Getting busy fast had been the plan.

'Listen up, everyone.' Nixon strode out of his office, his mouth tight, eyes serious. 'There's been an accident north of Wanaka involving a campervan and car. The first patients will be here in less than thirty.'

'How many are we expecting?' Emma asked.

'Two from the car in critical condition. One's on the way in the helicopter, the other by ambulance. The reports coming in on the remaining casualties suggest arm fractures for two plus a suspected skull fracture.' Nixon seemed to be talking directly to her.

Seemed to be, because his gaze had reached her and stopped. But she was probably wrong. He had no reason to seek her out. She was glad that the confusion between them had gone, replaced with calm and, yes, damn it, that irritating caution. Caution she now believed hid past hurts.

Emma focused on the scant details he was providing and ignored the fluttering in her belly. They had to work together.

But did he have to look so delectable with that stubble on his chin? Those broad shoulders filled out his scrubs in a way she'd not noticed before. Emma shivered as need clogged her veins. She'd been fooling herself to think this desire for sex with Nixon was going to disappear in a haze of reality. She wanted him. All of him. That was her new reality.

'Emma.' Her new reality spoke directly to her. 'Welcome back. Sure you're up to this?'

'Better than going bonkers at home.' She glanced around the department. Her world might be topsy-turvy right now, but here at work she knew who she was, and what was expected of her. And damn it all, she was more than happy to see Nixon despite the misunderstanding that kept arising between them.

'Don't overdo it, all right?' Nixon stood close, his steady gaze locked on her.

Closing her eyes, she drew in a long, slow, man-scent-laden breath. How had she not been aware of this before? Nixon had become more attractive and sexy and exciting in the time since she'd gone into labour. The tension gripping her eased off, replaced with a different kind of tightness. Sexy and inappropriate in the middle of an emergency department.

Looking around, she found something innocuous to say to quieten her body. 'I think Abbie's bringing Grace in today for you all to meet her. As long as she's not grizzly, which she hardly ever is.'

'I can't wait.' Steph smiled as she picked up a folder. 'We had a collection and put a basket of baby things together for them.'

The buzzer announced the arrival of their first critical patient, giving Emma an excuse to look away from those watchful faces so she could exhale and quickly swipe at a couple of tears.

'Emma, you're with me and Nixon until you're needed in triage. You can roll bandages.' Steph winked before handing out jobs to everyone.

Brushing her hands down the front of her top, Emma said, 'Right, let's get this show on the road.'

Nixon stood in front of her, his eyes tracking her hands on their trip down her belly to her thighs. 'About Sunday...'

'I'm sorry. I was out of line.' She waited for him to raise his head so she could eyeball him. But when he did she got sidetracked by the heat blazing out at her, and she forgot what she'd been going to say. 'We work together, we don't need to know the nitty-gritty about each other.'

His eyes widened with relief. 'You understand. That's good. I'd hate anything to come between us that interfered with work.'

Not what she'd meant at all. Her stomach clenched painfully around a lump of disappointment. 'It won't. I love my job and won't put it in jeopardy over something you don't want to talk about.' So much for backing off. She was protecting herself, her feelings, her heart. 'Here's our first patient.'

Soon she was in triage, time flying by in capsules of broken bones, fevers, chest pains, a probable concussion. Emma took readings and obs, made notes, reassured patients and sent them straight to ED or back to the waiting room according to the seriousness of their situation.

Emma wanted work to be a distraction from everything going on in her head, and she got it. When knockoff time after only four hours rocked around she was shattered. 'Hate to admit it,' she told Nixon.

His eyebrows rose in a quaint fashion. 'There's a surprise. Time you headed home to those walls you so want to destroy. Oh, what have we here?' He inclined his head at Santa Claus being wheeled in.

Emma chuckled. 'Been climbing too many chimneys, Mr Rodgers?' So much for going home. She wanted to help this man she'd known all her life if she could.

'Get away with you, girl. My wooden horse fell over as I was handing out the presents at the primary school.'

'So you were Santa at Rosie's school today. Rosie was that excited this morning I couldn't get her to eat any breakfast.' Emma found scissors to cut the red pants away from what appeared to be a very swollen ankle. 'Who's taken your place on the sleigh?' Disappointed kids were not an option.

'One of the teachers made up some story about Santa's helpers being busy so he'd do the job. The kids accepted that, probably thinking they'd miss out on their presents if they didn't.' No remorse showed in Mr Claus's face, just amusement at what a silly old coot he'd been, and flicks of pain whenever he moved his ankle, which he did too often.

'Are you always this restless?' Emma asked.

'Me? Restless? Like I've ants in me pants, that's me. Been like this for a while now. Night time's the worst. Wife keeps threatening to move me to the spare bedroom.'

Nixon raised his head. 'I'll check a few things while we've got you here. Any numbness anywhere? Walking tall or stooped?'

'No numbness, can't always straighten fully first thing in the morning. Getting old, that's all.' Behind the smiley face worry flickered, disappeared fast.

Was Nixon thinking Parkinson's? Emma shuddered, mentally crossing her fingers for this lovely old man, and plumped the pillows ready for him once they got him onto the bed. 'There you go, Mr Rodgers. Let's get you up here so Dr Wright can examine you thoroughly.'

'This is where I take over.' Nixon placed a hand under his patient's arm. 'I'm not having Emma flinging you over her shoulder this morning. Can you call us an orderly, Emma? Santa needs to go to Radiology. I'll give him the once-over while you're doing that. And then it's time you clocked off.'

'On it. You take it easy, Mr Rodgers.' The brazenness was dipping rapidly, the man looking more and more like a wizened old guy. 'Speaking of your wife, want me to call her and let her know how you're filling your afternoon?'

'No can do. She's in Auckland visiting the grandkids and doing the Christmas shopping. Bet I'll need a second job to cover that.' His smile was wistful.

'I can talk to her for you,' Nixon added his piece. 'Or you can if you're feeling up to it.'

'No, leave it for now. Get me sorted first.'

Emma glanced at Nixon, saw her concern reflected in his thoughtful gaze. Something wasn't sitting right, but if their patient didn't want his wife to know he was here then there was nothing they could do about it.

'Orderly,' he murmured, a slight lift to those full lips. 'Then home.'

Flip, flop. Her stomach did its new dance routine as she hurried away. How could one man's lips do this to her stomach? Lips she hadn't kissed, or touched, or any damned thing. *Lie down, hormones. You're on the way out, remember?*

Nixon pumped his legs hard, the cycle eating up the forty-five kilometres out to Glenorchy. Sweat streamed off him, moulding his spandex shirt to his skin. Salt stung his eyes and plastered his hair to his scalp under the helmet. To his left, wavelets on Lake Wakatipu glittered in the late afternoon sun. High above, two paragliders winged their way over the water.

Idyllic. That summed up Queenstown and its surroundings. Idyllic. The best move he'd ever made.

A car sped past him, the wing mirror a whisker off his elbow. He raised his fist and vented uncharacteristically loudly and rudely. The driver couldn't hear and he doubted there were people hiding in the bushes alongside the road to note his profanities.

But damn, did cussing make him feel better. Lifted some of the weight bearing down on him from the moment Emma walked into the department that morning. He hadn't slept a wink last night for thinking about that aborted conversation she'd tried to get started. Why would he consider telling her what made him tick when they wouldn't be going anywhere with it? He'd got by for thirty-one years without discussing the day his family died, so what would be gained by opening that can of worms now? A sinking feeling was going on in his gut. Like if he didn't open up his life would remain in this holding pattern. If ever there was a person he might be able to talk to, it was Emma. She'd understand what had driven him to withdraw from loving people. Wouldn't she? She'd been to hell and back and was still a very loving woman.

Pump, pump. He was pushing as hard as he'd ever done, needing his muscles to ache and his head to shut up. And Emma damned Hayes still managed to sneak in and wave at him. As if she were saying, 'Don't ignore me, I'm not going away.'

Yeah, got that in spades. We work together, and we both need our jobs, love our work, won't be moving out of the department any time soon. He had to find a way to stop thinking about her all the damned time.

Push harder. The body wasn't complaining enough yet.

The first outlying houses in Glenorchy came into view as Nixon sped around a long, sweeping corner. He glanced at his watch, pride lifting his mood. Not bad.

Then his phone chirped and dropped his mood back to ground zero.

Ignore it.

Except he was head of the emergency department. That wasn't an option. He braked hard, the cycle sliding in the loose gravel on the edge of the road as he skidded to a stop.

'Hello?' If he sounded grumpy whoever was annoying him might go away.

'Cameron here. Your Mr Rodgers's ankle is all put back together with some shiny steel. Yanky's paying him a visit tomorrow once he's fully recovered from the surgery.'

Yanky being the resident neurologist. 'You agree with me?'

'That our man might have Parkinson's? Yep, afraid I do,' Cameron confirmed.

'That'd knock him off his sleigh if he hadn't already come a cropper.'

'Quite a character, isn't he?'

Nixon asked, 'So what's up?' Cameron wouldn't have phoned to talk about their patient unless it was urgent.

'I'm knocking off. Feel up to a beer?'

Nixon's mouth watered instantly. He couldn't think of anything better with all the fluid pouring off his body at the moment. 'Could certainly use one. Only problem is, I'm out at Glenorchy—on the bike.'

He hesitated. He didn't often drop in for a beer with the guys, but cycling wasn't banishing Emma from his head. 'Where will you be?'

'The Thirsty Pig.'

'Put one up for me in forty-five. Pick an outside table.

I won't be smelling sweet.' Nixon stuffed the phone back in its pouch and took off for his destination, eager to get back to town and that cold beer. Just what a bloke needed after a bit of exercise in this heat. And meeting up with the guys gave him a strange sense of belonging as he spun around the end of the road and aimed for Queenstown. Not strange, more like comfortable. A welcome distraction from Emma. Damned good, in fact. It had taken nearly a year, but finally he was getting to know his colleagues outside work, pushing aside the usual hesitation he had about getting too pally with people. Queenstown was working its magic, drawing him in and showing there was more to life than being a great specialist and an aloof relative or friend. Was it Queenstown's magic or Emma's?

The front wheel wobbled dangerously and he fought to straighten it up without taking a dive onto the road. Pedalling hard didn't stop other questions popping up. Had he learned to be reticent from Henry? That'd been nagging him for days.

Focus, man. There's a beer at the end of this. Think of nothing else.

'Get that down your throat.' Cameron handed him a condensation-coated bottle moments after he leaned his bike against the outside wall and whipped off his helmet to join the surgeon and Yanky at an outdoor table.

'That's pure nectar,' he said appreciatively after pouring a third of the liquid down his throat. 'It's hot out there.'

'Only if you ride like a madman. Why do you do it?' Cameron asked. 'There're lots of ways of keeping fit and having fun without going hell for leather on two skinny tyres that don't look strong enough to hold your weight.'

'He's taken up kite flying,' Yanky got in before Nixon could come up with an acerbic reply.

The beer he'd been about to swallow snagged in the back of his throat. 'I what?'

'He what?' Cameron also spluttered, but then *he* began laughing. 'Kites? As in those things that are tied to string and lift off the ground only to crash back again, often getting broken in the process? I know I suggested tiddly-winks, but kites? For real?'

Yanky had plenty more to offer. 'There was a little girl attached to the other end of the string.'

Think I can hear a phone call coming in. At the very least a text saying I'm urgently needed back at work, or any damned place but sitting here with these two come-dians.

'Knew there was a reason I didn't do drinks with the guys.'

'Can't handle the pressure?' Cameron gave him a shrewd nod. 'Would that have been a little girl with dark curls and a stunning mother?'

'Shut up, man.'

Through a roar of laughter, Cameron said, 'I like it when people take my advice.' He drained his beer. 'Your round.'

'Your advice, your orders.' Nixon stood up, debating whether to escape or buy some beers. The beer won out. He was parched. Also, if he left here then he'd just go home and for once his swanky house wasn't at all appeal-ing. It was empty, cold—lonely. Digging his wallet out, he headed inside to the bar.

The guys weren't done with him. The moment his back-side hit the seat he got a grilling.

'Emma Hayes, eh?' was Cameron's opening shot. The man sounded smug.

'Been seeing her long?' Yanky wasn't any better.

'I am not seeing her.' Then what the hell had he been doing following her down to the park after Abbie had told him where to find her? Taking her pulse to see if she was ready to return to work? If any pulse had needed reading then it would've been his. It had been out of kilter for days, starting when he took Emma home to the family farm out in Gibbston Valley. Or had it begun its crazy erratic beat earlier when he'd sat beside her hospital bed while she'd slept? Or back on the day she'd sobbed out her fears on his shoulder? The day he'd tried to pull away, and hadn't quite managed.

'Why ever not? Emma's a great lady. A good match for you.'

The beer soured in his mouth. Coming here was a bad idea. 'I'm not a good match for her.' He made to push up onto his feet.

Cameron held up his hand. 'Sorry, mate, just ribbing you. But for the record, I think you are. She's got history that needs patience and caring and understanding.'

'She does and all—from someone more settled than me.'

'I hear her family didn't run you off the property last week.' That smirk didn't suit Cameron. 'That's got to be a thumbs-up, if ever there was one.'

Seemed nothing was private around this town. So he'd redirect the discussion, find out what he could. 'You ever meet the ex?' One thing he'd learned about this town was everyone knew everyone if they'd grown up here.

'Stitched him back together once after a brawl he got into and lost.'

'Hope you went easy on the pain relief.'

'No comment. It was no surprise he died fighting. He was getting more and more out of control by the time Emma's family ran him out of town. She did well getting away when she did.'

Nixon's heart died. Emma had been abused. He'd known

that, but was Cameron intimating more had gone on? 'Just as well the man is dead.'

'I'll drink to that.' Yanky nodded. 'Guess it's my round.'

He mightn't like how the conversation had started, nor where it had gone, but Nixon was glad he'd joined these two. He was unused to letting his guard down, but they'd taken the choice out of his hands and he wasn't offended or angry. It felt good to talk about Emma and learn she had so much support. Not that she'd ever ask for help from just anybody, but that it was there was good. The upside of smaller towns, he supposed.

He was released from feeling he had to protect her when there were already so many people on her side. Men like these two, her family, they'd been there at the worst. He was new on the patch. But damned if he could deny this gnawing need to guard her back—and that was even with the ex being deceased.

Just another person to do his best for. Like his patients. And colleagues.

Believe that and he'd believe a newborn baby could climb Ben Lomond.

CHAPTER SEVEN

EMMA DRAGGED HERSELF out to the car, pinged the locks and opened a window to let the heat abate a bit before she drove home. Thank goodness for Fridays. This particular one had taken forever to get here, three four hour shifts, but at last she'd knocked off work with the weekend ahead to do very little.

Everything had caught up with her, big time. Knowing she'd have to work through her feelings was one thing. She'd expected them to be all about having a baby for Abbie, and the emptiness she'd feel.

But she was being held back by other, alien feelings. Wants. Needs. Hopes. Call them what she liked, they involved her future and how different it could be. Bringing up Rosie on her own, without someone special to share the everyday dross and fun, was plain hard work at times. More and more she wanted to reach out and grab the fulfilment of those wants, needs and hopes. Those were the aspirations she'd grown up with and they were revisiting, teasing, tormenting her. She'd sworn she did not want to settle down with a man again, then along came Grace and she was losing touch with that idea. Knew she'd been wrong. Slowly, slowly, pinch by pinch, the idea of love and more children with someone special was making itself felt. Uncomfortable. Disconcerting. Worrying.

No wonder she wasn't sleeping at night. Nor during the day, which had to be a plus for her patients at least. She slid onto the driver's seat and tipped her head back on the headrest.

'Emma, wait. You okay?'

Emma jerked upright at the sound of Nixon's question. He looked harried, breathing fast, concern locking onto her. 'I'm fine.'

He shook his head. 'This is me you're trying to fool. It's not working.'

No surprise there. Dredging up a smile, she acknowledged, 'I came back too early, but what else was I supposed to do? Staying at home all day every day would've done my head in. Thank goodness for weekends.'

'Which is why I'm here, though maybe I should leave you to get some rest over the coming days.'

He had plans that involved her? She sat up straighter. 'Doing something interesting can be as beneficial as resting. In fact, resting doesn't work—too much climbs into my skull to annoy the hell out of me. I need a diversion.'

'So what are you doing tomorrow morning? You and Rosie.'

'Rosie's at a sleepover at her friend's tonight and staying all day for a birthday party. Me? Washing, vacuuming, getting in the groceries. Exciting stuff.' She added a smile to show he wasn't meant to feel sorry for her. This was how her weekends unfolded; nothing new there.

'Do you like flying?'

What was this? An opportunity to go somewhere out of town on a hot date? Hardly. This was Nixon. 'I don't mind it. Jumbos leave me cold but they get me where I want to go in a hurry.'

'Small planes, as in a four-seater.' He was relaxing now,

his airways back to normal speed. 'As in a scenic flight around Milford Sound.'

'You're kidding, right?' She'd grown up here and not once had she flown around the area just to look down on her home town. Her blood began to hum with anticipation. This could be fun. Especially if Nixon was part of the package. Hey, Nixon was a package—a sexy one. *Stop it.*

'Why would I be joking?'

'The smallest flying machine I've been in was a Robinson helicopter for my twentieth birthday and that was in the Abel Tasman National Park. I've never flown in a small, fixed-wing plane.' Judging by the determination in his stance, he was definitely serious. 'I'd love to go.'

'I'll swing by to pick you up at eight tomorrow. I've checked the weather and it looks superb.'

'No bumps.' The hum was raising its tempo, her blood no longer sluggish, her limbs tightening back to normal. Nixon had asked her to go flying with him. As if they were used to doing things together out of work hours. She could get used to this. 'Do I need to bring anything other than my phone for photos?'

'A light jacket. It will be cooler around the mountains. Those bumps? You're not a nervous flyer, are you?'

'Nope.'

Nixon stepped back. 'I'll see you then. Shame Rosie can't join us.'

'Yes, she'd have loved it.' But Emma would be happy having Nixon to herself for a few hours.

'Emma? What are you doing later since you're not picking up Rosie?'

'Going for a power walk along the lake.' Instant decision. Didn't want to sound completely pathetic with nothing to do this afternoon as well as tomorrow. Anyway, it was time to start getting a little bit fit again. 'Less emphasis on the power and more on the walk,' she added for clarity. Couldn't have him thinking she'd be doing something close to a run.

'Want some company?'

'Yes.' It came out before she could change her mind.

His gorgeous mouth twitched. 'Meet you about three-thirty at Steamer Wharf?'

'Sounds good.' She turned the ignition, keen to get away before he realised what he'd suggested. What just happened? Taking her flying tomorrow was amazing, and now he was joining her for a walk. After their disagreement at the park, she'd never expected he'd want to spend time alone with her again. Did that mean she was forgiven her deep and personal questions? Or he'd come to realise he'd overreacted and was trying to apologise without saying the sorry word? Guys did struggle with that.

Funny, but she didn't quite trust this alien sense of anticipation for some fun, was almost waiting for it to crash and burn. A shiver rattled through her. Dumb thing to think when she was going flying tomorrow.

'Let go the past,' commented Abbie when Emma barrelled through her open door minutes later to tell her her news.

'I thought I had.' Not completely, as it happened. 'But I know I want to.'

'Thoughts from then are bound to pop up when you start dating again. But shove them away, forget it all. Seriously, that's the way forward. Chin up, game face on, and go have a blast.' One look and Abbie had understood her confusion.

'Who said anything about a date?'

'Didn't we have this conversation a while back? Only it was you saying it about me and Callum.'

Emma felt her mouth drop. 'True, but—'

Abbie grinned. 'But it's different because it's you and Nixon and neither of you wants a relationship. I get that. So go have time with your boss and enjoy yourself.' She held her arms out for a hug. 'It really is that simple, Bestie. I know cos it worked for me.'

'Only after heartache,' Emma added as she succumbed to the hug.

'Good things are worth waiting for, and you, my friend, have been waiting a darned long time.' Abbie dropped her arms as Grace's cry reached them from down the hall. 'Someone's extra hungry today. You had lunch yet?'

'No. What've you got?'

'Bread and cheese. Creating delectable meals seems to have gone out the window. But it is fresh bread from the bakery.'

'I'll put sandwiches together while you satisfy Grace.' And by the time she'd slapped some bread and cheese together, hopefully her boobs would have returned to quiet, not this aching throb going on from the moment she heard the first cry. At least they'd had a morning off from the aches that still blasted her intermittently. Not a huge change in that since the birth, but it had to be coming soon. Fingers crossed.

Emma stretched her legs out on Abbie's couch and yawned. 'Why did I say I was going for a walk? I can hardly keep my eyes open.' She'd spent the afternoon with her friend, chilling out, having baby cuddles and handing Grace back with no difficulty. Emma didn't for a moment believe she was out of the woods, she knew there were still plenty of difficult moments ahead, but this time had helped.

'So, are you going to phone and cancel?'

Emma fixed her friend with a glare. 'As if.'

'Then move your butt, girl. You're wasting minutes you

should be using to drag your running gear on and redo your make-up before driving into town early so you're not late for your not date.'

'See ya.' Emma leapt up, and instantly regretted the hurried movement. 'Ouch.' She rubbed her stomach before rushing out and across to her apartment where she rammed the key in the door lock, or tried to. She missed and had to slow down.

Abbie's laughter followed her inside and down the hall to her bedroom where she tugged a drawer open so fast it came right out and hit the floor with a thud. Snatching up her running pants, she squeezed into them before searching for a loose tee shirt. No way could she wear her fitted sports top yet. Boobs and tummy too big. A complete refresh of make-up before snatching up shoes, phone, keys, a cash card in case they went for a drink afterwards. Expecting too much? Probably, but in for a walk, in for a drink. And if not, then she'd buy a takeaway to eat at home later. On her own.

Emma was doing light stretches when Nixon walked onto Steamer Wharf, and he had to pause. Sports pants fitted snug around her curvy butt, and when she leaned over to touch her toes the baggy shirt rose above her waist to expose creamy skin on her back.

Zap. A heat ray got him. In places he'd prefer not to acknowledge. Not that he denied his masculinity, but this was Emma. Emma as in friend, nurse, mother, and surrogate mother.

The oath he uttered was for his ears only. Who was he fooling here? The woman in front of him with her amazing body that not even pregnancy had turned heavy and cumbersome had found a way into places in his heart he'd firmly believed didn't exist. She hadn't entered in one hit.

No, this was Emma with her sweet nature and those fears that rocked her from time to time, with her generous heart and sadness that sometimes dulled the greenest of green eyes. She'd snuck up on him when he wasn't looking.

When he was avidly avoiding involvement might be closer to the truth. He could still avoid that. Forewarned was supposedly forearmed.

'Hey, you joining me?' the object of his desire asked, hands now firmly on her curvy hips.

Lots of curves going on here. Curves he'd only begun noticing recently. Curves he now wanted to clasp in his hands so he could lean in for a kiss.

Shut down, Nixon, or you're not going on any walk.

His body was sitting up to attention, and would bring him a load of unwanted attention if he didn't haul on the brakes. 'Sure,' he managed and lifted a leg to the bollard on the edge of the wharf. Leaning over, hands stretched to his ankle, he counted to ten before releasing the tension in his muscles. In most of his muscles. Not all were playing the game.

'What kept you?' Emma had strolled closer. Too damned close. 'Couldn't find your top-of-the-range outfit?'

'Cheeky.' Twisting slightly sideways, he managed to swap legs on the bollard without presenting his dilemma. 'Why are we walking when that's obviously running get-up you're wearing?'

'Not sure the body's quite ready for a run yet.'

He'd figured, but needed a conversation filler while he got everything under control. 'You ran before you got pregnant?'

'Most days I'd go out, often with Abbie. She likes to race whoever she's with, and always wins too, damn her.' Emma swigged some water from her bottle before clipping it on her belt. 'Ready?'

No. 'As I'll ever be.' Things were settling down. Hopefully hard-paced walking would finish the job. Hard? Gulp. 'Let's go,' he growled.

It was slow going through the tourists crowding the wharf and the extended areas where cafés and bars beckoned, but once they were beyond the town centre Emma upped the paced, striding out as if nothing could hold her back.

'Take it easy. No point in overdoing the exercise when you're already knackered.' Nixon matched her step for step, pulling back on the pace in an attempt to slow her down, happy to be beside her until they hit the narrow path further out of town. 'How far are we going?'

'Sunshine Bay, maybe up the hill, down the other side and probably back to town. Not far, but I'm thinking since it's been a while I'll quickly run out of steam.' She doubted she had the energy for more. '"I'll re-evaluate when we reach the lake road again. Do you run or walk much?'

'Cycling takes up most of my spare time. I started snowboarding last winter too.'

'You like seat-of-your-pants sports.' Not a question. 'I don't understand people wanting to take huge risks all the time. Are you an adrenalin junkie?'

The second person to pull him up on this in a week. Did he need to re-evaluate his approach to life now Emma was getting under his skin? He'd have to if their friendship developed into something stronger. 'I guess, though I don't see it as risky, more a way of totally focusing on something to banish all the minutiae in my head. Being distracted by wondering who's going to fill the roster next week or did I pay the power bill is dangerous. Getting injured is the last thing I want.'

'It's your go-to place when you need a break.' Emma shot him a speculative look.

'Yes.'

'Have you always done that?'

Since he was six. 'Mostly.'

Her mouth flattened. 'Right.'

Back to Sunday and that argument without even trying. He wanted to head back to town, but he hadn't got to being head of an emergency department by being a coward. So if he wasn't one then he should be opening up to Emma, explaining a little of what made him tick. But that meant exposing his fears. If his body hadn't already quietened down from the heated moments back at the wharf it certainly would now. This was scary stuff. Something deep at the back of his mind was nagging him to let go, to see where it took him. He'd already worked out Emma would be the only person he'd even consider exposing his inner demons to—if he got brave enough.

Deep breath. One, two, three. 'I lost my parents and brother when I was a child. Doing extreme things like climbing the tallest trees in the bush backing onto my uncle's property became my way of denying the mental images of them in the plane crash that killed them. I guess I haven't stopped.' The words rushed out so fast she probably didn't hear them properly.

Emma halted, tipped her head back to stare up at him, nothing but compassion in those beautiful eyes. 'Plane crash? Jeez, Nixon, that's terrible. I mean, you were a little boy. How did you deal with that?' Nothing wrong with her hearing, then. 'Sorry, I guess you've just told me how. But it's hard to comprehend what life must've been like for you. At least you had your uncle.'

'Plus older cousins.' His tone was flat, and that guilt he got when thinking about them rose. 'Henry took me in and raised me until I left for university.' His elbow nudged her to start walking again. 'Better than being submerged in the welfare system.' *And that, Nixon Wright, is ingratitude in full colour.* 'My uncle never hesitated when the news broke, and I was well looked after.'

'But they weren't *your* family.'

'Not in the way I wanted.' He hadn't been loved. Or so he'd believed, but seeing how Emma loved her daughter without being too effusive he began wondering if he'd been wrong. She wasn't loud about her feelings for Rosie, but nor was she silent. Because she hadn't lost anyone close? Uncle Henry had lost his wife, his cousins their mother, before his sister died in the plane crash, yet never hesitated to take a lost little boy into the family. Henry would've known what he was going through. That didn't mean he could be open and loving while dealing with a load of grief and his own two distressed children. No wonder the man was closed to everyone. It had become his way of coping.

Like mine?

'You were afraid to love them in case they disappeared overnight.' Emma saw it clear as day.

Loving anyone *was* terrifying. What if he lost them? Just because Henry didn't profess love to all and sundry didn't mean he didn't feel it. Henry would've been grieving when he'd opened his home for his sister's terrified son. No wonder love hadn't come Nixon's way in an obvious display of affection, the way his parents had shown him. If he'd hurt his uncle and cousins by thinking they didn't care then he had a lot of ground to recover.

Now she understood the determination and despair in Nixon's eyes when he'd worked on the little boy's mother in the car accident. Emma's heart cracked open some more for the little boy who'd been Nixon. He hadn't wanted the other child to suffer for the rest of his life—as he had. He'd have done anything to keep the mother alive.

Emma kept up her power walking—very little power, she grudgingly admitted, yet her lungs were burning. They headed up the hill past the international hotel and into the housing area. If she stopped she'd give into the clawing need to wrap Nixon in a hug. A hug to show him he wasn't alone. And that might signal the end of whatever they had going on between them today. He would back away. Again. And again. She wasn't ready to risk that. She wanted more time with him, more getting to know him.

When he was talking about losing his family, his words had been terse, biting on the pain, saying in no uncertain terms he hated discussing it and she was not to start pressing him for more. No problem on that score. Guilt tightened her muscles, her skin, for pushing him so hard last Sunday. No matter that she hadn't known what was behind his three-date rule and risky lifestyle outside work. She shouldn't have pushed him as hard as she had on Sunday. Kind of explained why he was a doctor, saving people when he hadn't been able to save his family. How did anyone cope with the sudden news that the people he loved the most were gone, that he was never going to see them again? No more hugs, kisses, laughter. As for a six-year-old comprehending it—impossible.

But Nixon *had* told her. A horrific accident had stolen so much from him. A plane crash. 'I don't understand how you're okay with flying.'

'Learning to fly was another tactic to put myself out there, face the same odds my family faced.'

'You're a pilot?' The words spluttered across her lips. 'You're flying us tomorrow?'

'Yes.' He watched her as he asked, 'That all right with you?'

'Of course. It never occurred to me.' But it made perfect sense. This was Nixon after all. 'I presumed there'd be someone else at the controls.'

'You can pull out.' He gave a strained laugh that said he'd be hurt if she did.

'What? Miss out on winging over Milford Sound? Sorry, Nixon, but you're stuck with me for tomorrow morning at least.' Longer if you're interested. She nudged him forward, walking behind him on the narrow pathway. Any excuse to check out that sexy butt and those long, muscular legs sending her heart into palpitations. Nixon was no longer just a sometimes friend, or any kind of friend, but a man she was looking at very differently. Where was that going to get her? Nowhere unless he lightened up some more with her. Or maybe it was time she showed him a little of how she felt.

Whoa. Her heart rate lifted, sending her blood zinging around her veins. Tell Nixon she cared about him? Really, really liked him? Lay her heart on the line? No. He wasn't ready to hear any of that. Was she ready for this? She wasn't sure, but it seemed she also didn't want to slip back into her box and hide away from life any more.

Now what was she going to do?

Nixon stumbled, righted himself and waited for Emma to catch up. He let her retake the lead to set the pace. No longer walking very quickly, she looked thoughtful.

His hormones liked that it was slower, giving him an opportunity to admire that sweet backside that had him in a lather far too often. He shouldn't be looking, let alone thinking about those curves. But they were meant to be appreciated. They were also a wonderful diversion from the revelation that he might've been wrong about Henry. He cringed with embarrassment. He'd held himself aloof from the only family he had. Did his uncle understand why he'd done that? His cousins? What did they feel about his attitude to their father when in fact he'd been given everything he needed to grow up into a successful man?

Instead he watched Emma, ignored the guilty ache these unasked-for questions were causing. He would deal with it in good time. Nothing he could do right this minute anyhow.

After a silent ten minutes they reached the road back at the bottom of the hill and Nixon turned towards town. Emma was tired but quite capable of seeing the challenge in doing another round. 'I'm ready for a beer.' Hopefully she didn't see through his attempt to head her off.

A light red hue coloured her cheeks, and not from excursion. Running a hand over her head, she shook her head. 'Definitely out of shape. I'm going to have to put in a lot more effort, just not for a few weeks.'

So she wasn't trying to prove a point. Got that wrong, along with lots of things about Emma. He did know there was nothing wrong with her shape. Nothing at all. 'Does that mean we'll stop for a drink when we reach the wharf?'

She looked at him over the top of her sunglasses, which had slid down her nose. 'Try stopping me.' Her tongue did a lap of her lips. 'I'm picturing a cold bottle of beer already.'

'Then let's hustle because I've got the same image.' Along with another one involving that tongue on his fevered skin.

The little pub hidden away down a back street was heaving with locals when they squeezed their way inside to the bar.

'Looks like we'll be better off out in the garden when we get these.' Emma looked around. 'Can't hear myself think in here.' Her eyes were wide with happiness.

'You don't get out often enough.'

'Tell me something I don't know.'

The wistful twinge in her voice didn't dampen her pleasure beaming out at him, making him feel oddly pleased. There'd been a moment back there on the hill when he'd have sworn Emma had been about to hug him, before she'd turned away, cutting further conversation and that maybe hug. He'd been grateful and disappointed. If she'd wound her arms around him he would not have been able to resist, would've held on tight, and a little bit more of his barricade would've cracked open. Dangerous. Gulp. To be that close to her, to let someone know his history and understand him, hell, but that would be wonderful. A release. Relief. If he had that, who knew what the future could hold?

Getting in deeper here, Nixon.

'You going to stand there having a conversation with yourself all night?' Emma winked over the rim of her bottle, her elbows wedged on the top of the high wooden bench they were using.

He found her a smile. 'Thought you couldn't hear a thing.'

'It's way better out here.' She swallowed a mouthful of her drink. 'You moved to Queenstown from Dunedin, right?'

He nodded. Where was this headed?

'Had you come up here very often before?'

'Of course. The mountain biking is awesome, and the skiing is right up there with the best in the country.'

'Of course,' she repeated his words with a smile. 'The adventure capital of New Zealand is a perfect playground for you. Reckon this is a permanent move or will you up stakes and move away some time? Get a job in a bigger hospital?'

It might be a question people asked each other every day, but for Nixon it felt loaded. Fraught with road bumps.

'Queenstown suits me. We get more trauma injuries per capita than anywhere else in the country and those are my specialty so why leave? But who knows? A fabulous offer might come along that I'd be stupid to turn down. Though I doubt there's too much out there I'd trade for what I've got here.'

'Not a big city guy, then?'

'Not even for holidays.'

'Damn. I always planned on going to LA and the fun park when Rosie was old enough.'

What did that have to do with him? 'Never been there, and can't say it's on my list, but then I haven't had a little girl to factor into the equation.' What would it be like to go to a theme park with Emma and her daughter? There'd be lots of laughter for one.

'What's your favourite colour?'

A laugh bubbled up and out. 'Green.' As in the colour of her eyes. 'What's yours?'

'Haven't got one.' She grinned.

'Okay, what's your favourite breakfast?'

'Pancakes with bacon, bananas and maple syrup.' One eyebrow rose. 'You?'

'The whole works: bacon, eggs, hash browns, mushrooms, et cetera. Holiday destination apart from that one for Rosie?'

'Wanaka, staying in the family beach house. Summer wouldn't be the same without going there.'

That was something he hadn't had. There'd been a rumpty little shack on the West Coast his dad went to for fishing and hunting, occasionally taking the family with him, but it had been sold when the estate was wound up and the proceeds invested for his future. 'Sounds wonderful.'

'It is. As of now you are officially invited to come and

stay with my lot over the summer. Bring your bike and swim shorts, beer and an open mind, and you'll have a load of fun.'

'Seriously?' Of course it was serious. Emma didn't do things by half measures. 'Invitation accepted. I am already looking forward to it.'

And to spending more time with you away from the hospital.

CHAPTER EIGHT

EMMA STARED OUT of the Aero Club window onto the air-field beyond where planes were tied down in neat rows. Past the terminal, an international flight was lining up in preparation for take-off. Beyond the airport boundary Coronet Peak rose into the sky, dominating the scenery with its sheer rock faces and snow-capped peaks.

Excitement made her squirm. Last night's beer and pizza had been a world away from her usual Friday night, but this was out of the park.

'Ready?' Nixon called across the room from where he and the flying instructor had been talking over weather and flight paths.

She'd tuned out minutes ago, but now they were about to go flying. Looking up at the man who was becoming more important to her by the day, she nodded. 'Are you?'

He grinned, not a tense muscle in sight. 'Always when it comes to flying.' Piloting a small plane must be his best place, his most comfortable environment. If that grin was anything to go by then she'd join him at every opportunity. It sparkled with heat, was filled with cheeky temptation, so that right about now she should be getting very afraid. Because damned if she wasn't falling into the pool that was Nixon. What lay ahead for them? Patience was usually her way—except when it came to Nixon and she wanted to rush through the tape, see where they arrived and what their future held. 'Settle down,' she warned, walking beside the man tempting her heart.

In one hand Nixon held something like a large compass, a map and a key. In his other hand he held…hers.

Did he know what he'd done? Had winding his fingers through hers been an intentional move? Or was he so focused on preparing for their flight that he'd done it without thought? Meaning that he accepted her as a part of his life in some way?

Emma kept quiet, tried not to squeeze her hand a little bit tighter to feel his strength, his long fingers between hers. She was holding hands with Nixon. Her feet danced. The sky was breathtakingly blue. The air clear and crackling. She'd got it bad.

They crossed to a plane with its wings on top. 'All the better to see the view,' Nixon explained as he checked fuel, props and wiggled the rudder, explaining everything as he went. 'Right, up you get.' He held the door open for her, his other hand on her elbow as she scrambled aboard, his fingers leaving pads of heat on her skin.

When Nixon joined her from the other side he passed over a set of headphones. 'We can talk to each other through these. Be aware that at times I'll be talking to the control tower.'

Belted up and headphones clamped around her ears, Emma watched Nixon run through pre-flight checks, talk to the tower, and then off with the brakes and the plane rolled forward. 'We're away,' she said more to herself than Nixon.

'Sure are,' he came back.

The moment they were airborne, the plane leant sideways as Nixon brought it around to head directly towards the Remarkables. 'Where are we going?' she managed in a semi-normal voice.

'We're getting out of the approach path because there's a commercial flight on finals. I'll turn as soon as the tower advises me to.'

Oh. Good. Great, even. 'Do you follow instructions the whole time?'

'No. I've filed our flight outline and before take-off I told traffic control what height I intend flying at. I'll be informed of other light aircraft within my range so that I can look out for them, otherwise I'm in charge.'

Emma laughed. 'Typical.'

'Sit back and relax. Enjoy the unfolding scenery. Drinks and meals won't be served on this flight, but we can make up for that when we get back.' Nixon listened intently to the controller and finally made a slow right-hand turn.

A small sigh of relief escaped Emma. All very well being told aiming directly for mountains was okay, but changing direction was far more encouraging. Staring out and down, she gasped. 'It's so pretty from up here.' Whenever she'd flown out of Queenstown on a commercial flight the plane had been up and gone so fast she'd never appreciated her town from above.

'We'll head to Mount Aspiring first,' Nixon told her.

'Cool.' The famous mountain peak looked colder than cool when they reached it. 'Those guys are mad.' She pointed to two climbers working their way up a ridge near the top. 'What if they fall?'

'They'd be history. Looks like they've got all the gear though. They must've set out about three this morning to be that close to the summit.'

Bonkers. 'Why risk your life for a view from the top when you can fly up here?'

'It's a calculated risk if you prepare for the worst, have

the right equipment, take note of the weather and act accordingly.' Nixon flew around the mountain. 'There's a lot of fun to be had if you take adventure seriously.'

Damn but zooming around the sky in a little machine with Nixon beside her was exciting. It wouldn't take much to give into the swamping need to kiss him and share the fizz in her blood, so she worked at going with the joy and beauty of it all instead. 'This is amazing.' Right now she was going to catch a rainbow and pretend she was as carefree as she felt. Because—because maybe her dreams could come true.

'Want to have a go?'

'What? At flying?' When Nixon nodded she shivered. 'Is it safe?'

'I'm not getting out,' he teased. 'Put your hands on your controls like I'm holding mine. I've got everything covered.'

'Funny how there are two sets of everything.'

'One for the instructor and one for the pupil.'

Gripping the controls, she said, 'What next?'

'Hold the plane level by keeping the controls where they are.' Removing his hands, he watched her sitting rigid for fear of moving the controls even a fraction. Putting one hand back in place, he said, 'I'm holding lightly. To make the plane go down and faster push forward slowly, not abruptly or too far.'

Her heart in her throat, she hesitated. *Wimp.* 'Right, onto it.' *Deep breath, push forward an incy-wincy bit.* Nothing happened. More pressure and suddenly the nose of the plane was dropping. She jerked backwards, bringing the controls back to where they'd been when she'd first touched them.

Nixon laid his hand over hers, gave her a gentle squeeze, sending her heart winging into orbit. 'You're doing fine.

Look, I'll show you.' When he pushed forward the plane began heading down on a slow line. 'To go up you pull back, again, not abruptly. You need to add a little more power when going upwards.'

Up they came, down they went. Up down in gentle movements until Emma started laughing with glee. 'This is awesome. I can't believe I'm flying a plane.'

'Next you'll be taking lessons and getting your own licence.' Nixon high fived her. 'Right, I'm taking over now.'

Relinquishing the controls meant letting go of a different life, an opportunity to do something for herself. A glimpse into a world of adventure she'd never experienced or believed she needed. 'No matter what, I'm still a mother and a nurse with all the necessary commitments. Nothing can change that.'

'You can be whatever you choose if you want it enough,' Nixon said.

Did I say that out loud? Must've.

'You think it's that easy?' Then why wasn't he letting go of his issues, becoming a man with love in his life? *Gulp. I didn't say* that *out loud, did I?*

'No, I don't. Just quoting someone who probably never had a problem in his whole sorry life.' Nixon was still smiling, telling her to keep having fun, because this was one of those special days that didn't happen often.

She leaned forward to peer over the nose of the plane. 'Is that Milford?' There was a long fiord with an airstrip and a few buildings at one end. Planes were landing continuously, no doubt full of eager tourists.

'Sure is. We'll stay away from the airstrip. Too many other planes for my liking.'

That was another reason she liked Nixon. He might do adventure but he didn't take risks with her or anyone else. Or probably himself. She certainly hoped not. She wanted him around for a long time to come. 'So we go up the Sound?'

'Up the right side and back down the left. We don't fly through the middle for safety purposes. I need room to turn the plane around in the unlikely event something goes wrong.'

Her tummy didn't tighten when he said that. She was confident in her pilot, and having the best day of her life. Recent life anyway. Putting her phone to the window she clicked photo after photo. 'I think I'm going overboard but who knows when I'll ever get another chance?'

'There'd be endless opportunities if you learnt to fly.'

'No, thanks. As much as I'm loving this, if I had spare money I'd rent a block of land and have horses. But I'm saving to buy a house, so any spare dosh gets put away. Out of sight, out of spending danger.'

'Not staying in the apartment for ever?' Nixon swooped the plane around in a circle to face the way they'd come.

'Owning my own place has always been a dream since I had Rosie. I grew up in that house out in Gibbston Valley. Dad farmed cattle then. All the special memories from my childhood are to do with there and I want that for Rosie somewhere down the track. Though what I'll be able to afford will be on a much smaller scale and not in such a fabulous location.'

'It'll be a start.'

'Exactly.'

She took more photos, settled back in the seat and breathed in warm, kerosene-laden air and smiled with happiness.

Nixon grinned. 'You are enjoying this, aren't you?'

'Oh, yeah.'

'Hate to tell you but we're heading home. The plane's booked by someone else at eleven and I need to refuel.'

'I'm fine with that.' The rest of the day was going to be tame after this. The rest of her life if Nixon wasn't starting to feel the same way about her. Since he'd brought her up here anything was possible. Wasn't it?

'Want another crack at flying?'

'Can I?' Not waiting for an answer, Emma sat up straighter. 'Can I try turning?'

'Wait 'til we're well away from Milford.' Nixon was scanning the sky in front of them, out of the side windows and then above as much as he could see.

'You do that a lot.'

'First lesson in flying: be on the watch for other planes. Don't rely on other pilots or air traffic control to tell you who's in your space.' He glanced at the control panel, then at the wings. 'Straight and level. You're onto it.'

Pride filled her. Anyone could do this, but she was doing it and that felt special.

'Let's try a turn. Move the control gently to the left. Again, nothing abrupt. Too sharp and too far and you'll flip us over on our back.'

'Yikes.' Emma let the controls go, suddenly terrified at how easily this could turn to catastrophe.

Nixon's hands were instantly in charge of his controls. 'Steady.'

'You frightened me.'

'Good. You need to be wary all the time.'

'Handing back to you,' she told him. 'I prefer to relax and enjoy my flight.'

'Emma Hayes, I don't believe you're chickening out that easily. Not the strong, brave woman of these past few weeks.'

Heat blasted her cheeks at the compliment, but it was nothing compared to the heat between them. Her hands seemed to reach for the controls of their own volition. 'Talk me through the turn.'

His low, measured voice instructed her as required, allowing time for her response while watching dials, wings, the nose, her. His calm approach gave her confidence.

Concentrating harder than she'd ever done for anything else, she turned the plane to the left, and kept turning because Nixon didn't tell her to straighten up. She held her breath, took a quick glance out of the window to see the land below moving in a circle. 'Ready to straighten any time you tell me.' Thump, thud. Her heart was leaping in its cage; excited, happy.

'A few more degrees and we'll be back on line.'

'I'm doing a complete circle?' How cool was that? Dealing with a cardiac arrest was going to seem tame after this.

'Watch that the speed doesn't pick up when you straighten. Keep the wings level. That's it. You're a natural.' Nixon slapped his hand on his thigh, his fingers tapping a soundless tune.

She wished it were her thigh those strong fingers were resting on. Her muscles tightened anyway, and her skin prickled with need as though he were touching her. If only she could let go of the controls to place a hand over his. Laughter bubbled up and out of her throat, filling the small cabin. 'This is awesome. Thank you so much for bringing me up here. It's the best time I've had in for ever.' She'd left her problems on the ground and was having unfettered fun with a man she couldn't get enough of. No wonder her heart was singing.

'We'll do it again.'

Truly? She couldn't wait. 'I'll hold you to that.'

His laughter died away as a thoughtful expression expanded across his face.

Emma waited to hear whatever was going on in his

mind, but he remained silent. 'It's okay, I understand if you don't get the chance. I'm usually fairly busy at the weekends too.'

'Stop it. I can't wait to take you up again.' His smile melted her. 'I haven't had a day like this, ever. You make me happy, Em.' He swallowed hard, stared outside for a moment, then focused on flying, taking over the controls and checking everything essential to a safe landing. Pressing the talk button, he spoke to Queenstown Air Traffic Control. 'Bravo Juliet Foxtrot on approach, three kilometres out, two thousand feet and descending.'

'Bravo Juliet Foxtrot, cleared for landing, out.'

'Cleared for landing,' Nixon repeated back before glancing across to her. 'You ready?'

She nodded, and watched the ground slowly come up to meet them at a steady rate. The touchdown was so soft it was as though they were still above the ground. Taxiing back to the aero club went too fast, and suddenly they were there, the prop slowing, stopping, and Nixon was pushing his door open, fresh air infiltrating the cabin and diluting the heat, the smells, the excitement.

'Welcome back to earth.' He smiled softly, again wakening her in places she hadn't known were still alive.

'I can't thank you enough.' But she was going to try. The time had come to move this forward to a whole new level, to express the kiss that had been building up since takeoff. All or nothing. And nothing was no longer an option.

Unclicking her seat belt, Emma leaned over the gap between them, her hands on his upper arms, her lips seeking his. Pressing her mouth to his, she breathed deeply, gathered in his man scent, his heat, his vitality, and kissed him with everything she had.

Nixon stilled, sat tight under her onslaught.

Unable to help herself, Emma kept kissing him, her

tongue beginning to explore his mouth. He tasted better than she'd imagined.

He moved closer, took over the kiss, his lips savouring hers, his tongue dancing with hers. His arms wound around her, drew her as close as possible in the awkward space they shared. The kiss moved to a depth she'd never experienced before. Nixon tasted of mint and heat and male. Under her hands his muscles were tight, strong, and knocking her heart out of shape. *Her* muscles were liquid as they pinged with heat.

Then she was set back, those wondrous lips gone, her mouth destitute.

'Sorry, Emma. I shouldn't have done that.'

'You didn't start it. I did.'

Not that she'd put any thought into it—it had just felt so natural, so right.

'I shouldn't have continued kissing you back.' His hands gripped the now useless controls in front of him.

'Fine.' If he needed space he'd get it. Using her elbow, she shoved her door wide and dropped to the ground, slammed the door shut and strode across the grass to the four-wheel drive to wait until Nixon was ready to take her home.

She was glad she'd kissed him, and stopping had been out of the question. Damn but could he kiss. Her toes were still curled and her blood hadn't returned to a normal pace. Might never. As for her heart—messy. Like putty, it had been moulded into a new shape far too easily. Now she had to find a way to straighten it out so she could face Nixon and not go into emotional overload, or do something more embarrassing than kiss him. What could be more embarrassing than that? Ah, well, there was always...

Nixon was taking his time topping up the fuel. That long body stretched across the front of the plane as he held the nozzle in place reminding her how he'd walked beside her yesterday as they'd headed up the hill in Sunshine Bay. Long, confident strides as if he were on the prowl, sexy as all be it, stirring her deep down whenever she'd glanced at him. No wonder she'd kissed him. She'd been buzzing all morning. It had had to come out somehow and what better way than in a kiss? She hadn't known a kiss could lift the lid off so many banked-down emotions.

Behind her the locks on his vehicle pinged as he headed over. Climbing in, she waited to be driven home, probably in laden silence that said they were back to where they'd been after their last disagreement in the park.

The four-wheel drive rocked as he climbed in, then the engine roared to life and they were heading back to town.

Emma wanted to talk to him, about anything, except that kiss. She would not apologise when it had turned out to be the best kiss of her life. 'What are you doing this afternoon?' she asked, her voice a bit squeaky and high.

'Em.' He slowed at an intersection, turned onto the main road. 'Don't get mad at me, but we can't do this. It's not that I didn't like kissing you, it's that we cannot get involved.'

He liked kissing her. Not all was lost. 'Because we work together?' That would be a ridiculous reason. 'Or because you won't give us a chance?' That would be tricky but with patience and need on both sides they could work it out.

'You're not ready.'

That could be true, and it could be totally wrong. 'What makes you think that?'

'Recently you had a baby for someone else and are still coming to grips with all the emotions involved. You can't really know what you want yet.'

Her mouth dropped open as anger flared. She forced it away. Nixon deserved her truth. All of it. 'You're right. And you're wrong. My emotions are extreme at the moment but they run true. I miss Grace in my arms even though she's not mine. My body wants her while my head and heart are working to let her go.' Her hands were clenched on her thighs and didn't relax when Nixon briefly covered them with his and gave her a squeeze. 'As for us, I have no idea where or how far we're headed. I only know...' she loaded her voice with honesty '... I want to find out. To do that I'm prepared to take some chances.' Then a little imp got hold of her tongue. 'For the record, I kissed you, I didn't propose.' *Careful. That's enough.*

Nixon braked sharply for a red light, his fingers tapping in an annoying way on the steering wheel. 'I still think it's too soon for you.'

'I think you're using me as an excuse not to let go and have some fun for a change,' she dragged out over a mouthful of disappointment.

'You might be right, to a point.' Green light, and he pulled away. 'I don't want a relationship that I can't walk away from at any moment. I told you what happened to my family and the result is I'm ultra-cautious about getting close to anyone. I could hurt you, Em, and that's not happening.'

More than honest. The lack of hope was obvious. She turned to see him clearly. 'When I kissed you I wasn't asking for a lifelong commitment. It happened. I'd had a wonderful time with you and I was buzzing. It happened,' she repeated, suddenly at a loss for words. Sensible ones anyway.

'Tell me, do you want more children?' he asked.

'Yes, one day, with the right man.'

'Is this a new thing, or have you felt like that for a long time?'

I see where you're going with this. 'For the past nine months I've been focused on having Abbie's baby, and doing it without breaking my heart or hers. I did that, and there are no regrets.'

Nixon turned his head her way and started to say something.

'Wait. I haven't finished. What the pregnancy's done is wake up my maternal needs and, yes, one day I do want more children, a family unit with a man, not only Rosie and me. She needs siblings and a dad too. The only new thing is I'm admitting it.'

I want to love a man, to be loved. To share a home, a life with him.

But now she'd well and truly scared Nixon off—if he'd even been at the starter's block, and with his hang-ups that was unlikely. 'Out-of-whack emotions and all, it's time to start living in a way I haven't for years. My life is no longer on hold.' That was enough. She'd raved on too much.

'Good for you.' He was silent after that, and for once she accepted it was Nixon's way of dealing with a load of information.

She'd put herself out there; better he think it through than make an impulsive decision that he later regretted. They were close to town now. Just ahead was the café she frequented when she had time for coffee and cake. 'Drop me off here. There's something I need to get for Rosie.'

He pulled into the kerb. 'We've done it again, finished a fun time with disagreement.'

Our way of putting up the shutters?

Was she also a scaredy-cat? Afraid to grab what she wanted and run with it, take a risk with her heart? But she'd initiated that kiss. That was a risk. Or would've been if she'd actually considered what she was doing before she did it. Was she really ready for a relationship? Had the past finally gone? Just because she rarely had the nightmares any more, did that mean she was free to start over?

Would she be able to relate to Nixon without looking over her shoulder?

Out of the four-wheel drive, she leaned in the door to eyeball Nixon. 'Not a disagreement, more like we're testing each other, digging for information and feelings. We're new at this. If I've upset you then I'm sorry. Thank you again for an amazing experience. I'll see you on Monday, and we won't go round with long faces.' Where did all this come from? She didn't do strong and forceful. Except finally she was done with meek and mild. Look where that had got her in the past. 'Please,' she added softly, far more like her.

'It's a deal.'

The best she was going to get today. 'See you.' She closed the door softly, not wanting to put him on edge again. Ducking around a group of German tourists, she headed for the book shop and a present for Rosie to take to the street Christmas party tomorrow. Might even grab that coffee and cake for herself. Would not think about a certain man and how well he kissed. No, damn it. Every sweet, hot, delicious moment and sensation was right there at the front of her mind. Why did he have to be so good when he wasn't going to follow up with another one?

CHAPTER NINE

'SOMEONE TO SEE YOU.' Abbie nudged her none too gently.

Emma looked around the throng of neighbours filling the front lawns of adjoining properties where they lived for the street Christmas party, not seeing anyone wanting her in particular.

'Talking to Callum. Tall, dark hair, not a street resident.'

Nixon. Her heart began its now familiar thumping. 'What's he doing here?'

'Umm.' Abbie scratched her chin. 'Could he be here to see my neighbour?'

'I guess.' Yesterday he'd said he'd see her Monday, not today. Had he missed her as much as she him?

'Grab him.' As Emma began to shake her head her nagging friend grinned wickedly. 'You know you want to.'

She sure did. Could be he liked random kisses after all. 'You don't know what you're suggesting.' Because she didn't believe she could keep her hands to herself around Nixon any more. Her gazed drifted to Rosie playing soccer with the other youngsters.

'I've got her.' Abbie nudged again. 'She'll be fine.'

She'd go to get away from that annoying elbow if nothing else. Moving fast, but not quick enough to look desperate, she headed towards Nixon, caught up with him as he turned in her direction. 'This is a surprise.'

'A good one, I hope.'

He wasn't sure of his welcome? Emma slipped an arm through his. 'I'm thrilled you came. Hope you're not put off by the crowd.'

'Not at all.' Nixon tossed his keys up and down, up and down, his eyes mostly focused on her, big thinking going on behind that gaze. 'I dropped by for a coffee, and to see if you needed a hand getting a tree to decorate.'

So he wasn't avoiding the kiss. Or her spiel about where she was at now. 'All done. Come and join in.'

He hesitated. 'We get offside with each other too easily.'

'Then we get on just fine again.'

'Which suggests we both have defining lines we're not prepared to step over.' Yet. Maybe never. Or possibly sometime in the future. One thing abundantly clear was she wanted to find out, to explore whatever it was between them that had her blood thickening and hope expanding in her chest.

He shoved the keys into his back pocket, took her hand in his as they started walking back to where Abbie sat with Grace. 'What's with the party?'

'Christmas. It's an annual event. We have a barbecue and the kids get presents after their game of soccer. It brings the street together.' The whole of December was about Christmas functions. 'Rosie is excited beyond reason, especially now she's got a tree. Every morning she asks if Santa's coming today. I'll almost be glad when it's over. Almost.'

'I can picture her on Christmas morning. There'll be no holding her back.' But it was her Nixon was gazing at, his eyes bright. His smile sent ripples of desire caressing her in places that hadn't been touched in ages. So that kiss hadn't been a failure. It had ramped things up, and she wanted to do it again. As she had time and again throughout the sleepless night.

'Is Rosie playing soccer?'

'You have to ask?' Emma relaxed into his side, holding her breath until he stayed with her, didn't step away.

'Not really.' His full-wattage smile further lit up her insides, and sent another twist of desire curling through her body and downward to that special place. 'About yesterday…'

She held her breath.

'I had a lot of fun. I'm hoping we can have some more.'

'You're on, starting now. There's cold beer in the chilly bins.'

'Way to a man's heart.'

'Cheapskate.'

His arm tensed as he drew a sharp breath. 'Just so you know, that kiss was out of this world. I pulled back because I was losing control and I hate that more than just about anything.'

Best answer yet to all the questions buzzing in her head. They might be all over the place but she'd take this as a step forward, another kink in his armoury ironed out. They would be having more fun together. 'Let's party.'

'Nixon,' shrieked Rosie as she looked up from dribbling the ball towards the goalposts made of cardboard boxes, immediately losing concentration and the ball to the boy running beside her. 'You came.'

'Yes, kiddo, I did.'

'You can be my daddy partner.'

Emma froze. Awkward. The man would be gone any second. She glanced at him from under lowered eyebrows. Saw him jerk, then shrug.

'Okay. What do you want me to do?'

Pardon? This was Nixon? The man who'd pulled away

from that kiss as if he'd disturbed a nest of angry wasps? Her eyebrows rose as she studied him. Yep, definitely the man she'd fantasised about all night.

'Get the ball and give it to me,' Rosie instructed, jumping up and down with glee.

Don't let my girl down, please.

Despite what he'd just said, he'd soon realise he'd had a brain fade and forgotten he didn't do personal. Emma's lungs started aching with the breath stalled in there. Forcing it out, she aimed for normal—if normal meant racing blood, thumping heart and disbelief as he said to her, 'Put a hold on the beer.' Then he jogged across to the kids and men—fathers—to join Rosie.

'She's too damned sassy for a kid her age,' Emma muttered as she rejoined Abbie, who hadn't missed a word of that exchange.

'Nixon looks relaxed about it all.' Abbie grinned her infuriating grin.

'Since Grace was born you've become this annoying smug—yes, *smug*—person. Well, can it. Bring back my old friend who understood where I was at in my life and left me to get on with it quietly.' Emma wheezed out the last sentence as lack of oxygen from not breathing throughout that tirade caught up with her.

Abbie laughed. And laughed. When she finally got some control she managed to splutter, 'Now I know how rattled you are.'

'I am not,' Emma ground through her teeth. She hadn't been, but she wondered if she was expecting too much. She shook off that though—now was the time to leap in and have some fun, maybe find love while she was at it. 'Not rattled, bewildered.' She held her hand up. 'No words of wisdom, please. I'm going to work this out my way.' Hopefully that would encompass another of those stupendous kisses. At least one.

'Here, get this into you.' Callum handed her a beer. 'Since I've suddenly been replaced as—' he flicked his fingers in the air '—quote, "daddy partner", I'll be the drinks waiter.'

He could stop laughing and all. Emma grabbed the beer and gratefully tipped a mouthful down her dry throat. Then nearly choked when Nixon looked across at her with such a smile of delight on his face as Rosie cheered loudly over a goal they'd scored. 'He's enjoying himself,' she muttered.

'What can I say?' Abbie gloated. Then twenty minutes later she said, 'Get that man a beer, Callum. The game's finished.'

Rosie was trotting alongside Nixon trying to keep up with his long stride, her hand in his. 'Mummy, did you see that? Nixon helped me kick a goal.'

'Clever clogs. You played really well.' Emma smoothed errant curls off her daughter's forehead and leaned down to kiss her cheek, whispering, 'Did you thank Nixon for playing with you?'

'Thank you, Nixon, for playing with me.' Rosie was jumping up and down between her and Nixon. 'I'm going to get a present, I'm going to get a present.'

Emma slapped a hand over her ear nearest that explosion, but too late. The sound reverberated through her head. 'Jeez, Rosie, down a decibel or three, if you can.'

'What's a decibel?'

Nixon chortled. 'I think your mother is saying you shout too loudly.'

'That's how I make her hear me.' Rosie had an answer for everything since starting school.

'Go on, join the other kids. The presents will be given out shortly.' Emma patted her bottom.

'Where's Santa?' Rosie's face fell. 'How will I get a present if he's not here?'

'You won't miss out, my girl. Have I created a spoilt little monster by any chance?' she asked the others.

'It's Christmas. This is what kids are like,' Abbie re-assured her.

'Did you get her a muzzle by any chance?' Nixon asked.

She nodded. 'A permanent one.' Somehow she'd stepped closer to Nixon, could *feel* him beside her without touching him. As if they were a couple—an in-tune couple, not a hit-and-miss pair of messed-up characters. A permanent kind of life. Oh, hell, what was she thinking? 'The barbecues are being cranked up. You'll stay?'

Don't say no, please don't say no...

'Love to, but shouldn't I have contributed something?'

'There's enough food to feed twice this many people, and I brought some beer so you're all good. Anyway, you took me flying. Should I have paid half the plane rental?' she asked sharply. It hadn't occurred to her to offer when her mind had been on other things. 'I never thought.'

'I invited you to join me. I didn't expect you to pay. The only stipulation was to have a great time, and you did that.'

Gazing at Nixon, she told him truthfully, 'I certainly did. Way beyond my expectations.' So was that kiss. 'It gripped me. I felt I'd left everything on the ground for an hour.'

'That's how I feel most times.' Back to smiling. Not that he'd really stopped since he'd arrived. 'There's a freedom up there like no other, away from people, except the ones yabbering in your ear from air traffic control.'

'No white lines and pedestrian crossings.'

'Sure you don't want to take it up?'

'Yes. I don't do much for me what with Rosie and work, but it's time I found something to get passionate about.

Holding those controls gave me confidence and nudged me into thinking about a whole raft of things I might like to take up, but I keep coming back to owning my own horse one day. If that sounds like mumbo jumbo it's because I spent so long getting over the past I forgot about the future.'

And you, Dr Wright, are shaking me up something shocking. Exhilarating even.

'We'll go up soon, take Rosie with us.'

'Yes, please.' Bring it on. The flying. And Nixon time. How long before kisses weren't going to be enough?

Settle, Emma. Getting ahead of yourself here. Until two weeks ago you weren't interested in any guy, or having fun and kisses and—and sex.

Whoa. Sex? It did follow on from the kind of deep and meaningful kiss they'd shared. But sex—with Nixon? Why not? With all the aches her body had going on? She shuddered. Maybe not.

'I'll go help Callum at those barbecues.' Nixon sauntered off.

'He looks like he belongs here,' Abbie muttered.

'Shouldn't you be watching Grace?' Emma growled.

'Just saying.'

Emma swallowed a laugh. 'Can I have a hold?' She reached out for Grace, who was staring up at her. 'Hey, gorgeous. How're you doing?' Snuggle, snuggle. Sigh.

'That sounded like a wish.' Abbie was watching her, no longer smiling or teasing, now in concerned-friend mode.

'Not for Grace, in case you're worried.' Yes, holding Grace still cranked up the hormones something terrible but it had got easier over the past few days. The gaps between feeling lost and needy for this baby were stretching longer and occurring less frequently. No, this feeling going on inside her involved Nixon and her own family.

'If anything's come of having Grace it's that I'm missing out on so much. Would it be greedy to want another baby? No, let me rephrase that. A family. The whole shebang. Loving man, more children.'

'What's greedy about that? It's what most of us want eventually, after we get the crazy stuff out of our systems. This anything to do with Nixon?'

'Lots.' There. She'd admitted it out loud. To the one person who'd treat it with the care it deserved. 'But I'm scared. It doesn't help that Nixon's not ready and nothing's going to happen.'

'You could try enjoying the moments. One step at a time. Says the woman who was never going to find love again, and *kapow*!'

A sense of well-being encompassed Emma. Excitement, caution, need, independence. Every emotion in the book rolled through her without tipping her sideways, instead leaving her with an easy acceptance.

'Very profound.' Abbie chuckled. 'We're two mature, life-damaged women and we've arrived at that? I like it. What will be tonight is you and Nixon sharing over-cooked steak and sausages off the barbecue along with soggy coleslaw made by our favourite elderly neighbour and baked spuds in tinfoil still hard in the middle. But, hey, you won't notice, because you've hardly noticed a thing since he turned up. Then you'll take Rosie home, tuck her in bed, and snog Nixon senseless. How's that?'

Perfect. 'Don't expect me to report in with a running commentary.' She handed Grace back to her mother with only a tiny backward glance. 'Better go see how Rosie is doing. I got her a pogo stick for her present.'

Seems Nixon had beaten her to helping Rosie. He was holding the stick and Rosie's arm as she tried to bounce along the path. 'Don't lift your feet off the step,' he instructed. 'That's it. Now lift your legs and the stick at the same time. Like this.' Without letting go of Rosie he did a good impersonation of bouncing on a stick when he didn't have one.

Rosie wobbled on the stick, concentrating fiercely, then bounced. A tiny bounce, but it was real.

'Go, girl,' Emma encouraged. 'Do it again. Yes, awesome.'

Nixon walked alongside Rosie, keeping her steady as she got the hang of the motion.

Then, 'Let go, Nixon. I can do it on my own.'

'Yes, ma'am.' But he kept his hands close, ready to catch her if—when it all turned to custard. After three bounces. 'Got you.'

He'd make a good dad for that baby she wanted. Bumps lifted on her skin. Far too soon, Emma. 'Okay, you two, come and get some dinner.' She couldn't watch any more now that idea had struck. Nixon helping Rosie with her kite last weekend had started the hope rising, and today was lifting it to a whole new level. But Nixon would say he wasn't used to playing with kids, and that he had a lot to learn. 'You're a natural,' she told him over burnt sausages and well-done steak.

'At what?' he asked before loading dressing-laden salad into his mouth.

'Being social.' No need to scare the pants off him. Now there was a thought. Her eyes did a quick cruise over his butt. A brilliant thought. Tempting. And would certainly put the kibosh on being friends afterwards.

Rosie was exhausted after her exciting afternoon and went to bed unexpectedly early without a whimper. 'Goodnight, sweetheart.'

'I want Nixon to tuck me in.'

Take a back seat, Mummy.

'Nixon, you're required.'

He strolled into Rosie's bedroom, taking up all the space, and leaned over the bed. 'Hey, sport, you did good on that pogo stick. And you got a soccer goal.'

'I'm clever, aren't I?' Rosie gave an impish grin and held out her hand to high five.

'Very clever. But it's time you went to sleep. You've got school tomorrow.'

Emma choked. Nixon sounded like a regular dad. He'd probably got it from his uncle speaking to him as a child. The number of times she said things to Rosie, told her off for a misdemeanour or praised her, in the exact same words and tone as her mother had used with her had her expecting to find her mum was sitting on her shoulder putting the words in her mouth.

Moving to the other side of the bed, she bent down and kissed her gorgeous girl. 'Goodnight, darling. Sleep tight, make sure the bedbugs don't bite.'

'There're no bugs in my bed.' Rosie shuffled further down the bed, tucking the blanket around her cute little face. 'Night, Mummy…night, Nixon.' Then, 'Mummy, is Santa coming tomorrow?'

'Not for some more days.'

'He's taking for ever,' Rosie sighed. 'I can't wait that long.'

'You're going to have to, my girl.'

Out in the kitchen Emma put the kettle on. 'Tea or coffee? Or there's beer if you want some.'

'Coffee, ta.' He came to stand beside her, that enticing butt parked against the edge of the bench. 'I enjoyed today.'

'Nothing wrong with a good old street party with the kids and oldies all mixed in. Abbie and I started it our first year here. Some of the older folk don't have family in the area and the busy build-up in the weeks before Christmas with parties and celebrations seemed lonely for them so we went door knocking and told everyone let's have a barbecue on the street.' Now it was an annual event.

'What I meant was I enjoyed hanging out with you and Rosie, with your friends. It was comfortable and fun, and…' he raised a hand to lift a curl off her cheek '…and perfect. I could get to wanting to do it regularly.'

Knock me down. 'You can join in any time you like.'

'It's that simple?' He breathed out the question.

Emma shook her head. 'It's getting to be, the more time we spend together.'

'Is that how you approach everything, Em?' His eyes locked onto hers. 'You didn't mind stepping out of your comfort zone and going flying with me. You obviously love your job and nothing seems to daunt you there. You're bringing up Rosie single-handedly for all the world like it's a breeze. But I see moments of wariness and worry clouding your eyes when you think no one's watching. I know you have trust issues, and understandably so, but are you really so at ease with me, with us?'

'Blimey. Don't hold back, will you?' He was asking things he would not answer if she reciprocated. She spooned coffee into a mug and dropped a teabag into another. 'Everyone has moments of uncertainty. I've told you some of mine. Having Grace gave me a huge jolt and got me thinking there was more out there if I'd just grab it. I've been afraid I'd get it wrong again if I ventured into the world of men and love, but suddenly I'm sick of hesitating. I want to put my toes in the water and to hell with the consequences. I've survived the past. I can survive the future.'

'You kissed me. Should I take that as a compliment?' Serious face on. Meaning?

'You're the first man I've kissed in many years.'

'Definitely a compliment.' A teasing smile appeared.

Emma dropped the teaspoon and leaned closer to him, drawn in by that smile and the intensity in his eyes, by the muscular body dwarfing her small frame, by the man scent pervading the air between them. 'You like compliments?' she whispered.

'Let me give you one.' Then his hands were on her arms, bringing her close, his head dipping to find her mouth. His lips covered hers, possessed hers, sent need spiralling out of control to every corner of her taut body. Melting against him, she returned the kiss, gave herself to him with no barriers in the way. Nothing but them. Together. Kissing. Needing. Wanting. Complimenting each other.

'Mummy, I'm thirsty.'

Emma jerked away from Nixon, her cheeks flushed, her heart disappointed. 'The real world of a single mum.' She sighed and grabbed a glass to fill with water. 'Sorry.'

'Don't be. It's how it is. Real.'

The smile Nixon gave her took the strength from her knees, leaving her incapable of moving while she took some deep breaths. Real? Was this sensation of losing her grip on reality real? This need for love and family clawing through her? Was that real? Should she be following up or heading for the hills while she could still think?

'Don't take this the wrong way, but I should be heading home before we take this too far.' There was a load of regret behind his words negating her sense of being dumped when things were heating up. 'You have a child in the next room we have to be mindful of.'

'It's not just about us.'

'No, Em, it's not.'

How many men would've considered Rosie when wanting to get close to her mother? They'd have been focused on that kiss and heading down the hall to her bedroom if the altering shape of Nixon's jeans was anything to go by. He wanted her. Her. The woman who'd had a baby not long ago and wasn't looking slim any more. Stretching up on her toes, she caressed his chin with her lips. 'Thank you. And goodnight.' She'd just fallen even further into the pool.

CHAPTER TEN

'THE CHOPPER CAME in as I padlocked my bike to the rack,' Nixon told Emma the next morning. He'd been watching out for her at the hospital car park, feeling like a lusty teenager any time one of his staff went past and he didn't walk in with them. But he was busting to see her face, listen to the cadence of her voice. Yeah, right, what he really wanted was a repeat of last night's kisses. Out in the car park? Got it bad, man. Then Emma arrived and he couldn't deny the happiness spreading throughout his body.

'Wonder what we're getting.' Exhaustion flattened her voice.

'Not much sleep last night?' Sleep had been elusive for him with a certain nurse bouncing around inside his skull. Watching her with Grace yesterday had settled something within him. Emma was coming to terms with what she'd done. Her bravery and strength stole his breath away and yanked at his heartstrings. She was one courageous woman. The kind of woman he could imagine spending the rest of his life with—if he found the same courage to let go of his lifelong hang-ups. How did he learn to do that? If he'd really copied Henry to becoming the man he was there were no examples to follow out of the quagmire.

'Darling daughter was up and down all night. Demanded drinks, needed the bathroom, wanted a story—

didn't happen—had to talk. Wanted Santa to visit.' Emma shivered. 'The joys of motherhood.' The soft smile she wore belied her shudders.

'Nights like that happen often?' How did she cope with work when they did?

'Sometimes she has a run of them then sleeps through ten hours for weeks on end.' Emma tried stifling a yawn, but it won out. 'I thought I'd have trouble waking her up this morning.'

Nixon's phone pinged. A quick glance, and, 'We're on. The chopper's patient is being taken into ED.' There was a spring in his step as they headed inside. Being an emergency specialist made him useful and needed. Helping people at their most vulnerable gave him huge satisfaction. Add in a weekend filled with Emma and it was surprising his feet even touched the floor.

Then he saw his patient and the gloss diminished. Trish and her husband Bill owned the greatest little bagel cart, his favourite go-to for quick, delicious food when on a bike ride. 'Trish, what brings you here?' Nixon walked beside the stretcher being pushed into the department.

Callum filled him in. 'Trish was walking her dog when she fell down the power track out at Arrowtown. We airlifted her to avoid a three kilometre hike out with the stretcher. Suspected broken ankle and sprained wrist. Obs are normal so it doesn't appear likely an event precipitated the fall.'

'Punch saw a hedgehog and took off, and I ran after him,' Trish grumped.

'Where's the dog now?' Her white and brown bitsa was a legend for lapping up attention outside Trish and Bill's cart.

'One of the ambulance crew that walked in took him out to meet up with Bill.'

'Bill's not here?' Nixon asked.

'He's coming in when he's arranged for someone to staff the cart,' Callum said before giving Nixon more medical details.

'Let's get you sorted, Trish. I'll check your ankle, but judging by the angle it's at you're headed to Radiology. We'll get pictures of that wrist too. Any other sore spots?'

Trish shook her head. 'No.'

'No headache, dizziness? Cramps? Something out of the ordinary?'

'Not a thing.'

'Hey, Trish. Heard you were here.' Emma arrived from dumping her bag in her locker and smiled at their patient. 'Came luxury class too.'

'Beats being carried out of the bush.' Then Trish's face dropped. 'If my ankle's broken I'm going to have to put it up, right?'

'Afraid so,' Nixon agreed. 'Bill will have full range of the cart for a while.'

'Don't smile about it, Doc. I'm the bagel queen, not him.'

'I wouldn't have said Bill was any kind of queen.' Emma chuckled. 'All bloke from top to toe, not that I've seen his toes, mind. Does he wear nail polish under his socks?'

'I heard that, young lady,' growled Trish's husband from behind them. 'Just as well I broke the speed limits to get here. Who knows what stories you'd make up about me given half a chance?'

'Bill, glad you're here.' Nixon nodded.

While Emma wrapped him in a hug. 'You didn't wait for Punch, then?'

'The medic said they'd drop him round at the house.'

Nixon shook his head. 'The patients those guys carry.

Let's get Trish onto a bed. I'm sure Callum wants his stretcher back so he can go rescue someone else.'

'More like grab a coffee and some breakfast,' Callum said. 'Good luck, Trish. Bill, if you need a hand with anything around the property while you're short staffed give me a call.'

'Sure will. There's a lot to be sorted before the auction next month.'

Emma stilled. 'Auction? You're not selling my favourite house?'

'Yes, lass, we are,' Bill started. 'It's getting too big for us, and neither of the lads are interested in coming back to live in Queenstown. We want a new house that doesn't need loads of upkeep and a section I can mow in five minutes not five hours.'

'Mum never said a word.' Emma's mouth drooped and the gleam in her eyes dulled. 'I have a lot of happy memories playing there with Trish and Bill's sons when I was little,' she told Nixon. 'Our families are close.'

'How many acres you got, Bill?' Nixon asked.

'Four and a bit. The house is big with five bedrooms.'

Emma's sigh was long and nostalgic. 'It's ideal for a couple with young children.' She shrugged, lifted those eyes to him. 'Need me for anything before I head to triage?'

A kiss. With some follow up! Knowing the feeling of her body in his arms, small and light, strong and hot, he had no chance of forgetting the desire she lifted in him. Yep, idiot that he was, still not a hundred per cent certain how ready Emma was, he wanted to hold her in his arms to repeat that kiss, to have a relationship with her. Which underlined how messed up he was, because relationships were what other people had, not him. 'I've got this.'

'Sure.' No tension today. But then last night had ended on a good note. A hot note.

Forget what it felt like to have Emma's lips on yours, her body pressed close to your chest. Just forget it, okay? Right now you're a doctor—with a patient waiting for your undivided attention.

Poking his head out of the cubicle, he looked around for an available nurse, wishing Emma were free. 'Carl, in here.' Back to Trish, trying not to give her any more pain as he touched the swollen ankle. 'I'd say you've fractured some tarsal bones. I'll arrange an X-ray now. Carl, can you clean that wound on Trish's upper arm and I'll put some sutures in shortly?'

Emma returned. 'We've got a twenty-year-old tourist in the waiting room who walked in off the street after riding his bike into the back of a truck. Broken nose, teeth, shoulder injury. Concussion likely. I tried to bring him straight through but he refused to budge.'

Nixon approached the guy sitting half sprawled on the chairs, covered in blood and looking miserable. In pain and angry. 'I'm a doctor. Do you speak English?'

'*Sì,*' a girl beside him answered. 'A little.'

So why hadn't they talked to Emma? 'Come through so I can examine you.'

'Rocco trying talk to insurance,' the girl explained. 'We wait 'til he know.'

Nixon shook his head. 'You'll come now.' The financial side of things was someone else's problem. 'Rocco needs medical help, now.' If he said *now* often enough, the message might get through. The guy needed stitches on his chin and forehead at least. His left arm was held against his chest. Broken arm or problem with the shoulder? Cameron wouldn't be thrilled at getting an unexpected surgery this early in the day.

Emma brought over a wheelchair. 'You come.' She nodded at the girl. 'Jen, call me if anyone comes in.'

The receptionist nodded. 'Will do.'

With Rocco on a bed, Emma began peeling away clothes so Nixon could see the extent of the injuries.

Nixon caught a whiff of strawberry that was Emma. He wasn't usually aware of the perfumes female staff wore, but his senses were hyper alert around Emma. Saturday, crammed into the Cessna, he'd breathed that scent, heard her every breath and movement, felt the air shift around them, known her excitement when she held the controls. Ever since, he'd been fighting those senses, trying to squeeze them back in their place and denying she'd piqued his interest on every level. He'd still gone to see her even when he'd also been busy reminding himself why they shouldn't have a fling. If it was going to be a three-date thing, there was only one outing left.

In the waiting room, a poster on the wall advertised a band playing on the foreshore this Friday night. When they had a spare moment he'd ask Emma if she'd like to go. Hopefully her mother or Abbie would babysit Rosie.

So much for being friends. Friends didn't kiss each other with tongues involved. Didn't share kisses that cranked up the heat in his veins, in his groin. Kisses that knocked the air out of his lungs. Kept him awake all night, every night. Emma was the reason he felt lethargic and groggy and had to fight to concentrate on his patients.

'Doctor, put these on.' Emma winked as she held out two latex gloves.

'Thank you, Nurse.'

'You want me to collect the suture kit?' She grinned. 'You do seem a little distracted this morning.'

She was flirting with him. 'Would you please go to the cupboard by Resus and get the kit off the third shelf and bring it to me?' He grinned back. So this was what it was like to get a little closer to someone. Fun, flirty, and exciting. As long as he remembered first and foremost why he was here. 'Rocco, I am going to examine your arm and shoulder.' He looked to the young woman. 'Understand? *Comprendo?*'

'*Sì.*' She rattled off something in what sounded Italian and his patient lifted his arm.

'*Comprendo?*' Emma laughed. 'Stick to your day job, Doctor!'

'Rocco, tell me where this hurts.'

Asking Emma out would wreck the three-date rule because this wouldn't be the last time. Emma was tearing down his norms, beating the barriers to the ground, intriguing him, tempting him into an area he'd never stepped in before.

His skin lifted as a chill touched him. *Don't invite her. Find a woman who wants fun for a night and walk away in the morning without a backward glance.*

He'd done that too often; now he wanted something different, something more sincere, something with possibilities.

Wanting was one thing…actually following through was another. There'd be consequences for both of them. Was he ready? Was he not? When would the point come when he threw caution aside and leapt in? Now?

Emma slipped her new blue blouse over her head and smoothed it down her breasts. Breasts that had mostly stopped aching every time Grace cried. They were starting to resume their old shape and size. The blouse with its downward pattern added to the slimmer look. The short black skirt hugged her hips and settled at mid-thigh.

Slipping on shoes with killer heels, which would give

her pain by the end of the night, she studied the result in the full-length mirror. Not bad considering she wasn't back to her figure yet. Excitement fizzed along her veins. A night out with a hot guy. A night where she could forget being a mum, and be a single woman having fun. A night that could lead to anything.

The doorbell buzzed. Old monsters tapped her brain, tightening her stomach. Was she doing the right thing? She trusted Nixon, believed he was genuine, so, yes, right as right could be. Slinging the strap of her purse over her shoulder, Emma headed for the front door and the man who was pressing the button a second time. 'Let's go party,' she quipped as she shut the door behind her.

The atmosphere was electric when they pushed their way through the crowd to a street bar for some beer. The band was in full swing and people were laughing, dancing, and drinking. Every language in the book seemed to be in the air, tourists and locals mixing comfortably. 'I haven't been to anything like this in years,' Emma told Nixon, who held her hand firmly.

'Sleeping Beauty awakens,' he replied, those beautiful eyes twinkling.

'Don't think that makes you a prince,' she retorted around a smile.

Downtown, they strolled around the crowd's perimeter to find somewhere to sit, watch and listen. But within minutes of settling on a stone bench Emma stood up to sway in time to the music. When she tipped her head back to stare up at the sky her hair swung from side to side. A glance at Nixon showed his eyes fixed on her hair and a thrill of excitement caught her. Say what he liked, he was keen on her. 'Hey.' She held out her hand. 'Get your butt up here and show me your moves.'

His eyes widened but he was on his feet in an instant. 'You're on.'

Bleeding heck. The man had all the right moves. Those long legs were whippet-strong, his body bending and rolling, and his eyes—locked on her all the time. Blasting her with heat, drying her mouth, softening her limbs and forming warm knots in her stomach and places beyond. Winding her arms around his neck, she continued dancing. When his hands spread across the small of her back she felt secure and safe and happy and—yes, damn it, totally ready for a whole lot more than kisses.

'We've got all night,' he breathed beside her ear.

Her answer was to move her hips against him, to sway in time to the music up against his chest, teasing her nipples tight. All night. The words repeated in her head. A promise? Oh, yes. That was her interpretation and she was sticking to it.

They danced until the band took a break. Nixon asked, 'You want to find somewhere for a meal?'

The air was warm, the sky sparkling with stars. 'How about street food from one of the carts and we take it down on the foreshore?'

'Sounds good to me. We can come back to dance some more afterwards.'

She slipped her hand into his, and they queued for kebabs, just like any regular couple. Except nothing was regular for her. 'Dating could become my favourite pastime.'

'Mine too.' Nixon ran a finger down her cheek, across her lips. 'Think we can do this without falling out at the end of the night?'

'I'm over that. We get on so well I don't like it when we have a spat. So, yes, we can, we will, go home happy with each other.' Her fingers on her left hand, the one out of his sight, crossed ever so slightly. No harm in adding a dollop of good luck to the mix.

Tasty food sitting on the foreshore amidst the crowd, a buzzing atmosphere, and Nixon dancing with her. What more could a girl want? She had it all. The hours flew past in a blur of heat, yearning, sore feet from those heels, and Nixon. Nixon's smiles, his kisses, his hands on her back and her waist and her shoulders; laughter that made her forget everything but him.

Then the band was packing up and the crowd spilling deeper into the town centre where the bars were waiting. Nixon draped an arm over her shoulders and tucked her close to him. 'Want another drink?'

'I hate admitting this but I'm ready to quit.' Nine-thirty bedtimes were her norm these days.

'I'm relieved,' he whispered. 'And I don't have Rosie to blame.' His chin grazed her cheek before his mouth covered hers.

'A couple of geriatrics, aren't we?' she said when they pulled apart.

'I didn't say the night was over. I'm just not interested in hanging around with half of Queenstown and a gazillion tourists any longer.'

The night wasn't over. Anticipation pushed aside her growing weariness. Her feet found a second life, all but skipping back to Nixon's vehicle. Then cold reality struck. He probably meant he'd have a coffee with her before heading back to his place. This was Nixon, the avoidance expert.

'Where's Rosie tonight?' he asked when he parked outside her front gate.

'At Mum's.' As in, not coming home until after breakfast. She held her breath. Should she make a move? Ask him in? But the words weren't there. She didn't know how to invite a man into her home for some loving, and was afraid of being turned down when she wanted it so badly.

Nixon got out of the four-wheel drive and came around to open her door, held her hand as she climbed down, kept hold of it all the way up the path, through the door, and along the hall to her bedroom. Not a word, not a questioning look. Confident and certain was this Nixon.

The insecurities fell away as he turned to her, took her in his arms and said, 'May I?' and kissed her thoroughly. A kiss deeper than any she'd experienced. A kiss that sparked to life all the desire and need she'd been trying to keep a lid on from the moment she'd opened her door to him earlier.

She was free, able to do what she'd wanted to do with Nixon for ages. He was giving her the opportunity and wouldn't back off.

Then that hot, tantalising mouth tugged away. 'This isn't too soon for you? It's only been a few weeks since the birth.'

It might hurt a bit, but somehow she believed that'd be lost in the heat and need and desire. 'Let's see how it goes.'

'I'll be careful.'

That was a bucket of cold water being tipped over her feverish skin. She kissed him to show she had no intention of going carefully. It must've worked because his fingers were at the buttons of her blouse, clumsily undoing them, his skin skimming hers. As soon as the buttons were dealt with she tugged the blouse off and tried to squeeze out of the tight skirt. Nixon's hands covered hers, pushed the skirt down over her butt, her thighs, to her knees, where it dropped around her feet. And then…one touch and she was quivering and tight and hot and cold. And crying for him to hurry.

'I don't want to hurt you, Em.' His fingers did some serious touching, whipping up a storm along her veins.

'You're not. You're—' She gasped around a shudder of need. 'You're— Let me touch you.'

'Wait. We've got all night.'

Yes, but there are two of us here. 'I won't last five seconds if you keep doing that.'

'Then I'll have to do it again.'

You're welcome.

As she gave into the shudders wracking her body her world spiralled out of control. She was sprawled across Nixon, his naked torso an aphrodisiac under her palms. Not that she needed one. Everything about Nixon turned her on. When had they got onto the bed? His erection pressed against her belly, his tongue now teasing her tender nipple, a tenderness she forgot as waves of need rolled through her when she'd barely recovered from the first onslaught.

Pushing up, tugging free of that exquisite mouth, she reached for him, held him, moved slowly, up and down.

'Condom,' Nixon gasped.

'Let's keep doing it this way.' It felt right, and eased her worry of being too close too soon after the birth.

'Emma,' Nixon groaned. Then he was back to arousing her, and they were together, moving as one, the pressure building. He brought her to the peak, restraining himself until she exploded, then quickly joined her.

Emma's breathing took for ever to return to normal. If that was making love then she hadn't lived. How soon could they do it again? Hell. She hadn't even got her breath back. Neither had Nixon. Her hand reached for his, her fingers interlaced with his. Hot, sweaty, strong, gentle. Now she knew what those hands had been made for. And she wanted to get to know them even more.

CHAPTER ELEVEN

NIXON WATCHED EMMA scooping Rosie up into her arms and kissing her on both cheeks. 'Anyone would think you'd been apart for a week, not one night.' He chuckled, acknowledging the warmth and tenderness in his gut, and his heart, for both these adorable females.

Making love with Emma last night, he'd felt as if his world had finally come together for the first time since his family had left him. It had been a revelation. Emma was so generous with her loving he'd been lost for a while. Then she'd grounded him, made unspoken promises of more to come if he was prepared to reach out and take a chance. He'd gone into this thinking he'd be able to knock the monkey off his back for good, return to being friends once the mystery of Emma was exposed. He had not expected to feel smitten, to want more, to hate the idea of closing the door on what they had. Friends they might've been, but now they were so much more. They were lovers.

For now.

For longer?

For ever?

That meant accepting he'd never again be abandoned by someone he loved, or at least making the most of every day between now and when—if—that happened. Might mean accepting he had been loved all along as he grew up.

'Nixon, pick me up,' demanded Rosie. 'I want a hug.'

'What madam wants, madam shall have.' He swung the bouncing girl up against his chest, savouring the closeness, absorbing the smell of soap and cornflakes and...? 'You had chocolate for breakfast?'

'Don't tell Mummy I ate a Santa off the tree.'

'It's our secret.'

Rosie wriggled and wriggled, her small hands batting at his shoulders. 'Can we take my kite to the park?'

Nixon looked over her head to Emma, and raised an eyebrow.

'Later. Wave goodbye to Grandma, Rosie.'

'It'll have to be the waterfront. I'm on call,' Nixon said.

'Not a problem.' Emma led the way inside her apartment and dropped the newspaper Kathy had brought on the table. After filling the kettle, she flicked through the pages until she got to the real-estate section. 'Trish and Bill's place is a feature.' She read the details. 'Shame nursing's not the highest paying job in town.'

'You'd buy the place?' Nixon asked. He'd heard the longing in her voice when she'd talked with Bill in ED, but hadn't realised how much she yearned for it.

'I would if I had a family, as in more kids and a partner. And the dollars. Plenty of them, since Queenstown's some of the most expensive real estate in the country.'

A home and family of his own. A chill slid down his spine. Too soon. Just because they'd slept together didn't mean they were setting up house.

Picking up the paper, he read about the property that had captured Emma's heart. He could see how it would be a great place for youngsters to grow up, could visualise Emma and Rosie in the yard playing with a dog, those horses she yearned for in the paddocks. Hell, he even wanted to see himself fitting into the picture. Domestic bliss. Except that wasn't on his horizon. Certainly wasn't part of his plans for the future, despite the feeling of well-being today. He was getting closer, but still had a long way to go before he moved into a home with a wife and children. A very long way.

The old fears began kicking up a storm. His feet were itching to run out of the door, his heart beating a heavy tattoo—*don't go, get out of here, don't go, get out of here.*

A hand touched his upper arm. Emma stood staring up at him. 'Don't torture yourself, Nixon. I am not asking anything of you. We're doing great, no arguments, all fun and agreeability. Leave it be.'

'I'm that obvious?'

Her head bobbed. 'Afraid so.'

'That's scary in itself.' It was. Women didn't get to know him well—he made sure of it. But then he hadn't met an Emma before. He stared into her trusting eyes, his fears receding, leaving him shaken but—but okay. Ready to stay with Emma for the day. He could even return to the conversation that had tipped him sideways. 'You want to own your home.' It was most Kiwis' dream.

'That's what I'm saving for.' The kettle clicked off and she poured the boiling water over the coffee grounds.

Emma had plans, she wasn't resting on the mess of her past, even though it lurked behind her eyes when she was tired or upset. She'd dealt with her marriage in a similar manner to how she was dealing with post-partum blues. Brave, strong, and doing just fine with the occasional flare up of distress. 'You ever want any more hours in ED just tell me.'

'I am not cutting back my time with Rosie. We'll get there when we do, and meantime we're not living in a hovel.' Sniffing the coffee-scented air, she asked, 'That house you're in is yours?'

'Yes. I bought it off the guy I replaced in ED. He was heading to Wellington and wanted shot of the place fast. It's handy to work, easily accessible, and will only improve in value over the years, so I signed a contract immediately. Made moving from Dunedin a lot simpler.'

His phone pinged. 'Hold that coffee. A hang-glider has crash-landed on Bob's Peak close to the gondola building. Multiple injuries. Patient critical.' He called in. 'I'm coming in.' He'd prefer to go to the site but the paramedics would be there and they knew what they were doing.

'Come back for lunch if you're finished in time,' Emma called after him.

With a wave he leapt into his vehicle and gunned the motor. Of course the traffic was diabolical, with sightseers gaping out of windows and forgetting to drive. The locals were obvious—they were the ones with their hands on the horns. If only he could legally stick a flashing light on his roof.

For the first time, being called into work for an emergency didn't raise the adrenalin, didn't create anticipation for the injuries he'd have to deal with. Instead his heart got heavier with every kilometre he drove away from Emma. At least he had lunch with her to look forward to— if he ever got through this damned traffic. More time with Emma was imperative to his well-being, and the sense of balance coming into his life. Didn't matter what they did, as long as he was with her. Keep this up and his cycle might become rusty.

'Move it.' His palm pressed hard on the horn. 'Get out of the damned way.' A patient could die while he sat in this traffic jam. If his bike had been at the back of the four-wheel drive he'd be parking up and riding to the hospital by now. But it wasn't. He'd been too busy thinking about Emma to do anything that sensible.

Finally he was racing through the hospital, his vehicle abandoned in a tow-away area of the health department's car park. 'How far away is our man?'

'Coming down now,' Carl told him. 'Resus one's ready.' The nurse handed Nixon a scribbled note. 'The general surgeon and neurosurgeon are on standby, and surgical are contacting Cameron.'

'Thanks,' Nixon muttered, his eyes sweeping over the information. Moments later they were dealing with the worst of worst-case scenarios. Fractures, blood loss, unconsciousness, internal injuries. Everyone worked fast, fighting the impossible, agonising minute after agonising minute, slowly winning, getting their patient ready for Theatre.

'No reaction from his feet or hands,' Nixon warned Cameron when he arrived dressed in gardening clothes.

'Damage to the spinal cord. Makes sense. Those impact injuries to his femurs and ilium suggest he landed feet first.' Cameron studied the X-rays on the screen in front of them. 'First things first, starting with that liver haemorrhage. It's going to be a long day.'

Especially for the man they didn't have a name for.

'He arrived at the car park this morning, set up his hang-glider and took off, only to go splat against the mountainside,' Nixon told Emma that afternoon. 'A hang-gliding instructor thought there'd been gear failure, but that hasn't been verified yet.'

'Can't he be traced through the car reg?'

'It belongs to a woman in Christchurch who's in Auckland for the weekend.'

'In the meantime, the man is alone and suffering dreadfully.' Emma sighed.

Nixon sprawled out on the lounger on Em's deck, and

begged the phone gods to keep the damned thing silent for the rest of the day. Exhaustion softened every muscle in his body. Hunger pangs cramped his gut.

'Get these into you.' Emma held out a plate with two salmon bagels and an icy bottle of water.

Placing everything on the table, he reached for Emma to pull her onto his thighs. It felt so right with her sitting there. 'Thanks for this. Coming in after a heavy time in ED to find you and sandwiches waiting is just...' his voice hitched '...just something I haven't had and it's wonderful.' Made him feel different, as if he belonged somewhere with someone. Pulling Emma close, he kissed her. It started gently, lips to lips, then deepened so that his blood stirred and desire overtook all thought processes. His hands slipped under her shirt, found those soft mounds.

Suddenly Emma pulled away, her breasts rising and falling rapidly. 'We can't. Rosie's in the back yard.'

Reality check. Yet while it meant tugging the brakes on his need, Rosie's presence didn't bother him. She was part of the deal. What deal? They hadn't come to any arrangement. Did he want to? What did he want from Emma? A meal? A date and sex occasionally? Or to share a beer on the deck?

Getting too clinical here, man.

It went to show how little experience of dating he had. In the past when he'd taken a woman out there was no comeback, no questions about where they were headed, no child to interrupt a hot kiss that was heading down the hall to the bedroom. This was a whole new deal.

Liking it?

Oh, yeah.

'You'd better stay for dinner.' Emma stood up. 'Hope you like chicken burgers. Saturday night dinners are Rosie's choice.'

'I'd eat anything if it means I get to stay.'

Her grin turned wicked. 'I'll see what's in my diary.'

The next week was a mix of excitement and exhaustion for Emma. While the post-birth tiredness had dissipated over the week since they'd first made love, having Nixon here kept her on high alert. Tonight he hadn't left after dinner, instead had taken her hand and led her to her bedroom to make love, not once but twice throughout the night. 'Thank goodness Christmas is almost here,' she murmured against Nixon's shoulder, steeling herself for the moment he got up to go home.

His hand was making lazy circles over her back. 'Think Rosie will make it without imploding?'

'She will, I mightn't. If I hear "how many more sleeps?" once more I'll scream.'

'I'll miss you two while I'm in Dunedin.' His hand pressed a little harder. 'I could stay here instead.'

'No, you've got to see your family.' He hadn't been dancing with excitement when he'd told her he was going to Dunedin for Christmas. More like apprehensive. 'I couldn't imagine not spending the day with Mum and Dad and the annoying brothers. It wouldn't be Christmas.'

'Your family is so together. Everyone loves each other so easily, comfortably.'

'You missed out there.'

'Once I'd have agreed.' He bit his lip. 'But I might be wrong.' A pause. 'Hate to admit this but I'm looking forward to spending time with everyone, seeing how the kids have grown. Getting to know Rosie has made me realise how much I've missed out on.'

'Could be your best Christmas ever.'

'Yeah.' A soft kiss on her brow before he told her, 'I'm back on duty on the twenty-seventh.'

Two days and nights without seeing Nixon. A lifetime. 'Glad you're having dinner with us tomorrow night before you hit the road south.' They'd agreed to get together with Rosie for presents and an early meal, then she'd head out to the Valley to join her family.

Nixon's hand left her skin, and the bed rocked. 'Time I headed home.'

She wasn't ready to have Rosie bouncing into her bedroom in the morning to find Nixon in bed with her. Not when they hadn't talked about where they were going with this, while they were still in the exciting, don't-get-too-serious phase. To introduce Rosie to the possibility of Nixon staying in her life before she and Nixon had made that commitment would be plain irresponsible.

Rosie's heart would be broken. Already she thought he was the best thing after chocolate Santas. So did her mother. 'Ever thought of coating yourself in chocolate?'

Nixon's head jerked up. 'What? You want to lick it off me, by any chance?'

'Now there's a thought.'

'I'm not going to ask where you're going with this one.' He slid into his chinos and shoved his arms into his crumpled shirt before bending over to kiss her chin, her nose, and then finally her mouth. 'See you later.'

'I'll hold you to that.' She wasn't working again until after Christmas, having booked the days off long ago. Having worked half shifts most of the month, she and Nixon had agreed she'd return to work full time on the twenty-seventh.

Another kiss caressed her lips, and she snatched a handful of shirt, tugged him closer. 'What's the time?'

'Unfortunately I do need some shut-eye before returning to the ED.'

'Damn.' She craved another round of lovemaking.

'See you.' Emma sighed as the front door closed quietly. Bring on the time when he did stay right through until morning.

Don't rush things.

Nixon wasn't ready for anything serious, and she probably wasn't either. Memories of bad times returned at inconvenient moments, coming more frequently these past weeks, as though the more she got to know Nixon and thought he might be the man for her, the more her mind reminded her how wrong love could go.

Picking up the adjacent pillow, she buried her face in it to inhale deeply, savouring Nixon's scent. They were a work in progress, which was currently giving her unbelievable pleasure.

Forget moving ahead. She was already there, wherever that was. Right or wrong, she'd fallen in love with Nixon. Totally. Helplessly—which was the scare factor. She understood being helpless as only those who'd been in her situation did. But while caution tripped through the excitement, deep inside where it mattered she knew Nixon didn't have a violent bone in his body. He'd protect those he loved to the end of the earth. If only he could admit that love.

Nixon had given her back so much she felt like the optimistic girl she'd been before she married. And she gave him plenty of passion, warmth, fun, and genuine care. Another yawn had her putting the pillow aside and snuggling under the covers, her eyes drooping shut. Better buy some vitamins in the morning.

'Mummy, it's a robot.' Rosie tore at the paper left on the box Nixon had given her.

'Careful, my girl. You don't want to break it.' Emma smiled at Rosie's excitement. 'We've only just started. There's all tomorrow to get through yet.' Her smile slipped.

She'd miss Nixon so much. Too much. It was only for two days—and nights. She rubbed her eyes with her thumbs. Her head pounded, and her breasts ached for the first time in days.

Nixon nodded. No easy smiles from him this afternoon.

'You okay?' she asked, trying not to let the grizzly mood that had been gnawing at her all day come to the fore.

'Busy day.' He concentrated too hard on opening the well-sealed box holding the robot.

Not what she wanted. She'd been looking forward to a few hours relaxing with Nixon over a wine as Rosie opened her present and he taught her how to operate the controls. So they were both in moods. Maybe this time of the year did that to him, reminded him of missing out with his parents and brother.

'Abbie came in for coffee and cake earlier. She's on a high about Christmas with her baby and how everything's going so well with Callum.' She hadn't shut up for a moment and Emma had felt drained when she'd picked up Grace and left. Not that she could blame her friend for feeling out of sorts. Hell, she didn't know what to blame it on, but if she had to pick a culprit she'd go with hormones. Always a good backstop.

'Hold the controls like this,' Nixon demonstrated to Rosie. 'Push that button.'

The robotic super girl lurched and fell over. 'I did it, Mummy. Look.'

Nixon stood the toy up again, and again, so patient. If she didn't know better she would have said he was an old hand at playing with kids. 'What time do you want to get away?'

He glanced up. 'Being Christmas Eve, the road will be chaotic, so about seven if that works for you.'

A couple of hours earlier than she'd expected, or believed from his comments when she'd first suggested dinner. 'I'll start cooking.' The salad was prepared, the peas podded, the spuds ready to be brought to the boil. She stood up in a hurry and tripped over a doll lying on the floor.

Nixon caught her as she reached out for balance and came to his feet. 'Steady.'

Emma breathed in Nixon's scent and felt tension in his hands. Something was wrong. Making eye contact with him, she saw worry and uncertainty coming back at her. 'What's up?'

'Nothing.'

Through the wall, Grace started crying, a loud, heart-string-tugging sound, and Emma's breasts tightened, her heart dropped, and a waterfall streamed from her eyes. Nothing, he'd said. It was just all too much. She fell against Nixon, wrapped her arms around his waist and cried, deep harsh sobs filled with sadness and longing and envy.

Nixon lifted her into his arms and sank onto a chair, holding her against his chest, his hand soothing her back, his lips brushing the top of her head. 'Rosie, take the robot to show Abbie, will you? I'll come and get you in a minute.'

'Can I?'

'Off you go.' A moment later he was pressing tissues from the box nearby into her hand. 'Hey, about time this happened.'

'This isn't baby hormones.' Emma sniffed. 'Not Grace ones.'

Under her backside he tensed. 'What do you mean?'

Because it had been a day full of yearning, feeling as though she was missing out and not knowing how to cope or where to find the strength to look life in the eye and tell it to go to hell, she opened her mouth and spilled. 'I want another baby. One of my own. Don't even think of telling me this is because of Grace. It's not.'

Nixon's chin rested on the top of her head. 'You're exhausted, Em. You've been rushing around pretending all is well in your court, that you're coping. Hell, you've avoided meetings with the counsellor, saying you don't need to download your heart. Give yourself a break.'

Pulling her face away from his sodden shirt, she stared at him. 'I know all that. You're still wrong. Not that it matters. Pregnancy's out when I'm not in a permanent, loving relationship.' What would he do if she told him her half of that picture existed? She loved Nixon, wanted him to be the father of her next child, but she'd gone off half cocked, hadn't waited until he was ready to hear what she was thinking. 'I'm sorry,' she blustered, afraid she'd scared him off for ever. 'You're right. I'm tired.' She sat up straighter, wiped her eyes and cheeks; his finger brushed her hair. 'Here's me being a cry baby and it's Christmas.'

Brushing her forehead with his lips, he gave her a lopsided smile. 'How about we skip dinner and you head out to your folks' while you're still awake? I can grab something from the supermarket as I go through Frankton.'

If her heart hadn't already felt like a lump of concrete that would've done it. He was bolting. Using her as the reason, but he hadn't been forthcoming with her since arriving, and now he was in a hurry to be gone. 'If that's what you want,' she said pointedly.

'It's best.' He stared at her with something she'd like to believe was love in his eyes, but her head screamed out that she knew better. She'd fallen for him, but doubted he felt the same. Pushing her case would be rushing him.

Clambering to her feet, she stared out of the window, seeing her hopes vaporising in the hot summer air. When Nixon draped an arm over her shoulders she couldn't help but lean into him, absorb his strength and heat. And hope against hope that time would bring her what she wanted.

'Merry Christmas, Nixon.'

CHAPTER TWELVE

EMMA GRINNED. A WIDE, excited grin that tightened his gut with apprehension. 'Hey, Nixon, we're having a baby. How awesome is that?' She was grinning and dancing around ED as if she'd won the lottery. To her she probably had.

Not to him. He didn't need a lottery of any sort. 'A b-baby?' Nixon stuttered. 'Really?' Not true. She was teasing. He watched her, and heat filled his veins. He wanted her. Despite her bombshell he wanted to get close and hold her lithe body against his, to make love slowly and tenderly. To look into her eyes as she came and fall into the depths of their togetherness. She couldn't be pregnant. Not when they hadn't discussed this or anything about their future.

Now Emma moved closer and closer, her hands rubbing her stomach—her swollen, pregnant stomach. Those small hands spread across the taut cloth of her scrubs, gently holding her belly. 'Hey, put your hand on here,' she whispered. 'You can feel him kicking.'

Nixon stepped back, his butt coming up against the desk. 'You've had a test?'

Her eyes rolled. 'Do you think we need one?'

He thought they were not having a baby between them. Not yet. Probably never. He wasn't ready to be a dad.

Clapping filled the department, banged in his ears, slammed around his skull.

'It's good, isn't it?' Emma persisted.

Nixon shot up on the couch, sweat covering his skin, his heart pounding so hard his ribs were about to snap. The sheet was tangled around his feet, his pillow on the floor.

'Santa's been,' shouted Thomas. 'Get up, Uncle Nixon. We've got presents.'

Nixon gulped and stared at the two boys in their pyjamas and dragging laden pillowcases through the room. What the hell? He was in his cousin's lounge. There was a Christmas tree in the corner. Voices were coming from down the hall. His watch said five-ten. The sun was barely up.

'Look what we found on our beds, Uncle Nixon.' Mathew brought his goodies over to be inspected.

Nixon's feet hit the floor and he pushed himself to standing. He needed out of here, fresh air and solitude: not excited kids with their Christmas bounty. Emma and a baby? It was a bloody dream. Dream? Nightmare more like. He shivered despite the early sunlight coming through the windows. 'Em?' he croaked. It was a dream, man. Yeah, but what he wouldn't do to have her wrap her arms around him and say it was only a stupid nightmare.

'Some tea wouldn't go amiss about now.' Henry strolled into the room looking unfazed at the early hour.

'Be right with you,' Nixon managed as he pushed past to go to the bathroom, where he snapped the shower on and stood under an icy blast of water. Tried to blot out the image of Emma's hands gliding over her belly. Over their baby. It had been a nightmare. It would fade. He could not ruin Christmas day thinking about what it meant. His life had been turning around; he'd been so happy being with Emma and her girl. But a baby? Not this side of the next century. That was going too far. He wouldn't know how to cope, how to love the child, how to be the parent he'd missed and wanted all his life.

The shower didn't work. The dream remained at the forefront of his mind.

Watching the boys unwrapping presents and squealing with excitement pushed Emma aside briefly, but she returned the moment the family sat down for brunch. The laughter and chatter, the mountain of delicious food, champagne—his family. Despite the dream, he accepted their warmth and involvement with him. The kids were great, and he was getting to know them better. But one of his own? He had not moved that far forward.

It wasn't for real.

The dream was a warning to go slowly, be careful. A reminder of how life went belly up when he stepped outside his parameters.

His phone rang. Emma. He couldn't talk to her right now. He didn't know what to say, doubted he could talk without fear clogging his throat. Fear of losing her. Fear of having it all: Emma, Rosie, a home, more kids. He wasn't going there. He was the wrong man for her. He was a mess.

The ringing stopped, was quickly followed by a text. 'Call us when you're free.'

Next Christmas?

Nearly two hours later Nixon stared at the excited scene on his screen. 'I see the puppy's a hit.'

Em laughed softly. 'Rosie hasn't let her out of sight all morning.'

'Nixon, have you seen Bella? She's gorgeous. I love her. Mummy says I have to teach her about going to the toilet outside.'

'That'll be interesting,' he quipped around a huge lump blocking his windpipe. If only he could be with Emma today. And Rosie. If only he hadn't had that dream and didn't feel a deep trepidation. He'd had a wake-up call, could no longer continue seeing Emma if he felt so stressed over the thought of having children. He glanced at the woman inadvertently causing him anguish. 'How're you feeling today?'

Em's smile appeared forced. 'Great. Had a massive breakfast as only Mum knows how to make. She's already busy in the kitchen working on Christmas dinner. I'd help but turns out Daniel's girlfriend loves cooking so I got shunted out, told to put my feet up. How about you? Having a good time with your family?'

Yesterday's dark shadows under her eyes hadn't disappeared overnight. Say what she liked, she hadn't fully recovered yet. 'We were woken just after five by two lads who'd discovered Santa's presents on their beds, and nothing quietened down until a few minutes ago when everyone except Henry disappeared to the beach with some of the toys.'

Emma's soft laughter warmed him when he needed to be strong and stepping aside. 'You're glad you're with them?' she asked.

'Yes, I am.' The loud, loving greeting from everyone when he'd walked in the door of his cousin's house last night had stunned him. His family cared about him, had probably always loved him. Today, when he wasn't denying Emma and what they could have together if he could deal with the gremlins, he'd begun giving it back, cautiously sure, but he was stepping into new territory—and enjoying it.

'Nixon, look what my puppy does.' No peace when Rosie was around.

The dog was licking Rosie's face. 'Yukky.' He chuckled, happy to be a part of this child's life. At the moment.

For how long was up to him and Emma. Once he'd worked his way through all his hang-ups. If he got through them.

'Here comes the gang,' Emma warned. 'Hope you're wearing your armour.'

The screen was taken over by her family, full of good cheer and a load of cheeky questions. By the time he hit 'end' Nixon felt as tired as Emma looked. Her family were full on—just like his, he realised. He'd noticed the easy care and love in her family before he had in his. They'd got him thinking about his past in ways he'd never considered before. They? Or Emma? Definitely Emma. She was becoming special. Becoming? Emma was the most important person in his life. Did he love her? Was it possible? Why not? She was beautiful, loyal, strong, generous to a fault. What wasn't to love about her?

'They sound like a great bunch.' Henry handed him a coffee. 'Emma someone special?'

Had he been listening to the whole conversation? Avoiding the loaded question, Nixon sipped the coffee and went with one of his own. 'Did I shut down immediately that day? Or did it take some time?' Then he clarified. 'We've never talked about it. Neither of us like talking about the deep and personal, but lately I find I need to know what makes me tick.'

'You withdrew the moment you were told about the accident.' Henry studied him for a long time. 'I've been waiting for this day for a long time. Sorry, lad, I should've found a way to bring it up but...' he shrugged '... I'm the one who never talks about our losses and unfortunately you learnt from me. Not the best role model you could've had.'

'I could've done a lot worse.' Nixon took another mouthful of coffee. Strong but not hitting the places that needed it. 'Any of that champagne left over from brunch?'

'Help yourself, and pour me one while you're at it.'

Henry sat down at the outdoor table and stared out over the lawn.

Nixon was in charge of roasting the turkey so he poked the massive bird with a fork, adjusted the oven temperature and took two full glasses outside.

They sat relaxed in each other's company. Nixon couldn't remember a time when he'd done this before. His visits were usually focused, busy and followed a standard formula. Check how everyone was, see that Henry didn't need anything, have a meal to celebrate whatever occasion had brought him here, and then head away relieved it was over until the next time. This time he'd come for two nights, not the usual one, and for once he had no desire to hit the road back to Queenstown in a hurry.

Yet he did because Emma was there. Despite his fright over a baby he still wanted to see her, hold that sensational body and breathe her in, listen to her happy voice. She hadn't been happy yesterday. Downright sad because of Grace not being hers. She'd have loved the dream. His gut twisted tight. Dream for her, nightmare for him. Hopefully after a good night's sleep Emma realised her hormones had been at play, nothing else. This morning that sadness still lingered, so who knew what she felt about babies today? As much as he couldn't wait to see her, the brakes were clamping down on his feelings, making him hesitate. He wanted her in all facets of his life. And at the same time, he didn't. What if he didn't love her enough and hurt her accidentally? What if he did love her enough and got hurt himself?

'Don't make the same mistakes I did,' Henry intoned. Talking about himself would be as normal as a worm flying past.

Nixon didn't move a muscle, afraid he'd distract his uncle and that'd be the end of this odd conversation. Just because Henry had admitted to being closed, didn't mean he intended talking about everything from the past.

'Being older, my kids knew me way better than you and didn't let me get away with a thing. But it was easy to stay aloof from you. You shut down, held in all the pain, the fear, the uncertainty. I knew what was going on in your head.'

'I've finally worked that out.' Now he could see it was so obvious. No hugs, no talks about his family. But he'd been cared for, safe, fed and clothed. 'You lost your wife, and then your sister.'

'It was a bad time.' Henry drained his glass.

Nixon went to refill it. It was Christmas morning after all and they were having quite the conversation. Damn it. He took the bottle outside. 'Tell me about Mum. I remember her always laughing, and she sang a lot.'

'You call that singing? Haven't I taught you anything?' Henry chuckled. 'But, yes, she loved to sing. But most of all she loved her boys. You were everything to her. You two and your father. I'd never known her to be so happy.'

Nixon sipped his wine, absorbing this knowledge. 'Thank you.'

Out on the street some youngsters played, shouting and laughing, reminding him of Rosie. Such a well-rounded girl because she had a wonderful, caring, fiercely protective mother. Emma didn't have any problems letting him get close to her daughter, to taking part in small ways in her life. Had Emma let her guard down? Was he worthy of her trust?

'Don't make the same mistakes I did.' There was a ton of regret in Henry's voice. 'I could've remarried, had another chance at happiness but I refused to let her in.'

'It's not too late.'

Henry sipped his drink. 'No, lad, it's not.'

* * *

'Doing anything exciting tonight?' Steph asked Emma as they headed into ED a week later.

It was New Year's Eve and Queenstown would be party central. 'Staying out at the Valley. Mum and Dad always have open house.' Emma laughed. 'Rosie and I have been there since Christmas.' The three days she'd been at work had been busy, and she was looking forward to the New Year public holidays for some rest. When would she start to feel normal again? This tiredness had gone on too long.

'How's that puppy coping with Rosie?' Nixon called from his office as she passed.

Emma's heart fluttered. She'd missed him. His uncle had taken ill on Boxing Day and Nixon had remained in Dunedin until last night, making sure Henry rested. They'd talked every day but it wasn't the same as being with him. There'd been a hesitation in his voice she couldn't pinpoint. Stepping inside the office, she told him, 'They're inseparable. How's Henry?' Damn but he was beautiful. That lean body and those tight muscles at the edges of his scrubs' sleeves. That mouth that did amazing things to her body.

'Back to his usual taciturn self,' Nixon replied fondly, which was unusual. He was normally guarded when talking about his family. How likely was it that they'd talked about the past and whatever held Nixon back?

Walking around the desk, she leaned in to kiss him, inhaled him, felt his shoulders under her hands. 'I missed you. You still game for tonight?' She'd invited him to join her at her family's home for the night. As in, stay over in the spare bedroom, and hopefully sneak down the hall to her room like two naughty teens when the lights went out.

Pewter eyes met hers, clear of any hesitation now. 'You bet.'

'Good answer.' She'd held lingering doubts that he was

going to continue seeing her when he returned. That melt-down she'd had on Christmas Eve had rattled him as much as her, though for different reasons. Shock had marred his face when she'd said she wanted a baby. As well it might. They weren't anywhere near ready for that level of commitment. Nor was she ready to carry another baby. She had to wait, enjoy being with Nixon and slowly bring him around to seeing he could have a loving life with her and Rosie. If he wanted to…and she thought he might.

Nixon cupped her head to draw her close again.

'Hmm,' Steph cleared her throat. 'Nixon, you're needed in Resus.'

'Right.' He was up and moving towards the door. 'Nothing like reality to remind me where we are.'

Following him, Emma envied the energy blasting off him as those long legs ate up the distance to Resus. Right on cue a yawn stretched her mouth.

'You're still doing that?' Nixon asked as he reached for the patient notes being held out to him. But then he was reading and she ducked out of answering.

Until the middle of shift when he caught her out again. 'Think you need your iron levels checked? The pregnancy could've caused anaemia.'

'My haemoglobin is around one twenty.' Not anaemic by any stretch.

'Let's get it checked anyway.' Nixon took her elbow and led her to his office. 'I'll fill out a lab request so you can get it done before you leave work.'

With Nixon acting on her exhaustion she felt worse. This tiredness was for real, not something her imagination had conjured up. 'Okay.'

Nixon printed a request form and signed it with a flourish. 'Don't put it off.'

'I said okay,' she snapped, letting the tiredness get to her. Instead of gaining more energy, her body was on a downhill slide and even her boobs had returned to aching at inconvenient moments.

'Go now while we're not busy.'

'Thanks.' She'd be a load of fun tonight like this. The lift was waiting, as though expecting her. She hit the floor number and leaned back against the cool wall. Her boobs ached. As they had when her milk was drying up. Or when she was in the early stages of pregnancy with Grace.

Emma straightened up fast. 'No way. Can't be.'

Women didn't get pregnant this soon after giving birth. Huh? Which nursing textbook did she get that out of? Just as breastfeeding didn't act as birth control, there was no downtime when sex was safe. But she and Nixon had been careful, always used condoms. Had to be low iron. Could not be any other reason.

It had been a month since Grace's arrival. No bloody way.

The lab form shook in her hand as she stared at the tests Nixon had requested. CBC and iron studies. Nothing startling, nothing to change the momentum of her life. Unless the CBC showed some abnormality with her white or red cells, or platelets, which hadn't occurred to either her or Nixon. But nor had that idea her brain had just thrown at her. Had they used a condom each and every time they'd made love? Yes, she'd swear they had.

The lift shook to a stop on the floor holding the lab. Emma shivered. Stepping through the door, she hesitated, wanted to run, head home to hide under the bedcovers. Go to sleep and wake up knowing she'd been silly even to consider she might be pregnant. Glancing down the hall, she saw Cindy, a pal from school who'd played goal shoot to her goal defence when she played netball in winter. If ever she needed Cindy, now was it.

'Hello, what brings you up here?' asked Cindy the moment she saw Emma.

'I need a blood test.' She shoved the form into Cindy's hand. 'I know it's not your job but can you take the specimen? I need to ask you something.' Lab technicians were trained to take blood samples.

'Come with me.' Cindy led her into a little used cubicle. 'Sit and tell me what's got you in a sweat.'

'You're working in biochemistry, right?' When Cindy nodded, she continued. 'Is there any chance you could run an HCG for me? I'll make it legit by paying, but I don't want the result going to the doctor who signed the form.'

Cindy's eyes widened, but all she said was, 'Sure.'

Within minutes Emma was on her way back to the department, the worry that had been gnawing at her for hours put to rest. It was as though, now she'd faced the real possibility she could be pregnant, she wasn't bothered. The panic had gone. Only to return if the HCG test showed positive.

Then she'd have to face reality and make some difficult decisions.

She'd have to think of Rosie, and her family.

Her job. How could she continue to work if she had a baby as well as a school-age child?

She'd have to confront Nixon.

Panic flared, returned harder and tighter than the first round. Emma backed up against the wall, out of the way of patients and staff, working at keeping herself from doing a face plant as her knees no longer had the strength to hold her upright.

'How long do you intend holding up that wall?' came

the deep, sexy voice of the man who would be propping up the wall himself if he knew.

The test would come back negative. She'd take some iron tablets and be back to normal in no time at all. It came down to the fact she'd worked throughout her pregnancy and gone back to work only days after the birth. She aimed for casual and confident, even though she must look like someone who'd camped out all week under a bridge. 'As long as it needs me.'

A firm hand on her elbow lifted her away from that helpful wall. 'You're starting to worry me.'

I'm worrying myself.

'Should have the answers to the tests within an hour.' *Click, click.* One vertebra at a time she drew herself up as tall as possible, but still short beside this man. That was one of the things she adored about him. He made her feel tiny and safe against his length and strength.

'We need to talk. If you're seriously unwell I'd like to know. No, damn it, I need to know. No argument.' Nixon looking out for her was awesome, and heartening. Make that heart-stopping.

Don't let me be pregnant.

That'd knock him back into I-am-only-a-friend-with-no-involvement. Even though he seemed different, that attitude still lurked on the periphery, ready to pounce. 'Let's get back to patients.' The focus on her was disturbing. What if they'd made a baby?

They had.

Emma sank to her haunches and stared at the phone in her hand as though it were a monster. Her head swirled with the connotations of her predicament. A baby. How careless was that? She'd started thinking another child would be wonderful, but that picture had a father for the baby in it, a caring parent for Rosie, a loving partner for her.

Careful what you wish for.

Now she got that message in black and white. No grey areas. Nixon would put his hand up, yes. Be a responsible man, yes. Give her his heart, doubtful. *A grey area.* Her head hurt.

It was New Year's Eve, the night she was taking Nixon home to her family as a partner, as someone she loved and wanted them to get to know a whole lot better.

'Em? What's wrong?'

Her worst nightmare had found her in the drugs room. No, that was unfair. Nixon was not a nightmare. He was a loving man she'd given her heart to and now she had to drop a bomb in his hand. She took the hand he held out to her and dragged herself upright.

Tell him. Not now. We're at work. Coward. Nothing's going to change the longer you leave telling him. You'll only make it harder on yourself.

But keeping Nixon in oblivion for a little while longer would give him a few more hours' peace.

Then she looked at him, found his worried gaze searching her face for answers, and knew she was being selfish. 'I'm pregnant.'

'We are?' Shock and disbelief warred across his face.

We are. That gave her hope. He hadn't disappeared down the corridor and locked himself in his office. Yet. She nodded, incapable of forming words.

'That's why you're so tired. I should've guessed.' He shoved a hand through his hair. 'Your iron and haemoglobin all normal?'

Again she nodded.

'I think I knew they would be. I feel as though a cloud has lifted from something I've been denying.' When she stared at him he rattled her with, 'I think I might've known deep down.'

Finally her larynx started working. 'We were always careful.'

One dark eyebrow rose in irony. 'Must've got a dud. Doesn't matter how it happened, the fact is it did. How are you feeling about this?'

How are *you* feeling? 'It's still sinking in.' Cop out, but true. 'I know I'll have it and keep it. Even if that makes me look like a careless slut.'

'Don't insult yourself. Or me.' His fingers brushed her cheek, took her chin gently and lifted her head so she had to look into his eyes. 'We need time to absorb what this means to all of us.'

He still wasn't running. It felt too good to be true. This man didn't get involved. Emma shivered and stepped away from those gentle fingers. She needed answers now, not tomorrow or in the new year. She wasn't going to get them. Nixon needed space. She needed reassurance. The only person in this picture who was going to give her that right now was herself. 'Here's the thing. I already know what it means. Been here before, remember?' She didn't give him time to reply. 'Only this time it's different. This time I want the father in the picture. I want a family: you, me, Rosie and the baby.'

He took a step back, cracking her heart in the process. No surprise there.

'I've fallen in love with you, Nixon. I didn't mean to, I knew you'd probably never feel the same way about me, but it's happened and I can't undo it.' The truth sucked big time, but if she didn't put it out there she wasn't going in to bat for her baby. Or herself.

Nixon took another backward step, and the cracks widened.

'I love you.' It was surprising how easy it was to say. It

was true, and right, and, hell, it was killing her on the inside. She stared at him, willing him to answer, to put her heart at ease. The silence was laden, heavy and chilly. Finally, she said, 'Time I got back to work.' She needed to get a grip or she'd be a danger to any patient who came near her.

'Take the rest of the day off, Emma.'

'It's all right.'

'No, it's not. You've had a shock.' He was ignoring the love factor. Wouldn't know how to digest that news. 'Go home, put your feet up.'

'You want me out of the way. Out of sight, off the radar, so I'm not reminding you every minute about the problem lying between us.'

'We need space while we get our heads around this. Don't you agree?'

'Not for a moment. I'm not skulking off when we're busy so *you* can avoid *me*.'

'Give me time, Emma. That's all I ask.'

'Yeah, and there lies the problem. You want time, not a baby or me or involvement.' Crikey, she had grown a backbone after all. Or was she being harsh? 'Sorry.' A yawn followed.

'Go home, Em. For your sake, not mine.'

Her bed beckoned, the quiet, the solitude; Abbie banging down the door to ask why she was home. 'No can do. I have a job to do and I'm going to do it. I don't run at the first sign of trouble.'

His nod was curt. 'I think I'll take a rain check on tonight with your family though.'

She might've seen that coming but it still hurt like stink. 'Avoid me as much as you like but we are involved now. There's nothing you can do to change that.'

Pain filled his gaze, tightened his face, then was gone, leaving—despair. He turned away.

Her heart thumped hard, for him, for her. 'Nixon?'

He turned slowly, one eyebrow elevated. 'Emma.'

The chill in her name froze her to the spot. Backbone remember? Swallow. 'I could've gift-wrapped the news, but we both believe in plain truth. I am pregnant, and I do love you. There's no hidden catch.'

'I didn't think there was.' He stalked away, disappeared into Resus, leaving her alone and frightened.

She'd fallen for a man who couldn't find it in him to admit to love. They were having a baby and he had no idea how to deal with it. Which left her stranded, in need of him, of his love.

'Emma, can you take the fractured femur arriving in two?' Steph stepped into her line of vision. 'Are you all right? You're not coming down with the stomach virus too?'

Suck it up, get on with life as you knew it before Nixon stole your heart. 'I'm good. Who's our patient? Local or tourist?' She got busy, burying herself in other people's problems and pain, ignoring her own, barely coming up for air, ignoring Nixon, until shift ended. At four o'clock she drove up her parents' driveway, walked inside and burst into tears the moment her mother looked at her.

Happy new year.

Nixon pedalled as if his life depended on it. Arrowtown had never appeared on the horizon so quickly, and he hadn't finished thinking through what he was going to do. He'd barely started. Focusing entirely on riding hard and safe was easier than the fear and trepidation kicking up a storm in his belly.

A baby. He was going to be a father. Nightmares did come true.

The township was quiet, the tourists gone for the day. Nixon wheeled along the streets, barely noticing his surrounds. Emma was pregnant with his baby. He got that in spades. But knowing, and then knowing what to do— different pages, different books.

A cat streaked across the road in front of him. Braking hard, he fought to remain upright and on the tarmac. Blasted animal. A broken collarbone wouldn't help anything. Heading for the park at the end of the main street, Nixon dropped his bike on the grass and sank his butt onto a picnic table.

The sun was dropping behind the hills but that wasn't why he was shivering.

Emma was carrying his baby. He was going to be a dad. Like it or not. Too late for choosing whether to chance becoming a parent. Too late to heed the warning from his nightmare. It was a done deal. Not that he wished the baby away. No, excitement stirred his blood, then reality kicked in and fear engulfed him. He knew little about loving someone. He wanted Emma. In his life. In his heart. Everywhere, all the time. If only he knew how. It should be as easy as sitting down and talking with her, explaining himself—if laying his heart on the line were his way. It wasn't.

Em had knocked his socks off saying she loved him. Her declaration had turned him hot and cold all at once. He wanted her love, needed to show her he loved her, but a lifetime of holding back was in the way. There were no guidelines. Anyway, it probably wasn't even possible.

'I love you.' Emma's words resonated endlessly, had kept him on edge for the rest of shift. Every time he'd seen her he'd wanted to rush over and shake some sense into her head, make her see he was the wrong man to be looking at a future with. 'We're having a baby.'

Riding was supposed to settle his head, but his heart wasn't in it. He was running away. He and Emma were having a baby. She'd been stoic when he'd said he wasn't going to her family dinner, not showing relief or disappointment. Which had rubbed him up the wrong way. He'd wanted a reaction, something to guide him through this murky situation. But no. She'd left him to make up his own mind—about everything.

'Don't make the same mistakes I did.'

Sure, thanks, Henry. I'll keep that in mind.

The man who'd talked to him last week for the first time. The man who'd taken his real father's place as best he could. Should he ask his advice? No, this decision was his alone. But no harm in getting some input. Digging his phone out of his cycle pants, he pressed a number. 'Henry, it's me.'

'I'm sixty-five, not ninety-five. My phone is state of the art.'

'Of course.' Nixon had given it to him for his last birthday.

'What's up?' Straight to the point.

Hang up or tell Henry? Flight or fight? Gulp. 'I don't know what to do. I'm going to be a father.'

Henry was quiet, and Nixon could see the frown forming between his bushy eyebrows and the meditative look in his eyes. Then, 'This anything to do with Emma?'

'Yes.'

'You love her?'

Go for the throat, why don't you?

'I—' Swallow. 'Yes.'

'Does she know that?'

You know she doesn't, you old bugger.

'It's not so easy.'

Another silence, then, 'Yes, Nixon, it is. If you truly love her then you open your mouth and tell her.'

More silence. He had no answer to that gem. Because Henry was right. That was how people communicated. Most people. Just not him. 'I've never said those words to anyone in my life.' Not that he was telling Henry something he didn't know.

'Time you started. It's not that you don't know how to love.'

His eyes moistened, damn it. Henry was digging under his skin, scratching the painful scars. He didn't know how to say I love you. Did he just open his mouth and spill? Or did there need to be a lead in? Not an orchestra or roses; he got that. But to say those three words—once they were out, there was no taking them back to protect his heart. He'd be vulnerable. Emma mightn't walk away from him but she could get injured, die. The other day she'd been so exhausted it had crippled her. What if it had been worse? Something other than pregnancy doing that to her? He'd have lost his heart, the woman he loved. Or equally bad: what if he failed her? Found his love wasn't strong and true? No, he was sure about that.

Scrubbing a hand across his eyes, he coughed. Henry was waiting patiently. Damn but he owed this man. 'Henry—'

'It's all right. Go and tell this special woman how you feel. Then bring her down to meet us. If you're going to set up family we're going to be part of the picture. All of us.' Then he was gone.

It was that easy? Yeah, sure. Nixon began riding back to Queenstown, taking a different route, riding slower as he let Henry's advice wash over him, into him.

Tell her.

Family. Emma. Children. A home. A baby.

He passed a real-estate sign with a photo showing a large family home set in paddocks. The house that had been advertised in the paper before Christmas. The house Emma thought would be perfect for her and Rosie and anyone else she might love.

His speed fell away as he stared over the fence at the house coming into view from behind a row of birch trees. Placing his feet on the ground, he took in the wide verandas, the bay windows, two chimneys, the rose-filled gardens. Yes, Emma could be happy there. But this had nothing to do with them and their current situation. This house was not going to tell Emma he loved her.

Or was it? What if he showed Emma how much he loved her? He could do that. He could. Words weren't the only way of putting his feelings out there. His heart pumped faster, harder, and the need to act expanded through his chest, became urgent. If he couldn't do this for Emma he didn't deserve her. Then what would his life be like? Empty. Lonely. Unbearable.

Emma looked up from the bacon she was cutting into ever smaller pieces on her plate. 'Expecting someone for breakfast?' she asked her father. The house was quiet the next morning as most people slept off last night's party.

'Nope. Sure you didn't invite a certain someone?' Her father winked as he glanced out of the window.

'What?'

Rosie was racing for the door, Bella at her heels. 'Nixon!'

'What does this mean?' Emma whispered, trying to ignore the hope thrashing against her heart. Good? Or bad? Were they getting together, or was it over before it got started?

'Why don't you go and find out, love?' Her father patted her hand.

Nixon had been blunt about wanting time to himself yesterday. Every time a car had come up the drive last night her heart had lifted in hope, and dived back down when it hadn't been Nixon. She hadn't slept a wink all night for fear he'd reject her. Was that why he was here now? To tell her he couldn't be the man she wanted? Or—

Her legs refused to lift her up. Remaining seated, shaking on the inside, she refused to acknowledge the fledgling hope firing in her gut. This could all be the biggest let-down of her life.

Then Nixon was standing at the end of the table, Rosie's hand wrapped in his. 'Sorry to barge in like this, but I need to talk to Emma.'

She tried pushing up from the table; again her legs failed her. At least her neck muscles worked and she could meet his steady gaze. A lot steadier than her heart.

Her father held his hand out. 'Come on, Rosie. We'll take Bella to the pond.'

They both watched them leave as though that were the most important issue right now. The air stalled in Emma's lungs. 'Do you want some coffee?' she finally asked to fill in the tight silence.

'I'll get it.' He stepped across to the table and picked up a mug. Coffee splashed on the tablecloth when he poured.

Finally she couldn't stand it any longer. 'Tell me.'

He looked at her for a long moment, an emotion she couldn't identify in his eyes. 'I'm sorry about yesterday. It was a shock and I didn't handle it well.'

'You needed time to get your head around the baby.' He'd known almost as long as her.

'Not as much as what else you told me.' He hesitated. Emma waited for her world to implode.

'I've struggled with putting my emotions out there since the day they told me my family was gone. I think I believed if I didn't say a word it wouldn't be true. Later I couldn't find the words, so I kept quiet. To my detriment. To your detriment.'

Hers? That had to mean something good. Didn't it? 'And?' She was rushing him. But, hell, how could she not? She wanted this over, no matter what he told her.

'I want us to have a future, Em.' More coffee splashed on the cloth and Nixon carefully placed the mug on the table. 'The four of us.'

She liked where this was going, but they were only at the beginning. 'As in, a family?'

'Yes.'

Her heart jerked, stabbing her painfully. 'Are you doing this for the baby's sake? Because you have a responsibility towards it? I can't accept that. It's all or nothing for me.' Where had the strength to say that come from? On the inside she was a bubbling mess of fear. Her mouth was a desert.

Nixon pulled some papers from his pocket. 'You'd better see this.'

A legal document. No way. She wasn't signing any damned piece of paper that put the baby entirely in her custody. Or took it away from her. She stared at Nixon, saw the man she'd given her heart to, saw the strength, the honesty, the big heart, the fears and the care. He would not do that to her. Or his child. Reaching out, she asked, 'What is it?'

'Take a look.'

Slowly unfolding the document, she gasped. 'It's a sale and purchase agreement.' Quickly lowering her gaze, she read some more. 'Trish and Bill's place?'

'Yes.'

'I don't understand.'

'I looked around the property last night, and negotiated with the agent this morning. It's ours.'

Emma's butt was glued to her chair. 'Ours?' Did this mean…? She had no idea what it meant. Or rather, she was afraid to contemplate it in case she was wrong.

Nixon smiled that long, slow, heart-stopping smile of his as he moved closer. Reaching down, he pulled her up into his arms. 'Yes, ours. As in our home for our family. I know you love the property. I agree it is amazing, perfect really.'

'You're serious?' she squealed. Of course he would be. Nixon would never say so otherwise. 'We're going to live there?'

'You and me, and Rosie and the baby. And Bella.' He nodded. 'Yes, Em. That's what I mean.'

'But—' Her hands moved up his chest, up to his face. 'You want to live with me? As a family?'

'As your husband. Will you marry me?'

A hundred questions pushed forward as her smile started a slow widening and softening, turning up at the corners, lightening her heart. Nixon had proposed. That had to mean he loved her. Didn't it? The smile slowed, held position. 'This really isn't for the baby's sake?'

'No.' He looked up at the ceiling and puffed out a breath. 'Not at all. It's you I want to spend my life with. You and our family.'

Unbelievable words from Nixon. He'd come a long way. But he hadn't said he loved her. Not a dickey bird. Disappointment railed against elation. Nixon wanted to be with her for ever. It should be all she wanted. Call her greedy, but it wasn't enough. He'd buy her a house but not say those important three words. Even if only once. Once was enough. She'd cherish them, hold them close. But she had to hear them. Tipping back in his hold, she said, 'You bought this house because I said I loved it?'

The air quivered between them. 'Yes.'

'An impromptu decision?' Please say no.

'No.' Phew. 'And yes.'

Great. Now what? 'Can you elaborate?'

Thump, thump, went her heart.

I know it's hard, but please, I need to know.

'It happened very fast, but it feels right.' Nixon shoved his hands deep into the pockets of his chinos and strolled, oh, so deliberately, across to the bay window to stare out at Rosie playing in the pond. Then he turned to her. 'When Trish mentioned they were selling, this longing filled your eyes, a longing that got to me, made me wake up to the fact I wanted a part of that. Wanted it with you. You've got to me, Em. Under my skin, in my head, in…'

She took a step forward, said softly, 'Go on.'

'You're there all the time, even when you're someplace else.'

Another step. 'That's how it is for me too.' One more step.

'I want to be with you for the rest of my life. I want to marry you, Emma.'

'I want to marry you, Nixon. I love you,' she added as she reached him.

He looked away, swallowed, turned to face her, reached for her hands, held them as though they were fragile as spun sugar. 'You want me to tell you?'

She nodded. And waited.

Finally, 'I love you,' he whispered, a shiver in his fingers.

Up on her toes, reaching for his mouth with hers, her heart going crazy against her ribs, she kissed him. Long and deep and filled with love. Then she pulled back.

'Thank you. Yes, Nixon, I will marry you, because we love each other.' Then she went back to kissing him, knowing he couldn't say any more, he'd laid not just his heart but everything about him on the line by uttering those words. He'd shown her his love, he'd put it out there in actions—and in the best three words ever. 'I will never hurt you, Nixon.'

'I know.' Cocky right to the end now he'd got over the biggest hurdle of his life.

She grinned. 'So we've got ourselves a house, huh?'

'With lots of bedrooms for the family we're going to keep adding to.'

'You're getting carried away, my man.'

'My man, huh?' His kiss was full of promise and the future, and, yes, lots of love.

'Happy New Year,' she whispered against his mouth. What a way to start.

EPILOGUE

Next Christmas...

'Mummy, can I open Jack's presents from Santa? He's too little to do it,' Rosie pointed out earnestly, the excitement that had dragged them out of bed twenty minutes ago temporarily reined in while she waited for permission for her next adventure.

The stocking at the end of her bed hadn't taken very long to deal with and she was struggling with not being allowed to open any more presents until all the family arrived for brunch.

'When Dad's here you can.' Emma held baby Jack against her breast as she sat curled up in the leather rocker Nixon had bought her for nursing when he was born. It was her favourite go-to place inside the house, and this morning—yawn, it wasn't six o'clock yet—the decorated pine tree with the presents underneath filled her vision. Another Christmas. They seemed to come around awfully fast. But she didn't mind. There was always something wonderful happening at this time of year.

'Get this into you.' Nixon placed a mug of tea on the table at her elbow before dropping a kiss on the top of her head. 'Jack more interested in his breakfast?'

'Make the most of it. Next year will be different.' She

smiled up at this amazing man who'd stolen her heart and delivered his in a million ways ever since.

'Dad's here now. I can open Jack's stocking.'

'Bring it over to me and we'll do it together.' Nixon sipped his tea and dropped onto the floor beside Emma's rocker.

Rosie upended the stocking. 'What do you think Santa's got him, Dad?'

Emma's heart expanded with warmth. Dad. From the day she'd told Rosie Nixon wanted to adopt her and be her daddy she had never called him anything else. And Nixon had filled with pride and happiness and love.

Love. He still didn't say those three words very often. After the day he proposed she'd had to wait until their wedding day. Standing on their front lawn, surrounded by their families and friends, he had said, 'I love you, Emma Wright,' as he slid the wedding band onto her finger.

He'd said it again the day the adoption was finalised, and then when he held Jack in his arms for the first time.

Every time Nixon told her his face was filled with awe and love and everything she could ask for. It was enough. She didn't need to be told every day or even every week. Because he was constantly showing her. The cups of tea in bed first thing in the morning, the paintwork in the bathroom, the laundry hung out before he headed into work. Those kisses that melted her bones.

'Look, Jack. You've got a book like I had when I was little. It's made of really thick paper so you can't rip it.' Rosie reached for another parcel, squeezed and shook it. 'What's this?'

As though he knew he was missing out on something, Jack pulled his mouth away from breakfast and wriggled so he could see his sister. Emma cleaned his face and sat him up on her knee. 'There you go, wee man.'

'Go easy. You don't want to break it.' Nixon gently removed the parcel and laid it on the floor. 'Take the paper off slowly.'

'It's a caterpillar. A long one with funny pictures on its bumps.' Rosie leapt up and brought it over to Emma and Jack. 'See, Jack?'

'Careful.' Emma put a hand up between Jack's head and the toy, and when Rosie stepped back she reached for her tea. 'Right, guess we need to get dressed and ready for the influx.'

'No rush.' Nixon looked up at her. 'No one will be here for a couple of hours.'

'You're forgetting my family turn up when they're ready, not when we might be. Mum will be taking over the kitchen before you know it.' She was doing Christmas dinner here as Nixon's family were all driving up from Dunedin this morning.

Nixon just grinned. 'Rosie, can you bring me that red envelope with the big green bow on it, please?'

'Who's it for, Dad?' She placed it in Nixon's outstretched hand. 'Can I open it?'

'Not this one, my girl.' He stood up and lifted Jack into his arms before handing Emma the envelope. 'Merry Christmas, darling.' His eyes were filled with love and hope. Hope that he'd done the right thing?

Her heart fluttered 'What is it?' she asked as she slid a finger under the back of the envelope and opened it. She tipped out the contents. Two photos. Of a beautiful black horse. Her head tipped up as she sought those wonderful grey eyes again. 'For me?' she whispered.

Nixon nodded. 'But you have to meet her first, see if you like her. If not we'll find another one.'

Emma leapt up and wrapped her arms around her husband. 'I love you so much. And not because you're buying me a horse, but because you're you. Wonderful, caring, kind...' Her throat filled up and happy tears streaked down her face. Crying had never really stopped since she'd had Grace, only this past year without exception they'd been happy tears.

'Carry on. I'm enjoying this,' Nixon murmured against her ear.

'And cheeky,' she managed.

His lips caressed hers. 'I love you, Emma.'

Wow. He'd said it again. That was a bigger present than any other he could give her.

'Merry Christmas.'

* * * * *

Don't miss the first story in
THE ULTIMATE CHRISTMAS GIFT *duet*
THE NURSE'S SPECIAL DELIVERY
by Louisa George

And if you enjoyed this story
check out these other great reads
from Sue MacKay

FALLING FOR HER FAKE FIANCÉ
PREGNANT WITH THE BOSS'S BABY
RESISTING HER ARMY DOC RIVAL
THE ARMY DOC'S BABY BOMBSHELL

All available now!

MILLS & BOON®

MEDICAL ROMANCE™

THE ULTIMATE IN ROMANTIC MEDICAL DRAMA

A sneak peek at next month's titles...

In stores from 28th December 2017:

Just can't wait?
Buy our books online before they hit the shops!
www.millsandboon.co.uk

Also available as eBooks.

MILLS & BOON®

EXCLUSIVE EXTRACT

One sizzling encounter with trauma doc Major Elle
Caplin is all it takes to tempt Lieutenant Colonel
Fitzwilliam to break his one-night rule…!

Read on for a sneak preview of
TEMPTED BY DR OFF-LIMITS
the second book in Charlotte Hawkes's
HOT ARMY DOCS *duet*

Fitz forgot everything. He simply indulged. For what
seemed like an eternity, his mouth slid over hers. When he
pushed, she pushed back. When he held back, Elle sought
him. He trailed kisses down her jaw, her collarbone and to
the hollow at the base of her neck. Her shivers of pleasure
stoked his need. And each time he returned to those plump,
pink lips, her mouth reached for his and her tongue met
his in the same sinfully sinuous dance.

As he gave himself up to the sensations, as each kiss
from Elle threatened to undermine every defence he'd spent
years putting in place, the plink of those warm droplets on
his ice-block heart growing more insistent.

Before he could help himself, he'd released the curtain
of reds and golds from its military bun, inhaling its familiar
fresh, floral scent as his hands buried themselves in its
luxuriant depths. He could recall exactly how it had felt
brushing over his naked skin that night and his body
tightened.

'Gabrielle,' he groaned, unable to make up his mind
whether it was a groan or a warning growl.

And still he kissed her, sometimes gently and reverently,
other times hard and greedily. As though he never wanted
to stop. He didn't know when he backed her up so that she

was sitting on his desk with him standing between her legs, or when his fingers crept under the hem of her tee, or when he lifted it over her head and dropped it in a puddle on the plans he was supposed to be going through.

He needed to stop. Needed to remind her—remind himself—what kind of a man he was. How he would inevitably hurt her.

Don't miss HOT ARMY DOCS:
ENCOUNTER WITH A COMMANDING OFFICER
Available now!

TEMPTED BY DR OFF-LIMITS
Available January 2018!
www.millsandboon.co.uk

YOU LOVE ROMANCE?

WE LOVE ROMANCE!

For exclusive extracts, competitions and special offers, find us online:

- **f** facebook.com/millsandboon
- **🐦** @MillsandBoon
- **📷** @MillsandBoonUK

Visit millsandboon.co.uk